Praise for *Triangle* ...

"... readers will applaud Daigle's emotionally intense saga, which revolves around an endearing heroine and her relationships. This is a high-quality release—from the exceptional editing, eye-catching cover art, and tightly woven storyline, to the subtle thematic exploration of the power of love, forgiveness, and redemption. Readers will surely savor the story."

— *BlueInk Review*
Starred Review

"*Triangle* kind of snuck up on me. I suddenly found that I couldn't put it down. I loved the developing depth of the characters, especially Merran, as well as the unexpected twists and turns in the story. The tantalizing glimpses of Azelle's culture and beings through the storyline of Merran's early life and the visit made by Tamara, Merran, and Alarin to Azelle were awesome. Thanks for such a wonderful experience of possibility ..."

— *Diana Riverstone, Artist, WY*

"In *Triangle*, Sara Daigle delivers and picks up where *Alawahea* ends. It fleshes out the lives of the characters I came to love in her first novel and introduces more. Sara's writing is compelling. She raises thought-provoking ideas about culture, language, attitudes, and family through the drama the characters must face as they choose to continue to be involved with each other. I recommend this series to my clients who are seeking romance novels."

— *Tara Galeano, L.P.C., Boulder, CO*
Boulder Sex Therapy

"*Triangle* is a great story etched in top 'science fantasy.' I appreciated that it was not just another 'space western.' It's a story of people involved in complex relationships, playing out in a time and place that makes those relationships both easier to relate to and yet more complicated."

— *Dr. Kevin Mills, Boston, MA*

"The series' second installment, *Triangle*, introduces provocative new characters and plot twists while adding dimension to the beloved characters from *Alawahea*. With Sara's fluid writing style and energetic storytelling, you'll not be able to put it down. While the subject matter focuses on other worldly characters and ideas, it's very relatable and remarkably human."

— *Andrea Nelson, Kansas City, MO*

"In *Triangle*, Sara L. Daigle examines the intricate bonds of relationships. Her characters are endearingly and realistically relatable as they wade through the clashing of cultural sexual norms. Compassion and wisdom champion resolution. Daigle artfully draws the reader into a contemporary storyline interwoven with humor, poignancy, and self-discovery. I happily read far past my bedtime!"

— *Linda M Hicks, Westminster, MA*

"Fantasy romance was never my genre until I read *Alawahea* a couple years ago. Since then, I have been impatiently waiting for the sequel, and it certainly did not disappoint. The characters feel familiar and consistent and the storyline has great continuity. Sara did a phenomenal job with keeping the reader on the edge of their seat and wanting more. I really look forward to getting to know Tamara, Alarin, and other Azellians more deeply in the upcoming installments."

— *Tatiana Finkelsteyn, Denver, CO*
Founder, IQ Wired, Inc.

"*Triangle* is a personal exploration of the characters' lives in the second book of The Azellian Affairs. The story simmers along as we learn more about Azelle's culture and inhabitants. Sara's powers of description continue to bring her world to life. It will be fun to see where she takes Tamara, Alarin, and Merran next!"

— *Kirsten Wolpert, Phoenix, AZ*

"Reading *Triangle* was equally as riveting as *Alawahea*. Sara's books have deepened my journey into myself. Once again, I felt myself in the storyline. The characters took me on an extraordinary ride exploring my greatest desires in life, love, and relationships. By the end of the book, I felt even more empowered to design my destiny!!"

— Wendy Groves, Pagosa Springs, CO

"Sara L Daigle has created another exciting page turner with new twists and turns. The mystère of her well-developed characters kept me intrigued and their intertwined storylines had me on the edge of my seat. I can't wait for book number 3!"

— Meghann Conter, Denver, CO
Founder of The Dames www.thedames.co

"… this sci-fi tale offers complex, imaginative liaisons and worldbuilding."
— Kirkus Reviews

Triangle

Triangle

The Azellian Affairs
Book Two

SARA L. DAIGLE

MERRY DISSONANCE PRESS   CASTLE ROCK, COLORADO

Triangle
The Azellian Affairs, Book Two

Published by Merry Dissonance Press, LLC
Castle Rock, CO

FIRST EDITION 2018

Daigle, Sara L., Author
Triangle: The Azellian Affairs, Book Two
Sara L. Daigle

Publisher's Cataloging-in-Publication data

Names: Daigle, Sara L. (1970-), author
Title: Triangle : the Azellian affairs book two / Sara L. Daigle.
Description: First trade paperback original edition. | Castle Rock [Colorado] : Merry
Dissonance Press, 2018.
Identifiers: ISBN 978-1-939919-54-0
Subjects: LCSH: Romance fiction. | Metaphysics--Fiction. | Fantasy fiction.
BISAC: FICTION / Fantasy / Romantic. | FICTION / Romance / General. |
FICTION / Visionary & Metaphysical.
Classification: LCC PS374.F27 | DDC 813 DAIGLE–dc22

ISBN 978-1-939919-54-0
1. Fiction 2. Romance/Fantasy 3. Visionary & Metaphysical

Book Design and Cover Design © 2018
Cover Design by Elena Karoumpali
Book Design by Andrea Costantine
Editing by Donna Mazzitelli, The Word Heartiste

*For my dad who taught me about being a storyteller,
and for the Norrises and the Norris/Colwells, with whom
I share the joy of reading and learning*

Chapter One

The intercom beeped insistently. The dark-haired young man who sat at the desk glanced over at the persistent blinking light.

"Allyn knows I'm in the middle of a meeting, Ki'i. He should be fielding all my calls and not letting any of them through," Merran Corina, ambassador from the planet Azelle, said to the half-visible presence hovering above the chair in front of his large mahogany desk.

"Apparently, your attention is urgently needed," Ki'i replied, a ripple of deep green flashing across Merran's vision. Speaking with the normally invisible being was always a visual treat. To people it liked, the Dorbin showed itself on the visible spectrum as an energy field of vibrant color. "I am not offended, Merran. We can always conclude our business at another time. We ambassadors cannot afford to let the little things disturb us."

Merran smiled at the ghostly being. "As much as I appreciate your ease, Ki'i, you know as well as I do, if it weren't for our personal relationship, you'd be dreadfully offended by an interruption."

"I don't know that I'd say *dreadfully*," Ki'i responded with fond amusement. "We Dorbin lack the emotional volatility that you corporeals enjoy. But I do have to admit my fondness for you does make it somewhat less … *irritating* than it would otherwise be."

Merran leaned back against the thick brown leather of his office chair. "Well, whatever your reasons for being calm about this, I appreciate your tolerance. How about we pick this up again, say next Tuesday at this time? By then my regular assistant will have returned and we should be able to have an uninterrupted meeting."

"Certainly," Ki'i replied, shimmering slightly, the green transmuting into a delicate blue tinge. "You have put considerable effort into learning about our plant life, which is appreciated, but I remain hesitant about the specifics. Those you have put forth lack your finesse, yet you are not willing to give yourself over to the care of our plants. May I ask you a personal question?"

"Of course."

"Those who have a physical form usually have difficulty with all things Dorbin, yet you seem to understand the interaction and impact between physicality and the energetic more than even most Azellians do."

Merran nodded. "I haven't been to Dorbin myself, but I am certainly very familiar with the effect of non-corporeal beings on physical beings. I spent some time with the *aarya* and among the *urro*."

Ki'i moved in a gesture that conveyed agreement, a magenta spark flaring through the room. "Ah yes. The *aarya* and the *urro*, the split race that originated on your planet many eons ago. I have heard of the *aarya* and the *urro*, of course. They are nearly as old as we Dorbin, and also lack a physical form. However, they live

12

isolated from the physical beings of your planet and few of your people have contact with them, or am I not remembering that correctly?"

"Yes and no. Yes, the *aarya* live isolated from most of the physical beings on the planet, centered in our Temples, interacting only with specific, carefully trained individuals we call Keepers. You are correct about that. The *urro*, however, live among their followers," Merran replied. "I am one of those former *urro-ken*. Before I became an acolyte at the Temple, my childhood was spent among the outer caves with the *urro*. That experience gave me my familiarity with non-corporeal beings."

Ki'i drifted closer, the filmy form almost overlapping the big desk. "You were a follower of the *urro*?"

Merran shifted in his chair, the leather sighing softly with his movement. Although the Dorbin normally displayed no emotion beyond fond amusement, Ki'i was emoting something quite different from *normal*. The being was almost … anticipatory … something Merran had never felt from the Dorbin before. "Are you familiar with the *urro*?"

Ki'i did not answer the question directly, but simply asked, "So you are very familiar with the merging?"

"Yes, I am. Very much so. I had a *meynsur*. Do you know what that is?"

There was an even stronger surge of something from Ki'i, almost intense enough to be considered excitement. "I do. A *meynsur* is a non-corporeal partner with whom you share your physical body and your psyche. If you had a *meynsur*, you were very close to permanently merging."

Merran smiled faintly. "I was close to permanently sharing my psyche with another being, yes. I went to the Temple instead.

The *aarya* took me in and made me an acolyte."

"You did not want to permanently merge?"

"I wouldn't be here, talking to you if I had. The *urro-ken* aren't allowed off Azelle."

"But you did not stay with the *aarya* either."

Merran inclined his head. "My call to be of service to my planet was not in the form of becoming a Keeper isolated among the *aarya,* so I left to come to Earth."

"Ah." The ghostly being was silent for a moment. "Did you mind another being sharing your body?"

Merran frowned at Ki'i. Half-suspecting where Ki'i wanted to take this conversation, Merran considered in a flash of inspiration that this might just provide the leverage he needed to accomplish what everyone had long considered virtually impossible: getting the Dorbin to agree to trade with anyone. He thought he had managed the impossible when Ki'i had begun training him in plant care a few months ago, but the talks had foundered once the Dorbin ambassador realized Merran would not be involved long-term. Did Ki'i want to merge badly enough to agree to allow someone other than Merran to care for the plants? Most of the other corporeal races in the galaxy had nothing the Dorbin wanted badly enough to offer trade concessions. "What is this curiosity about merging? Forgive my directness, but are you asking to merge with me?"

Ki'i's image faded slightly as another surge of something that might have been called desire lapped over Merran's psi awareness, just before the Dorbin's form flared into shimmering rainbow-colored brightness. "I would like to experience a body, yes. Perhaps when you are in the midst of a very strong physical reaction ... such as a pleasurable physical reaction?"

Merran stared at Ki'i, surprise making him blunter than he normally would have been with the Dorbin. "Are you asking to merge with me while I have sex?"

"If that is not difficult for you."

"Uh … I'm not in a position to be able to allow that."

"Do you not have a *diarhman*?"

"I do have a lover, yes."

"Then you need his or her agreement perhaps?"

"Um … yes, of course, I would need her consent, but it's complicated. It's a fairly new relationship, she's been raised on Earth, and it's not only the two of us who are involved."

"There is a third?"

Merran rubbed a hand over his face, feeling the scrape of rough hair against his skin, wondering how the conversation had gotten here, to his sex life. The Dorbin, who were as non-physical as the *aarya* and the *urro,* viewed sexuality differently from the physical beings who experienced it. *The Healers desperately want psi-active medicinal plants from Dorbin,* he thought to himself, behind heavy shields, making sure Ki'i would not pick up the thoughts racing through his mind, or the surge of intuitive awareness that had served him well over the years during negotiations. *And I can sense that Ki'i desperately wants a chance to merge with me and share my physical form. I don't know exactly how yet, but we may have a way to rescue this deal.*

For the first time since the talks with Ki'i had stalled, Merran thought he might have a chance at success—if he could just figure out how. He took a deep breath and let it out slowly. *It isn't a matter of figuring out,* he reminded himself, *just an opening to possibility. Kyarinal,* he told himself. *All that is possible becomes possible. I just have to relax. A way will be shown.*

The intercom beeped again, reminding him that Allyn had some kind of emergency awaiting his intercession. He dragged his attention back to Ki'i and their conversation. "Yes, there is. And the third will most definitely not be okay with the merging. He's Azellian, and though he's open-minded enough to be my friend despite my childhood in the outer caves with the *urro*, I don't want to ask him to participate in even a temporary merging. The prejudice against the *urro-ken* is quite intense, Ki'i. I know you don't fully understand it, but please accept that it is so. You have been observing our cultures long enough to know that we corporeals have strange customs. This is one of them."

Ki'i said nothing for a long moment, a silence during which it took Merran all of his self-discipline not to fidget. As a virtually immortal being, Ki'i had a rather vague sense of time and it was difficult to get it to understand the concept of being in a rush. "I accept what you are saying. I am wondering, then, if you might be willing to participate in a merging with me," it finally said.

Merran's instincts prickled. Given the Dorbin tendency toward secrecy, there was a very good chance these talks might stall out again, but this might truly be the way to get this deal done, if Ki'i wanted to merge badly enough. "I am willing to discuss a temporary merging as part of our discussions, but we will need to come to an agreement about how and when. Let's talk more about this on Tuesday?"

"Yes, that is acceptable. I look forward to it," Ki'i said, drifting toward the door, disappearing through it as if it weren't there— and for the Dorbin, it probably wasn't.

Merran watched the ambassador go, wondering briefly—and not for the first time—what it would be like not to have a physical body, then turned his attention to the blinking light on his phone.

"Yes, what is it?" he asked, tapping the intercom, his tone sharper than he meant it to be, but he let it stand. He hated days when his assistant Janille called in sick. She didn't do it often, but when she did, the embassy just seemed to dissolve around him. He spent more of his time refereeing chaos than he did working.

"Ambassador, I'm sorry to interrupt you, but I have someone on the line insisting they must speak to you. I didn't know what to do," Allyn Darvyne said, the tension in his voice obvious to Merran even without Merran's ability to sense another's mental state. Allyn was a good kid with definite strengths, tolerant and relaxed most of the time. Unfortunately, his inability to multi-task and his easygoing nature meant that he was not nearly strong enough to fend off the sometimes aggressive callers as this job— Janille's job—required. Not for the first time this week, Merran cursed the flu bug that had taken out half his staff during this cold January.

"All right, Allyn. I'll take it. Could you bring in the file on Justern Memaxthal?"

"Certainly, Ambassador." There was an obvious ocean of relief in the young man's response.

Merran shook his head and tapped the computer screen to accept the video call, making sure his expression was neutral and calm as the screen cleared to reveal an attractive younger woman who had a sour face and a tight expression. "Corina," he said.

"Ambassador Corina." The woman sounded surprised, almost shocked, but hastily covered her astonishment and stammered into her intro, talking quickly, as if afraid Merran might cut her off. "I'm, uh, Elise Winters, a correspondent with the *Women's Issues Quarterly.* Do you have a few moments to answer some questions?"

Merran frowned. "No, Ms. Winters, I'm sorry. I am heading out to a meeting. You will need to schedule a time with my assistant." He reached to cut her off.

She leaned forward, as if grabbing for his wrist. If they'd been in person, she probably would have—and been summarily shoved aside by his bodyguards. "Wait, Ambassador, wait, please. We are a small magazine that is looking to raise our profile, and an interview with you would really help."

Merran, who had been the target of the tabloids far too often during the past six and a half years of his tenure as ambassador, hesitated for a moment. In the past month, he'd hired a publicist to help him manage his media and online presence. Even though Dana Redmond had gotten him some very high-profile, prestigious interviews, he still got hounded by the tabloids, which preferred to write about who he was seeing rather than what he was accomplishing. Though he did sometimes give those types of sensationalized celebrity interviews, it was never without a thorough checking of the media outlet first. "I have brought a publicist on board, Ms. Winters. Dana Redmond of the Janus Media Agency. If you would like to speak with her, please feel free. She can answer your questions or schedule an appointment between us."

He ended the call firmly and sat back, closing his eyes and resting his head against his chair's high back. Groaning, he reached up with his hands to rub the muscles of his neck as he rolled his head slowly over the soft leather of his office chair, massaging the tension at the back of his head. He had been hoping that things would slow down for him so he could focus on more personal matters—like the new, but fragile, relationship he'd mentioned to Ki'i. Unfortunately, it didn't seem like it was turning out that way.

Although hiring a publicist had helped him route elsewhere

the endless calls for interviews, his love life seemed just as uncertain as ever. His relationship with Tamara Carrington, a young college student who had just discovered her Azellian heritage and related psi abilities at the end of last year, seemed to have potential, but she'd been out of town during the college's semester break and hadn't called him once. Although he didn't mind, since he wanted her to be independent and think for herself, what did bother him was that he hadn't heard from his friend Alarin during the exact same time period, which was definitely not normal, considering what had happened between the three of them.

Last semester, Tamara's unusual, explosive Awakening to her psi abilities had dragged all three of them into an intense psychic—and sexual—link. That tie, which forced a deep emotional and telepathic bond between them, supported his empathic sense that something was not quite right. Alarin's avoidance of him was not a good sign—normally his friend would have reached out mentally or by phone to spend time together, or simply to talk, especially as he had no classes at the moment. Calling Alarin on his cell phone had resulted in no response, and his friend had remained tightly shielded to any mental hails as well, making Merran wonder if Alarin was suffering from an intense bout of jealousy.

Merran had no proof that he was jealous—Alarin certainly had not said anything—but Merran knew Alarin well. He did not share sexual partners easily, and never had, even during their youth on Azelle. The feelings between Tamara, Alarin, and himself were not at all casual, which was very likely exacerbating whatever Alarin was feeling. But as long as Alarin was not talking, there wasn't much Merran could do to reassure him or mitigate Alarin's feelings of jealousy. It didn't help the situation that Tamara had been raised purely human, having been taken away from her Azellian mother at birth by her human father to live on Earth. She worked hard to hide it, but Merran knew she was far from comfortable about her psychic link with the two men that forced all three of them to share emotions, thoughts, and physical pleasure. He wondered if maybe she was avoiding him as well.

He rubbed his hands over his jaw, again feeling the rough scratch of facial hair against his fingertips, the sudden physical sensation reminding him that life went on, despite his inner turmoil. He lowered his hands and clicked on his email. The students were due back on campus within the next couple of days, so soon enough he'd get his answers: if Alarin and Tamara still weren't talking to him, he'd just have to reach out to Tamara to find out what was happening with their three-way relationship.

A knock on the door interrupted his thoughts. "Come in," he called.

Allyn pushed open the door, carrying a file folder. "The Justern Memaxthal file," he said as he placed the folder on Merran's desk. Allyn stood in front of the desk, looking nervous, his hand still on the smooth cover of the file.

"What is it, Allyn?" Merran asked, as he reached across his desk to pull it out from under his assistant's tense fingers.

"I thought this issue was resolved on Azelle, when Justern was found innocent last month."

Merran nodded. "He was. But unfortunately, he was not found innocent here on Earth, and considering that the crime was committed here on Earth, we've had to fight this through human appeal channels. That hasn't been as easy as you might think, considering our 'proof' is psi in nature."

Not long ago, fellow Azellian and exchange student Justern

Memaxthal had been found guilty of raping a human girl. *That case is going to have far-reaching consequences*, Merran thought, *not just because a number of Azellian abilities were openly revealed, but also because I am still dealing with the political ripples of the case itself. The girl's father is furious at the overturning of the verdict by the Azellian courts and wants Azelle to extradite Justern back to Earth. The Azellian Council is backing Justern, thank the* aarya, *but it's tricky. Wars have started over less, even among friendly planets, and the last thing we need is a war.* He didn't mention any of that to Allyn, though. *He doesn't need to know about something that might never happen. And, if I have anything to say about it, it never will.*

"Are you making some progress?" Allyn asked, concern written across his face. "I know Justern personally. He and I trained together."

Merran shrugged. "It's hard to tell," he replied evasively. "Diplomacy is an art ... and sometimes a damned uncertain one. Justern's trial and subsequent exile were political hotspots, and the human authorities are trying to make a point with him. I'm doing everything I can, hoping that it will work out for the best." As Justern's friend, Merran had a personal stake in trying to make this come out right, but if it came to choosing between Justern and peace between Azelle and Earth, Merran knew what he'd have to do. He fought the urge to sigh and turned to the phone. "Get me a cup of tea, will you, Allyn?" he asked as he dialed his friend and fellow Azellian Greg Tenricth's number. As a Healer and as one of the people who had been *very* involved with the drama last semester, Greg's insights would be invaluable. *One impossible task at a time*, he thought to himself. *I'll deal with the fourteen others later.*

"Certainly, Ambassador," Allyn said, and walked out of the room, closing the door behind him.

※ ※ ※

Not far from the embassy and the downtown area, Tamara Carrington shoved open the door with a shoulder and threw her bags down on her neatly made bed, grateful that she'd taken the time to make it before going on semester break. There was something cheerful about coming back to a neat room instead of a disaster area. She pushed a lock of soft brown hair out of her eyes, looking around the familiar room, the indirect southern midday light and east-facing windows making the room bright but not uncomfortable. Another semester about to begin, hopefully less chaotic than the last one had been. So much had happened last semester—from the death of her mother, whom she had recently found out was actually her stepmother, to the discovery and exile of her half-brother Justern, to the revelation of her own mental abilities and half-Azellian heritage—that she didn't think she'd be able to top it in a million years. Of course, she hoped she didn't even match it.

A light knock on the door interrupted her scan of the empty room, as a mind brushed across the shielding that swathed her. She thinned her shielding enough to recognize the Azellian mind at the door and felt her heart skip a beat and speed up. She took a breath, forgetting to release it, as waves of dizziness made the ground seem unsteady under her feet, anticipation and nerves causing her to feel shaky. This semester break, she'd done nothing but talk to him awkwardly a few times on the phone, with her father and sister listening in on every conversation. Her father had lived on Azelle for a year, even had an affair with an Azellian woman (which had resulted in her own birth), but for some reason, Peter Carrington had decided that his daughter needed to take time before leaping more deeply into a relationship with an

Azellian. That had led to stilted phone conversations and miserable separation under the pretense of a "family vacation." *Dad probably did it on purpose, to "teach me a lesson,"* she thought to herself, her body forcing her to breathe even as the rest of her forgot about everything but the rush of emotions. *Forget that I have no idea what that lesson was and that the time away was the worst time of my life.*

Tamara opened the door, more than a little breathless, and felt her heart leap to her throat at the sight of the tall, dusky-skinned redhead who stood nonchalantly at the door. She and her family had just returned from the "vacation" late last night, and she hadn't had a chance to see Alarin until now. Had he missed her as much as she'd missed him? "Alarin," she said in a voice that sounded higher than normal. She stepped back so he could walk into the room.

"Hi," he answered, his musical accent lilting in her ears, the thrill of it moving through her from head to toe. He let the door swing shut behind him as he entered, looking around the room. "You cleaned before you left."

"I made my bed," she said. "I hardly call that cleaning. My closet is a mess, the bookshelves are chaos, and don't *even* look under the bed." She scowled at the room. "Classes start in two days, and I barely had time to relax. So much for a vacation!" She came to stand beside him, not quite touching him, hugging her arms around her stomach in an attempt to control her emotions. After being away, she felt shy and awkward in Alarin's presence— especially since he seemed to be relaxed, as though their relationship was nothing more than the friendship it had started out as. "Did you manage to get an apartment?"

Alarin nodded. "The argument that I need a place for the

next year and a half so I don't have to move out every three to four months apparently worked. That and the school wants us Azellians off campus." His tone remained neutral, despite the reference to the mess last semester created when Tamara's recently discovered half-brother Justern had been falsely accused of the rape of a human woman and deported back to Azelle. That situation was still messy and they were still working through all the implications of it. He walked over to the dresser to lean against it. "How was your vacation?"

She shrugged and gave him a look from the corner of her eye, recognizing that neither of them wanted to talk about the repercussions, so she let him change the subject. "Miserable. I would have preferred staying here with you."

Alarin grinned delightedly. His mind immediately slipped around hers, as though he'd been waiting for that encouragement, and slid underneath her shielding. The touch raised shivers up and down her spine as he brushed up against the erotic centers in her brain. "And I would have preferred to have you stay," he replied, stepping forward and pulling her into an embrace.

She wrapped her arms around his slender waist and rested her head on his chest, feeling his wiry strength. A tension she didn't know she was holding in her shoulders drained out through her arms and feet and the top of her head. He dropped a kiss lightly on her hair. "So you missed me?" she asked softly.

He didn't answer in words, leaning back instead so he could lift her chin, tilting her gaze up to meet his. He lowered his head, brushing a kiss across her mouth. Her breath caught in her throat as a tingling sensation raced down beyond her stomach. She deepened the kiss, pressing herself against him.

He made a sound and pulled her more tightly against him,

kissing her aggressively, his mind twining itself around her so intensely she could barely tell where he began and she left off. He shoved the bags off the bed, using those mental abilities that had been revealed last semester. Not releasing her mouth, he walked her backwards and pushed her down to the surface of the bed. His hands found their way up under her shirt, touching her sensitized skin lightly, his long fingers cupping her breasts through her bra. If she'd had any questions about him missing her, they were washed away in the urgency of his touch, the almost desperate pressure of his mind and body against hers.

Their lovemaking didn't last all that long—probably not surprising, considering the length of time they'd been separated—but it was extremely intense, minds and bodies wrapped around each other in an intimate embrace that blurred the boundaries between them. They lay, still intertwined on the bed, as their hearts slowed and their breathing returned to normal. Belatedly, a thought occurred to her after it was over. "Uh, Alarin?" she asked, shifting slightly, so his weight was a little less centered on her chest.

"Hmmm?" he asked, sounding very sleepy and content. He moved so she could breathe, but he didn't completely pull away from her.

"Uh ... how do you think this impacted Merran? We didn't give him any warning and I know he's at work right now."

She felt the tension spill through him. He rolled off her and stared up at the ceiling. She shivered, hugging her arms to herself, the always constant link forged between them at her Awakening giving her a glimpse of the poorly understood, roiling emotions coming from Alarin. Last semester, Tamara had been cast into the Azellian world of psi, Awakening traumatically to her own mental abilities and leaving Alarin, Merran, and herself tied in an emotional and mental bond that linked them all through sex. Merran always knew when Alarin and she were together and vice versa. The two men shared her mentally, whether she—or they—wanted to or not.

"Merran's fine," he said, after a few moments of silence.

"Are you mad at me?" she asked, finding herself unable to look at him.

Alarin shifted on the bed beside her. "No," he responded. After a few minutes of uncomfortable silence, she felt the flare of hurt despite the shields they tried—unsuccessfully—to maintain between them. "But why is it that the first thing you ask about as soon as you see me is what's happening with Merran? I haven't seen you in weeks and that's the first thing you ask about?"

"Hey, wait a minute," she protested, pulling herself onto to her elbow. "I only mentioned Merran because I was concerned that our activities might have inconvenienced him, since he can sense it any time we're together," she added with an obvious frown on her face.

"Did you call him last night? You certainly didn't call me."

She sat up. "I didn't call anyone last night, Alarin. We got home at midnight, and I went right to bed. I didn't even speak to Merran while I was away ... it's actually been longer than that. Not even one phone call. What's going on?"

Alarin rolled over to face her. He reached out to trace a fingertip over her lips and jaw, cupping her cheek lightly in his palm and guiding her to lie down next to him again. "I guess I was a little thrown off balance because you were concerned about Merran. It just seemed like we'd hardly had a chance to spend five minutes together before you started asking about him."

Tamara made a sound and moved closer. "Why wouldn't I be

concerned that we might have interfered with Merran's day? He has a job, Alarin, and our activities can impact his job, whether we like it or not. It's not like we waited until tonight, when he's not in the middle of meetings."

He pulled her more tightly into his body, stroking a hand over her hair.

She could feel his remorse. "I know, I'm sorry. I reached out to him just now. Merran said it was fine, that he had a moment or two before he went to a meeting, and that we had pretty good timing, considering what could have happened. You don't have to worry."

She leaned into the embrace, resting her head on Alarin's shoulder. She could feel his body respond as she cuddled closer, even despite their activities a few moments ago. He rested his chin on her head, wrapping her in his arms as they lay quietly on the bed.

"Uh, Alarin?" she asked after a moment.

"Hmmm?" he replied, that sleepy content sound having returned to his voice. The rest of him wasn't nearly so sleepy though.

"As much as I'm enjoying this, we really shouldn't be doing this right now," she reminded him.

He lifted his head. "Right," he said, shifting away from her and getting to his feet.

If she thought it was hard to ignore his nudity during a normal conversation, it was nearly impossible when he was in this state, half-aroused and tousled from their earlier activities. He seemed quite unselfconscious about it, but her fingers twitched as she sat up. She wanted to finish what they'd started ... badly. Even knowing Merran was busy and couldn't afford to be distracted right now was hardly enough to dampen the fires. She closed her eyes to avoid looking at him.

A feather-light touch brushed across her eyelids. She opened her eyes to see Alarin's fingers brush down the side of her face, certain parts of him still standing very much at attention, especially as he stood in front of her. "Having trouble?" he teased.

She raised her eyebrows and leaned her head into his palm. "Uh, you could say that," she muttered.

He grinned, and she could feel his delight. He dropped his hand to her wrist and guided her hand towards his stomach, brushing her fingers against his skin, just above where she really wanted to touch. He stayed very properly wrapped in his own shields, however, so the contact was only physical.

"Alarin," she warned breathlessly, "you're teasing me."

"I'm the one who's being teased," he replied, sounding nearly as breathless as she was. "And I don't mind. Merran's connection is with you, not me. What we do to me shouldn't affect him."

She wanted to believe what he was saying, but she didn't trust either him or herself. It was too easy to forget themselves. "No, Alarin. Not right now. Tonight, okay? We can experiment tonight, and maybe we can find the edges of this ... thing."

"All right, fine. We don't have all that much time anyway. I sense Kari coming up the stairs."

"What?" Tamara leaped to her feet, reaching out to verify that what Alarin had said was true. "Shit," she blurted out as she grabbed for her clothes. "God damn it. Why didn't you warn me sooner? I know, I should have been scanning the area around me, the way Greg taught me to do, but you know that doesn't come naturally to me ... which is why I don't do it most of the time." She tugged on her jeans, fastening them hastily. "Will you put some clothes on?" she demanded, glancing over at him. He watched her, unconcerned and amused.

"Why?" he asked lazily.

"Because Kari doesn't want to see you standing there half ..." she waved a hand at him.

"Half what?" He leaned back against the oak dresser, making his body lengthen and certain parts of him leap out into sharp relief.

Tamara blushed violently and leaned over to pick up his jeans and underwear. "Half, half ... you know. Naked. Without clothes. I don't want her to see any of you at all, much less that," Tamara retorted, pointing at his groin and throwing his jeans and underwear at him as the sound of the dorm's interior fire door slamming shut became apparent to both of them.

He grinned at her and pulled on his underwear and jeans, but he didn't bother with his shirt or socks. Tamara tugged on her own sweater and ran her fingers through her hair to straighten it, then quickly pulled on her socks.

The knock on the door made Tamara jump, even though she was expecting it. She glanced over at Alarin, who'd replaced the bags on the bed, but the covers were still rumpled, providing mute testimony to their earlier activities. He seemed calm enough, his erection gone, and there was little other evidence of their love-making still left in the room—just his lack of a shirt and socks. She knew it was as much of a concession as she was going to get from him, though. She hated it when friends interrupted them, or figured out what they'd been doing, but he never cared. Indeed, it had been a fight to get him to wear anything at all when friends knocked on the door. He never dressed when it was Greg doing the knocking, and to tell the truth, Greg never seemed to care either. She couldn't get over it, though, and she didn't want to find out if her human friends could handle it or not.

Tamara straightened her shirt and pulled open the door. "Kari, hi!"

"Hey Tam. Oh, I'm sorry, am I interrupting something?" she asked, as she peered around Tamara to see Alarin standing there wearing nothing but a pair of jeans, his arms crossed over his bare, muscular stomach.

"No, you're fine," Tamara said, glaring at Alarin, who grinned at her unrepentantly. He loved to tease her about her uptight attitudes. "Will you put your shirt on, please?"

Kari eyed Alarin appreciatively, whose grin widened. He uncrossed his arms and turned slowly in a circle, ignoring Tamara's request. "Like what you see?"

Kari raised her eyebrows. "Hmmm. Absolutely. You never told me he was *this* hot, Tam."

Alarin bowed to her. "Thank you," he said, leaning over to grab his shirt off the floor.

"Don't hide that mighty fine chest on my account. I'm quite content to gaze."

"Hey!" Tamara protested. "Kari!"

"I wouldn't hide my mighty fine chest, as you put it," Alarin replied, talking to Kari, his green eyes twinkling brightly, as he slipped the t-shirt on over his head and pulled the long-sleeved button-down shirt over it, "but you heard her. She told me to put my shirt on. It doesn't bother either of us, but I think it's disturbing Tam."

"I'm not sure why. If I had that in my bed, I'd be parading it all over campus," Kari said, glancing sideways at Tamara, who could feel her cheeks burning.

"Will you stop talking about my boyfriend like he's a piece of meat?" Tamara demanded hotly, knowing they were teasing her, but unable to restrain her indignation. "Aren't you offended, Alarin?"

He grinned wider. "Of course not. It's too much fun watching you get upset."

Kari giggled. "You should know by now that we love teasing you, Tam."

Tamara did know, and that was one reason she never ever wanted Kari to walk in on them. *I'd never live it down,* she thought to herself. "Are you ready for the spring semester to start?" she asked Kari, trying to change the subject.

Kari sobered and shrugged. "As much as you are. I thought I'd come by to see if you want to head over and grab some lunch. But considering lover boy's here, you probably have better things to do."

"Dinner sounds great," Tamara said, glancing at Alarin. Balancing unconcernedly on one leg, then the other, he slipped on his socks and sneakers. "Are you hungry? Did you want to join us, Alarin?"

He looked up. "Given the amount of energy we recently expended, I'm starving, actually. I'd love to join you."

Tamara blushed ferociously, as Kari raised a hand. "Hey, I don't get to share in it; I don't want to hear it, kids."

"Kari!" Tamara protested again.

"I said I didn't want to hear it, didn't I?" Kari asked with an unrepentant grin. "It's not like I asked for details. Come on, lovebirds, let's go get dinner." Alarin and Tamara trailed her as they left the room to walk over to the cafeteria for lunch.

As they walked, Tamara slipped her hand into Alarin's. He squeezed her hand lightly, just a gentle pressure on her fingers. She'd missed him, and more than that, she felt this odd hunger to touch him. Not necessarily to lead to anything more, just to touch him. He let her, his mind wrapping around hers in a mental echo to hold hands. It had taken a little adjustment for him to get used to her need for physical touch and for her to get used to the way he used mental touch like she did physical, but now that they had, Tamara loved it.

The cafeteria was not yet full, since it was still a couple of days away from the start of the new semester, but Tamara could feel the mental pressure of the people in the cafeteria on her shields anyway. She let Alarin's hand go as they separated to see what was being offered, but they remained in light mental contact the whole time. Enough so that when Alarin saw the other Azellians sitting at a table by themselves, she felt it, and she agreed that they should join them.

Alarin got to the table first, Tamara not far behind. "Welcome to Earth," he said in Azellian. Tamara didn't hear him speak Azellian often; it changed his voice and made him rather exotic sounding. A thrill washed up from her stomach to pull at the top of her head, and a peculiar sense of possession pulsed through her. She took a deep breath. Now was not the best time to get lost in emotional forays—not with five newly arrived Azellians sitting there quite able to read any nuance of emotion she let past her shields. "I'm Alarin Raderth. How was the trip from Azelle?"

"Long," a young woman said. She was handsome rather than pretty, her nose prominent and slightly too large for her face, but her cheekbones were high and well-defined. She oozed physical confidence in a way that made Tamara vaguely jealous, especially when the woman gave Alarin a frankly appraising look. "So you're the famous Raderth who came to Earth."

Alarin grinned. "I don't know about famous," he said, "but I am a Raderth and I am on Earth."

Even sitting down, it was apparent that the woman was slender, willowy, and athletic looking, a body type Tamara had always wanted and most emphatically did not possess. She slipped in the empty slot beside Alarin, trying not to feel possessive, but failing miserably. Alarin didn't seem to sense her discomfort, which in some ways was a relief, but in others made her even more nervous. She was doing her best to shield from the other Azellians, but she was most definitely not shielding all that well from him, their psychic link preventing them from shielding effectively from each other. For him not to notice her upheaval meant he was either ignoring it or too distracted to notice, neither of which made her happy.

"I'm so pleased to meet you, Alarin. I'm Francyne Mennak Corvik," the athletic, handsome woman said. Her interest was plain to read. "I hope to get to know you better over the semester." She smiled at him, her eyes intent. Tamara took Alarin's hand, which rested on the table. He let her touch him only briefly, before moving his hand away. Tamara could feel a flush crawl up her cheeks as she tried to tell herself that it was just his lack of interest in touching that made him let her go so fast, not an interest in Francyne. Indignation warred with uncertainty within Tamara. Francyne gave Alarin a warm smile, ignoring Tamara completely, as she picked up on his dismissal. Tamara wasn't sure what Alarin's attitude about Francyne was, but she certainly knew what Francyne's was about him. Alarin's aura read clearly like a man who'd done what they'd just done—and she knew her aura matched his. For Francyne to be ignoring it meant she'd do things that Tamara didn't trust. She looked steadily at Francyne, who still didn't acknowledge Tamara's presence.

"I, for one, have been dying to know how a Raderth managed

to convince his family to let him come," a very slender young man with wide shoulders said, leaning forward and interrupting them. He had the same effortlessly confident air that Francyne did. But with deep dimples that appeared when he smiled and an infectious quality to that smile, it seemed considerably less like arrogance and more like charm. Tamara met his dark brown eyes and somehow knew he had quite deliberately interrupted to break the tension.

Alarin looked over at him. "The same way a Healer and a Memaxthal managed to get himself onto the roster of Azellian exchange students," he said with a grin. "Ignoring family strictures. Hey, Rory. Didn't expect you to make the leap to come to Earth. Long time no see. How have you been?"

"Not bad, not bad at all," Rory replied. "Much better than I was on Azelle." He looked at Tamara. "May I ask who this lovely lady sitting next to you is?"

Tamara flushed slightly. "I'm Tamara Dorvath Carrington," she said, using the Azellian form of her name somewhat self-consciously.

"Dorvath Carrington?" a petite brown-haired woman who looked barely old enough to have Awakened, much less to be in an exchange program, said in a high voice. "Are you related to that Carrington who got thrown off the planet for interference in internal Azellian affairs by getting an Azellian woman pregnant?"

"He's my father," Tamara replied, trying not to feel sheepish or defensive, but not really succeeding. "My mother was Jasmian Dorvath."

"So you know Justern Memaxthal, then?" Rory asked, interest sparking in his eyes. He leaned against the table, pressing his weight into his forearm, which made the muscles in his arm stand out sharply. *For a man who is as thin as he is, he's quite muscular,* she caught herself thinking before she cut it off abruptly.

"I'm his half-sister," Tamara admitted, feeling heat rise up her neck to her cheeks.

Rory grinned at her, his dimples turning into deep grooves down his cheeks. "We're cousins of a sort, then. I'm related to Justern through our fathers. It's somewhat distant, as our families aren't that closely related, and you're related to the Dorvaths, not the Memaxthals, but it's a connection. I'm Roryn Mennak Memaxthal, by the way. You can call me Rory."

Tamara let out the breath she hadn't realized she'd been holding. With one sentence, Rory had managed to somehow make her feel included. *Greg, Alarin, Merran, Mellis, and Justern never made me feel this way,* she thought, *that I should be ashamed of my family connections. I don't even know how Francyne did it, but she did. I feel like the lowest thing on the planet right now.* "Pleased to meet you, Rory," she said, feeling a rush of gratitude toward the handsome young Healer. Rory's grin softened into a smile.

Alarin didn't seem to notice, or maybe wasn't reacting to, the unspoken superiority at the table. *This is not at all like the last time I met Azellians,* Tamara thought, feeling out of her depth and uncertain about what do or how to act.

Rory continued the introductions, rescuing her yet again. "This is Francyne Mennak Corvik as you already know," he said. Sitting next to her was a quietly pretty young woman who lacked the flashy good looks of Francyne and the other Azellians at the table. "Malinna Sorved Serryn, who has relatives who work at the embassy." A faint moue of distaste crossed Francyne's face as she sniffed at Malinna, and Tamara knew she wasn't going to like Francyne. On the other side of Alarin was a young man with midnight blue eyes that looked almost black, even in the bright fluorescent light of the cafeteria. Tamara had to look twice to make sure his eyes were actually blue. "That's Damiar Corvik Darvyne over there. He's related to Francyne, if somewhat distantly, and more closely to Greg Darvyne Tenricth, whom I believe you know quite well. Sitting next to you is Sharynn Mennak Memaxthal. She's a very distant cousin of mine and of Francyne's." Sharynn was the petite woman with a pleasant expression on her face who had asked about Tamara's father. She smiled warmly at Tamara, and Tamara smiled back.

"It's great to have five more of us on Earth. Do you want someone to show you around? I'm more than happy to do it," Alarin commented, looking around the table.

"There are actually six of us," a new voice said, and Tamara looked up to see a dark-haired beauty standing above them, her gentle elegance making even the handsome Francyne look dowdy. "Hello, Alari."

Alarin didn't reveal anything on the surface, but Tamara could feel the shock reverberate down to his toes through the still active connection between them. Before she could react, he slammed up shields between them, heavy shields that only imperfectly hid the tangle of conflicted emotions the bond allowed her to access, even despite his shields. "What are you doing here, Idara?"

Shock reverberated through Tamara, too, and she wasn't nearly as accomplished as Alarin at hiding it. *This is Idara? Idara Tenricth, Alarin's ex-girlfriend? God, she's gorgeous. No, gorgeous isn't the word for it. Model beautiful, elegant, hot, drop-dead stunning, Aphrodite come to Earth. Alarin left this poised, elegant woman to take up with me? They must have looked absolutely breathtaking when they were together*, Tamara thought, her brain racing. Idara's elegant beauty matched Alarin's own aristocratic good looks, complimenting and adding to them. Insecurity suddenly slammed through Tamara, and she fought to hide her reaction.

"Greg's been telling me so much about Earth that I thought I should come to find out what's so fascinating. You don't need to worry that I'll get in the way." She set her tray next to Tamara and sat down. Alarin vibrated with tension. Unlike Francyne, who seemed to want to pretend that Tamara didn't exist, Idara looked straight at her. "I'm Idara Darvyne Tenricth. Greg's sister. You must be Tamara Carrington. I've heard quite a bit about you from my brother. It's a pleasure to finally get to meet you."

Before Tamara could say anything in return, Alarin broke in. "You don't need to be a *shiia*, Idara," he said sharply. "Leave her alone."

Idara blinked her large brown eyes at him. "What?" she asked, sounding wounded. "I did nothing but introduce myself."

"I'm out of here," Alarin said, slamming his chair back as he got to his feet. He grabbed his tray and stalked toward the dish return.

Not understanding what had happened, but not really wanting to spend any more time with these Azellians whom she didn't know, Tamara got up and followed him. She wasn't sure what had just taken place, but she knew she didn't want to be alone with Azellians who were doing things she didn't understand, even if Rory was being nice.

She passed by Kari, who was just getting her food and about to sit down.

"Tam? What's going on?" she called out.

Tamara watched Alarin slam out the door and made a motion with her two fingers and hand, mouthing the words, "I'll call you later."

Kari nodded and headed for a group of people she and Tamara both knew, as Tamara hurried after Alarin.

Tamara broke into a jog to catch up with him. "Alarin? Alarin!" Alarin didn't slow his long-legged stride much, just shortened it enough that Tamara could join him. "What just happened in there?" she asked as she came up next to him. Sullenly, his aura flared a turquoise green, the link between them telling her he was still in the grip of some powerful emotion, although she couldn't quite figure out what it was. She grabbed his arm. "Will you slow down and tell me what happened?"

Alarin turned on her. Tamara stepped back for a moment, out of breath and just a little frightened by the anger that was evident on his face. "She's the reason I left Azelle," he muttered in English, then added something in Azellian that Tamara didn't understand. It was either slang or another dialect Tamara didn't know. Maybe both. "I can't believe Merran okayed her coming," he continued in English. "I can't believe he'd do that to me."

"Maybe he didn't know," Tamara suggested, guessing that by "her" Alarin meant Idara.

Alarin gave her an expressive look that told her what he thought of that idea.

"Well, he's not omnipotent," she defended herself. "Ask him, if it's got you so upset."

"I'm planning to," Alarin snapped, turning on his heel and lengthening his stride, which forced Tamara to run to keep up.

As she trotted beside him, she thought about Alarin's reaction. When Alarin told her he'd had a girlfriend at home, she hadn't expected that ex-girlfriend to look like she'd stepped off the pages of a fashion magazine. Idara was beautiful, elegant, and tall. She could easily make Tamara feel short, dumpy, and ugly. She hadn't, but Alarin had reacted as though she'd done something much more offensive than sit down and introduce herself. What exactly had she done? What had Tamara missed? Idara hadn't been nearly so unpleasant as Francyne, with her air of superiority and her attitude of holier than thou ... yet Alarin hadn't reacted to that. As a matter of fact, although Idara's elegance and beauty were intimidating, she didn't seem to use them as a weapon. She looked nothing like her brother, nothing at all, but there was a quality to her, a similarity to Greg that made Tamara think she was nice underneath the emotional tension between her and Alarin. Francyne, on the other hand, was nothing short of a bitch. The strength of her reaction to Francyne surprised Tamara, but she didn't pause to question it.

Tamara trailed Alarin to the embassy, although he didn't say a word as she followed him. His shoulders were clenched, his fists tight against his sides as they approached the gates and she tried to catch her breath. He wasn't the slightest bit winded, and it bothered her on some level, as though he'd left her behind ... again.

"Alarin, Tamara," the guard, a young woman they both knew, said. "We don't usually see you this early in the day. Something happening?"

"Hi Eryka. Is Merran in?" Alarin asked, mitigating his tone just enough that he wasn't being rude, but still letting all his urgency through. "I need to see him. It's very important."

"Let me call in and see, Alarin. I think he might have left for the day. I saw his assistant leave, anyway," she added, stepping back into the booth.

Alarin waited, thrumming with tension as she called up to the office.

She returned a few moments later. "Merran's in and he's got some time available. Go on in," she said.

Alarin nodded. "Thanks, Eryka."

"Thanks," Tamara echoed, and they entered the embassy grounds. Neither of them spoke as they walked up the winding path that led to the entrance of the main embassy building, a beautiful large mansion and grounds that had been purchased by the embassy and converted to an office complex. As they always did, the doors opened silently to accommodate their entry. Tamara sensed the feather-light brush of a mind scanning them with psi as they entered, but no one said anything or confronted them as they proceeded into the building.

Alarin paid the doors no attention as they closed behind him. He headed for the large marble winding staircase in the huge entrance hall of the mansion, up toward Merran's office. It was silent in the office complex, many of the offices closed for lunch. Alarin's aura flared in the dim interior of the embassy, building up in a well-known intensity toward a crescendo Tamara wasn't sure she wanted to be near. She followed anyway. Maybe she'd learn what had actually happened.

Chapter Two

"All right, Dana. I'll review the final proposal and give you an answer by tonight," Merran said, leaning back in his chair as he focused on the woman in front of him. "I don't know that I like that I'll be—"

The office door opened abruptly, slamming into the wall and interrupting him. Alarin stomped in, his aura flaring brightly in the shadowed corners of Merran's office, glowing so strongly that Merran glanced surreptitiously at Dana Redmond, his human public relations director, to see if she noticed. She didn't seem to perceive anything unusual, much to his relief.

Merran felt a slight surge at the sight of Tamara looking somewhat lost and forlorn. He hadn't seen or talked to her in weeks and hadn't quite realized how much he'd missed her. She was heavily shielded, but the link between them told him she was uncertain, confused, and even frightened by the aggression Alarin was projecting.

The young man moved forward in a cloud of his fury and slammed his hands down on the desk in front of Merran. "You asshole," he said in the street dialect of the *urro-ken* who lived in the caves outside their hometown of Azorantxl. It was a dialect Merran didn't realize Alarin knew. Merran's full-blooded High Council siblings certainly didn't speak it. How had full-blooded High Council Alarin picked it up? The dialect was uniquely appropriate for swearing, though. Most of what Alarin was spewing was *nothing but* swear words. Alarin continued to swear at Merran for a good thirty seconds before switching to the cleaner, more formal Azellian they all spoke. "I left Azelle to get away from her, Merran. How could you let her follow me?"

Merran got to his feet, not liking that the redhead towered over him from that angle. His own temper ignited, a flash response to abuse him right back flared within him, but he drew on years of experience in tense situations to help him not overreact. Ignoring Alarin's outburst, he looked at Alarin and then at Dana, deliberately bringing Alarin's attention to the fact that there was someone else in the office. "I apologize for the intrusion and my compatriot's rude behavior, Dana. Apparently, I have a crisis on my hands that I need to take care of right away," he said in English, his tone polite and businesslike.

Alarin's temper tantrum slipped into embarrassment as Dana, a tall, attractive brunette dressed formally in her designer business suit, kept her calm and poise. She leaned over and collected her brown leather briefcase. Getting to her feet, she assured Merran. "That's all right, Ambassador. We were pretty much finished, I think. And you do have to take care of crises as they pop up." Her tone was correct and very professional, without a hint of judgment that Alarin had burst in and started screaming in Azellian.

Alarin flushed a deep red from the bottom of his neck to the tips of his ears, unable to control the intensity of his physical reaction to his embarrassment. Visibly shoving down his temper to bring himself under control, he turned to her. "I'm sorry for the intrusion, Ms ..." he said in English, the force of his anger draining away with his words. "I didn't realize Merran had a meeting. The guard said he was available."

"Redmond, Dana Redmond," she replied, holding out a hand. "You must be Alarin Raderth?"

Alarin nodded and shook her hand. "I'm flattered that you recognize me," he said, his native politeness resurging from the shattered shards of his temper. "I apologize again for my rudeness."

Dana smiled at him, and some of the tension drained from the room. "It's all right, Mr. Raderth. As I said, we were nearly finished anyway. Will you email me your final thoughts?" she asked Merran. "I'd like to get the interviews set up tomorrow."

"I'll have an answer for you tonight," Merran replied, making sure he was as heavily shielded as Alarin. "Thank you, Dana."

"You're welcome, Ambassador." She glanced at Alarin. "Nice to meet you, Mr. Raderth, Ms ..."

"Tamara Carrington," Tamara said, extending a hand.

Dana shook it and smiled warmly at her. "Pleased to meet you, Ms. Carrington." She turned back to Merran. "I'll talk to you tomorrow, Ambassador. Nice to meet you again, Mr. Raderth, Ms. Carrington."

Alarin gave her a short bow and Tamara murmured a polite response as Dana walked to the door and exited. As soon as she was out the door, Merran turned on Alarin.

"What in the name of the *aarya* was that all about, Alarin?" he asked, his tone still cold and distant, reigning in his temper with an effort. "I have an office to run, you know." *Give us a moment, will you, Tamara? I'll contact you when we're done.* He sent the request to Tamara's intimate level. Tamara left as he requested, slipping out of the office quietly. Merran turned his attention back to Alarin. "What's with barging in here and flailing around like a madman?"

Alarin's aura flared, but it lacked the intensity of just a few moments ago when he'd slammed his way into the office. "You know what I'm talking about."

"No, actually, I don't," Merran said slowly, enunciating his words carefully and slowly. "What has you so upset you felt the need to come barging in here, swearing at me in the *jygar* dialect, and demanding to know why I let her come? Who's here? What are you talking about?"

"Idara. Idara's here … as an exchange student." Alarin stared down at the swirling design on the area rug carefully laid over the russet cherry wood floor planks, refusing to meet Merran's eyes.

Merran raised an eyebrow, relaxing slightly. At least Alarin hadn't started swearing again. Although his friend's surprising facility with the vulgar, if creative, *jygar* dialect had been quite impressive, he didn't really care to hear more of it. "Idara?"

"Yes," Alarin snapped, starting to pace. "Larger than life and just as pushy. She's not going to give me up without a fight, Merran, and you know how she fights. Why, in the name of the *aarya,* did you authorize her to come?"

Merran ran a hand through his hair. "I authorized five exchange students. Idara was not among them. My assistant, Jamian, greeted the students when they arrived the day before yesterday. I just found out about her arrival when he and I met this morning, and since then, I've gone from one meeting to another. I haven't had a chance to even think about her presence here or its implications, Alari."

Alarin stopped on the other side of Merran's desk. "Like I believe that. Nothing happens in your exchange program without your approval. You didn't even warn me! I thought we were friends. Friends don't do that to each other, Merran."

Merran yanked open a drawer and pulled out a computer tablet. He swiped a finger across it to activate the screen and threw the tablet across the desk at Alarin. "Look at the roster of students I authorized if you don't believe me."

Alarin stared at the list of students. "But I thought she had to ask you first."

Merran snorted. "Why would I think Idara, of all people, would even want to study on Earth? I know her almost as well as you do. Never in my wildest dreams would I think she'd want to come to Earth, much less seek out a visa to actually do it. She didn't go through me to get a visa." He took a deep breath and let it out slowly. "As for my say in the exchange program, since the fiasco with Justy, the Council has taken over the choice of candidates. They can, and apparently did, send people they didn't tell me about."

Alarin snorted. "As if."

"Don't believe me if you don't want to. I don't care." He looked steadily at Alarin, picking up on the emotions behind Alarin's outburst. *They definitely feel more personally directed at me than just being upset about an unwanted ex-girlfriend showing up,* he thought to himself as he relaxed and opened himself to the unspoken messages his friend was giving off. *At least he's talking to me, finally.* "What did she do?"

Alarin took a deep breath. "She showed up at lunch and started in on Tam."

"Did she harm Tamara? What did she do?" Merran asked again, and just the faintest hint of protectiveness crept into his tone, despite his effort to stay neutral.

Something, maybe that note of protectiveness in Merran's voice, set Alarin off again. His temper flared. "She started in on Tam, all right. Does it matter? I'm not spending the next two years dodging her in every class I have. Get her off the planet!"

Merran took a deep breath and let it out slowly. "What *exactly* did she do? Tell me what she did, Alari, and I will lodge a protest with the Council. Enough of those and I'll force them to recall her. But I have to lodge a protest first or I'll be censured myself."

Alarin blew air out his lips in frustration, the brief flash subsiding. "She was harassing Tam."

"Do I have to call Tamara in here to ask her myself?" Merran challenged, pulling up the reserves of patience he normally stockpiled for a particularly recalcitrant ambassador or dignitary. *Alarin is acting so strange,* he thought to himself. *Almost paranoid.* "Tell me what Idara did to Tamara, or I will call her in myself."

Alarin's jaw clenched. "Tam didn't even understand what happened," he muttered. "It's not going to help for you to call her in."

Merran took a deep breath. "Then you tell me what she did," he said. "There is nothing I can do unless you tell me, formally, so I can lodge a protest."

Alarin narrowed his eyes and looked at Merran, his expression as unpleasant as the dark emotions leaking from his shielding. "My telling you does nothing. As the wronged party, Tam has to be the one who lodges a protest, or am I not remembering the rules correctly?"

Merran scowled. "Will you stop treating me like I'm out to get you, Alarin? So what if you tell me and Tamara doesn't? As you said, Tamara didn't understand what happened. It doesn't make it any less hurtful, and I do have some leeway in the rules. Tell me what she did!"

Alarin stared down at the desk. "She reminded all the Azellians at the table that Tam is human and not High Council," he muttered. "While she emphasized her own High Council connections."

"Is that all?" Merran asked, relaxing abruptly. "From the way you were acting, I thought she attacked Tamara."

"Is that all?" Alarin lifted his eyes and glared at Merran, his aura flaring. He said something in the *jygar* dialect again, then continued, "Is that all? I knew it! I just knew it! You just want her here because it will distract me and you'll get Tam all to yourself."

So there it is. I can feel it now. Jealousy. Even as Merran listened to the now clear projections of jealousy, insecurity, and fear rocketing around his office, he said, "Whoa, whoa, whoa. Wait a minute. How did we get from Idara being rude to Tamara to me wanting Tamara all to myself?"

"I'm not blind, Merran. You're in love with her. Fine. You want her, take her. I'll just go back to Azelle and you can have her." Alarin straightened and switched to English. "If I'm back on Azelle, I might not have to listen to your fucking either." He turned for the door, reaching out with psi abilities to pull it open.

"No, you don't," Merran snapped. He held the door shut under the pressure of his mind. "We're dealing with this right now, Alarin Dorvath Raderth. You are *not* walking out of here thinking that I am trying to make a play for Tamara, or that Idara is my way of doing that."

Alarin refused to turn around. They struggled for a moment, but Merran won. "Let me go, Merran. There's nothing to talk about."

Merran came around the other side of his desk. "You're jealous."

"I am not."

"Yes, you are. You're so jealous you can hardly see straight. Why?" Merran asked, walking over so he stood between Alarin and the door, forcing Alarin to meet his eyes. "You spend ten times more time with her than I do. You've made love to her so many more times than I have that my sex life has become pretty much exclusively experiencing what you two are doing. I haven't had physical sex with Tamara or any other woman in a while. What are you afraid of?"

Alarin twitched.

"You're afraid I'm going to get sick of it and demand my fair share of time, aren't you?" Merran asked ruthlessly.

Alarin held his body and mind under control this time, giving Merran nothing but blank shields.

"Or are you more afraid that I'll step back and give you free access to Tamara?" Merran asked, a sudden curiosity welling to the surface.

Alarin's breath caught, but his shields didn't waver.

"Is that it? This whole drama was to give yourself an excuse to leave Earth, to leave Tamara and what you feel for her?"

"I'm not you," Alarin muttered under his breath.

Merran ignored the comment. "You are very capable of handling Idara, Alari. She probably is here to try to test the boundaries you've set up, but you are very good at distancing yourself. As for her behavior toward Tamara, you know as well as I do that Idara will listen to you. You tell her to stay away from Tamara, she's going to obey. Not that she has much of a choice, if you use your Raderth willpower to force her to do what you want. Let go of this jealousy, Alari. I will step away from Tamara, if that's what it takes."

Alarin lifted his head and stared at Merran. "How can you do that, with the bond between us that forces you to share in Tamara's sex life? Do you want to restrict yourself to a vicarious sex life? How long do you think that will last before you start demanding your share of time with Tamara?"

"What do you want, Alari? Forget Tamara. Forget about me. Forget all the rest of it. If the bond weren't between us, what would you do?" Merran asked, leaning back against the door and crossing his arms in front of his chest.

Alarin's breathing caught slightly, and he said nothing.

"I thought so. You love her; you want to be with her. She feels the same way, you know."

Alarin frowned, looking up. "What do you mean?"

"She loves you, Alari. I'm an empath, remember? Even without the bond, I know quite well how she feels about you. And I, for better or worse, can't give her what she needs," Merran replied, feeling suddenly tired. While Alarin had been working himself into a jealous rage, Merran had been sensing the cracks in their relationship and had tried to talk about it with Alarin before it got to this point. That Alarin chose to get angry and throw a temper tantrum, not taking the more reasonable approach to talk through his troubles around their odd little arrangement, made Merran very tired.

Alarin took a deep breath and let it out slowly. "No matter what you say, the bond between us does make a difference, Mer. No matter how we feel about it, we're irrevocably tied together. It's going to destroy us if we don't deal with it."

Look who's talking, Merran thought to himself sarcastically, but he kept all hint of that emotion buried under heavy shields. Instead, he studied Alarin as he spoke. "Not necessarily irrevocably," he responded quietly.

Alarin's eyes widened. "What do you mean?"

"I've been talking to Greg about it for some time now. Pretty much ever since it became glaringly apparent that Tamara and I have not been spending time with each other. He says he thinks the bond may have been established at Tamara's Awakening, but that our activities after that served to strengthen it. He thinks the sexual sharing part will fade with time, if Tamara and I don't renew it by being together."

Alarin stared intently at Merran, unable to suppress the surge of hope that spilled through his body. "What? How does he know that?"

"Because the intensity of my participation in your sex life is fading off the longer I'm away from Tamara. At the risk of condemning myself to a hell of you two rabbits going at it, I can ignore you two having sex if I have to, whereas not that long ago, there was no way I could have ignored it to save my life." He made sure his tone was calm, as if it didn't matter. As if he didn't care. *The funny thing is I do care, just not as much as I care about you two*, he thought to himself.

Alarin was silent for a moment. "That doesn't change how Tam feels about you. You're lying to yourself if you think she doesn't love you."

"No matter what Tamara may feel, the reality is that I've already chosen to be married, Alari. To my job, to my life as an ambassador. She deserves more than my occasional attention when I have the time, and I sense that she already knows that. It's not something I can see changing. Me? Married, with kids? Not in this lifetime."

Alarin eyed him narrowly. "Ambassadors don't have to be single. Being married to your job is your choice."

Merran shrugged. "I just said that. I've thought about it quite a bit since Tamara's Awakening and the establishment of this bond, Alari. For better or worse, I can't give Tamara my full attention. For better or worse, since you and she have been having sex, she's come to depend on you, come to love you. I don't mind stepping back. Once our link through sex is gone, it will be even easier."

Alarin scowled at him. "You still love her. The link you have with her is not just sexual."

Merran shrugged again. "We're friends, too, Alari. If I step back, I'm not going to betray you with Tamara just because she and I care about each other. Are you afraid she doesn't love you as much as she loves me?"

Alarin took a deep breath and let it out slowly. "It's a thought."

Merran raised an eyebrow. "And a baseless one. Whose bed has she been in pretty much constantly since her mother's death?"

"Because yours hasn't been available."

Merran snorted. "You haven't been paying attention, Alari, if you think she's chosen you because I'm not available. She turned me down several times before she left on vacation."

"She did?" Alarin asked slowly, his tone lightening considerably.

Merran spread his hands and let Alarin read the truth from his mind. "She's sensitive enough to have picked up on the nuances long before you were ready to admit they existed. Of course, she was pretty clever at making me think there really were other reasons she couldn't have sex with me, but she's managed to tell me no quite a few times. In fact, I've had only a handful of sexual encounters with her on the physical level since you and she started having sex. If anyone should be jealous, it should be me. In truth," he continued thoughtfully, "it's for the best. I'd rather have you and Tamara happy than Tamara with me. I care about your and her well-being more than I care about who's in my bed."

Alarin relaxed abruptly. "I didn't know that. She ... never told me."

"Why would she? I'm not sure she was consciously aware of what she was doing anyway. Now go. I have work to do, and you have a relationship to build and nurture." He stepped aside so Alarin could pull the door open and leave. "You do anything to hurt her, though, and we'll have words," he said, only half-joking.

"Stand in line. I think Greg would be there first."

"You're probably right. Take care of her, Alari."

"If she lets me. You know how prickly she gets about her independence." He put his hand on the door and looked back at Merran. "What about the bond? How long do you have to continue in enforced chastity?"

Merran sighed. "I don't know." He ran a hand through his hair. "Hopefully it will fade before Festival descends upon us."

Alarin frowned, doing some mental calculations regarding the upcoming Azellian spring ritual. "They told us it would affect us on Earth, but does Festival really impact us that strongly here?"

Merran made a sound. "Oh yes. The *aarya*Song travels quite well through the galactic aether."

Alarin's eyes widened. "They told us before we came to Earth that humans don't know about it. How have we kept it from them? I mean, if the Song is heard so clearly here, how have we been hiding it?"

"It's one of the reasons Azellians don't live anywhere else on Earth but near the embassy. The Council usually warns us at least a few hours before it happens, and we've negotiated with the *aarya* to send out a call before the Song gets into full swing, so the Azellians can gather here on the embassy grounds. You'll feel it. So will Tamara, since she interacts with us on a psi level. We close the embassy, chase off the humans, and let the Song take us."

Alarin blinked. "Humans haven't even been curious about it? I can't believe that no hint of it has ever gotten out during the fifty years Azellians have been here."

"Oh, hints have gotten out. Don't tell me you haven't heard the rumors. Why do you think my reputation is what it is? We play the media, work the story, write Festival off to a holy day, and that gets us the tolerance we need. It's worked well in the past, and probably will continue to work well if we continue to restrict exposure to it."

"I still can't believe humans accept this," Alarin said. "Or that all our kinsmen here on Earth accept the restrictions."

Merran shrugged. "Do you want to be caught among humans when out of your head with Festival?"

Alarin shuddered. "No. The *aarya* preserve us, no."

"There you are."

"It's that loud?"

"As if we were on Azelle."

"Shit," Alarin muttered, leaning his arm against the door.

"What?"

"You know how Tam is about frightening new experiences … and unusual sex in general," Alarin replied. "How is she going to react to Festival?"

Merran laughed. "Ah, well, I suggest you get her used to the idea. You have, oh, a few months to do it. Good luck with expanding her sexual horizons before Festival does it for her."

Alarin snorted and pulled open the door. "Thanks so much."

"You're so welcome."

As they opened the door and headed into the outer office, Tamara stood up from where she'd been seated in one of the waiting room chairs. "Is everything better?" she asked, looking from one to the other.

Alarin slipped an arm around her waist, leaning over to kiss her. "Everything's fine," he said after he'd pressed his lips against her temple.

Tamara didn't glance at Merran, but he could feel her soft question inserted on his private level under his shields. *Is it, Merran?*

Merran gave her the mental equivalent of a hug and sent back reassurance, although he didn't speak in words. She relaxed visibly and let Alarin cuddle her close to his body. Merran blinked, keeping his own emotions carefully shielded. He did care about Tamara, Alarin, and his friendship with Alarin, but sometimes, like now, when he would have liked to greet his lover with a passionate kiss and some intense lovemaking in his office, it was difficult. He turned back to his office and the cold comfort of work.

A few hours later, high in the World Tower not far away from the embassy and campus, Tamara sprawled on the plush soft leather armchair in Greg Tenricth's apartment. Since the whole revelation had come out about his identity and his psi abilities, he'd moved to the secure World Tower, just a few floors below Merran. His Healing talent made him the focus of all kinds of attention, and living on campus would have become impossible, even if the college had been willing to allow the Azellians to live on campus anymore. It made visiting him a little more of a pain, but Tamara had caught him at home this afternoon on a rare day off.

"How did you manage to get a day off?" she asked, looking around the obsessively neat apartment. Merran's apartment was almost as neat, except for his office and closets, where it looked like someone had exploded paperwork and clothes everywhere, or her own place, which also had its hidden messy areas. Greg's, however, was perfectly arranged and perfectly cleaned, making Tamara wonder why he was now in the midst of cleaning. He moved around the room, dusting off the few personal objects he'd displayed to decorate the place, as Tamara sat in his armchair.

"By sticking to my guns. I am actually scheduled to be four days on and three days off. It's partially my fault that I keep booking my days off," Greg replied calmly. He shook his head. "Healing isn't something I can turn off and on at will, but today I just needed to take the time."

"I'm interrupting then," Tamara said, shifting so her legs were on the floor as she leaned forward. Greg shook his head. She felt the slightest pressure against her shoulder, as though he'd touched her, although he was six feet across the room. "It's not a bother, Tam. No more than Merran or Alarin are. I can still clean while we visit," he said, dusting off a large polished wood statue of a tree. It didn't look like it needed dusting, but then she wasn't nearly as picky as Greg.

"What is that?"

Greg touched it lightly, brushing his fingertips over the silky wood with a caressing gesture, an unconscious sensuality the other Azellians showed but Greg did not often display. "It was a gift. I Healed a Miir symbiont some years back and its host gave me this."

55

"You Healed a Miir?" Tamara asked, surprised. The Miir were even more secretive than the Azellians were reputed to be. *Although the Azellians have never been particularly secretive around me,* she thought.

"A Miir symbiont. Most people have such an anthropomorphic bias, whether human, Atheran, Tyr, or we *umanaarya,* as we Azellians call ourselves. The beings we see as the Miir are actually nothing more than the eyes and ears of the Miir intelligence. They have little or no native intelligence themselves."

Tamara stared at him. "What do you mean?"

"They are conduits for the larger Miir whole. If you go to Miirjl, the whole planet is forested, covered in a thick stand of what we'd call trees. About half of them aren't."

"Aren't what?"

"Trees. At least not as we know trees, anyway."

Tamara's eyes widened. "The Miir are trees?"

"No more than you are apes."

Tamara blinked. "So the beings that move around and interact with humans on a limited basis are …"

"Symbionts."

She struggled to process such an alien thought. "How do they react to our tendency to cut down trees?"

"Badly. It's one of the reasons the Miir are found in very few places on Earth. They tend to avoid areas where humans harvest lots of trees, which is pretty much everywhere."

"How did you learn so much about them?"

Greg grinned at her. "Earth is not the first place I've spent away from Azelle. I've been an unusual Healer from the time I Awakened."

Tamara heaved a sigh. "That I can believe. I've always thought that Healers were the least likely to travel away from Azelle."

"I don't know that the proportions are any different from the non-Healers who want to leave Azelle; there are just fewer of us than there are non-Healers," Greg replied, moving on to another shelf on the corner cabinet in the entryway of the apartment. "I know quite a few Healers who love to travel, to explore alien bodies, and to learn about new biologies." He glanced back at her. "In more ways than one."

Tamara managed, with something of an effort, to control her blush. "Ah, so you mean not every Healer is as celibate as you are?" she half-teased, although she knew embarrassing Greg was as impossible as embarrassing Alarin.

Greg gave a small smile. He slapped the dusting rag against his leg and hesitated for just a moment. "It's complicated, but not all Healers are as celibate as I have been, no."

Tamara blinked at him. "Not all Healers are homosexual, are they?" she asked curiously, thinking about the new Healer arrival, Rory. Tall, charming, roguishly handsome, he exuded that same undefinable, but potent, sexuality she'd noted in Alarin and Merran. He'd certainly appeal to many of the girls on campus—he'd appeal to her if she didn't have her hands full with Alarin and Merran.

As he usually did, Greg saw right through her, either knowing her well enough or reading her because she'd been leaking curiosity. "Rory's most certainly not. I'd suggest moving carefully around him, though. You're used to me, and Rory has a very different style. He's also … fresh from Azelle."

"Which means?" Tamara asked, her face heating up as it usually did when she talked about subjects like this with Greg.

"It means, I'd suggest that any move on Rory's part you

consider from the point of view that Rory may misunderstand you. He likes women, a lot, and though he is a Healer, he's not nearly as interested in working all the time as I am. Not all Healers are workaholics. Or therapists. I like both physical and emotional Healing, but Rory does nothing but Heal physical complaints. He's not the slightest bit interested in counseling or teaching beyond the bare basics. While I'm gone, I suggest you not consider him a replacement for me."

It took her a moment to process everything Greg had said. She did indeed have a counselor-teacher-type relationship with Greg, although she'd never really thought about it that way before. "Wait a minute, wait a minute," she blurted, processing the last bit of what he'd just said. "Gone? Gone where? Where are you going?"

Greg came around the corner of the white leather couch. "Ather. There's a plague there and the Atherans are asking for help."

"For how long? When? When did you find out about this?" Greg's warnings about Rory evaporated in the shock of finding out he was leaving.

He perched on the arm of the heavy couch. "I don't know … soon … and about three days ago. Merran found out about it through his contacts, then asked me and I said yes."

Tamara pressed her hands against her head. "Plague? Is it dangerous for you?"

Greg shrugged and said neutrally, "Depends on the plague. The differences in Atheran and Azellian genetic makeup are significant enough that it's unlikely, but there is always some risk."

"Some risk? Why go then? You can't go. You can't. Greg, what would we do if we lost you?" She tried to control the fear and worry that began to spread through her, but she knew she was leaking emotions past her shields.

Greg moved so he faced her. "I'll be fine. Even if I'm not, I have little choice in the matter. I'm a Healer. Sick people call and I go." He crouched in front of her, swirling his hands lightly through her aura, soothing her, both hands smoothing out the roils in her aura and the disturbances in her emotional state. Her shields steadied under his ministrations. "You can be sure I'll be back if it's in my power."

Tamara took a deep breath and let the calm spread from his fingers through her. "I'm not worried about what is in your power. Just what's not."

Greg leaned forward and kissed her lightly. He stood up. "You're sweet to be worried about me, Tam, but I'll be fine. I'll make sure I take extra care."

She blinked at him. "You'd better."

He smiled again. "Now, you didn't come over here to discuss my plans or talk about Miir symbionts. What's up?"

Tamara fought the blush. "Can't I just want to visit?"

Greg raised an eyebrow. "Sure. Do you? Or are you trying to pretend because I talked about how not all Healers are counselors and you don't want to see our relationship that way?"

"How do you *do* that?"

Greg smiled. "Not all Healers are counselors, but we do have a leg up when it comes to training and sensitivity. And I know you pretty well. We haven't shared ourselves quite the way you, Merran, and Alarin have, but I've studied quite a bit about you while I've trained you to access and use your psi."

Her blush slipped out from her control. She suddenly didn't want to talk about it.

He sat beside her on the couch. "Trouble in paradise?"

Tamara shrugged, not liking that he knew her that well. "Yes.

No. Maybe. I don't know. It's not working, Greg. The agreement we made during my Awakening is pretty much defunct. Nothing left. Alarin gets jealous if I even mention Merran, and Merran ... well ... he's been so busy I don't think I've gotten to spend more than a couple of hours with him in the past few months, outside of the office."

"You knew going in that Merran is committed to his work first and foremost."

"I know. I know. It could be worse. I mean, I like Merran, enjoy spending time with him, care about him, but ..."

"But what?"

"But I can't see depending on him on a day-to-day basis. He carries such a wall in his head. Even when we were ... when I Awakened ... I didn't get through it, not really. Certainly not now. He won't share with me, not the way Alarin will, and that makes it hard to have an open relationship with him."

"It's common for sensitive empaths to do that, to build barriers to keep others out, and it is pretty much the way it is for channeling empaths like Merran. Other people's emotions overwhelm an empath, so they stay hidden behind thick walls, which sometimes looks like they are cold or don't care. To add to that tendency, Merran had a rougher childhood than many, and he's driven. It means he holds everyone at arm's length."

"I can accept that. It's part of who Merran is and nothing I can change. Or would even want to. I mean, Merran's drive and ambition are too deep a part of who he is. But what does it mean to us, as a couple? Or a trio, for that matter? How do we work it out?"

"Have you ever thought about letting him go? Not trying to push yourself or him somewhere he's not able to go?"

Tamara held herself very still, probing at that thought.

"Completely, as in break up with him?" She hesitated, finding it hard to admit that she might have had a part to play in why she and Merran hadn't spent any time together. Yes, he was busy and spending most of his time in meetings, but he'd invited her several times before she left on vacation to stop by for a romantic evening and she'd turned him down, afraid of Alarin's reaction, and not wanting to spark off a fight before her father dragged her out of town. "Maybe, just a bit. But it's hard to let Merran go, to see him draped over someone else. I'm not sure how I would handle it."

"I think you're safe. Merran doesn't drape himself over anyone, not even you. I bet you're one of the only women in his life that has even seen his barriers. Most of the time, he doesn't let them get that close."

Tamara's stomach fluttered a little, and she sighed. "I guess we have to do something, because it's going to come crashing down around our ears if the three of us keep trying to make this work. It's obvious that Alarin's not going to tolerate it if I spend *any* time with Merran." She buried her head in her hands.

"Why do you think there's a problem with Alari?"

Tamara lifted her head to meet Greg's calm gaze. "Alarin's been so touchy lately." She lifted a hand and rubbed her forehead. "Not wanting me to do anything with Merran, not even talk to him. He's jealous, I think. I don't know. He won't talk to me about it."

Greg got up and went into the granite-and-stainless-steel kitchen. "Do you want some tea?"

Tamara nodded and got up, too, trailing him to settle down on a tall barstool that stood underneath the stone pass-through to the kitchen. She rested her arms against the cold surface, then sat back, as the chill of the countertop seeped uncomfortably through the sleeves of her blouse. "Lemon, if you have it."

Greg poured water into the teakettle and touched the button to start the heating cycle. He reached up and pulled out two large mugs and two small plates, retrieving a bright yellow box from another cabinet. He unwrapped the box, took out two tea bags, and settled them on the two plates.

She watched him for a few seconds, then asked, "What do I do about it?"

"Have you talked to Merran?"

"Not yet. I haven't had the chance."

"Talk to Merran. Emotionally, he's got less riding on this than Alarin does and he's more likely to be logical about it. Who knows? He may even have a solution for you."

Tamara's eyes widened. "Have you talked to him?" Greg shrugged noncommittally. He met her eyes calmly, without a flicker of reaction. He might know her, but she knew him, too. "You did! You talked to him about this. What did he say?"

Greg put his hands up. "I don't get in the middle when I have a choice, Tam. You know that. Talk to Merran."

Tamara's mind raced as she thought about it. She squirmed on her chair. "What about that bond thing we have? What are our solutions? Doesn't it kind of take away our options? I thought you said it was permanent."

Greg raised an eyebrow. "Nothing is permanent. Everything renews itself ... changes ... based on how we react to it and what we do to develop it, or not. This bond may not be any more permanent than ... love." He flashed her a quick grin. "Not that I want to burst your romantic ideals, but even the love we call romantic love isn't permanent. Or really even designed to be."

A weird sensation crawled through her stomach. "Does that mean ... what does that mean?"

Greg shrugged, putting his hands out. "I've said as much as I'm going to, Tam. Talk to Merran directly."

Tamara sighed. "Fine. When?"

"Now, that, my dear Tamara, is something I can't help you with. Schedule an appointment."

She could feel herself relax a little. "Scheduling an appointment is a good idea. And probably the only way I'll get a chance to talk to him without someone interrupting us."

The teakettle reached boiling and clicked itself off. Greg poured their tea. Smiling at her, he shifted topics. "Now, while I'm gone, I want to be sure that you do your focusing exercises every day, Tam. Otherwise your shielding may slip. And as an empath, it will be uncomfortable to you and the people around you. Other people's emotions can really mess with yours when you're not shielded, and things can get blown out of proportion. If you start projecting things back at people, it will be uncomfortable for them," he reminded her as he poured.

"I know, I will, I promise," Tamara replied as she leaned back in her chair. "Speaking of psi, I heard you guys talking about family talents before I left on vacation and have been meaning to ask you about it. What did you mean by family talents?"

"That's a longer conversation."

"Are you doing anything right now … besides cleaning?"

He smiled. "Good point. All right, you know all Azellians are psi, right?"

"Yes."

"Well, there are certain psi talents that are passed down from father to child in certain families. We don't know why that is, but it has formed a strong piece of our societal structure. Those families that have these talents are considered to be 'High Council' families, the ones who currently rule Azelle. The rest simply have a variety of psi talents of varying strengths. You know what many of them are—able to read minds, to move objects without touching them, to see things in a distance even when not physically present, to sense others' emotions, things like that."

"What's your family talent?"

"Psi healing," Greg replied. "All of us Tenricths have the ability to soothe and calm others. Not all of us go into Healing, but a large number of Healers are Tenricth."

Tamara looked down at her tea. "Alarin's is what?"

"Charisma and coercive willpower. The Raderths are extremely charismatic and can literally force others to do their will, if they want it strongly enough. The effect doesn't last, especially if you truly disagree with whatever they're trying to do, but people often find themselves doing things they didn't mean to do around a strong Raderth. It makes the Raderths very headstrong and stubborn as well. Most of them are pretty obnoxious."

"Alarin's not like that."

Greg shrugged. "Alari is nicer than most Raderths," he said. "And when he truly cares, he makes the effort to mitigate his behavior and inclinations. But don't make the mistake of thinking he's not a Raderth. He's got their family talent in full measure."

Tamara remembered seeing Alarin force people to do things before; when Justern had been accused of raping a college girl, Alarin had compelled the young woman to remember what had happened. When Tamara read the young woman's mind during the forced recall of the incident, it had led to Tamara's brother's acquittal on Azelle, although Earth authorities, without access to those mental abilities or memories, had not come to the same conclusion. The situation was still in flux, with the young woman's family fighting to get Justern to pay for his "crimes" and Azelle flatly refusing to admit that there had been any culpability on Justern's part—it was an unpleasant situation all the way around. Tamara pushed away thoughts of her brother and focused instead on Greg's words. Alarin's ability to force himself on others was a frightening talent, for sure, yet she knew, to the bottom of her heart, that he would not hurt her—any more than Greg would. "What about Merran?"

"Merran is a Corina. He's a channeling empath."

She frowned. "Like me?"

"Not exactly. You aren't a Corina, so your empathy takes on a different form than his. The Corina talent is very much about being able to receive and send huge amounts of psi energy in the form of emotion. Merran can channel emotion and manipulate it, project it back on itself, or turn it into something else entirely."

Tamara blinked. "I can't do that. I mean, I can sense other people and sometimes make others feel what I am feeling, but not what you're describing."

Greg shook his head. "Your empathy is different from Merran's, so I would guess that your empathic ability came from the other side of your heritage, not your mother. It's our understanding that human psi exists, but we don't know much about it. Your psi is definitely Azellian overall, or you wouldn't be able to hear us, or we you, but you don't seem to have a family talent, not the way the rest of us do."

"Dad's not psi," Tamara objected.

Greg shrugged. "He's not psi the way we are, no, but he is also almost impossible for us Azellians to read, unlike most humans who are open books to us. He may very well have some kind of psi talents, considering your abilities. Or maybe you're just expressing

Azellian talents differently because you have a human father and it's changing how your Azellian psi is expressed."

Tamara blinked and shook away the novel idea that her father might have some kind of psi talents. "Did my mother have a family talent? My birth mother, I mean, of course."

"She was a Dorvath, so she would have been clairvoyant, able to see some of the future and the links between actions and results. Not as strongly as Alari's father, Galadrian, but enough to get a sense for where things are going next."

"I didn't inherit that."

"No, it passes from father to child. Your father's not Dorvath."

Tamara rubbed her eyes. "Wow. So complicated. What about Justy?"

"He's a Memaxthal, so he can project illusions. He's strong enough to make you think you are somewhere else entirely than you are. Or hide himself when he doesn't want to be seen."

Tamara blinked, remembering a few times while her brother had been on Earth when he'd essentially "disappeared" from a room or conversation. Had that been his talent? Each time, she'd thought he was just being subtle about leaving and she hadn't noticed. "So he can literally go invisible?"

"If he wants to, he can make you think he's in a room, or not in a room, or he can even make you think he's someone totally different from what he is visually."

"That's scary. God, are all the High Council family talents that frightening?"

"They can be. Yet each one has a weak spot, and each one of them can be defeated by someone who has access to other levels of perception. None of our talents work on any of the *aarya*, for example, or the Keepers, who spend all of their time with the *aarya* and have access to completely different levels of perception. Of course, for those of us *umanaarya* who are limited by our current level of perception and awareness, we are all trained quite carefully in what is and is not acceptable, as you know from our sessions."

Those endless training sessions, which had a stronger reason for occurring than she'd known. "So basically, I'm responsible for my own behavior."

Greg laughed. "Yes, exactly." He gave her an affectionate mental hug. "You will be fine while I'm gone, Tam. Just do your focusing and meditating exercises and you won't have any difficulty with your psi getting out of hand."

Tamara took another swallow of tea. "Yes, maybe, but I'm going to miss you anyway."

"It will go by quicker than you know."

"I hope so, because I'm already looking forward to you coming home." Tamara cradled the mug between her fingers. "Can I, uh, ask you a question about your sister?"

"Ida? Sure."

"What's between her and Alarin?"

Greg raised an eyebrow. "Why?"

"I met her earlier today. She seemed nice enough to me, but Alarin got really upset about how she was behaving. He actually lost it. I didn't understand what was happening at all."

"Lost it?"

"He got really angry and went to confront Merran. They worked it out, but neither of them explained it to me, and now I'm really confused. I don't know what to think about Idara or her relationship with Alarin, or his with me, for that matter."

Greg turned to pull a tin of cookies out of the walk-in pantry closet. From what Tamara could see, the pantry was as carefully organized as the rest of Greg's apartment. Coming back out of the pantry, he pulled the top off the tin and tipped a few cookies out onto a plate. "Want one?"

Tamara looked at the cookies and then up at Greg. "Is this your way of saying you can't answer me?"

Greg grinned at her. "Good guess, but no, I'm just trying to figure out where to start. It's complicated."

"I'm just full of complicated questions today, aren't I?"

Greg laughed. "I don't mind. I love teaching and you are a great student. I'm limited on what I can talk to you about when someone comes to me as a Healer, of course, but Ida is a different story. She's my sister, not my patient. Her relationship with Alarin was always weird. Our mothers arranged the match with each other and then forced Alari and Ida into it."

"I remember someone telling me that last semester. But I really can't imagine anyone forcing Alarin into anything, especially not now that I know him."

"It was strange for all of us who know him. He's never talked to me about it, probably because Ida's my sister, but I suspect the only reason he agreed to the arrangement at all is because it was convenient at the time. As for how he feels toward you, you'll have to ask Alari that. But I can tell you he certainly never acted toward Ida the way he does toward you. Alari tends to be very ... protective of his lovers. He never was like that with Ida. Apparently, he is with you."

Tamara snorted. "Protective? I'm not sure I'd call it that. Jealous is more like it."

Greg put the lid back on the cookie tin, then turned and put the cookies away, closing the pantry door with an audible *click*. He turned back around and returned to his mug of tea, picking up a cookie. "I don't know what happened or why, and it's not mine to share if I did. But as for his relationship with Ida, it's over. And she knows it. From what Ida told me about coming here, she wants to learn more about herself away from the pressures of our family, not chase Alari. No matter what she chose to tell our mother."

"I really didn't get the impression that she was chasing Alarin when I met her today. Good to know I was reading her correctly. Alarin's response made me wonder if I was missing something."

"You're a pretty sensitive empath, Tamara. Trust your instincts, not what you think other people think. After I went away to Healer training, and Mother figured out I was never going to give her grandchildren, she put quite a bit of pressure on Ida to follow a certain path. Ida's far too strong and opinionated for that. Probably why she and Alari never really worked out ... they're too much alike. As for how she feels now ... Alari breaking up with her was the best thing that ever happened to her. It gave her a chance to be herself. Coming to Earth is opening up even more possibilities for her, too. It will be nice to see her truly acting how she wants, not how she thinks she has to."

Tamara could hear in his voice the affection Greg had for his sister, and she already knew the support he could—and did— offer to those he cared about. "I wish I had a brother like you," she blurted without thinking about how that would sound.

Greg chuckled. "Well, thank you, Tam, that's very sweet. You do have a great brother, you know. Justy might be somewhat immature right now, but he's really sweet and caring underneath it all. And he's just as interested in seeing you become who you really are as I am."

"Oh, I know, I know. I didn't mean that the way it sounded. Justy has been really great at keeping in touch with me since he left, and he has been wonderfully supportive and caring. I wish he could live closer so I could talk to him like this, though." Her growing relationship with her recently discovered half-brother was one very bright spot from last semester. "No criticism meant about Justy, just appreciating what an awesome brother you make."

Greg gave her an affectionate mental hug and a mischievous grin. "You do know that even if we were related, I'm still going to Ather, right?"

Tamara returned his hug with a brush of her shields against his. "Ha-ha, I didn't think it would change anything. I'm just … well thank you for being a wonderful Healer and a good friend."

"You're welcome, and thank you for being you too." Greg handed her the plate of cookies. "And to celebrate our mutual awesomeness, do you want a cookie?"

Tamara laughed, and they drifted on to other subjects.

She lingered until the early winter twilight fell, the sun dropping behind the high silhouette of the mountains. Greg's apartment didn't look out over the mountains the way Merran's did, but instead faced the glory of the other high-rises in downtown. Approaching nightfall announced its arrival through the twinkling fairy lights that sprang up in their windows. "It's getting late," she said, as she glanced at the clock behind Greg and slid off the chair. "I've got to get back. Alarin and I usually go get dinner at five-thirty."

Greg came around the counter to give her a physical hug. "Thanks for coming by, Tam. I'll see you before I leave, I promise."

She returned the hug. "You'd better," she warned. "We're going to miss you." She had to fight her momentary feeling of tears, then pulled herself together. Greg didn't need an emotional scene. She took her leave more hastily than she wanted, trying to rein in her emotions—which Greg probably already sensed—and left his apartment, closing the door gently behind her.

She got on the elevator, trying to hang on to the calmness that time with Greg always cultivated in her. It was one of the reasons she loved to spend time with the Healer. As she stood quietly on the descending elevator, she rested her head against the polished walls of the elegant interior, watching as the numbers marked the floors going down one by one.

The elevator doors whooshed open on the first floor of the building and Tamara jumped. Merran stood in front of her, his sport jacket slung over a shoulder, his briefcase in his opposite hand. As usual, she hadn't been scanning ahead of herself, so seeing him there took her by complete surprise.

He studied her calmly and appeared unsurprised. He'd probably been aware she was in the building from the moment he walked in the door and penetrated the outer shields of the high-rise. "Hi," he said, standing in the entrance of the elevator.

"I, uh, didn't expect to see you," she said, getting over that first rush of shock with an effort.

"Still not scanning ahead of yourself, I see." His dark hair was ruffled, as though he'd had a hard day, which was very possible. Although it usually took quite a bit to get him to the point that he was continually running his hands through his hair. She felt a strong desire to smooth it down, and it made her jumpy. Tamara hadn't spent private time with him in a long while, and it felt odd for it to be just the two of them here together.

She flushed slightly. "I'm trying to get the hang of it, and most of the time I do, just not when I'm thinking about something else. It's not automatic habit yet."

Merran smiled. "It will come with time, Tam." It wasn't quite a lecture, but come to think of it, her relationship with Merran had always been somewhat counselor-teacher-supervisor—despite the fact they'd been sleeping together.

"You're off early." She stared at the bank of buttons. Merran stood in the doorway of the elevator, leaning against the doors to keep them from closing.

"I have a meeting with Greg in an hour," he said neutrally, not offering anything more.

"To get him set up for going to Ather?" Tamara lifted her eyes to meet his. "He told me this afternoon that he was leaving." She let her unhappiness with the situation show. Merran most likely had been the one to set it up. He and the Healer had a tendency to put duty before self—a way of thinking Tamara had never internalized. She understood it intellectually, but emotionally, it was much harder.

Merran shrugged noncommittally, his eyes and mind guarded.

"Why?" she asked, trying not to whine, but probably not succeeding too well. "We need him here."

"Not as much as the Atherans do. There aren't many Healers who would risk their lives for Atherans."

"There's a reason for that. They aren't very nice to non-Atherans."

"They are no more xenophobic than humans are."

His tone remained neutral, but she winced anyway. There wasn't anything to say to refute his comment, so she took refuge behind anger. "What if he gets sick and dies? Have you thought about what that's going to do here? Greg may be the only Healer willing to risk his life for Atherans, but he's also the only Healer willing to spend time on Earth."

"There's another Healer on Earth now." Merran stepped fully

into the elevator and tapped the button to the floor just below his. This wasn't the elevator he normally took to get to his apartment. That elevator was a dedicated one, with a complete security system to get to his penthouse apartment. Tamara knew there was a staircase from his penthouse apartment that went down to the main levels. She'd never seen him take that route before, but apparently he was today. Probably so he could spend time with her. That thought made her uncomfortable.

"What are you doing?"

Merran raised an eyebrow. "Do you really want to discuss this in the elevator? Besides, I have to get changed. I don't particularly want to stand around in my business suit all day. It's not that comfortable." He loosened his tie and pulled it away from his neck.

Tamara felt a curious sense of panic, and the only thing she could think was that Alarin wouldn't like it. "I can't go with you up to your apartment," she blurted, not thinking about how her words might be received.

Merran gave her a look. "Afraid I'm going to ravish you the moment we step into the apartment?"

She blushed furiously. Not ten minutes ago, she was wondering when she was going to get a chance to get him alone to talk to him and now he was standing in front of her … confusing her. *I'm not ready to talk to him, not yet. But with Merran, who knows when the next time will come around?* She cleared her throat. "No, no, of course not."

A grin hovered at the edges of his mouth, but he did not let it express itself fully. "I think you don't mean that." He gave her a look that said she was leaking more than she meant to.

She blushed harder. "We, uh, need to talk."

"Then come up with me and talk while I get ready for my

meeting with Greg. I promise to behave." She suddenly felt silly. It was Merran. She knew Merran, and forcing her would never cross his mind. But then, forcing her wasn't entirely what she was worried about. Her confusion increased.

She didn't say anything as the elevator doors slid open to reveal the hallway on the floor just below the penthouse. Merran stepped out of the elevator and walked to the entrance of the staircase that led up to his apartment. He went through the usual security protocols to open the doorway to the stairs, with Tamara right behind him. They didn't speak again until Merran unlocked the doors that led into his residence, revealing the spread that was Merran's penthouse apartment. It was messy, for Merran, with books and papers lying around on the coffee table in the living room and clothes scattered in various places. "You've been busy," she commented, looking around the cluttered space.

He threw his briefcase on the table and slung his suit jacket over a chair in the dining area. "My cleaning lady moved away and I haven't found another one to replace her yet."

"Ah, so that so-clean apartment was the result of a cleaning lady. I never would have guessed." She wouldn't have, either. Merran always lived in a neat place, and she'd never met the cleaning people, not even when she'd been staying here more often.

"There aren't many people I allow in here. It's a rather intensive search process," Merran replied, walking toward the bedroom, pulling his tie over his head and unbuttoning his shirt as he went. "Takes awhile."

Tamara followed him, hesitating uncertainly at the door.

"You can come in further," Merran commented, sticking his head out of the closet. "I'll change in the closet, I promise."

The bedroom had memories, too many memories. Hell, the

whole apartment did. *It's a mistake to come back here*, she thought, *no matter how this conversation goes.* They'd had some good times on that large, canopied bed ... She shivered.

"What happened?" Merran asked, coming out of the closet wearing dark blue tight-fitting jeans and a tucked-in white tailored t-shirt. It accentuated his muscular chest, his silky dark chest hair visible under the open v of the neckline. "You suddenly stopped talking."

Tamara turned on her heel and walked quickly out of the bedroom, blinking away sudden hot tears. She took a deep breath. She wasn't ready for this talk. Something in his manner, and in Greg's earlier, made her think that maybe the solution to their problems was going to hurt.

Merran came out of the bedroom, closing the door behind him as Tamara stared over the chaotic mess in the living room and dining room. It helped to see the disorder. Being this messy made it not seem so much like Merran's apartment.

"I've been meaning to get a hold of you. You're right, we need to talk," he said carefully, after a few moments of silence, introducing the subject she didn't want to address.

Tamara took a deep breath. "About?"

"About us."

"What ... what about us?"

Merran gave her a look. "You know what about us."

Tamara kept herself still, afraid to move or shift. She felt like her world was going to slide out from underneath her. "What about us?" she repeated, not wanting to acknowledge Merran's statement.

"It's not working, with the three of us," Merran replied, after a moment in which she had the strongest impression that he'd tested her shields. She wasn't sure, though, because she was concentrating so hard on blocking everything out that she had little attention left for anything else.

"Greg said you might have a solution for it," she said, grateful that her voice was neutral and unemotional. Too bad the rest of her didn't reflect that. She held herself together with an effort that wasn't pretty.

"It's your solution actually." He turned and walked into the kitchen to pour two glasses of water.

"Mine? I haven't come up with any solutions lately. As a matter of fact, I'm so confused I don't know which end is up."

Merran stepped around the kitchen island and handed her the glass. "Don't sell yourself short, Tamara. You have come up with a solution, and a good one."

She took the glass and stared down at it, sloshing the water around the sides. As much as she hated to admit it, she did know what he was talking about. Her recent avoidance of Merran had been instinctive—an effort to smooth out her relationship with Alarin, but it was also an answer of sorts. Just not one she was certain she was completely ready for. Breaking it off sexually with Merran, assuming the bond let them—since, like Greg said, it wasn't truly permanent—was the easy part. But would it also be possible to stay friends? After having been so much more? Of course, Merran being Merran, how much more had there really been? It was so chokingly awkward right now. Could they work past this? She sipped the water, trying to fight off the thoughts tumbling around in her head.

"It's possible," he said softly, either reading her emotions or mind, or simply knowing what was affecting her so badly. "Anything is possible."

Tamara looked at him. It wasn't fair that he was so calm. What was it Greg had said? Merran had been less emotionally invested in the relationship than Alarin was? "Have you ever done it before? Been just friends with an ex-lover?" she asked, her voice not sounding like her own, hugging her arms to herself as she held the glass of water carefully against her body. Merran stayed very properly wrapped in his own shields, not offering her any physical or mental contact.

Merran studied her for a moment. "Sort of."

She lifted her eyes to meet his, then dropped the gaze. "What does that mean?"

"It means I've done a version of it before. Yes."

"With who?"

"Mellis. Among others."

"Mellis?" Tamara frowned at him. The young Azellian woman had come to Earth with the first batch of Azellian students last semester and they'd become friends, but she'd left with Justern when he was sent back to Azelle.

"It was before I became an ambassador, right after we both Awakened. She was my lover off and on during much of our adolescence."

"I knew you'd been with each other; I just didn't realize you considered her an ex-lover. She said it was pretty casual. Was she the reason you left?"

"Not at all. She was only a casual lover. It was never serious between us." Merran did reach out then, but only physically, dropping his hand before he touched her. "You deserve so much more than I could ever give you, Tamara. Alarin is the better choice and you know it. Don't damage your relationship with him over some fantasy about me. I'm married to my job, and that's that. You and I both knew that going in."

Tamara blinked and lifted her chin. "You never were in love with me, were you?" she asked bluntly, not sure if she wanted to know the truth, or why it seemed important, but maybe it would help her to let go.

Merran sighed. "Do you want the truth?"

"Yes." She clenched her jaw.

He gave a faint smile. "You probably did come closer than anyone else to making me regret what I've chosen for myself. As for being in love the way Alarin is, the way you are with him?" He spread his hands. "No."

She knew she was being ridiculous. He was right. Unconsciously, she'd already made that fateful choice to choose Alarin over him, but letting go was harder than it sounded, at least for her. She might have chosen this unconsciously, but to have him say it …

Hot tears burned at the back of her eyes. She would not cry in front of Merran. She couldn't, because it wouldn't change anything and would just make them both miserable. Well, it would make her miserable. She didn't know what it would do to him, and frankly, at the moment, she didn't care. The desire to flee suddenly flooded her, and she twitched.

He must have sensed some of what was going on in her mind, because he stirred. "Tamara," he said sharply, cutting through the emotional firestorm that gripped her and threatened to make her burst into tears. "Look at me."

She refused to lift her eyes to meet his, fighting for control.

He reached out again and put his hand under her chin, lifting her face to his. His touch on her skin burned. "Don't. Don't rip yourself apart over a decision we both made weeks ago."

She fought the tears, fought the desire to run away, to hide.

In truth, it wasn't control that made her stand there, letting him touch her. It was the complete inability to move. Paralyzed by her emotions, she literally couldn't move. An eerie calm filtered through her, and some of the firestorm released her from its grasp.

His mind touched the outer edges of her shields, and she felt the warm brush of him against her shields. "I'm sorry," he murmured, letting his hand drop away. "I never wanted to hurt you. I shouldn't have even tried to be a lover, but I did. That's how close you came to making me regret my life, Tamara. Never before has anyone come that close. I just can't see you and Alarin break up over this when I know I can't be the one you turn to. Please forgive me for my misjudgment."

"I have to go." She refused to look at him. She wasn't ready for the naked truth in his eyes.

She could sense that he wasn't happy. He was almost desperate in his fear that he'd irrevocably damaged their relationship, too, but it wasn't love—at least not the boyfriend-girlfriend type. He did care about her, just not in the way she'd hoped from their more intimate encounters.

She pressed the elevator button and stepped onto the elevator.

"Tamara. Don't go like this. Please."

She lifted her eyes to meet his. "I . . . I . . . need time," she managed to say. "Time. Space." Thankfully, the elevator doors shut and cut off the sight of him standing there, radiating fear, concern, worry—and pain. She couldn't deal with him right now; all she had within her was the strength to deal with herself and the new knowledge she had to wrestle with about their relationship before she could reach a new state with him. She rubbed her eyes fiercely as the elevator took her down to the entrance and away from the source of her pain.

Chapter Three

Merran stared at the elevator as the doors slid closed, a hollow, empty feeling in his stomach. They might have both made the decision, but it hurt to see Tamara flee like that, running away from him as though he'd ripped out her beating heart. Closing his eyes, he took a slow, deliberate breath, and tried to ignore the sharp jab of regret and self-directed anger. He opened his eyes again, scowling as he jabbed a finger at the elevator button. Time to go see Greg. Maybe that would help.

A few minutes later, he knocked on the door to Greg's apartment, and at Greg's cheerful mental hail, walked inside.

"What happened?" Greg asked as soon as he saw Merran.

"Tamara and I ended it."

"Oh. Have a seat. You want to talk about it?"

Merran sank into the thick cushions of the couch. "No."

"Okay. We'll talk about my trip then," Greg said, sitting across from Merran on an overstuffed white leather chair that matched the couch. He settled back and crossed one leg over the other. "How long do you think I should make an effort to stay? You know the Atherans. They're going to want me to stay far longer than we want me to."

"You're the Healer. You'll know when it's time to leave." Merran stared down at his intertwined hands. "Did I do the right thing?"

Greg let him change the subject. "With Tamara?"

"Yes. I care more about her and Alarin than I do about whether or not she's in my bed. But ..."

"But you love her and it's hard to let her go."

Merran frowned. "The word love is a little strong."

"Is it? You just stepped away from someone because it's more important to you to let her go so she can be who she needs to be rather than try to hold her to satisfy your own desires. Sounds like love to me."

"She loves Alarin. He loves her. Enough so that he accused me of trying to break them up."

Greg raised an eyebrow. "He's obviously jealous."

"Extremely. Worse than when we were adolescents exploring our sexuality. He swore at me in *jygar*. I didn't even realize he knew it. He's a Raderth. Raderths don't spend time in the outer caves."

"No, but Healers Heal anyone from *umanaarya* to *urro-ken*, and his sister is a Healer, Mer. Kyla taught him enough about Healer psi-training techniques that he was able to help us train Tamara in how to use her psi. Why wouldn't she have taught him a dialect that is uniquely suited to expressing strong emotions in the most colorful way possible?"

"Do you know *jygar*?"

"Of course. I've gone to the outer caves to Heal before, too.

If I couldn't communicate with the *urro-ken,* how could I Heal them?"

Merran frowned at his friend. "I didn't know that. So when I used to say all that stuff in *jygar* ..."

A smile flashed across Greg's face. "I understood what you meant, yes." His smile faded. "This is beside the point, though. Alarin doesn't share well, and Tamara isn't used to sharing. She wasn't raised that way. You know that."

Merran rubbed a hand over his face. "And I'm never going to be the person she wants me to be. But ... there's a part of me that wonders if ... what if things were different?"

"With Tamara, or just in general?"

"Either ... or both maybe."

Greg looked at him steadily. "Are you saying you want a relationship?"

"No, not really. Tamara and I ... it's like neither one of us is really quite seeing the other. She wants me to be something I'm not, and I ... my relationship with Alarin means more to me than being with her does. Is that love?"

Greg shrugged. "Do you need to define it?"

"I guess not." Merran sighed. "But there's this regret. Like I should have done something different."

"You're allowed to mourn what might have been, even if you know it couldn't work with you and Tamara. Although you want Tamara and Alarin to be happy, and you love them both, Mer, there is sadness in having to step away."

Merran stared at his hands. "My usual method of moving on is to bury myself in meaningless sexual encounters. I can't do that, not with Tamara sharing my psyche the way she does. And my sharing her psyche while she and Alarin ..." He shuddered.

"Sharing in the mental residue of their lovemaking is not going to help me move on."

"Ah, now that I can help with," Greg said, moving so he could kneel in front of Merran. "I've been talking to people I know at the Temple in an effort to figure out just what a bond does to the people involved," he said. "It both enhances and blocks psi. The bond doesn't last forever, if it's not constantly renewed. Although breaking it can be very dangerous, if it has had a chance to get itself tied to your psyche. How long has it been since you had sex with Tamara?"

"A month or so. It's definitely been a while. Except for this afternoon, I haven't really even talked to her since she left on vacation … much less had sex with her."

Greg lifted a hand. "May I touch you?" he asked.

Merran nodded and leaned forward slightly. He could feel the warmth of Greg's hand on his forehead and the slight tingling sensation of Greg's mind as it scanned lightly over him.

Greg sat back after a few minutes, removing his hand. "Well, the bond is still there for sure. I can see it linking the two of you. But it is thinner than it was last semester. I think I can block it so you can't hear Tamara and she won't hear you anymore either. It will still be there, and very strong emotions might rip through my barrier, but it will prevent the two of you from sharing each other's sexual encounters."

Merran blinked. "Please. By the grace of the *aarya,* please."

Bowing his head, Greg wrapped his fingers lightly around Merran's wrist and closed his eyes. Warmth spilled through Merran, a warmth that coated and soothed.

"That feels weird," Merran said after Greg had pulled his hand away. "Like I'm in a box or something. Sound is … muffled." He put a finger in his ear and jiggled it, but it had no effect.

"It's not sound that's being blocked, it's your empathic talent," Greg said, getting to his feet and settling on the couch next to Merran. "The bond seems to have linked you and her together through your respective empathic talents. I just temporarily blocked your empathy, to give you both a chance to have some space. The block might blunt your ability to channel emotion a bit. It will dissolve on its own in a few months, but for now, it should give you the space you need."

A tension Merran didn't know he'd been holding spilled out of him. "It's worth it, if it gives Tamara and me some distance from each other."

"What can you sense now?"

Merran closed his eyes and listened. The low-level pain and anger was gone, as was the sharp ache of regret. "Silence. Blessed, blessed silence."

Greg smiled. "It worked then. I'm glad."

"You're a miracle worker, Gregerin Tenricth."

Greg's smile stretched into a grin. "You would have gotten there yourself, eventually. I just accelerated things."

"Well, whatever it was, it helped. Thank you. So, do you want to go over the details about how long you'll be on Ather?"

"I'm a Healer. I'll know when it's time to leave."

"Okay, if you're sure."

Greg looked at him, cocking his head. "You just told me, not five minutes ago, that I'd know when it was time to leave, Mer."

"I did?" Merran shook his head. "I don't remember."

Greg studied him for a moment. "The spillover between your and Tamara's emotions, and your ability to hear her and Alarin's sex life might be gone, but you still need to give yourself some room to grieve, Mer. Despite what you think, I suspect you cared more than you want to believe you did. And although your tendency is to bury yourself in your work, I believe that because of how you've felt about Tamara, your judgment may be off right now. When was the last time you took a break from everything?"

"I don't know. Years maybe. Are you telling me you think I should go away for a while?"

"It might be a good idea."

Merran shook his head. "I can't right now. There's too much going on. I've got several media interviews scheduled for the next few weeks and a sensitive treaty with the Dorbin that I'm in the middle of."

"You need to take care of yourself, too, Mer."

"I will," Merran said. "I *will*," he said with more emphasis as Greg gave him a disbelieving look.

"How effective are you going to be negotiating treaties when your head is somewhere else?"

Merran scowled, irritation rising through him. "As soon as I finish up this agreement with the Dorbin, I'll take some time off. All right?"

Greg frowned at him. "Okay," he said. "As long as you promise."

"Yes, yes. I promise. Now will you tell me what you're planning to do to help the Atherans so when the Council finds out you went to Ather, I can make sure I've got something to present to them as to why I allowed a Healer under my jurisdiction to go to Ather and risk his life? I need the Council to back me, or the Healer Conclave, who is technically in charge of all Healers on and off Azelle, will have my metaphorical head for letting you go."

"You don't have to explain yourself, Mer. I'm going as a private citizen, and you can no more control a sacred Call from patient to

Healer than you can stop the sun from rising, but I've got an idea about how all the political mess can be avoided." Greg replied.

"Good. Tell me, then. The political mess is what I want to avoid." As Merran listened to Greg's plan, he was grateful to be distracted with other thoughts, at least for a while.

✳ ✳ ✳

That night, in the hush of late evening, Merran stood at his office's huge window, staring out over what was not actually the view he normally looked at from his office windows. When upset or disturbed, he liked to look out over the holographic projection of Azelle that he'd commissioned some years back. To the uninitiated, the endless waves of red sand hinted at the harsh solitude that Azelle offered. For any powerful psi worker, however, the holographic panorama induced a peaceful Zen-like state. The silence and solitude were restful—the sand absorbed sound and even thoughts, a meditative haven for those who knew how to access it.

He stared out over the dunes, thinking about his past, remembering the strong voice of his mother, Pelera. Curious and brave, she'd left the outer caves at seventeen, determined to find out more about the world she lived in. The *urro-ken* habit of sharing their psyche with another being was the overt reason the *umanaarya* on Azelle found the *urro-ken* distasteful, but over a thousand years, their isolation and exclusion from the rest of Azellian culture had become an institutionalized prejudice. The *urro-ken* lived in poor conditions, compared to the rest of the population of Azorantxl. Caves sheltered them, as caves sheltered the city of Azortantxl itself, but the *urro-ken* caves lacked any type of amenity enjoyed by the other inhabitants. Dark, dank, isolated, lacking running water and artificial lighting, the outer caves were known as Azorunt, which meant "place abandoned by beauty" in the harsh, ugly *jygar* dialect. There was much truth to that: Azorunt was a place with hardly anything that was beautiful about it. Yet, after his mother returned with her young son to Azorunt, Merran had grown up with little comprehension of the poverty of his circumstances or the lack of beauty in his surroundings.

Scrabbling for what he wanted, taking it and holding it with all his strength was just the way to get things in his world, and he'd gotten good at it, dominating the other children with a compelling combination of personality and persuasion. His mother had told him of another way of living, and he had youthful impressions from when his father had been alive of a different way, but he had little care for something that seemed so far away and fantastical. He'd listened, but it hadn't been until much later, after her death, that he'd been tempted to leave Azorunt. Merran closed his eyes, remembering his mother shortly before she died as she told him about the hostility she'd faced—and the shelter she'd found with his father.

"The merging leaves a residue in our psyche, but I thought that because I had not yet merged, I would be able to hide who I was when I went to Azorantxl," Pelera said to a much younger un-Awakened Merran, as he crouched on the floor by her pallet, covered by a thin, threadbare blanket that barely provided any sort of warmth in the wet, humid cave they called home. A fire burned in a fire pit, throwing elongated shadows on the cave walls, generating a little warmth, but it did not stop the shivers that jarred through her thin frame. She had called him in from the usual day's routine of roughhousing, fighting, and negotiating with his peers, insisting he sit by her as she told him of his father. He stared at the woman who lay in front of his eyes, dying by inches.

He'd heard various parts of the story his entire life and could remember the man who'd had such a brief but strong impact on him and his mother, but there was an urgency about her now that caught his attention and brought the information to him in a totally new way.

"But it did not work. They speak differently and they act differently, even without the residue of merging. We are not the same as they are, little Mero. They are *umanaarya*. We are *urro-ken*. And the *umanaarya* knew what I was. They rejected me. I found shelter with a sympathetic boy about my age, but he could do little to protect me, so I found someone stronger. Someone who had the political clout to be able to prevent them from harming me. Your father. Jarid Memaxthal Corina. His mate had just died, and he was willing. Even though he had two adult children from his mate, he loved me enough to agree to conceive you.

"When you were little, he died, and you and I had to flee to Azorunt again. But before he died, we got to live in the most incredible luxury, Mero. I want that for you, my beautiful boy." She coughed, the hoarse spasms wracking through her body, and spit bloody sputum into a bowl by her bed, reaching a shaking hand out to take his. He gripped her cold fingers tightly. "You deserve better than what I have given you, my son. So much better. You deserve to be everything you can be ... even Leader. Promise me that you will try to do better for yourself, my little Mero. Promise me you will leave this pit and make something of yourself. When I die, go to the *umanaarya*. Force them to accept you. Prove to them that you are every bit as good as they are. Promise me." She tightened her fingers on his.

"Yes, Mama. I promise." Merran stared at her, the implications of what he was hearing hardly registering as she clung to his hand.

She'd always told him to live in the moment, not to worry about the past. But even as she struggled to breathe, her breath wheezing in and out of her lungs in short spurts, the story spilling out of her in pieces that matched her breathing, he knew his world would never be the same again.

Pelera's death came not two days later, and with it, his world changed irrevocably. Hard on the heels of his mother's death, Merran stumbled into Awakening with a vengeance, his psi roaring to life with a ferocity that no *urro-ken* understood or knew what to do with—his *umanaarya* High Council empathic talent forcing him to sense everyone around him whether he wanted to or not, isolating him from his fellow *urro-ken,* who did not share his abilities and did not understand how to help him manage them.

Almost immediately after an uncomfortable, unpleasant Awakening, one of the *urro* approached him, asking him to merge. Seeking surcease from the hell of his psi's Awakening among people who did not understand, he agreed. Non-corporeal and genderless, filled with an ancient awareness that knew more about psi than he could have imagined, the *urro* who picked him indeed blunted his empathy with a perspective far beyond his, providing much needed relief from the pressures of his psi. His *meynsur*—his *urro* partner—tried to convince him to permanently mate psyches. Sorely tempted, but remembering his promise to his mother, and knowing that if he accepted the *urro,* he would never be accepted by the *umanaarya,* he refused. By nature highly independent and consumed by curiosity over what his mother had told him about the other half of his heritage, he left the *urro* and sought out his father's family instead.

Merran returned to Azorantxl and quickly found his

half-siblings. That memory could still make him wince. His older brother, Junian, had not handled the knowledge of a younger half-caver brother well at all. His older sister, Alerra, was much friendlier and open, but stinging from Junian's harsh rejection and drowning in the fury, hatred, and resentment his older brother threw at him through their shared empathic talent, Merran fled to the High Desert. An *aarya* found him kneeling in a sand dune, like the ones in the holographic projection outside his office window, as he prayed for release from the hell of his psi's Awakening and his brother's rejection.

Merran slowly became aware of the shimmering, non-physical presence beside him. The *aarya* said nothing, communicated nothing to him, just rested beside him in gentle, accepting presence, but suddenly Merran heard the rush of life that roared in and around him, and felt the deep, slumbering presence of the very planet itself. He touched the edges of that awesome, overwhelming presence and felt the warmth of inclusion, a deep spreading calm that poured through him, soothing back the meaningless emotional upheavals of his life. Nothing seemed to matter as a result of the serenity he suddenly felt—not the pain, not the fear or the upheaval—all fading into a peace that seemed unbreakable. It felt almost identical to the perspective the *urro* had offered, but there was a difference. The peace welled from within and was not controlling him from outside. Somehow, rather than give it to him, the *aarya* guided him to this sense of peace, and the difference was powerful and lingering.

Drawn by the power of that meeting, Merran went to the Temple, where the *aarya* lived. Staying at the Temple allowed him to explore the depths of his being, finding a joy in living in the moment that he'd known before in the caves, but had lacked the experience to appreciate at the time. He enjoyed his newfound awareness and rejoiced in his physicality, surrounded by others who not only understood his psi, but shared it. He might have stayed with the *aarya,* choosing to live his life as a Keeper, one of those who share the *aarya* perspective and live among them on a daily basis. But, once again drawn by his promise to his mother—because, in their way, the *aarya* are as isolated from the rest of the galaxy as the *urro*—after about a year he walked away from that as well, seeking resolution with his father's family.

Merran's time in the Temple helped him reconcile the fact that his older brother resented and hated him, a combination of prejudice for Merran's *urro-ken* upbringing and resentment of the place Merran's mother had taken in Junian's father's life after the death of Junian's mother. Junian never accepted Merran—he still didn't—making Merran wonder sometimes how much of his drive now was his promise to his mother and how much was an unspoken need for a paternal figure in his life. That need translated into a desire to have his unresponsive, hostile older brother tell him he was proud of him, something that Merran could now admit was hopeless, but still drove him anyway. Whatever pushed him forward—and he acknowledged it was a combination of things—the restlessness inside would not leave him in peace.

Merran raked a hand through his hair and rubbed his eyes, seeing nothing but the memories continue to roll by. After he returned to his family, his much older half-sister, Alerra, took him in, gave him a place to live, and provided him with sanctuary through the tumultuous years of his adolescence and further exploration of his psi. He met each one of the band that came to be called Merran's misfits—his niece Charina, who was Alerra's daughter, and Justern, her cousin on her father's side. Through

Charina, he met her friend Mellis, and through Mellis, Alarin, and through Alarin, Idara and Greg. They explored their psi with each other, those who weren't too closely related also sharing their physical bodies, enjoying the freedom of being young and alive.

More importantly, his band of friends gave Merran a place where he could truly be himself, without restriction or judgment. They knew of his past and truly didn't care, which gave him a haven against those who did—and there were plenty who tried to torment him over his past. His ability and willingness to fight, learned thoroughly during his childhood in the caves, prevented most people from taking it very far, but he still felt it, that judgment and resentment, the prejudice, the whispers that circulated among his peers who were not his friends.

His childhood in the wild streets of Azorunt gave him more experience at physical confrontation than most of the *umanaarya* had, blessing him with a set of valuable tools to resist the pressures and prejudices of his peers. Using a balance of violence and diplomacy to effectively keep hostility at bay, he learned to cultivate the attitude that most High Council Azellians learn from birth. As he began to act more like them, ruthlessly changing his *urro-ken* mannerisms and accent, the frequency of torment from his peers faded and he took his place among them, his promise to his mother slowly taking shape. Over time, though, the peace and joy he'd experienced while seeking refuge with the Temple called to him and he chose to return to the Temple, to formally become an acolyte, learning to see things as the *aarya* did. His friends supported his choice, and he maintained contact with them through the years of his acolyte training.

Though he'd told Ki'i that his calling was to come to Earth to become ambassador, the truth was a bit more complicated.

While what he'd told the Dorbin certainly was true, the reality of it had been a little less smooth. At the Temple, he'd fallen in love with another acolyte. For two years, he reveled in being in love, and in general lived life to its fullest with Kaelynn at the Temple and his friends outside of it. Then, two years after starting their affair, Kaelynn left the Temple quite abruptly, heading to Earth. He followed her, scrapping the three years of acolyte training and his friends. Although she welcomed him at first, she quickly disabused him of any idea he had that she shared his sentiment, breaking his heart and openly fleeing from him once again. At the time he blamed his *urro-ken* heritage for her abandonment, but he realized after a while that it had truly been for the best.

Using his acolyte training and perspective, he pulled himself clear of his broken heart and began to take interest in his surroundings, seeking out his next step in his promise to his mother. Loving the rough and tumble environment of human politics, facing the end of his visa if he did not find a job, he inveigled his way into the Azellian ambassador's good graces, negotiating a spot onto the ambassador's staff. With his powerful empathic abilities and careful strategizing, he managed to get himself invited to some very delicate treaty negotiations between the humans and Azellians. When the ambassador died during one of those negotiations, Merran brazenly continued the effort, using skills he'd developed as a child in Azorunt to cover up the ambassador's death so skillfully, no one noticed the ambassador was no longer alive.

Leaning on those talents developed during his childhood even further, he managed to win some very important concessions for Azelle, fully using his native charm and persuasiveness— and more than a little of his psi. When he returned to the Council on Azelle to report what had happened, Merran's role in successfully negotiating the treaty despite the ambassador's death meant the Council readily awarded him the ambassador position.

Merran grimaced at the projected image of endless sand dunes in front of him as the internal movie continued to play out. After becoming ambassador, he'd convinced most of his fellow misfits to come to Earth and be exchange students. It had been wonderful at first, but rapidly began to fall apart. Justern had been accused of rape and deported, taking Mellis back home with him. Greg had remained on Earth, as had Alarin, but Merran's relationship with Alarin was in shambles because of this bond they both had with Tamara. Had his walking away from Tamara rescued his relationship with Alarin? He couldn't be certain, and though he knew he'd done what was necessary for himself and his two friends, the idea that he might very well have damaged his relationship with both of them hurt far more than he would have expected. Reaching out, he turned off the holograph to reveal instead the brightly lit Denver skyscrapers.

Staring out over the lighted windows of the downtown area, he thought about his emotional turmoil. On Azelle, he would have gone for a walk into the High Desert, reaching into that unfathomable peace deep within the heart of the planet. He didn't have that option here, although Earth, too, had a deep thrumming energy that fed and supported its inhabitants. It wasn't the same, though. He rubbed his temples, suddenly longing for Festival, the Festival that would reestablish his connection with Azelle, drawing him back into the song of the *aarya* and their gentle guidance. It would come around again, as soon as the winter storms ended on Azelle, but until then, he had to use alternate methods to shift his mood.

A sudden restlessness gripped him. Despite the lateness of the hour and blowing snow, he made his way out into the streets of Denver, calling a cab and having it drop him on the 16th Street Mall. The mall was surprisingly busy, even with the cold winds and continuing snowfall. Although it was almost midnight, people were walking, window shopping, and paying no attention to him. No one seemed to recognize him or even care, and Merran could feel the depth of their disinterest.

The impersonality of the city's aura soothed, in some odd way, the emotional pain that had been dogging him ever since he told Tamara that they had to go their separate ways. Greg had helped him block the remnants of their link, and since then he hadn't felt a thing from Alarin and Tamara. No sexual energy reached down their link, either because they weren't doing anything or because he couldn't feel it anymore. His feelings about losing the link were mixed. He missed the sense of sliding into Tamara completely, a lovemaking that involved mental as well as bodily release. Yet, blocking their connection had been the best thing to do. It meant he was now free for the first time in months, alone in his head, and he had to admit that felt wonderful.

Almost unaware of his surroundings, he wandered off the outdoor mall and walked past a small, hole-in-the-wall bar with an old-fashioned sign out front that read *Roger Tolle's*. It glowed neon blue, red, and green, designed to catch the eye and draw attention to the open front door. Laughter spilled out from the interior of the bar, loud music impinging on even his distraction here on the street. The feel of the place was friendly and open, willing passersby to enter. Drawn by the possibility of stretching out his escape from the weight of the world and his own thoughts, Merran stepped into the interior of the bar, his coat draped over his shoulder.

Evidently, he wasn't the only businessman in the city who had chosen to stop here, even though it was so late and the weather cold and forbidding. Men and women crowded along the long, scarred oak bar that ran the length of the back of the tiny dive, a clean, bright, long mirror behind, which made it look as though the room were larger and more crowded. More people pressed against each other at the few tall wooden tables scattered throughout. There wasn't a formal dance floor, but several people gyrated to the near-deafening music coming from loudspeakers high on the walls. The sound and press of people was suffocating inside the bar, all non-psi, all half or fully drunk, and exactly what Merran needed. He made his way to the back, slipping in between a hollow-eyed man with lanky brown hair nursing a drink while staring morosely at the line of liquor bottles reflected in the long mirror behind the oak barrier, and a wiry salt-and-pepper-haired man who was intently hitting on the woman sitting next to him.

From long experience, Merran knew which drinks could affect his Azellian metabolism and which ones his psi and body would burn off before the numbing effect of the alcohol could take hold. The bartender leaned toward him. "What can I get you, buddy?" he shouted over the music and the din of the crowd.

Merran ordered a drink that he knew would affect him—after he had enough of them, that is. "Do you know how to make a Geneva Slider?" he asked, making sure his voice cut through the high decibel level of the late-night establishment, using just a little of his psi so that he didn't have to shout.

The bartender took the request in stride, even though he probably didn't get such an order every day. Or maybe he did. The only people who ordered a drink that strong were the ones who drank regularly, had built up an immunity to the alcohol itself, and undoubtedly spent a large portion of their time in a bar. The bartender nodded and Merran slipped some of his little-used currency across the bar rather than his credit card. He wanted to be anonymous tonight and not bring himself to the attention of the media.

The bartender, who was probably only a few years older than Merran, wore a beard like many of the younger human men did, his short blond hair shaved on one side, the other hanging long over his eyes. His arms were covered in tattoos, and his white t-shirt cut high on his arms to better show them off. He slid the fluorescent blue drink toward Merran, flipping the money into the register with a nod, then moving on to the next customer, a tall woman at the other end of the bar. Merran sipped his drink, the alcohol hitting him softly, blunted by his body's automatic response to the introduction of a drug. Too much, too powerful for even his body to block, though, with each sip the alcohol seeped its way deeper into his brain—dulling the noise in the bar, soothing his hyperactive thoughts, numbing his emotions, and lulling his conscious mind into a state of dreamy contemplation—as the alcohol burned down his throat, simultaneously heating up his stomach. For the first time in what felt like years, Merran relaxed. His shielding slipped, too, but he didn't care. The alcohol-amplified emotions from the men and women around him flooded into his head—a combination of loneliness, desperation, lust, fear, and excitement settling into the pit of his stomach and making his body stir.

Like many bars, this one was about frantic isolation, fear of being hurt, and the desire for immersion in a simpler way, a way that tried to pretend emotions weren't involved. Merran had played that game for a long time, and sometimes he thought he still did.

He took a gulp of his drink, trying not to think about it—the alcohol pouring through him, slamming into his memories and eroding them, veiling them in a shadow of mist—before his body got the upper hand and burned off the effect. To get drunk, he knew it was going to take more than one Geneva Slider. After ordering a second drink, he returned to his study of the others crammed into the small space, turning on his stool to scan the room.

A leggy, slender woman with an elaborate hairstyle caught his glance, and he felt her body's reaction to him immediately. Lust. Pure simple lust that right now was extremely attractive to him. He looked at her appraisingly. She was less pretty than statuesque, a large-boned woman with strong features, her blond hair tied up in a complex weave at the back of her head, dramatic blue eyes ringed by dark makeup. She smiled at him, revealing bright white teeth that softened the planes of her angular face.

Merran returned the smile, lazily, and she took it for an invitation to move closer. "I haven't seen you in here before," she said, leaning in to shout in his ear, slipping in between the salt-and-pepper-haired man who, too intent on his own conquest, didn't object, but rather used the opportunity to move into the space of the pretty little thing he was currently chasing.

Merran's nostrils flared as he caught the scent of her, a faint flowery fragrance mixed with the sweet smell of a fruity alcoholic beverage, probably the one she was cradling in her hands. "That's because I haven't been here before," he shouted back, leaning into her ear rather than using psi, taking the opportunity to smell her and brush his silk-clad body against the bare skin of her upper arm. Goosebumps marched across her skin and she shivered. He could sense a tingling sensation spread up through her body, his body reacting to hers as the alcohol lowered those inhibitions he'd built up during the past few years in reaction to the media explosion about his "exploits." It was probably not a good idea to let down his guard; in fact, he knew it was a terrible idea, but in this time and place, he didn't care. He leaned into her a little more closely. "You smell nice," he said, his mouth brushing up close to her ear where he could lower his voice enough to make it seductive.

She turned her head so that she could look at his face, putting her mouth inches from his, then she stepped back off the barstool as she put her hand on his arm. Merran turned. Instead of talking to him, like he expected, she licked his ear and bit at his earlobe. It startled him, although it shouldn't have, since he'd started the game. He shuddered at the touch of her mouth on his ear, and on the sensitive skin at the base of his earlobe and neck as she moved downward. "I have to go to the bathroom," she murmured into his ear, sliding her body sensuously up his back and rubbing her breasts against the silk of his shirt. "Why don't you come join me?"

Merran was Azellian, and quite experienced, but because he'd never tried the human bar scene before, it took him aback that she was being quite so blunt. He'd gotten used to having to do at least a little courting to get into a woman's bed, even if they both knew it was just sexual, but this woman was nothing but pure physical hunger. She didn't care who he was or what he wanted—she just wanted sex. She was aching with the need for it, for physical contact and the touch of a man. Without meaning to, he read farther. Scarred by a father who had never given her any love, who had offered beatings in the place of affection, who had scorned and raped her, who made her hate herself and men far more than she cared about anything else, she chased after the thing she hated and craved. He'd met women before who just wanted sex, but nothing like this.

He shook his head, desperately dragging sluggish shields up around his mind, the physical response she stirred dying under the onslaught of her self-hatred as though it had never existed. With her, it could be nothing but rape, her need too open, too raw for him to be able to perform, much less to want to. He gulped another swig of alcohol, which did nothing for the stability of his shields, but cut the gush of her desire to a dull enough roar that he could redirect, somewhat clumsily, her attention to the man sitting next to him. She shifted her attention to him, and he responded quite enthusiastically, unable to see into the inner depths of her mind, clueless as to her true motivations. Merran could sense the two of them a short while later, going at it in a stall in one of the bathrooms, but he forced himself to ignore their encounter and ordered another drink. After that, he disregarded the other women who tried to hit on him, too afraid to look deeply into the women who would be driven to a bar like this for companionship, or even just a sexual encounter, too fragile himself to let anyone else near enough to breach his shields. In his current state, with his shielding so delicate, it wouldn't just be sex, and he really didn't want to analyze anyone else.

His assistant Ketiana found him after his fifth Geneva Slider, when the alcohol finally started to affect his coordination, but before he'd reached the level of passing out. He didn't notice her approach, despite the fact his shields were virtually gone, effectively deafened by the chaos and cacophony of sounds around him.

An arm slid past him on his right, as he peered owlishly at the hand that planted itself on the bar. He turned his head and looked up at her, trying to focus. "Katie," he said, slurring her name, the "tee" coming out more like "chee."

"Merran," she hissed in English. "What the hell is going on?

We had a Council meeting scheduled for tonight, but you missed it. I've been looking all over for you. It wasn't until your shields collapsed that I was able to find you. What are you doing here?"

"Getting drunk," he drawled slowly, his words almost undecipherable.

She picked up the half-full glass and sniffed it. "The *aarya* take it, Mer. What the hell is that?" She took a tiny sip and winced. "By the *aarya's* eyes! What are you trying to do, kill yourself? Come on, I'm going to take you back."

"Okay." He was far too drunk and relaxed to care what she did.

Ketiana grabbed his arm and pulled him to his feet. He sagged, and she steadied him by sliding his arm around her shoulders. By the time they got to the door, he was liberally draped over her body, his weight on her more than on his own unsteady feet. "At least you're an easy drunk," she muttered to him as she shoved him into the backseat of the limo waiting outside. He slid bonelessly to the floor and passed out, the world going dark around him.

❈ ❈ ❈

His body woke him the next morning with a violent need to void itself. He stumbled out of bed, barely aware that he wore little more than his skin as he scrambled for the bathroom, making it just in time.

He sat trembling on the floor, cradling his throbbing head and wondering if his stomach were going to rebel again, or if it was safe to move. The cold of the tile floor seeped into his backside and made his physical discomfort worse, but he didn't want to change positions. It felt like any movement would either cause his head to fall off or his stomach to come crawling out of his mouth. It cramped at the thought and he moaned.

A knock on the door of his bedroom wasn't enough to make him get up.

"Finally awake?" Ketiana's voice sounded amused as she came into the bathroom. Merran buried his head in his legs and curled around them, resting his forehead against his knees. "Awake and suffering, I see."

"Go away." He refused to look up at her. "Leave me alone."

Instead, she came closer, leaning against the sink. "What were you trying to do last night?"

He lifted his head to meet her gaze. "None of your business," he said, his voice shaky enough that the effort to be authoritative failed miserably.

She raised an eyebrow. "You make a pliable drunk, but a lousy hangover sufferer." She handed him a sports drink. "Here, drink this."

He shook his head, his stomach lurching at the thought.

"It will help rebalance your body and will make you feel better, I promise. Now drink it."

Acquiescing to her authority, he took the drink from her. As soon as the liquid touched his mouth, he realized how thirsty he was and sucked down the entire bottle. Miracle of miracles, it stayed down. His stomach roiled a little, but then began to settle and accept what he'd put in it. He felt a little better, his headache subsiding slightly.

"Now, get up and get dressed. You have a meeting in an hour with a journalist." She eyed him critically.

"An hour? I thought that meeting was going to be at three thirty this afternoon." Merran pulled himself to his feet, using the sink for support.

Ketiana didn't even flinch at his state of undress, ignoring it effortlessly. "It is afternoon."

"Really?" Merran stared at her. "What time is it?"

"Two thirty."

"What?" Merran's jaw fell open.

"Two thirty. Now get dressed."

Merran ran a hand through his spiky hair. "I need a shower first." He made a face. "I stink."

Ketiana opened her mouth.

"Don't say it. Get out and let me take a shower."

"What, don't you want me to join you? You certainly asked me to last night." Her eyes flicked down the length of his body. A grin played at the edges of her mouth.

"I what?" He pulled a towel from the rack and wrapped it around his waist. "When?"

"You said, and I quote, 'Make me forget that I ever knew her, Katie.'" She cocked her head. "Her being Tamara, I suppose."

Merran glared at her. "I did not say that."

"You did. I swear it by the *aarya*." She grinned at him for a moment, then said softly, "It will fade with time, you know."

"What will?" He sounded as miserable as he felt.

"The heartache." Ketiana straightened and walked to the bathroom door. "The pain. As I told you last night when you were sobbing your heart out in my arms." She closed the door behind her softly.

Merran had a nasty feeling she was telling the truth. He stood in the middle of the room, flashes of memory coming back to him—Ketiana's arms, a confused impression of her body, his own sobbing. He looked down at himself. Had they? She didn't say whether they had or not—although something about her attitude said not, which relieved him. He and Ketiana had been lovers once, but not since he'd become ambassador, and he didn't want even a casual sexual encounter to interfere with their working relationship. He pulled the towel off his waist and touched himself. No residual stickiness, except from his own body's excretion of alcohol as fast as it could. He made a face. He reeked. Even he could smell the waft of stale drink coming from his body. No way did he have the physical control last night to do anything, no matter how much he may have wanted to.

Merran sighed and pulled open the glass door to turn on the shower. No matter what did or didn't happen the previous night, he had other things to worry about this afternoon, including how he was going to get through a difficult interview with this monstrous headache.

He had to admit that he felt physically better after the shower, but emotionally, he was still somewhat of a mess. What had possessed him last night to get drunk, sob in Ketiana's arms, and pass out? Wearily, he rubbed his forehead and stared at himself in the mirror. The dark shadow across the clean shaven parts of his jaw made him look older and scruffier, like some sort of villain in a play. His dark hair stuck up all over his head in a riot of little spikes, ruffled from the toweling he'd given it. His dark brown eyes were shadowed by circles in his skin, his face whiter than his normal tanned look, and it still had faint green tinges to it, his lips ringed with a faint white hue, paler than their normal color. He didn't look that imposing or that amazing to himself, but he'd always known what he could do with his looks and used them to their fullest. They had given him a level of confidence, even arrogance sometimes, that his High Council training had refined into an art. He knew how to be authoritative, to take control, and, in response, people listened. He knew how to run an embassy, to negotiate a treaty, to read people to a fine level using both his psi and powers of observation. Why then did necessity hurt like this? He turned his back resolutely on the mirror, wrapped the towel around his waist, and walked into his bedroom.

The room stank almost as badly as he had before his shower. He made another face.

"You got sick more than once." Ketiana spoke from her position just outside the door, where she stood looking at a computer pad in front of her. "I managed to get the trashcan to you, but there were several near misses."

Merran's head pounded, but it wasn't just from the hangover. He made his way into his large walk-in closet. "Were you with me all night?" he asked, trying to keep his tone mostly civil, although embarrassment made him want to growl.

"Pretty much. I didn't think you wanted me to deposit you at the hospital or call in a Healer, so I watched over you."

Merran took a deep breath. "Thank you," he muttered, not wanting to admit the need that had driven him to that point.

Ketiana looked at him steadily. "Being in love sucks sometimes."

Merran went very still. "I am … was not in love with her."

Ketiana raised an eyebrow. "Oh really. So you felt the urge to skirt the edges of death just so you could get a release from a casual fling? Tell me, Ambassador Corina, do you always celebrate the ending of your relationships with a colossal drunk?"

He didn't flush, but it took some effort on his part to avoid it. He pulled on his clothes with short, jerky motions. "Tell me, Assistant Ambassador Dorvath, don't you have anything better to do than deconstruct me and my emotional state?"

Ketiana's nostrils flared. "Yes, however, my job description does include running interference for the ambassador if it becomes necessary. Last night, it became necessary. I doubt you or your cleaning person would have enjoyed cleaning up the mess you made last night if I hadn't been here."

Merran sat on the edge of the bed, fastening the buttons at his wrist and down the front of his chest. "Do you feel it necessary now to continue to bring up what might just be something I'd rather forget?"

Ketiana looked down and he could feel a flash of something beyond irritation from her. Hurt? His head throbbed a little more. She was also angry, which he could tell from her posture as well as from the emotions leaking from the edges of her shielding. She turned to walk away.

He sighed. She didn't deserve the emotional abuse he was directing at her this morning—afternoon. "Katie. Wait."

She halted, keeping her back to him.

"Thank you for taking care of me last night. I ... appreciate it. Despite what you think, it is not in your job description to mother me through a colossal idiocy on my part." He leaned against the doorjamb, letting his shielding relax slightly. "It was the move of a friend, not an assistant, and I do appreciate it. I'm not entirely sure why you came to my rescue, but I understand that you did, and I'm ... sorry. I won't do it again."

She turned. "I know what it feels like, to be where you are," she said softly, her anger smoothing away. "Maybe I wished I'd had someone do that for me."

Merran took a deep breath in through his nose. Denial stirred again, but he couldn't avoid the fact he'd reacted quite violently over what had been supposedly just a casual relationship. The problem was, he still loved her. He loved Tamara more than he had ever realized while dating her, but it didn't change anything.

Maybe it didn't even mean anything, which shook his world and made him feel sorry for himself. "Maybe we can compare stories sometime."

A smile flashed across her face, etched with a deep sorrow he recognized immediately, even though he'd never seen it before from her. "Maybe. Finish getting dressed, we're running out of time."

Merran reached down to pull on his shoes.

She walked away, then stuck her head back into the room. "Oh Merran?"

"Hmmm?" he asked, tying the laces on his shoes.

"You're welcome. See in you in a few."

He made an affirmative noise and put the finishing touches on his ensemble. When he came out of the bedroom, he felt much, much better—even his headache was beginning to fade. By the time they headed out to face the interview, he felt almost like himself again. Ketiana followed him down the elevator and out to the street, her heels clicking on the cement as they headed for the limo that waited in front of the steel and glass high-rise. The sound made him wince, sharp enough to poke at the lingering headache, but he didn't say anything to her about it as they climbed into the limo and Ketiana gave the driver the command to go.

His publicist had arranged for him to meet the reporter in the Janus Agency's office in the Lower Downtown area, known as LoDo to its inhabitants.

Ketiana pulled another sports drink from the limo's fridge and handed it to Merran.

"If I drink too many more of these, I'll have to stop the interview multiple times to use the bathroom," he said, but he took the drink from her anyway.

"Better that than throwing up in her lap."

"Haha," he said, unscrewing the top and taking a sip. "Who is it I'm meeting again?"

"Her name is …" Ketiana glanced down at the tablet on her lap and swiped her finger across its surface until she got to the notes she was looking for. "… Elise Winters. The story she gave Dana was that she wants to raise the profile of her magazine by interviewing you. Are you ready to face a reporter who is going to try to get information out of you that you don't want to give?"

Merran made a face. "Probably not, but I'll do what I have to."

Ketiana studied him for a brief moment. "I'm coming into the interview with you."

"You don't trust me."

"Do you trust you?"

"Right now? Not particularly." Merran took another sip of the sports drink and rested his head against the seat. "Fine. Come with me. Answer questions for me. Keep me from making an ass out of myself."

"That's going to take some doing," she said, but there was a hint of amusement around her mouth. "Why don't we just cancel this?"

"Because we have to cooperate with the media, and canceling it is going to piss her off. The last thing I need is to get a reporter pissed because I treated her poorly. Journalists tend to get nasty when I do that. And this particular reporter works for *Women's Issues Quarterly*. That magazine has been overly concerned with my behavior and not focused enough on my accomplishments in the past. I'm intending to set the record straight this afternoon. Starting it off with a cancellation because I have a hangover isn't going to look good."

Ketiana frowned at him. "That's pretty prepared for someone who's as hungover as you are. I thought you didn't feel good, didn't know who you were meeting, and weren't prepared."

"Once you told me the name, I remembered the other details. I never face an interview without some preparation."

She made another face at him. "I think you're going to be able to handle this interview just fine."

"Oh, so now I can go in on my own?"

"Yes. I'll wait for you outside. Good luck." She gave him an affectionate mental hug that blurred the usual firm boundaries between them.

Merran allowed the hug, rather grateful for her care. "Thank you." He went in to talk to the reporter.

By the end of the meeting, his head was throbbing again and his stomach was upset. Elise Winters had bombarded him with hostile questions, a reporter who knew him only from his media image, a woman with a strong prejudice against men in general and him in particular. His shields still a bit wonky from his binge the night before, it was virtually impossible to hide from her determination to write a nasty article rather than a positive one, so he cut the interview far shorter than she wanted.

He stalked out of the room and ran into Ketiana.

"So it didn't go well?" she asked.

"I don't want to talk about it."

Ketiana raised an eyebrow. "That bad?"

"Worse."

She was silent until they got into the limo again. "Not going to be a good article?"

"Not unless I want to smear my name into hell and back," Merran replied, resting his head against the seat.

"Do we need to have a talk with Dana about just who she schedules for interviews?"

Merran shook his head, closing his eyes. "No, this one was my fault. Dana told me, quite clearly, that the magazine was hostile toward me. I told her to set it up anyway, because I thought I could change anyone's mind."

"And you can't?"

"Apparently not." In truth, he hadn't tried. After it became glaringly apparent that Elise Winters was not interested in anything but his sexual exploits—although not in a *tabloidy* way, rather more like someone who wanted him to be a stalking horse for all the men that had treated her badly—Merran had lost his temper and cut the interview short. "She was more interested in talking about how chauvinistic and arrogant I am rather than consider anything positive I've done." He sighed and ran a hand through his hair. "Get me home, Kate. I want to climb into a dark pit and disappear forever."

Ketiana nodded and wordlessly helped him up to his apartment. She ordered some food, paid for it, and shared the meal with him without saying anything. Merran mindlessly ate what she put in front of him and went straight to bed without paying much attention to her.

He thought Ketiana might try to impose on his solitude, but she didn't. For a split second, he was sorry about that—there was again silence from his link with Tamara and Alarin, and he knew they couldn't be abstaining this long. To have that link silenced opened doors for him that had been closed since he'd formed the link with Tamara, but as much as he might want a physical connection, Ketiana wasn't the one to explore with him the limits of his new freedom. For one thing, they worked together, and for another, Ketiana was being far too mothering right now. She'd responded to his vulnerability, and having sex with her would just increase that—dangerously so, even though she was Azellian and well used to the vagaries of sex, love, and friendship.

He threw himself on his bed and lay on his back, staring up at the ceiling as he heard Ketiana move around in his apartment, straightening up and letting herself out, the elevator dinging as it arrived and she left. *How crazy is this? Free for the first time in months but unable to do a damned thing about it.* A smile tugged at the edges of his mouth, appreciating the irony, if nothing else. He sighed and closed his eyes, remembering the reporter and her attempts to make him look worse than he was. *This is the last time I override Dana on her recommendations,* he thought to himself, letting exhaustion tug at him. His body, still somewhat upset at him for the overindulgence of the night before, took the upper hand and pulled him into sleep before he could do much more than start to think about relaxing.

After the breakup, Tamara struggled with a peculiar sense of drowning, but she managed to hold herself together enough to hide it from Alarin. At least she thought she had—Alarin mentioned nothing about it, but he certainly seemed much calmer now. He was in a cheerful mood, even playful. Tamara's own mood was strange, as though her mind had split in two. A part of her participated in Alarin's playfulness and pretended everything was just fine, but the other part was melancholy, even depressed. Merran and she might not have had as many day-to-day interactions as she and Alarin, so she didn't precisely miss him, but there was a hole, a gap in the number of people she could turn to.

Besides Greg, Alarin, and Justern, Merran had been one of those people. Now—well, it remained to be seen where they would end up. Question was, could she be just friends with someone she had loved? But had she loved him, really? If she had, why didn't it hurt more? Had she always seen him as only a friend? And if he was just a friend, telling her they couldn't sleep together should have hurt less, right? It was beyond her abilities to sort out what she really thought, so she pushed the whole thing into her subconscious and threw herself into her schoolwork.

Late one afternoon almost two weeks later, she sat studying in her room. The almost empty room was oddly relaxing to study in, maybe because Alarin's apartment was cramped, now that most of her clothes and other personal belongings were there. She and Alarin hadn't talked about her moving in with him; it had just sort of organically begun to happen. That first night in the apartment, after Merran ended things, had led to quite an intense session between them—their first completely solitary session actually. She hadn't sensed Merran's presence with them at all that night. Afterwards, she hadn't discussed that phenomenon with Alarin, but for the first time in her and Alarin's relationship, he seemed to gain confidence, as though all the time before, he'd been playing second fiddle to her relationship with Merran, as if he were the "other man." Now? Well, things had changed, most emphatically.

A knock on the door interrupted her thoughts. Hastily, because, as usual, she'd been forgetting to scan for people nearby, she perused the area outside the door and recognized Kari's familiar mental patterns. Something had her excited. Tamara got up and answered the door. "Hi Kari." She didn't bother to pretend she hadn't realized Kari was there. Normally she kept the odd things she did to a minimum, but today she didn't care.

"Hey girlie," Kari said, unconcerned as she bounced into the room, her eyes sparkling. "Whatchya doin'?"

"Studying," Tamara replied, returning to her desk.

Kari perched on the bed. She glanced down at the smooth comforter. "Not sleeping here, are you?"

"Why?" Tamara leaned back in her chair.

Kari grinned. "You never make your bed. For it to be made means it hasn't been unmade." She rubbed her hands together.

Tamara glared at her friend. "I don't *never* make my bed."

"Almost never."

"Fine. I'm spending the nights over at Alarin's apartment. What's got you all bouncy?" she asked, somewhat grumpily. She hadn't told Kari about her change in status.

Kari ignored her question. "Did you move in with him?"

Tamara shrugged. "Essentially. Not that my dad needs to know that. I'm going to get a lecture on tying myself to Azellians again." She frowned at Kari. "Out with it. I know you didn't come over here to see if Alarin and I moved in together or not."

Kari grinned wider. "Perceptive little thing, aren't you?"

"We've known each other for a while, after all."

"I have a date." She clasped her hands together and managed to look smug.

"Oh my God, don't tell me Danny finally asked you out!"

Kari shook her head. "Better actually."

"Better?" Tamara frowned. She'd been out of it lately, but not for *that* long. Who else had Kari been chasing for years but their fellow classmate? "I didn't realize you were interested in anyone else."

"Better, better, best. I'm going out with Damiar Darvyne. I'll finally get a chance to taste what you've had with Alarin."

"Who?" Tamara asked blankly. Wracking her brain, she couldn't remember who Damiar Darvyne was. Azellian, obviously, but who was he? She couldn't remember anyone at the embassy with that name.

"Damiar Darvyne, one of the new exchange students? God, Tam, you've been out of it this past week. Of course, you didn't go to the welcome party for the new exchange students either. We really hit it off. Over the past week, I've talked to him at least ten times. We have almost all our classes together. He's really hot too. Not someone I'd expect to look twice at me, but he seems to be as interested in me as I am in him."

"Which one is he?" Tamara vaguely remembered having seen him when she and Alarin met the students in the cafeteria before … she cut off that particular line of thought abruptly. That had been right before her life turned upside down.

Kari grinned. "He's the cute one."

"The one with dimples and dark eyes? The Healer?"

Kari did a double take. "Rory? You think Rory's cute?"

"No, of course not," Tamara said hastily, to cover up the fact she did think just that. "I just don't remember any of the new Azellian exchange students very well."

Kari gave her a strange look. "The only other guy among the new students? The one with the gorgeous coppery bronze hair that comes down to his shoulders? He's also got the longest lashes and darkest blue eyes I've ever seen on anyone before. I never thought I'd find a guy with long hair and without a single tattoo attractive, but I think he could wear a man-bun and I'd find him sexy."

"Oh him." She'd noticed a guy with striking dark blue eyes that day when she'd met all the new Azellians, now that Kari had described him, but he hadn't impacted her mental radar much at all. The altercation between Alarin and Merran right afterward had distracted her pretty thoroughly.

Kari frowned at Tamara. "Are you okay? You've been in kind of a weird mood lately."

Tamara shook her head. "I'm fine. Just tired. I've got papers to write for the semester of hell. Worse than last semester. So what's Damiar like?"

"I'm not sure but I can't wait to find out." Kari rubbed her hands together in anticipation. "I wonder what color the other hair on his body is. I guess I'll get to find out too."

"Kari!"

Kari grinned. "What?"

"That's not something I wanted to hear! You already have it planned that you're going to sleep with him?"

"Sleep? No. Have sex? Probably."

"The first time you hang out? He's going to read your mind, you know." Despite the Azellian effort to keep their abilities quiet since Justern's trial and the subsequent revelation of Azellian psi through Greg's Healing of him, their psi had become an open secret among most humans. Kari, who might not have known about all of Tamara's secrets, certainly knew her friend had psi, and she knew the other Azellians did, too.

"Ah, maybe not the first or even the second. But given the chemistry between us, soon."

Tamara shook her head. "You just completely blow me away, do you know that?"

"We can compare notes. He has a roommate, though, and so do I. Can we borrow your room?"

Tamara stared at her. "What?"

"You aren't going to be needing it, so can we borrow it?"

Tamara's skin crawled. "Uh, no."

"Why not? You have a whole apartment. We don't even have privacy."

A thought occurred to Tamara. "Is Damiar's roommate human?"

"No, he's sharing a studio apartment with Rory just off campus."

A grin tugged at Tamara's lips. Given both Merran and Alarin's complete unconcern about privacy for what humans considered the ultimate in private matters, Kari would find herself probably not needing Tamara's room. What sense of decorum they'd bowed to was purely because of Tamara's own discomfort, and she knew it. Fresh from Azelle, with an Azellian roommate, Damiar would be even less worried about it. Kari might find herself in for more than she'd bargained. "All right, sure. Fine. Go ahead. Use my room if you need to."

Kari frowned at her. "I was sure you'd put up more of a fight than that. What's got you looking like the cat that swallowed the canary?"

Tamara shrugged. "Azellians are different," she said, suppressing her smile. "It should be interesting to see how you adjust to it."

"Like how?"

"I don't want to spoil it."

Kari made a disgusted sound. "That's not fair."

Tamara grinned. "Nope. Talk to me again after the first time you sleep with him."

Kari's cell phone rang then, and she looked at the number. "It's him," she said, giving Tamara a look. "We're not done with this conversation, Tam. Hello, this is Kari." Tamara listened unashamedly to her end of the conversation. "Hi." Her voice softened.

"Yeah. Sure. How about twenty minutes? See you then." She hung up.

Tamara stretched. "Off to see the boyfriend?"

"He wants to check out something at the arts co-op and knows I'm an art major. He knows I have a key. Don't jinx it by calling him my boyfriend."

Tamara laughed. "All right. Call me later."

"You'll be at lover boy's?"

"Probably, but call me anyway."

"Okay, talk to you later," Kari promised, and she left. Tamara laughed to herself. Feeling much better, she returned to studying.

Her cell phone rang after she'd almost managed to finish the work she'd intended to do that day. She swiped her finger across the face of the phone. "Alarin, hi," she said, unable to stop her smile.

"Hey, Tam-*ala*. When are you coming home?"

"I'm almost done. Maybe another twenty minutes."

"Good. I have a surprise for you."

Tamara's stomach clenched. "A surprise?" She didn't do well with surprises.

There was laughter in his voice as he replied, having either picked up on her emotions or the tone of her voice. "I'm fairly confident you'll like this one. See you soon."

"Bye." She hung up her phone. Alarin's little announcement meant that she had absolutely no concentration left, so she wrapped up her studying five minutes later. Closing down her room, she paused, both hearing and sensing a group of students chattering and talking as they came through the fire door from the outer hallway into the more intimate space of the lounge area, their thoughts loud and rather boisterous. Sometimes it was hard to live in the middle of so much mental chaos. She thickened her shields, suddenly grateful for the haven that Alarin's shielded apartment provided. She could have shielded her room, but she'd decided not to bother, since they were so rarely there. Picking up her book bag, and using her psi to help steady it on her shoulder, she pulled open her door.

One of the students, whom she knew only because she'd had him in a couple of classes, waved to her as she passed, and she waved back as she headed out the door of the dorm, not giving him the opportunity to say anything to her. She walked across the block to the nearby twelve-story public apartment complex and made her way upstairs to Alarin's apartment.

The smell of food wafted out from underneath the door, and she frowned slightly. Was that coming from their place? If so, it was unusual; the kitchen rarely got used, and Alarin hadn't revealed any ability to cook in the time she'd known the Azellians. As a matter of fact, given that Merran's kitchen was only used for tea once in a while, she'd almost thought Azellian men didn't perform kitchen tasks. Rather than use her psi, she put her key in the lock and unlocked it manually.

She pushed open the door and entered the foyer, dropping her book bag on the floor by the door. She couldn't quite see the kitchen from here, but those smells were strong, and she could hear the sound of Alarin humming.

"Hello?" she called, although she expected that Alarin knew very well she'd come in, particularly once she'd passed through the shields. With a virtuoso ability she both admired and envied, he monitored the status of the shielding around the apartment with a part of the mind she hadn't used yet. She'd explored his mind thoroughly enough to know that he had access to levels she'd never dreamed existed. Both he and Greg had tried to get her to access those levels, too, but it was hard, painstaking work, and Greg ... well, Greg would be gone for quite some time, so she expected the lessons would be on hold until he returned from Ather.

She pushed the worry for Greg to the back of her mind as she felt the familiar warmth of Alarin's mind entwine itself around hers. "Hello," he said, coming around the corner, wearing nothing but an apron and holding a wooden spoon stained with brown. Incongruously, the apron said, "Mother's Kitchen" in bold black letters. Tied over his naked body, it looked silly and sexy at the same time.

Tamara's eyebrow shot up. "My my. What have you been up to?" She glanced at the spoon in his hand. "What's that?"

"A spoon. I thought I'd cook dinner tonight. And provide ... entertainment."

Tamara giggled. "You're doing that," she said, coming forward to wrap her arms around him. Although most of him was exposed, he felt warm, his free arm sliding around her body as he pulled her closer to him. "What's with the outfit?"

"You don't like it?" he asked, rubbing against her.

"Uh, it's interesting," she said as she scratched her fingers lightly down his back, "but it's not designed to allow you to complete dinner or prevent us from getting rather thoroughly distracted." She sniffed. "What's cooking?"

"Ah," Alarin replied, tapping her nose lightly with the spoon, leaving a smear of whatever it was on the tip. "A very special human recipe, which I discovered, after much digging and searching, is your favorite. It's called, I believe, Swedish Meatballs. I've also cooked mashed potatoes, and a vegetable, which I am also assured is your favorite, broccoli. For dessert, I went a bit Azellian, though, and made some *pyrit*."

Tamara hastily blinked away sudden hot tears, overwhelmed and touched that he'd made her favorite comfort foods.

Alarin leaned forward and kissed the smear off her nose. "I take it from the tone of your reaction that you're happy?"

"Happy? You could say that. I didn't know you could cook."

"I was our family cook's favorite because I liked to putter in the kitchen with him. I haven't had much opportunity since we arrived on Earth. I know you've been a bit depressed these past few weeks because of Greg's leaving and—" He stopped. "For other reasons. I thought you might need a little cheering up. The apron was to add a little spice, and because it's been ages since I've been able to go around like this. The dorm wasn't exactly a place I could spend time without clothes on." He hugged her tightly. For all his state of undress and her closeness, his body wasn't nearly as excited as it usually was in these situations, and she knew that he was worried about her reaction.

Tamara held him tighter, suddenly awash in emotion and unable to speak. She stood on her tiptoes and kissed him ferociously—passionately. He made a sound, low in his throat, and kissed her back, responding to her hunger. By the time they pulled apart, he was as thoroughly excited as he'd ever been, wearing the cocky, self-assured grin she hadn't seen in months. She'd realized recently that Alarin had struggled a lot more than she'd imagined since starting to date her. And she knew, for the first time on a deep level, that despite the hurt it had caused her, Merran had been right. She'd made the decision, albeit subconsciously, but it had taken Merran to actually say it out loud. She probably would have dragged it on and caused more damage. "You're going to burn the food," she said breathlessly, after another long, passionate embrace.

"I don't care," he replied, breathing hard, his eyes unfocused. He leaned his head forward to kiss Tamara's neck.

"I do. My taste buds," she squirmed as he hit a particularly sensitive area, "my taste buds … are all happy for what I'm smelling." She gasped as he slid his hands around her back. "At least turn it down? Alari. Please?"

He stopped and lifted his head, grinning impishly. "All right."

She shivered as he stepped away from her, turning toward the kitchen and the dinner. She trailed him into the kitchen, giving herself plenty of room to watch him walk in front of her—she had to admit, it was a very nice view—then slid her arms around his waist as he stirred the meatballs and turned them down to a low setting. The mashed potatoes were put to the back of the stove to keep them warm, and he stuck the broccoli in the microwave. Alarin turned to her after he was done and lowered his head to kiss her again. "I like it," he said, after they came up for air.

"Like what?"

"You don't call me Alari very often." He brushed her hair off her shoulders. "I like it."

Tamara pulled his head down to hers. "I'll call you whatever you want, Alari, if it will get you to kiss me."

He grinned and kissed her again.

The dinner didn't quite burn—but the whole interlude was rather more rushed than normal, because Tamara's stomach growled insistently at several key moments, sending them both into peals of laughter and disrupting the mood. Afterwards, they served up dinner and ate, Tamara, much to Alarin's amusement, putting on a robe and primly spreading towels on the chairs before they sat down.

"I can't eat dinner naked," she protested his teasing as she laid the towels on the chairs, "and we don't need to get our butts all over the chairs. For one thing they're not our chairs, and for another, it's just disgusting."

Alarin laughed. "You're adorable." He straightened the apron that had gotten rather twisted during their earlier activities. "And I hope you enjoy the food."

"I still want to know," she said, after she took a bite and found the meatballs to be absolutely perfect, the mashed potatoes exactly as creamy as they should be, and the broccoli as crisp as she liked it, despite the delay in service, "how you found out that this is my favorite meal. Did you call my dad?"

"Your sister actually."

"My sister ... Andreya? You actually talked to Andreya?"

"I did. She gave me the recipes and told me how you liked everything." He looked at her steadily. There wasn't quite a challenge in his eyes, but it was close. A challenge of what, though?

"She actually told you? That's a surprise. Hell, I'm surprised she bothered to figure out my favorite meal. I'm surprised she didn't tell you to cook things I can't stand. Like oysters. Or raw fish. That's her usual speed, Ms. Competitive. We might have reached some level of communication between us, but not that much."

Alarin shrugged. "I think because you told her about your Azellian background during your vacation, it made a difference. She was certainly chatty enough with me, and I was listening for rancor, believe me. Just so you know, I wouldn't have made oysters or raw fish. Besides the fact that I'm not too fond of them myself, I can usually tell when someone's lying to me."

Tamara made a vaguely noncommittal sound, although he

was probably right. She had finally come clean with Andreya during their vacation, admitting to her that they were only half-sisters, that the woman they both called mother hadn't been hers, and that she was in love with Alarin—although she hadn't gone so far as to share about her relationship with Merran. Come to think of it, Andreya had seemed much less touchy during the vacation, and except for Tamara's misery that Alarin wasn't around, their time together had passed rather pleasantly, at least between her and Andreya.

She shook her head, pushing the memories away. "Maybe. The vacation went better than I expected between her and me. Maybe it's because Dad and I are having a rough time. Andreya doesn't feel like the child who was left out anymore."

"Oh? You didn't tell me he was giving you a hard time."

How could she tell him that her father was against her relationship with him? She shrugged. "Dad's just worried about me. That I'll end up the way he did. It's more about his family's prejudices and his experiences than it is about me." She finished the last of her meal and sat back, rubbing her stomach. "Hmmm, that was really good. Really, really good." She looked up at him and grinned. "I think I'll keep you. Fantastic cook, fantastic lover … what more could one ask for?"

He opened his mind to her, inviting her in. "Meld with me."

She hesitated only for a moment, then let her shields thin so that she could wind her mind around his. The familiar sensation, fast becoming something she craved, spread through her body. She let the rhythms of their connection take her deep, as deep as they'd ever gone, before spiraling out into an ecstasy that consumed her and left her pleasantly exhausted. She was only vaguely aware that Alarin had gotten them to the bed, but as she curled around him and drifted off to sleep, and as she sank deep into his embrace, she was perfectly content and happy with her world.

✳ ✳ ✳

The ringing of her cell phone jerked her out of a sound sleep the next morning. Scrambling over a startled Alarin, she grabbed for it. "Hello?" she said, trying not to sound sleepy but knowing she'd failed.

"Tammy?" It was her father's familiar voice. "Did I wake you?"

"Dad?" She stretched. "No, that's all right. It's ..." she looked at the glowing digital clock by the bed. "I didn't realize it was so late. I have to work this morning anyway ... in two hours. What's up?"

"I wanted to double check and see if you were going to be coming home for dinner tonight. Your Uncle Jim and Aunt Nancy are in town."

Tamara glanced at Alarin, who grinned at her from his position sprawled on the bed. He sat up and reached for her, pulling her quite firmly into his lap. He wrapped his arms around her waist and rested his head on her shoulder. "Of course," she said into the phone, as Alarin kissed her shoulder, pressing himself against her with increasing intensity. It was hard to concentrate with him doing that, but she forced herself to pay attention. "What time's dinner? I work until three."

"That's fine. You can come by when you're done with work. Oh, and Jim and Nancy told me quite firmly to invite your boyfriend too. Apparently, Andreya has been telling them you are involved with someone and they want to meet him." Peter's voice was deceptively casual. In the months since she'd become involved with the Azellians, he'd met Alarin, of course, including right after the first time she and Alarin had slept together, but since she'd started dating Alarin openly, he hadn't been particularly welcoming. He'd probably explode if he knew they were effectively living together.

"I'll ask Alarin if he wants to join us for dinner," Tamara replied, trying not to catch her breath as Alarin escalated his attempts to distract her. Mention of his name made him stop momentarily, though, and he looked at her with a question in his eyes. "I'll call you later today and let you know what he says. Are you going into work this morning?"

"No, your aunt and uncle are arriving in town at noon, so I'm going to work from home this morning. All right, honey, give me a call later," Peter said, sounding distracted. "I have another call coming in. I'll talk to you later. Bye."

"Bye, Dad," Tamara said and hung up the phone. She leaned over to put the phone on the bedside table. Alarin caressed her as she came back into his arms and wrapped her arms around his neck.

"Are you all right?"

"I'm fine." She shifted so her legs wrapped around his waist. "Do you really want to come to this dinner thing tonight? In the middle of my half-crazy family?"

"Of course." He kissed her nose lightly. She rested her head against his shoulder and he pulled her tighter, opening his shields simultaneously and inviting her to read the truth in him. "It's your family, Tam-*ala*. As much as they frustrate you, I can accept them. I can even understand your father's barely restrained hostility."

She lifted her head. "You know about that? I mean, he's not precisely hostile, just worried about me."

Alarin snorted. "You're not on the receiving end, *akila*. He's being polite, but he would be quite content if I went away forever. Of course I know he's not at all happy that we're together. But it doesn't matter in the long run. It's not his choice to make."

She put her head back down and nuzzled her nose against his neck, breathing in the warm, slightly spicy scent that was Alarin. "That's true," she murmured, distracting him by kissing the side of his neck. Although she would perhaps have rather just cuddled, he responded quite enthusiastically. It wasn't until she was alone in the shower, letting the hot water hit her head and shoulders, that she had a chance to think about how things were going. Alarin had most definitely changed since Merran ended their relationship. Just before he left, Greg had told her he'd managed to block Merran's presence. It looked like it had worked—and was holding. Even though Alarin had always thrown himself passionately into their lovemaking sessions, this past week he'd been downright demanding, taking every chance he could to drag her off alone, seeming to take intense sensual delight in simply touching her.

Had Merran's presence made him *that* uncomfortable and put such a huge damper on him? What she had come to expect as a once- or maybe twice-a-week frequency had almost quadrupled, even quintupled, this past week, and Tamara wasn't sure she was comfortable with the change. Her frequency with Merran had never been all that great to begin with; Merran had too much on his mind and was too buried in work to have much energy left for anything else, but she'd considered that she and Alarin were well matched. This week, however, his stamina was leaving her in the dust. She sighed and turned off the water. Maybe things would calm down once he'd reassured himself that she was here, with him, and wasn't going anywhere.

Her cell phone rang from the other room. As she dried herself off, she heard Alarin answer it. "Just a minute, Kari, let me get her," he responded. Oddly enough, he didn't tease her in his usual fashion.

He knocked on the bathroom door, and Tamara opened it, a puff of steam tumbling out as she did. "Kari?"

He nodded and handed her the phone. He ignored her state of undress, as though they were both fully clothed, even though he wore nothing either. It was odd but not odd at the same time. Alarin had an ability to shift from noticing nudity to ignoring it completely with an ease she sometimes envied, because she was always aware when she had no clothes on. He turned back to the kitchen where he continued to clean up from last night's dinner.

"Kari. Hey. What's up?"

"Just checking to see if you have to work today." She sounded odd, almost choked up.

"Yeah, I do, but what's wrong? What's going on?"

"Nothing big." She was silent for a few moments, as if struggling to gain control over tears. "It can wait."

"What happened?" Tamara asked, straining to pick up something from the tone in Kari's voice and the connection between them through the phone. Merran was good enough to read someone over the phone, but Tamara hadn't quite gotten the hang of that yet. She chased down a possibility. "Did something happen between you and Damiar?"

Kari's breath caught. "Yes and no."

"What does that mean?"

"When do you have to go to work?" She sniffed again. "I don't want to start the story, then get interrupted." She was most definitely crying.

"About an hour. I can call work and see if I can come in late, though." Tamara offered. "Things are pretty relaxed over there on Saturdays."

She could sense the silent tears over the phone, but what Kari said was, "No, I don't want to bother you this morning. Can you come by after work?"

"Sure," she said, then remembered the family dinner. "Shit. I have a family dinner. Let me see what I can arrange and call you back, all right?"

"It's all right." Tamara could barely understand her through the tears. "I'll be fine."

"I'll call you back." Tamara hung up the phone.

"She all right?" Alarin asked from the kitchen.

Tamara shrugged. "I don't know. She's crying. It's got something to do with Damiar, I think. When I talked to her yesterday afternoon, she was all excited about the possibility that he was interested in her."

"Damiar? Rory says he's got a lover on Azelle."

"Ah, so he probably turned her down." Kari's upset suddenly made sense. "No wonder she's upset."

"Actually," Alarin replied dryly, "he probably didn't."

"Huh?"

"Humans are a rush," Alarin explained, his voice oddly toneless, as he rinsed off the plates and placed them carefully in the dishwasher. "They don't have shields and can't block the responses to us and our sex." His expression grew guarded, and he continued, "Especially not when we're ... helping to intensify the reactions. I've done it to you a few times; you know what I'm talking about."

She blushed. The couple of times he'd actually touched the erotic center in her brain with his psi, it had been so intense she thought she'd die. She hadn't quite gotten the hang of it to be able to reciprocate, but she was working on it. It wasn't something that was easily taught, especially because she went out of her head when he tried to show her. It wasn't something Greg could really show her either, since she didn't have that type of relationship with him. "Yeah, I do."

Alarin shook his head. "I personally haven't had sex with any pure humans, so I don't know for sure if they react the same way as you do to me, but Justy used to talk quite a bit about the rush he got from them." He glanced at her. "So did Merran." He cleared his throat over the moment of discomfort Merran's name caused between them. "Anyway, Damiar probably did some level of sexual interaction with her, as a curiosity thing, then told her he had a lover."

"Cheating on his girlfriend? Would he do that?"

"It, uh, depends on the context."

"Context? What context? Any sexual contact is cheating, isn't it?"

"Not necessarily."

"Not necessarily?" Tamara's voice went up. The conversation suddenly wasn't about Kari and her culture shock, but about Alarin and Tamara, and Alarin's Azellian attitudes. "What constitutes not necessarily!?"

Alarin turned to her. "Now's not a really good time to get into this. Don't you have to go to work?"

Would she ever understand Azellians? Tamara trembled from the force of emotions suddenly churning in her. Jealousy, possessiveness, and anger, fueled by fear, made her want nothing more than to confront Alarin and demand an explanation. "Fine. As long as you promise to tell me what you would consider acceptable sexual contact with someone else."

"Me? Why none," he replied, as though he suddenly understood something. "With a human or an Azellian, male or female.

I've been on Earth long enough to know that our definitions of sexual contact can be very different from yours, but Justy's trial gave me some insight into exactly how touchy humans can be about it. So I've pretty much avoided the whole thing completely." He shrugged again. "We didn't get much training about human cultural attitudes before we got here, but I'm sure Justy's trial has changed things. I'd better talk to everyone and make sure they all understand how important it is."

Tamara took a deep breath and made an effort to calm her raging emotions. Alarin's calm, matter-of-fact attitude about it helped, but she still could feel the culture shock race through her. He seemed to be respecting her feelings, but the differences implicit in what he'd said, in the very definitions of the words, made her unwilling to blindly accept that he was being trustworthy, as she defined it. She pushed the concern down—there wasn't much she could do about it now—and got herself ready. As soon as she was dressed, she placed a video call to the embassy number.

"Azellian Embassy Denver, how may I help you?"

"May I talk to Janille?" Tamara asked. "It's Tamara Carrington."

"Just a moment, Ms. Carrington, I'll connect you," the receptionist, a fresh-faced young woman she didn't recognize, said.

"Corina," Merran's voice startled her, and she had to keep herself from blushing, immediately grateful that Alarin was in the other room.

"Merran. I, uh, I was trying to reach Janille. What are you doing answering your own phones?"

"Janille's on another call and my intern hasn't come into work yet. Speaking of, when are you coming in?"

"I ... uh ... was hoping you didn't need me this morning. That I could switch to tomorrow from eleven to three. I've got some things that have come up here. Family stuff," she added, intending to use her aunt and uncle as an excuse, but feeling oddly like she was babbling. Merran was making her nervous in a way she hadn't felt since she first met him. She hadn't seen him at work since their breakup—she suspected he'd been avoiding her. Since she was happy to avoid him, too, she'd been grateful for the reprieve. "Uh, my aunt and uncle are here. In town."

Merran was silent for a moment, probably reading more than she wanted him to. "Tomorrow's fine. It will still all be here." He hesitated, then said, "Of course, tomorrow's Janille's day off."

Which meant it would be just him and her. That was almost enough to make her change her mind, but remembering Kari's tears on the phone, she shrugged. "Whatever. I'll see you tomorrow."

"Tomorrow then," he said and hung up.

Tamara stared at the phone, trying to get control over the strange emotions beginning to bubble up. She wasn't precisely upset by the unexpected contact, but it was definitely uncomfortable. She sighed, then used the video application on her phone to call Kari, wanting to see her friend rather than just hear her voice.

Kari answered almost immediately. "Tam?"

"Hey Kare," Tamara said quickly, seeing that her face was swollen and red. "Where are you? I switched work until tomorrow and can spend the morning with you."

"I'm in my room," Kari replied. "I can't go anywhere looking like this."

"I'll be there in five," Tamara answered and hung up. She left the bedroom and entered the kitchen, where Alarin was still in the midst of washing off counters and the table. "I got the day off from work and am going over to talk to Kari," she told him. "What will you be up to while I'm at Kari's?"

131

Alarin shrugged. "I think I need to find the others and talk to them right away, before this becomes a problem. I'm going to hop in the shower and then pay them a visit."

"Do you want to meet back here at three to go over to my dad's?"

"Sure. Contact me mentally if anything changes."

"Ditto." She stepped close to give him a quick kiss. He kissed her back, and Tamara headed for Kari's.

Kari opened the door, eyes bloodshot and swollen. A pile of unused tissues were stacked on the bed, pushed up into a pyramid.

"Okay, tell me what happened," Tamara walked over to the rumpled bed, settling down on it and pointing to the other side. She rested her back against the wall as she patted the bed for Kari to sit down.

Kari took a moment to pull herself together, then plopped down on the other side of the tissue pyramid. "I don't know why I'm so upset, really. I'm actually really pissed more than anything. I've been on this crying jag, though, for hours now."

"Start at the beginning. You said you were going over to meet Damiar at the arts co-op."

Kari took a deep breath and settled herself against her pillows. "I did that and things went really well. I mean *really* well. We really clicked. First we went to dinner, then we talked for hours, and I mean *hours*. One thing led to another and the next thing I knew, he was in my head making me feel …" She shuddered. "It's indescribable, Tam. I can't even begin to explain it. It was like he was touching something inside of me that just made me … explode." She flushed slightly. "I mean, I wasn't actually going to have sex with him on the first date. This wasn't exactly sex, though. We didn't touch once. He could do that without touching me? How?" She wrapped her arms around herself. "It was so intense. I just … I just can't explain it." She blushed harder and glanced at Tamara. "He got off too. Even though I didn't touch him either. It was like …"

"He rode the orgasm with you," Tamara said flatly, trying hard not to be embarrassed about the subject matter. It wasn't that she didn't know about it; it was something that Alarin liked to do to her, and he most certainly enjoyed it enough to climax with her. "It's something they can do. Give you pleasure and ride the result with you."

Kari looked at her. "Without touching you?"

Tamara nodded. "It has to do with the brain. From what I understand, touching that part of our minds directly bypasses the physical, and it is quite a bit more intense, because there's no lag time, or other nerves involved. Something like that. It's very complicated. Greg could probably explain it better than I can. It's a psi thing."

Kari shivered. "Is it something Alarin has done to you?"

Tamara blushed. "Sure," she said, looking down at her fingers as they rubbed against the edge of the bed. She deliberately stopped her hand's restless movements.

"Can you do it?"

Tamara squirmed a bit. "I don't have the hang of it yet. It's a bit arcane. I can't visualize the spot in the cortex well enough to reach it, partially because Alarin can't show me without sending me into spasms … and Greg can't either because as soon as he'd try, the result would be the same as if Alarin tried it, and Greg and I don't have that type of relationship." She rubbed her heated cheeks and firmly changed the subject. "All right, you and Damiar clicked, he rode your orgasm, then what?"

Kari blew her nose. "Then he told me he has a girlfriend on

Azelle." She leaned over to drop a soggy tissue in her trashcan. "He … he said he isn't interested in anything long-term with a human."

Tamara moved across the bed to hug Kari. "Oh, Kari." She held her friend tightly, not knowing what to say.

Kari hugged her back, then threw her arms in the air. "It shouldn't be a big deal. I mean, he has a girlfriend. So what? She's on Azelle, he's here. Why do I even care?" She grabbed a tissue from the stack on her bed and blew her nose. "But I do care. We had such an awesome time together. I want a relationship … but then to find out he has a girlfriend and isn't interested in a relationship with a human? If he wasn't interested, why did he do that to me? Why get me all …" she made a hand gesture that Tamara wasn't entirely sure how to interpret, but she supposed it meant the erotic mental stimulation Damiar had done, "… to just end it. Bam! Over? I want … I just … I don't know." She shook her head and took a deep breath. "I really need someone to tell me I wasn't a complete asshole and idiot last night."

Tamara shook her head. "That I can say for sure. You were making assumptions, and from what you told me, you weren't at all off base … from our perspective. I mean, he'd spent the afternoon and evening with you, had an intimate moment with you, then rejected you."

"Thank you." Tamara could hear the heat in her voice. "What do you mean 'from our perspective'?"

A firm brush across Tamara's shields made her jump. She hastily unshielded and touched a familiar mind. Alarin stood outside with Damiar and Rory. Alarin entered her head as she thinned her shields, slipping to her intimate level. *How is she?*

Upset, Tamara sent back. *Angry. Confused. She's trying to get me to explain something I'm not sure I understand myself.*

Let me read it, Alarin instructed. *I can maybe get to the bottom of this and see if we have damage control to do.*

No, I'll take care of it. Tamara knew Kari really would not like Alarin getting involved, and Alarin could get carried away with being bossy and taking control. He'd probably force Damiar to apologize and blow it up into something it didn't need to be. As a matter of fact, his presence outside might be a prelude to just that. And that, Tamara was certain, was the wrong approach. *It's just a misunderstanding. I'm handling it. Kari's going to want to avoid Damiar for a while.*

Why? Alarin sent back. *He should really apologize.*

Does he know what he did wrong? Tamara sent to Alarin's personal level, then she reached out and touched the surface levels of Damiar's mind. He acknowledged her greeting, but she couldn't read anything from him other than polite acknowledgment.

He knows it's dangerous to do what he did last night ... that he needs to be very careful. Alarin's response was curt. He sounded just a little miffed.

Then let me handle it. Trust me, Alarin. I know Kari better than you do, and I know what she's going to be okay with. Let her get some time and perspective. Then, if Damiar wants to apologize, he can. If you force Damiar into it, I think you'll do more damage on both their parts. Tamara begged. *Please, Alari. Let me deal with it?* She could feel his resolution waiver under the force of her plea as much as from any true understanding of what she meant. Something about her calling him Alari really affected him. Touching his private level as she was, he couldn't hide the rush of pleasure it gave him. She filed away the knowledge and withdrew, vaguely aware that Kari was trying to get her attention.

"Tam? Tamara, are you in there?" Kari asked, waving a hand in front of Tamara's face.

Tamara blinked at Kari. "Sorry, I was just trying to figure out how to answer your question," she said, her mind racing to catch up. "It concerns issues I'm not sure Alarin and I have worked out yet. I mean, Azellians define sex and sexual contact very differently, and I still don't have a complete understanding of it. I doubt Damiar even realized he was doing anything we'd call sex."

"Huh? Giving me an orgasm isn't sex? Having one himself? That doesn't make sense."

Tamara shrugged helplessly. "I told you I don't understand it myself. My personal feeling is that it is sexual contact and it should only be done between partners, but I don't think Alarin necessarily does."

"Alarin doesn't run around giving other women orgasms. Does he?"

Tamara flushed again. "No, of course not. He told me that he tries to avoid anything that might trigger my issues in that regard, because he knows very well that we have such different definitions. And all Azellians are super sensitive about triggering anything like what happened to Justy."

A very strange expression crossed Kari's face. "I didn't understand Joely, but now I kind of do. It's very weird. I mean, Joely's never been the most stable person, and she definitely loves to be the center of attention. If Justern did something that confused her, made her think it was something that it wasn't, I can see how she might have gotten confused and then interpreted it as rape or something. Not that what Damiar did was rape, but it was certainly very embarrassing for me to have him blow hot and cold like that. And since Joely is so unstable anyway ..." She shivered and pulled her knees up to her chest, hugging her legs close.

Tamara shook her head. "I read her memories, Kare. She

might have felt violated, and she might have handled it badly, but she very emphatically also used the opportunity to punish Justern for the other men in her life who had done similar things to her. All of us who could sense such things knew she was acting it up for the court case. As for what she originally felt about the whole thing, who knows? By the time the court case rolled around, she'd worked herself into hysteria." Tamara took a deep breath and pressed her hands against her cheeks. "It was one of the things that pissed us all off so much. If she'd been more reasonable about it, we could have worked things out and kept it from going that far. As it is, she's effectively barred Justy from ever coming back to Earth. And with the Council blocking my application to Azelle every time I try, what are the chances I'll ever get to spend time with him again?" She blinked away hot tears. It had been a rough time. As Merran had suspected, the diehards on the Council, even despite some major changes, still refused to grant Tamara a visa. She was, after all, the daughter of Peter Carrington, and there were Council members who had been a part of the drama of her father falling in love with, and impregnating, an Azellian woman who intended to marry another man. The marriage had gone through anyway, and Tamara had been sent to Earth to live with her father, never knowing her mother, but the hard feelings on the Council remained.

Kari reached out to touch Tamara's hand. "It's all right, Tam. You'll get there. Eventually. Maybe not as a college student, but if you and Alarin keep going the way you are, you'll end up there one day. It's not like they can keep you off Azelle if you become the wife of an Azellian."

Tamara shook off her momentary melancholy. "You're probably right." She waved a hand. "We're not talking about me or Justy, though. Are you okay?"

Kari shrugged and let her legs drop to a cross-legged position. "Yes, I'll be okay." She stared down at her legs. "It's more embarrassment anyway. I mean, I kind of jumped to some conclusions and still feel rather stupid about the whole thing."

Tamara reached over and hugged her friend again. "You aren't stupid, Kare. Not even close."

Kari stared down at the bedspread. "You know," she began. "You said you could read memories. Could you ... you know ... read them?" She lifted her eyes to Tamara.

Tamara dropped her arms and quelled a shudder. "Uh, I don't think so," she said, pushing back and staring at Kari with wide eyes.

"Why not?"

"Because you're my friend, Kari, and because anything I read from you I get to share in. And believe me, I don't want to share that particular memory," Tamara said, making a face. "It took me quite a while and some little adjustments from Greg to get out of Joely's memory. It was really pretty unpleasant. Horrific was more like it."

"Oh." Kari was silent for a moment. "You're so lucky. You found someone. Watching you and Alarin ... I guess I just want that for myself, too. Maybe I'm pushing for a relationship too hard. And assuming that things were happening with Damiar that weren't there."

"It will happen, when the timing's right," Tamara assured her as she reached out to give her a hug. "Whether it's with an Azellian or human, it will happen. Don't worry about it."

Kari returned the hug. "Thanks, Tam. I don't really want to leave my room, though. Not for a month or two."

Tamara laughed. "As pleasant as that might sound right now, that's really not a good idea. It would get rather smelly in here."

Kari threw a pillow at her. Tamara caught it and threw it back. Kari put the pillow behind her and leaned back.

"Come on, I'm starved. Let's go get some lunch and forget about the whole thing. I ran out of my apartment so fast this morning I didn't get to eat breakfast."

Kari put her legs over the edge of the bed. "Fine. Let's go to The Grill, though, please? It's not on campus, and we're less likely to run into other students."

"That I can live with," Tamara replied. After Kari took a few minutes in the bathroom to make herself presentable, they left the dorm. Apparently, Alarin had done as Tamara asked and taken the two Azellians away with him, since she didn't see him at the doorway waiting.

The afternoon passed pleasantly, and Kari seemed to recover more as the day wore on. They lingered over lunch at The Grill, which was unusually, but fortuitously, quiet on a Saturday. By the time three o'clock rolled around, and she and Alarin left to visit with her family, Tamara actually felt as if Kari might be coming back to her usual bouncy self, which was a relief. She hated seeing Kari so distressed.

✳ ✳ ✳

After Tamara canceled coming into work that day, Merran stared at his desk. He'd been avoiding her since they broke up—not difficult, given his always packed schedule—but when he saw the caller notice pop up, he decided to answer it. Tamara was raised as a human, so from his experience with human women, he'd rather expected it to be somewhat uncomfortable between them when they finally did speak. Despite expecting it, he found he didn't care for the sensation of stiff, awkward tension at all, and was relieved to discover from their brief conversation that Tamara wasn't going to be dramatic about their breakup.

There had been a few people over the years who hadn't taken breaking up well. One had tried to starve herself to death to get his attention back, startling him with the force of her reaction to a relationship that hadn't been all that important to him. It had taught him to be cautious about whom he chose as a partner. As unguarded as he'd been with Tamara, unlike everyone else who had come into his life since that long ago relationship with Kaelynn, he was deeply grateful that she seemed to be handling it fairly well. At the same time, a sting of pain zipped through him. She might be handling it well, but he was still plagued with a sense of sorrow and regret. He'd given her up, but his relationship with Alarin showed no signs of improvement, what closeness he did have with Tamara was now damaged, and on top of that, he had a heartache to go with everything else. He pushed aside the thoughts and buried himself in work again.

A few hours later, the intercom buzzed, and Merran tapped the phone to accept the call. "The Dorbin ambassador is here for your meeting, Ambassador," Janille said calmly, her mind giving him what details he needed through mental contact.

"Send the ambassador in, please," Merran replied, thickening his shields and shoving down his unruly emotions.

The Dorbin didn't enter through the door. The non-corporeal being simply appeared in Merran's office, the door still quite firmly closed.

"Welcome," Merran said, getting to his feet. "Thank you for agreeing to meet again on a Saturday to get this finalized, Ki'i. Please, sit and let us finish discussing the details about getting those plants to us and arranging payment for them."

"The honor is mine." The ambassador drifted closer and settled into a chair in front of the desk, as Merran sat down again.

Merran nodded and rested his arms on the desk. "We have agreed to an exchange. You will merge with me for an evening. You will allow a physical psi user other than myself to come to Dorbin to commune with your plants. We have agreed to this. But my concern is whether the plants can survive elsewhere other than Dorbin."

Ki'i flared, bright yellow spikes appearing in its filmy aura. "The transition of our plants to another planet will be simple, once a connection is made. They do not require much to grow, but they do require a link to another who is able to commune with them. Once that communion has been achieved, the plants will grow wherever you wish to take them."

"Good. That sounds easy enough."

The Dorbin ambassador's yellow spikes mellowed into a beautiful turquoise green, rippling through the air in a rainbow of color. "Complication is not required." Amusement tinged the air with a brighter green. "Their caretakers will need to be chosen carefully, however. Those who choose to be joined with our plants may find themselves changed."

Merran blinked. "Like the Miir? Are you saying your plants are sentient and will choose a symbiosis with mobile beings?" *That complicates things,* he thought to himself, wondering why Ki'i had not mentioned this earlier, like when Merran had learned how to take care of the plants himself, or when they'd talked about merging as payment for the plants. Merran would have a hard time finding an Azellian who was not *urro-ken* willing to be taken over by another awareness. Since most *urro-ken* were not allowed off Azelle, it might well be a nearly impossible task. He tried not to let his frustration show. This was where talks had foundered the first time. Although his willingness to merge with Ki'i had facilitated the Dorbin's agreement to allow another caretaker other than himself, Merran hadn't realized the full extent of what would be involved. His mind raced through the possibilities, testing. When the talks had moved forward again with Ki'i's agreement to exchange the plants for an opportunity to merge with Merran, he had decided to ask his assistant Jamian, because of Jamian's experience with the non-corporeal *aarya*. As a former Keeper, who had received specialized training and spent a good chunk of his time with the *aarya*, Jamian had experience with non-corporeal beings. *The question is, how will Jamian take the idea of sharing his psyche?* Merran thought behind heavy shields. Although he'd shared his intentions with his assistant, this had not been part of their conversation. Jamian had agreed to become a caretaker, but Merran now wondered if this final piece would be a deal breaker. The plan was to have Ki'i test Jamian, which now seemed even more critical.

Ki'i was silent for a moment, as if choosing its words. "Our plants are not sentient as the Miir are, no. But they are … aware."

A hint of an idea tickled the back of Merran's mind, a step that might start to heal the thousand-year-old rift between *urro-ken* and *umanaarya*, if Jamian agreed to the assignment. The sheer audacity of the idea made his mind shudder as the room whirled slowly around him, energy thundering through his body in the way it usually did when something fundamental was shifting around him. He blinked and let it happen, knowing he would be able to process it later. For now, he just let the possibility roll through him unimpeded and unprocessed. *Kyarinal. All that is possible becomes possible,* he said in his mind, and allowed the possibility he could feel take shape. *Alawahea. It is as it is.* He forced himself to speak, as if nothing had changed. "If I introduce you to the one whom I have in mind for this training, would you be able to tell if he will have a successful transition? My intention, as we corporeals are mortal and have limited life spans, is to train multiple people to care for the plants over generations."

The Dorbin didn't seem to notice anything unusual. Its aura shimmered a beautiful blend of orange, red, and pink, shading into blues and greens on the edges, as if the sunset had just painted the interior of the office. "You have given this thought. This pleases me. Yes, I would like to meet this choice."

"Let me call him in." Merran reached over and picked up the cool plastic of the handset, reaching out with his mind at the same time and brushing up against his assistant's shields. "Jamie, if you would come in here, please?" He spoke into the phone, but it was his mental touch that conveyed to his assistant the urgency for him to come into the office.

A few moments later, a very tall man almost ten years older than Merran opened the door and walked into the office. Long and lean, Jamie looked as though he missed more meals than he ate, but as a former Keeper from the Temple, who had once shared his mental space with the *aarya* themselves, Merran knew he would not buckle under alien perceptions. "You wished to see me, Ambassador?" He spoke formally, as he usually did. As a former acolyte who had experience with the Keepers, Merran found him less unnerving than many of the rest of the staff did, so he usually worked with Jamian directly. That familiarity had not softened Jamian's formality into something less structured and more relaxed, however.

"Jamie, come in," Merran said, getting to his feet and giving Jamian a bow. "This is Ambassador Ki'i from Dorbin. Ambassador, this is Jamian Tamyth Memaxthal."

The Dorbin ambassador floated up out of its chair and turned to face the newcomer. Jamian bowed. "Ambassador," he said in his deep, calm voice. Even years after having left the Temple, Jamian still exuded the deep peace that was part of being from the Temple. It made him a very good assistant, more so sometimes than the volatile Ketiana, but because he did not see things the way everyone else did, he was also rather unpredictable and somewhat unreliable at times.

"Ah," Ki'i said, floating closer to the former Keeper. "May I?"

Jamian inclined his head, and the Dorbin ambassador "reached" out, filmy tendrils of energy visible against the dark background of the office wall, flaring brilliantly against Jamian's shields. Merran watched as Jamian lowered his shields easily and the Dorbin ambassador dimmed, as though parts of its being were soaking into Jamian's tall form.

A few moments later, Merran realized that was exactly what was happening, as Jamian's aura shaded into an odd, blended color of coffee and cream, rather than his normal clear brown, with spikes of green and blue flaring and disappearing, like the glistening scales of a water snake disappearing into murky water. Merran had seen auras meld before, of course, when a couple shared intimacy, but it had never looked like this. This reminded him more of what an *urro-ken's* aura looked like after their *meynsur* permanently merged with them.

Shudders gripped Jamian's big frame. He panted in short, intense bursts, fists clenched tightly, but said nothing as Ki'i's form dimmed almost to nothing. He shivered again, his skin rippling, reminding Merran that the merging could express itself sexually—or at least it had with the *urro*—creating a sensation in the body not unlike orgasm. Although Merran could not read the former Keeper—Jamian kept whatever he was feeling under tight shields—a deep, distinctly sexual groan escaped the big man, as Ki'i's form slowly brightened again. As the Dorbin exited Jamian's body, Jamian let out his breath, then quite deliberately took a deep inhale, carefully unclenching his fists and stretching his fingers.

Ki'i returned to hover in front of Merran's desk. "This choice will do very well," it said, emanating pleasure. "Our plants will thrive in communion with him. And he will bring wisdom to us in the sharing."

"I'm glad to hear it," Merran said. "Thank you, Jamie, you and I will talk later. Unless you need a moment?"

Jamian inclined his head, his aura back to its normal translucent brown. "Thank you, but I am fine, Ambassador." He bowed deeply and left, moving a little more stiffly than normal, but better than Merran had after similar experiences with the *urro*. *Keeper training apparently includes how to function after a merge*, Merran thought to himself, watching Jamian leave. His assistant didn't seem to be at all disturbed by the merging, which was a very good sign.

"All right," Merran said, bringing his attention back to Ki'i. "Everything is in place. One evening merged with me in exchange for your plants." Watching Ki'i merge with Jamian reminded him how it had felt to allow the *urro* access to his body, something he hadn't done in years. He'd never reached Keeper status at the Temple, and the *aarya*, though as incorporeal as the *urro*, never merged like this with acolytes, although from Jamian's calm reaction to Ki'i's approach, he wondered if they did with Keepers. A pleasant, almost sexual anticipation stirred his body, and he could feel himself reacting rather more strongly than he expected—or maybe he was picking up Ki'i's excitement? It was hard to tell, because the Dorbin was emoting all over the office. Merran let himself ride the anticipation, remembering the other perk of merging with an ancient being—disassociation from his emotions. It would be wonderful to get a break from the nagging grief and regret. And if the merging had the sexual effect it seemed to have on Jamian, he would count it a bargain well made. "Come, we will make our way to a part of Denver to the east, an area my fellow Azellians do not frequent. I'll want privacy for the merge, so I will take us to a hotel first." Ki'i sent agreement.

They didn't say much as he and Ki'i headed across town, far away from those parts of Denver that Azellians patronized, using a nondescript embassy car that would not stick out. After he checked in under an assumed name and paid with cash, Merran made his way to the hotel room with a rising sense of excitement. The door had no sooner closed behind him when a very familiar, long forgotten sensation tickled through him. He abruptly understood Jamian's reaction in the office as a sense of sharp ecstasy doused him, his nerves firing pleasurably as Ki'i's energy filtered through his skin. He was vaguely aware that he'd gone to his knees, his body shuddering in reaction—how had Jamian kept on his feet in the office? Unlike with the *urro*, however, after a few moments, Ki'i's presence slowly blunted the pleasure his body felt, the sensations being picked up and filtered by Ki'i's awareness rather than his as Ki'i took control of his body. A faint, half-felt sense of alarm spilled through him—in the anticipation of this moment, Merran had negotiated nothing about how Ki'i should treat his body while in control of it—but then the alarm, too, was gone, washed away in a sudden darkness that swallowed him whole. Sinking into that darkness, Merran abruptly lost all sense of anything at all, his psyche disappearing under the weight of the alien being that possessed him.

Chapter Four

The next morning, Merran woke to the sun in his eyes, a nasty taste in his mouth along with another pounding head. He sat up, then collapsed back onto the bed with a groan. What the hell had happened last night? The last thing he remembered was reaching a final agreement with the Dorbin ambassador regarding both the negotiation for the Dorbin plants the Azellian Healers wanted so badly and the merging Ki'i wanted almost as strongly. Ki'i had met and approved of Jamian as a liaison. Once Merran realized merging with Ki'i would have a sexual side effect he did not want either humans or Azellians to witness, they had gone to a hotel far away from the embassy and any Azellian who might be able to perceive Ki'i's alien presence within Merran … and done … what?

He reached for hazy memories, using techniques his time as an acolyte at the Temple had taught him to refine and sharpen. He could remember merging with Ki'i, the sensation of an alien being sliding into him familiar from his experiences as *urro-ken*.

Although it felt similar to merging into the mind of a lover, the merge with Ki'i had been distinctly different, in that the alien awareness fit over Merran's like a glove. And unlike Merran's experiences with the *urro*, who were very careful to share the psyche and not take it over, Ki'i had been in total control of Merran's body last night. It certainly explained the haziness of his memories, but not the feeling that he'd gotten drunk again and was now suffering from yet another hangover.

Merran sat up gingerly and looked around. He was not in his apartment or his office, or anywhere he recognized. It looked and felt like the hotel room he'd rented last night, although his psi was still a bit wonky from the hangover—or from Ki'i's presence—so he couldn't be sure it was the same one. He could still feel the alien inside of him, but Ki'i had relinquished control back to him, so he could see and hear and touch as he always did. There was no one else in the room with him, thank the *aarya*, but Ki'i's presence added another layer to his psi and he could sense a tingle from the pillow beside him. Reaching out his hand, he brushed his hand across the pillow and picked up the faint fading mental residue of a woman. With that memory, he suddenly had a vivid sensual recall of sliding into a woman's body, Ki'i's elation rocketing through him strongly enough to distract Merran from even the most basic physical function of sexual intercourse.

A firm knock on the door made him wince, the thunderous sound echoing in his head. Merran swung his legs over the edge of the bed, halting for a moment as his stomach began to rebel. Instead of trying to make it to the door, he reached out mentally to brush up against shields he knew well.

Katie? What are you doing here? He unlocked the door with his telekinetic abilities—apparently those abilities were still functional despite the sluggishness of the rest of him.

Ketiana came through the door forcefully, allowing the door to slam shut behind her as Merran closed his eyes and pressed his hand against his temple. She came to a halt, staring at him, her eyes wide and horrified.

"What?" Merran asked, looking down at his naked body, hastily reaching to drag a sheet over his waist. "What's wrong?" He didn't move, not trusting his stomach to stay where it belonged. "Do I look that bad?"

Ketiana found her voice, but it took a moment. "Worse," she said. "What the hell have you done to yourself?! Your aura … it looks really wrong."

Merran winced. He'd forgotten that his aura probably looked strange, if what he'd witnessed when Ki'i merged with Jamian in his office was any indication. He knew better than this—if Ketiana figured out what she was seeing, he could be in deep trouble with his superiors. The *umanaarya* distaste for the merging and the *urro-ken* was deep-seated and illogical, buried in a past that no one could remember, even in legend, but it existed, and Merran understood this well. He took a deep breath and let it out slowly. Fortunately, it appeared that Ketiana didn't know exactly what she was looking at, and her reaction was more because of concern rather than the disgust fellow Azellians usually directed at the *urro-ken*. "It's nothing. I just got a little drunk last night."

"Alcohol doesn't change the color of your aura, Merran. What did you drink, poison?"

Merran shrugged, the heater whirring on with a click, spilling a draft of warmish air across his bare shoulders. He got to his feet, dragging the sheet behind him. Although Ketiana was Azellian and nudity was not really a problem, given his vulnerability recently and her tendencies to mother him, he wanted some cover. It didn't help that he could still feel Ki'i entwined with his psyche. *Let me handle this,* he sent to the Dorbin. *Please.* Ki'i sent affirmation in return, a bubble of amusement filling their shared body. It helped.

"There may have been other substances involved." From how his body felt, there hadn't been anything but alcohol, but it was better that Ketiana think he'd experimented with something rather than learn that he'd allowed another being to take over his body, especially without any restrictions, limits, or boundaries. Merran knew Jamian, with his Keeper training and perspective, would have handled finding him like this better, but, then again, Jamian wouldn't have come looking for him in the first place, so he was back to wondering why she was here. "Nothing to worry about. It will go back to normal soon. Why were you looking for me? How did you know where to find me?"

Ketiana moved to sit next to the flat-screen TV on the long dresser. She tapped her forehead. "My Dorvath clairvoyance gave me a warning that I needed to find you. Tracking you down wasn't easy, because whatever you did to your aura also changed the shape of your mind, but once I got to the right part of town, all I had to do was follow the trail of the man who was causing trouble, dancing on tables, inciting fights, and trying to pick up women *and* men. I found you last night, but since you had a woman with you, and you brought her to a hotel, I figured I'd leave you alone until your date left this morning."

Merran swore in *jygar.*

A smile tugged at her lips. "Men? I didn't know you were interested in men."

"Hah," Merran grumbled, mentally cursing himself for letting Ki'i take the wheel and drive without having first negotiated what he could and could not do. It had felt good to no longer have direct contact with his physical body and emotions, especially the ache of releasing Tamara, but leaving the Dorbin in total control of his body had been a terrible idea. Another little bubble of something—he'd call it Ki'i's amusement rather than last night's dinner—danced at the base of his esophagus, and he had to swallow hard. "Was I recognized?"

"I wouldn't have recognized you, so probably not, no—the only saving grace after a stunt like that." She studied him for a moment. "I know it hurts about Tamara, but you can't keep doing this, Mer. You're not thinking straight. I think you should take some time off."

Merran hated to admit it, but Ketiana was probably right. Letting the Dorbin, with its alien mores and thought patterns, take over his body completely, without consideration for the possible consequences, had been very risky—and definitely not something he normally would have done. If he could keep Ketiana from realizing that his lack of judgment was far worse than she knew, he could also maybe keep her from reporting him to the Council. That particular result didn't bear thinking about. The Azellian Council would recall him and he'd be exiled back to the outer caves for allowing another being to merge with him like this.

"Time off?" Greg had mentioned taking time off, and he'd considered it seriously enough to come up with an idea of how he could manage it. At the time, though, he'd decided against it because of the outstanding negotiation with Ki'i, but after last night, if Ki'i had any further questions, they could wait to discuss details.

"Time off. You know. Away from the embassy. Give yourself a chance to get some perspective. Three months would be good. I know you have the vacation time built up. We each get six weeks a year and you haven't taken a vacation in three years?"

Merran blinked. "Yes, but that doesn't mean I can afford to take that much time off. And I have to be back here before Festival. It's hard to tell when the winter storms will let up on Azelle, but it will definitely happen within the next three months." He gave her a sharp look. "Unless you'd like to have me celebrate Festival among humans?"

"Two-and-a-half then. This is not just a vacation, Merran. How long has it been since you've gone without any worries or concerns of any kind? How long has it been since you've taken time to do whatever you want and not had to make any more earth-shaking decisions than what clothes to wear or where to eat lunch? How do you expect to make any big decisions in the future, if you don't make the time to connect with yourself first … especially now?"

Merran took a deep breath and let her think she'd talked him into it, although the evening with Ki'i had pretty much made him realize he could use some time off. "All right, fine. I'll go on an extended ski trip and be back before Festival starts. No commitment on exact time though. I want to be sure I don't chance getting caught away from the embassy."

Ketiana raised an eyebrow. "Skiing?

Merran shrugged. "I'll start there."

Ketiana studied him for a moment. "Aspen?"

"I don't think so. I know the security is better in Aspen, but there are always too many celebrities and just as many reporters there. I may move in those circles regularly as the ambassador, but if I'm truly going to take time for myself, I need to be in a place where we can hide my presence. If I'm getting away, I'm getting away. It will give me the chance to be a nobody for the first time in years."

Ketiana looked at his hair and face. "You're not going to have much luck at hiding those features, Mer. You're too well known as it is. Wherever you go, you're going to have an entourage of reporters."

Merran reached up and tugged on his hair. "Was I recognized last night? I was here in east Denver, without a single disguise, and you said no one recognized me. Why? Because they didn't expect to see me in such a place. But to be safe, I can grow my hair long and dye it, and let my beard grow too," he added as he conjured an image in his mind's eye. "I'll vaguely resemble me, but since no one expects the Azellian ambassador to be a ski bum, and if I don't act like Merran Corina, they'll never figure it out. People see what they expect to see, and nothing else. My accent is good enough that I can get away with speaking English and not be identified as an alien, and my psi, well, I'm quite used to being discreet."

Ketiana gave him a strange look. "You've thought about this before, haven't you?"

"I've thought about how I could be a regular person before, yes. I just never prioritized it."

"Do you think you'll go back to Azelle at all?"

Merran shrugged. "Probably not. I can't be anonymous on Azelle. Too difficult to dodge mind readers, and I don't think there is a single person on Azelle who doesn't know who I am. Humans are more fun anyway."

Ketiana snorted. "It's your vacation. Just don't break too many hearts, will you? I'll see which bodyguard I can assign—"

"No. I'll go alone."

"You can't," Ketiana protested, shocked at the suggestion. "I suggested you get away, but I can't send you out alone!"

"I go alone, Katie. I can't be anonymous with a bodyguard.

You know that as well as I do. I'll be fine. My psi is *quite* strong enough to warn me about people who want to cause me harm. And if no one recognizes me, then I don't need a bodyguard. I'm far from helpless."

Ketiana threw her arms in the air. "I'll get censured for this. The Council will be horrified if they find out you went away completely unprotected."

Merran shook his head. "You obeyed a direct order from me. Since I'm doing as you asked, you aren't going to report my lack of judgment and I am still your direct superior."

Ketiana glared at him. "You're impossible." She took a deep breath. "At least give me a rough idea where you are while you're gone, will you? So I know we don't have to search for your replacement."

"You'll know where I am at all times. I'll even call you every now and again."

Ketiana was silent for a moment. "I don't …"

"Ah, Katie. You're absolutely wonderful. I'd kiss you if I didn't stink. Thank you for being so supportive while I try to work through … all this insanity." He looked down at himself. "I need to shower and get out of here. See you later, at the office?"

"Fine." Ketiana stood up and moved to the door. "Fine." She stopped and looked over a shoulder. "You sure you don't want me to stay?"

She didn't mean it as a sexual innuendo; he clearly read her distrust that he would do as he said. It wasn't a surprise she didn't trust him. He wasn't sure he trusted himself after last night's ridiculous stunts. "No, I'm fine, thanks," Merran replied, turning for the bathroom door and stepping inside as he closed it behind him firmly. As soon as he sensed she had left, he leaned against the counter and said, "All right, Ki'i, fun's over."

The Dorbin left him, pulling free of Merran's psyche slowly, the sensation sending shivers through Merran's body, reminding him that the experience hadn't been all bad.

"Thank you for a very fun evening," Ki'i said, appearing as a shimmery spot at the corner of the bathroom. The being motioned toward the outer room. "Your people really do not like the merging. I could feel your fear that your assistant would realize my presence with you."

"I could be recalled and exiled for it."

"I may not understand, but I accept that it is. I will leave you now so you can begin your well-deserved vacation. Shall I coordinate a visit to Dorbin with your assistant Ketiana?"

"No, you're going to work directly with Jamian, who you met."

"Agreed. Thank you, Merran." The being disappeared through the wall, dissolving from Merran's sight and mental awareness.

As soon as Ki'i left, Merran stared at himself in the mirror. Had his breakup with Tamara truly affected his judgment? Or had something else been working through him? It might have taken a weird night of possessed debauchery, but he'd managed to do what no other Azellian ever had: he'd gotten the Dorbin to agree to share their psi-sensitive plants. The *urro-ken* weren't allowed off Azelle—or very rarely allowed off Azelle, much less given positions like his—yet it was his *urro-ken* background that had paved the way for this triumph. *Take that all you Azellians who have ever held my heritage against me,* he thought to himself, with a sudden grin. *The irony of it is actually funny.* He shook his head and climbed into the shower. *Do you see, Mama?* he asked the silence in his mind. *I did something no other umanaarya could do, and I did it because I am urro-ken. Can I bridge the gap between us?*

Is it possible? As he lathered his hair, the shining possibility he'd glimpsed in his office showed itself. *Kyarinal,* he murmured to himself as he ducked his head under the strong spray of water, feeling the soap slide down his face and neck. *What is possible becomes possible. I wonder where it will take us.* He finished his shower and dried off, the glimpse into the future fading back into obscurity, as he got dressed and checked out of the hotel.

Several hours later, after a long and very satisfying conversation with Jamian about his hopes and plans for the Dorbin psi-sensitive plants, and after successfully getting in and out of the embassy before Tamara came in for her shift, he headed into the mountains toward the condo Ketiana had rented for him. Suddenly feeling younger and stronger than he had in years, Merran whistled a cheerful tune as he leaned back and drove the car he'd borrowed toward the mountains and freedom.

Tamara let time pass in a haze of schoolwork. She avoided the new Azellians scrupulously, and her life settled into something resembling a routine. Even at her internship, she managed to keep herself fairly isolated, working primarily with Janille. Much to her relief, Merran didn't make an appearance, called offworld according to Ketiana, who seemed to step into his shoes easily. Tamara stayed out of the political wrangling that surrounded Ketiana's sudden ascension and refused to speculate with the rest of the staff as to why Merran had left so abruptly. Even Alarin's incessant sexual demands on her eased as he relaxed—just as she'd hoped they would. She prayed that everything would stay calm in her life, at least for a while.

Late one afternoon, she was seated at the kitchen table in

Alarin's apartment, studying between classes. She'd pretty much given up her room completely to Kari, who had moved out of hers and into Tamara's, seeking privacy away from her roommate. Unexpectedly, Tamara heard the apartment door lock turn and Alarin walk in.

"Hey," she said, looking up to see him. "You're home early. I thought you had a study group."

"I forgot my chemistry book." He came over, kissed her rather distractedly, and grabbed the heavy book from the pass-through countertop.

"You going to be home for dinner?"

He shook his head. "Probably not. We have a huge mid-term coming up and we need to put several hours of studying in. I might even be late tonight. Depends on how much we get done. Francyne is having trouble with English and I'm having to coach her through it." He threw the comment over a shoulder as he turned to leave.

"Francyne?" Tamara asked as an odd feeling spread through her. "Francyne Corvik? The Azellian bit—woman we met at the beginning of the semester?"

Alarin nodded, giving her a strange look, probably because despite her effort to cut off the expletive, he heard it anyway. "She's in the advanced chemistry class with me. She knows her stuff, let me tell you, but because she's got the language handicap, I've been tutoring her in English. I thought I told you that."

"You told me you had a study group." Tamara wasn't sure which bothered her more—that he hadn't told her tutoring Francyne *was* the study group or that he was tutoring Francyne. "I thought that meant you had a study *group*, not that you were tutoring Francyne alone."

Alarin raised his eyebrow. "What's got you all upset? It is a study group. We're at the library, studying. There are two of us, which constitutes a group."

Tamara glared at him. She hated it when he split hairs and made her feel like the one who was overreacting. He hadn't told her about his tutoring of Francyne, and she suddenly decided that bothered her more than knowing he was tutoring her. She could still remember Francyne's suggestive comment that she would like to get to know Alarin better. And now she had—and Tamara hadn't even known about it. Could she trust Alarin? Was he doing things he shouldn't be doing? Had he done things with Francyne that Tamara wouldn't approve of? Jealousy raged through her, and she felt helpless against the roar of it.

"What?" He'd picked up on her emotions—their bond was undoubtedly making her transparent to him. "Are you mad that I am part of a study group or that it's with Francyne?" He put his book on the table. She saw his temper ignite. "Excuse me if I am just a little homesick and want to spend time with Azellians once in a while. Greg's gone and Merran and I still have some things to work out before I can spend time with him. Who do you expect I'm going to hang out with if not the new students? Do you want me to feel more like an exile than I already do?"

"No, of course not," Tamara replied, feeling tears prick at the back of her eyes, guilt adding to the jealousy until she felt so terrible that she didn't know what to think. Did he really feel like he was that isolated? "I just—"

"Just what? Are just so suspicious of me that you think I would betray our relationship? I can't believe you don't trust me."

"I am not saying that. I do trust you. I don't trust her after how she treated me when we first met, but I trust you. But you still should have told me you were tutoring Francyne."

"Are you saying I purposely tried to keep something from you?" Alarin pulled himself up to his full height, and she could feel the surge of hurt. "Fine. I'm going to tutor Francyne. I'll be back later." He grabbed his book and stalked out of the apartment, slamming the door behind him.

After he left, Tamara burst into furious, heartbroken tears, sobbing too hard to see straight. She gasped for breath, muttering to herself as she made her way to the bathroom, so angry and scared she could hardly think. How had they gotten from it being his fault for not telling her about Francyne to her fault that she didn't want him to spend time with his fellow Azellians? She screamed in frustration, throwing the bottle of shampoo that got in her way, then collapsed to the floor, swearing and sobbing.

The fit took a while to cool off, but she finally got herself back together, feeling drained, exhausted, and shell-shocked. *Kari.* She had to talk to Kari. They could go over to The Grill and get something to eat and talk about what assholes men were. Wiping off her face and staring at herself in the mirror—she looked pale and wide-eyed, but normal enough—she pulled on her coat and left the apartment, going across campus to the room that had been hers until recently. She kept her mind carefully blank as she walked.

She didn't scan ahead of herself and slipped the key into the lock without checking the room first. She pushed the door open and stared in shock. Kari was sitting on top of a young man—she recognized Damiar belatedly—and they were quite enthusiastically going at it, even though they were both fully dressed. Kari was making sounds, echoed by Damiar. It was quite obvious that either Damiar had come to terms with his lover on Azelle or that this was another "not sexual contact" thing, which she most emphatically did not want to hear about right now. They certainly were enjoying themselves—that was apparent. Neither of them seemed to notice her, so she backed out of the room hastily, locking the door behind her. When had Damiar come back into Kari's life? Why hadn't Kari shared it with her? Shaken by what she'd seen and feeling like she had nowhere to go, Tamara fled.

After letting the shock pass, she found herself wondering where she could go. Everyone she'd come to depend on these past few months wasn't available, and she fought that sense of complete and utter loneliness. She didn't intend to reach toward Merran, didn't even expect to have him answer, from wherever he was, but as she walked through the rapidly darkening streets, her mind reached out toward the only other person who had not yet turned away from her tonight. Far sooner than she expected, she brushed up against a familiar mind, getting startling images of a roaring fire in a marble fireplace, of warmth and women's voices in the other room.

"Michel?" one of the women called out, and the images were abruptly cut off as Merran quite firmly slammed the door that had opened between them. The force of it made her stumble, and tears of self-pity burned her eyes. Blindly walking through the campus streets, she made her way back to Alarin's apartment, feeling like she had nowhere to go, no haven she could call her own. Once at the apartment, she sat huddled in a corner, letting the falling darkness envelop her as she sunk deeper into her self-pity. Alarin was going to leave her for Francyne, whom she remembered as being tall and gorgeous; Greg would die on Ather; and Merran, well Merran hated her now. Both her mothers were dead, and her brother was stuck on Azelle, unable to develop anything more than a long-distance relationship with her, and to top it all off, as she sniffed, she felt like she was getting a cold.

There was sort of a pleasant indulgence to the wallowing she was doing; it made her feel justified, and it was fun in a masochistic sort of way. She knew, though, that if Alarin showed up before she'd had a chance to pull herself together, it was going to lead to another fight, and she didn't want that. Merran's actions earlier reminded her that for better or worse, she and Alarin were in it alone, that if she screwed things up with Alarin that would be it. She knew she was being somewhat theatrical, but she didn't care—right now it felt good. When feeling sorry for herself paled, she entertained herself with the thought of Alarin and Francyne together—although because that particular image burned, she hastily realized it wasn't one she should be imagining.

Alarin didn't get back home until late, after she'd given up and gone to bed. He moved quietly, as though he didn't want to wake her, but she'd been unable to sleep, too tortured by the unwanted images in her head. He climbed into bed and lay unmoving next to her, a small, artificial distance between them in the double bed. Tamara's muscles screamed at her, wanting desperately to close that small distance and touch him, needing the reassurance of physical connection. She didn't know if he'd welcome the touch or hurt her by pushing her away, but she tried anyway. She moved her arm across the distance to brush against his side.

"You awake?" he murmured as she moved.

"Hmmm. Sort of," she said sleepily. Several questions flew through her head, but she quickly discarded all of them as being too accusatory. She finally settled on, "What time is it?"

"Late." His skin was cold to the touch, and she shivered. She wanted to apologize, something to end this awkwardness between them, but one thing she'd figured out tonight was that she had nothing to apologize for. Still, something had to break the ice between them.

"You get what you wanted done?"

"Mostly."

"Is it cold out?" She brushed her fingertips over his skin.

"It's snowing." The faintest tremor went through him, so slight she almost didn't sense it. "We're supposed to get a huge storm over the next couple of days."

"We get those this time of year sometimes." She expanded her touching, brushing her fingertips across the firm lines of his stomach toward his lower areas.

Whatever his feelings were right at the moment, his body was quite happy to be there. She teased him lightly, sliding herself across the bed toward him. "Snow always …" he gasped as she wrapped her fingers around him and tugged gently.

"Snow always what?" Tamara asked, quelling her rising feeling of triumph. Alarin, in one of his mercurial shifts of moods, had gone from touching her constantly to not at all during the past week, and it had contributed to her feelings of jealousy—she hadn't realized until this moment just how much. Of course, she hadn't been too accommodating either, lost in her studies. She forgot sometimes that psi made things more difficult, that Alarin could sense her withdrawal and responded to it in a way human men couldn't and didn't. Maybe this business with Francyne was her fault after all. She pushed away the tiny frisson of guilt as Alarin rolled over, shifting so he lay against her.

Lowering his head to kiss her, he didn't answer her. His shields remained close around him, despite the leaking of emotions through them, but passion slowly eroded their strength. She could taste the desperate joy in him, even despite the shields, the fear so oddly echoing her own. Was he actually afraid *she* was leaving *him*? It hadn't occurred to her that he might feel that way—but it did, in some ways, make sense. It hadn't been all that long since Merran had stood between them, when she'd straddled the fence using Merran as a shield against the powerful, passionate feelings Alarin evoked. She could feel the echo of isolation in him, and she opened her mind to his, welcoming him into her depths.

He surged into the breach in her shields, even as he mirrored the movement with his physical body. He poured himself into her, his mind sliding around hers with that intense, sensual intimacy that only psi couples could attain. He moved his body against hers, and she rose to meet him, their movements becoming almost frantic. She cried out as he touched that intimate part of her mind and knew he followed her even as the sensations exploded through her body and mind. He caught her, supporting her as she tumbled from the heights, collapsing on top of her, as breathless as she.

She came to herself slowly, lethargically, feeling deeply satiated and content. "I want to know how to do that," she told him as he rested on her. "I want you to be on the receiving end of it for once."

He lifted his head, bracing on his arms as he looked down at her. "You'll either get it eventually or you won't. Either way, I don't care. I like making you feel like your body is going to fly apart and you might just explode into a million pieces. I like taking you where no human can." His voice was soft, tender, and carried a host of emotions he never talked about. He pressed himself against her as he leaned forward to kiss her, sliding out of her as he rolled away, just enough that he could pull her close to his body.

She cuddled next to him; feeling loved and held, her loneliness eased. "I love you, Alari," she whispered as she felt his body jerk toward sleep. The words came easily, but she didn't think he'd heard them. His hand on her side twitched a little as she lay energized and sleepless against him. She turned her head to see him lying on the pillow next to her, his total relaxation making him look young and vulnerable. "I love you." The words sent an odd tingle through her, and she knew they were true. "No matter what, I love you," she murmured again to his sleeping form. It was the first time that she'd said those words to him, accepting their meaning in her own head. She cuddled closer to him and closed her eyes, basking in this fragile moment of happiness.

Chapter Five

A few days after their fight and makeup session, Tamara woke once more to a ringing phone. Their relationship had smoothed out after that fight. She didn't mention Francyne, and Alarin was careful to tell her who he went out with—mostly Rory and Damiar, carefully avoiding the female Azellians as much as possible. She scrambled out of bed, reaching for her cell phone, which somehow always seemed to find itself on the other side of Alarin. By now, well used to Tamara's tendency to clamber over him, Alarin did nothing but open one eye and pin her across his chest with his arm.

Tamara momentarily struggled with the phone to see that it was Kari's number on the display.

"I gotta get this," she muttered to Alarin. "I told you about Damiar and Kari, didn't I?"

Alarin opened the other eye. "Uh-huh," he murmured affirmatively. Then he gave her a sleepy grin and slid his hand down her back to her legs. "Actually, you didn't precisely tell me. I read it when we were—"

"Yeah, yeah, yeah," Tamara said, hastily cutting him off. "I told you I have to get this."

Alarin laughed, a throaty masculine sound that made Tamara's stomach twist in her abdomen. She glared at him and answered the phone.

"Hello?"

"Tam?" Kari's voice sounded far more alert than her own did. "Sorry, did I wake you? I thought you'd be up by now. Do you guys want to go to the parade downtown?"

"What parade?" Tamara asked, shifting so she slid off Alarin, who turned over and listened unabashedly to the conversation.

"The one on the 16th Street Mall. They're supposed to be having a festival this weekend to celebrate something. I'm not sure what. We just want to go to the parade."

Tamara exchanged a look with Alarin. "We?"

Kari sounded sheepish this time. "Damiar and me."

"Ah," Tamara replied, trying not to sound too judgmental.

"Things changed." The sheepish tone in Kari's voice increased.

"Apparently," Tamara said, letting some of her surprise show through her voice. "More than a little it seems. Well, I hope it's a good thing for you. Maybe we can talk later ... if we join you at the parade?"

"That sounds good. I hope you guys can make it."

"Let me ask Alarin and I'll call you back. It sounds good to me, though."

"Talk to you later then," Kari said cheerfully. "We'd like to meet up at ten or so to get a good position before the parade starts at ten thirty."

"Okay. I'll talk to him and call you back. Bye." Tamara hung up the phone and turned to Alarin. "Did you get that?"

"Most of it. Sounds like fun."

"Did you know they've been seeing each other?" She slid down next to him.

"I had an idea." He pulled her close. "Apparently, he left Azelle for similar reasons to mine."

Tamara propped herself up on one elbow. "Similar reasons… you mean he's actually ended things with his lover? To take up with Kari?"

"He said he was thinking about it. Looks like he did." He pulled her down again. "Despite what happened before, Damiar is not a bad guy. Give him—them—a chance." He ran his hands down her body, trying to distract her.

She snuggled against him but didn't let him distract her that much. "I don't get it, though. Will he change his mind again?"

"He could." Alarin finally gave up on trying to divert her attention and slid a leg over hers instead.

"But that would …" She struggled to sit up. "That would hurt Kari!"

"What are you, Kari's love-life monitor? *Alawahea,* Tam. Let things happen as they will. It will either work or not. You can't control it, and you said yourself that Kari wants a relationship. So let's see what happens."

Tamara settled back and shook her head. "I don't like it. I mean, what if he does change his mind again?"

Alarin kissed the back of her neck. "It's her life and her choices. It's not for us to interfere, whether or not you want to."

Tamara heaved a sigh. "I suppose you're right."

"Of course I am." He let his hand trail suggestively down her body. "I'm always right."

She scowled at him. "If we're going to meet them at ten," she said, ignoring the cheerful arrogance in his comment, "we'd better get moving." She wrinkled her nose at him. "You take such long showers after all."

"Ha," he said, sitting up and letting her go. "I think you're thinking of yourself there."

Tamara called Kari back to let her know they'd be at the parade, then slid off the bed, putting her hand on the dresser table as dizziness assailed her momentarily. Her stomach roiled unpleasantly and she fought the sensation. *What is going on?* She'd felt fine a moment before.

"Are you all right?" He caught her discomfort and came close.

The scent from his skin was suddenly nauseating. Tamara shivered violently, trying to control her sudden desire to retch.

"Tamara?"

Tamara put her hand up and hastily sat down on the bed again. "I'll be fine. Just give me a moment," she muttered, willing her recalcitrant body into submission. What was wrong with her? Her whole body suddenly seemed alien to her, overly sensitive and unpleasantly unbalanced.

Alarin frowned down at her. "Are you sure?"

"I'm fine," Tamara snapped, suddenly irritated, fear rushing through her. What if she wasn't fine? What if there was something wrong with her? Emotions exploded through her with the force of a freight train, and she struggled to keep from bursting into tears. Something wasn't right. "Go, take your shower."

Alarin left her, slowly, hesitantly. Tamara scowled at him as another wave of fear passed through her and left her shaking. She took a deep breath as he closed the door behind him. She would be fine, she told herself. She *would* be. There was nothing wrong with her. This was just a blood sugar crash or something like that. It had all the hallmarks of one. Getting to her feet, and still a bit dizzy, she made her way into the kitchen to figure out what would be appetizing. Right now, nothing was, but she forced herself to eat some of the crackers they kept on hand. The nagging sense of nausea faded a little, but she still didn't feel particularly stable or in control of her body. She took another deep breath, and the feeling of instability eased up a bit.

By the time Alarin was done with his shower, she felt better and more able to take a shower herself. She took a fast one and got dressed.

"Feeling better?" Alarin asked when she came out of the bedroom wearing a warm sweater and loose jeans.

"Much," she said, giving him a smile. Maybe it was just a slight stomach bug. She did feel almost normal again. "Ready?"

"Let's go."

They walked to the 16th Street Mall area, Alarin using his psi to find Kari and Damiar. Rory was with them, as well as a petite, vaguely familiar woman who was standing next to him. After a momentary lapse during which her memory was frighteningly blank, Tamara remembered that her name was Sharynn Memaxthal.

"Tam!" Kari said, slipping an arm around Tamara and giving her a one-armed hug.

Tamara looked over at Damiar. He seemed somewhat hesitant and awkward, she thought to herself. Kari looked, well, radiant actually. Tamara glanced over to where Alarin was talking animatedly with Rory and suddenly saw how very isolated Alarin must have been feeling. Even though they'd made up after their fight, and Alarin had stopped spending so much time with Francyne, there was a part of her that suddenly understood what he must be going through. She wrapped her arms around herself and tried not to shiver.

"Are you all right?" Kari asked her.

"Fine," Tamara replied, trying to quell her immediate irritation with the question. Why was everyone asking her that? She looked meaningfully at Damiar. "I definitely want to hear what's happened with you two. When does the parade start?" she asked, deliberately changing the subject. It was cold, a cold that seemed to bite into the bones. Weather never lasted very long in Denver, but sometimes she wished she lived in a climate that never got cold.

"Soon," Kari squinted up at the sky. "It feels like it's going to snow."

Tamara nodded. "I hate winter sometimes," she said, somewhat surprised at the intensity of emotion that burst out of her. She rubbed her arms through her coat.

"Come on, if we get lucky, we can sit in one of the bus kiosks," Kari said, leading the way through a crowd less thick than it would have been if the weather were nicer. There were still too many people for Tamara's taste, though. Their minds seemed to press upon her shields, in a way she'd never felt before. Another shiver raced through her as a wave of nausea assaulted her again. Her shields thinned and her dizziness returned with a vengeance. As the blood roared in her ears, she felt like her feet weren't connected to her head anymore.

Tamara must have lost a few moments of awareness, because when she came back to herself, she was lying on the sidewalk, with Rory crouched above her, his hands running lightly just above her body. She could see his aura clearly, a beautiful nimbus of light surrounding him. Streamers of light spilled from his fingers and curled oddly around her stomach and lower abdomen. She gasped as her lower abdomen gave a little leap, pulling away from the silver filaments.

Tamara, Rory's voice breathed through her patchy, thinned shields to her intimate level.

What's wrong with me? She tried not to panic.

Rory's hand drifted closer to rest lightly on the top of her lower abdomen. *Nothing's wrong. You're reacting quite normally.*

To what? She shivered, her stomach roiling again unpleasantly as adrenaline surged through her.

Rory moved one hand to her head, leaving the other on her abdomen. *Now that isn't going to work. You're a powerful projector, you know. Pregnancy, especially a first one, can make your shielding go erratic, and you will make everyone uncomfortable if you project your emotions at them.*

What? Tamara struggled to sit up, feeling shockwaves go through her, even as her intuition whispered otherwise. *But that's impossible!*

Rory raised an eyebrow. *How so?* he asked, helping her sit up. She could feel his slight amusement. *You are saying you have not participated in any sexual activity at all?*

The combination of irritation and chagrin pouring through her left her shaking and weepy feeling. *No, I'm saying we've taken precautions. I've only been with Azellians.*

So? Rory asked. *We are fully fertile with humans. As I'm told you know quite well, since you're half-human.*

Tamara could feel the blush crawling up her cheeks, and she suddenly wished it were Greg crouched beside her. He already knew the tangled web they'd woven between them. An awful awareness suddenly spread through her. *Whose child is it? Alarin's? Or, God forbid, Merran's?* Her mind raced to do some very important calculations. *How far along?* she managed to ask, thickening her shielding enough that she didn't completely leak out everything about their bizarre relationship.

Ten weeks or so, Rory replied clinically, and she felt warmth spread through her body again. Her emotions didn't calm down any, but she felt a sudden giddy sense of dizziness, as though she could reject the knowledge with every atom in her body. In the middle of that, she sensed an odd weakness, a spreading desire to protect the tiny thing that made her body so alien. How had she not noticed that her period hadn't come? Vacation—she hadn't noticed on vacation that what was due never showed up, then the upheaval of her breakup with Merran ... ten weeks? Could her body have changed so much in ten weeks without her knowing it? Except—was it really a total surprise? Hadn't her emotions been all over the place in the past month or so? She'd definitely become more insecure since the new semester began. Was this the reason why? She trembled, despite the soothing warmth of Rory's hand on her forehead and the long clean strokes of his other hand through the roils of her aura.

Don't tell Alarin, she begged Rory, as a fresh round of tears threatened.

It's not going to take long for him to figure it out, Rory replied neutrally. *I'm surprised he hasn't already. He's going to hear an echo. To say nothing of the fact that you're going to start showing signs of it, if you haven't already.*

Tamara swallowed hard. *It's not fair,* she sent to him. *I'm only twenty-one. Too young for this. I haven't even finished college. I can't have a baby now.*

Rory studied her. *You know you can terminate it,* he said, his voice still expressionless. He didn't seem like he cared one way or another.

No, Tamara said sharply, as she reacted violently to that thought. A surge of protectiveness washed through her. *I can't.* Her mind sank slowly to touch that other cradled in her abdomen. Helpless, unable to even survive on its own, the fetus seemed to beg for her protection.

You will not have long to hide this from Alarin. If he hasn't figured it out just watching, Rory said, leaning back on his heels. He pulled his hands back.

Wait, Tamara sent to him. *Can you tell the paternity of the baby yet?*

Rory's eyebrow went up.

Don't ask. It's … complicated. Tamara said. A memory bubbled up, and she had to shield hastily to prevent Rory from reading it. About ten weeks ago, she'd been at the end of finals. Alarin hadn't been quite as vocal about his jealousy at that point. And Merran. Well, suffice it to say, she hadn't really counted it as *time* with Merran, since it had taken place between two meetings and not been entirely satisfying. He was distracted by work and she too nervous about the timing and the location to relax entirely. It could have led to this, though, as easily as the more leisurely encounters between her and Alarin. *Can you tell?*

No, Rory replied. *Not yet. It's not developed enough yet.*

But you'll be able to tell later, won't you? Tamara asked, anxiety pouring through her. The speed at which her emotions raced through her left her unbalanced and uncomfortable.

We could guess, he answered after a brief hesitation. *It will be much easier if you wait for the baby to be born. She or he is going to show a mental array that will be visible to those of us who can see it.*

Doesn't that have to wait until puberty? Tamara asked, remembering Greg's lessons.

It's easier at puberty, unmistakable. If I tried it at the birth, I'd be guessing, but Alarin's mental array is quite distinct, so I could probably tell you whether or not he is the father, Rory answered, slowly, as if thinking through the reply. *Although you have human blood, so I'm not sure how that will affect the fetus and its psi development.*

What do you do in cases like this? Tamara asked, belatedly remembering Greg's mention of something about Festival and babies that were sometimes born nine months later.

Judge by the mental array at birth, by the talents the mother sometimes takes on of the child's during the pregnancy, Rory replied. *The final assessment is done at puberty and Awakening.* After a brief pause, during which Tamara was almost certain he was thinking through several possible responses, or anticipating a reaction from her, he continued. *You could always go to the hospital and have a paternity test done. Your science is quite adept at these sorts of things.*

No! Tamara protested. That would mean telling her father, her family, Alarin, and God forbid, Merran. What the hell would Merran do with the awareness that he had a kid? How did Azellians slip up anyway? *Are you sure I'm pregnant?* she asked, still trying to deny what she knew deep down inside as truth.

Yes.

I still don't know how it could have happened, Tamara muttered. *I didn't think Azellians could have unwanted pregnancies.*

Accidents happen, Rory replied with a shrug. *Particularly when one or the other isn't paying attention. Or both.* He stood up.

"She'll be fine," he told Alarin in Azellian, leaving Tamara to shield herself from the other Azellians crowded around them. They were starting to draw a crowd of humans too. "We should probably get her inside, though. It's really rather cold out here."

Alarin leaned down to help her up, using a combination of arms and psi to help her stand. She felt fine, completely normal, belying the dizziness that had washed over moments earlier. "What's wrong with her?" he asked, hugging her tightly to his body.

Rory looked at her.

"I'm fine, Alari," she replied. "Just a bit dizzy. We did forget to eat this morning," she reminded him. *We'll talk about it later,* she added on Alarin's private level.

He wasn't mollified by her verbal explanation, but he respected her mental request. "Let's grab something to eat now then."

Tamara was abruptly ravenous. "Yes, let's," she agreed, and the group of them made their way inside the Tabor Center to get some food before the parade got underway.

Food helped her physically, but did nothing to soothe her mental or emotional state. As she picked at her breakfast sandwich, Kari leaned over and said, "Let's go to the bathroom." She turned to Damiar. "Be right back. You guys be fine on your own?"

"Of course," Damiar said, sounding amused.

Alarin gave Tamara a sharp look, and she knew he was not going to settle for her evasions too much longer. Kari's invitation gave Tamara a chance to escape, though, so she took it. She got to her feet and followed Kari to the bathroom.

At the door of the women's room, however, she shook her head and pulled Kari toward a sheltered area far enough from the bathroom that she didn't have to smell it. *It must be the pregnancy,* she thought. Her sense of smell had suddenly gone haywire and it was making her feel sick again. "Too smelly in there. Let's talk over here, by this plant. Unless you do have to go to the bathroom?"

"No, I'm fine. What's going on, Tam?"

Tamara shook her head, not ready to admit to the magnitude of her mistake. "What's up with you and Damiar?" she asked. "I thought you hated him."

"Hated? No, I never hated him, Tam. I was hurt, yes, but he apologized." A smile tugged at her lips. "He was very sweet about it."

"So what about his girlfriend on Azelle?"

"It's over. He told me that he broke it off after what happened between us. He didn't mean for it to get as far as it did, but after it happened, it made him realize that things weren't going so well with his girlfriend after all. I really like him, Tam. He's a great guy."

Alarin had said something similar. Tamara felt herself relax slightly. "Okay, if you're sure. I just don't want to see you get hurt, Kar." Tears built in her eyes, startling her with their intensity.

Kari hugged her. "I know, and I appreciate it. Now tell me what's going on with you."

Tamara stared at the potted tree beside them, the leafy foliage providing a comforting sense of the outdoors. It was a real plant, surprisingly, and looked happy enough in its location. If there weren't heavy clouds threatening snow outside, it would have been sunny in this corner. Gathering her courage, she hugged her arms around her middle and opened her mouth, then closed it again.

"What? What is it?" Kari asked.

Tamara shuddered, and the tears building in her eyes spilled down her cheeks. "Oh, God, Kari, I've wrecked my life!" She buried her head in her hands, fighting to hold on to what composure she could.

Kari grabbed her arms, pulling her hands away from her face. "How? What do you mean? What are you talking about? Wrecked your life?"

"I ... I ... I'm pregnant." She forced the words out, somehow, past the rock in her throat. She took a sobbing breath and shivered.

Kari stared at her, open-mouthed, for a good ten seconds. If she hadn't been so upset, Tamara might have found it amusing. Her friend let her go, slowly, staring down at her stomach. "You're *pregnant*?" She blinked at her. "How? I thought ... I thought you said Azellians took care of stuff like that themselves."

Kari might be a good friend, but considering she didn't know about the tangled mess of her relationship with Alarin and Merran, Tamara wasn't about to tell Kari that she had no idea which young man was the actual father. She took in another sobbing breath and let it out slowly, trying not to slide into hysterics, although the temptation was strong. "They do, unless ... well, mistakes happen with them, too, apparently."

"What are you going to do?"

Tamara shook her head. "I don't know. I don't know." She hugged her arms tighter around her middle. It was hard, not really showing yet, but she could imagine that she could feel it. A baby bump. She was going to have a baby bump ... one day very soon. Another shudder ripped through her body.

"Have you told Alarin yet?"

"No, I just found out myself this morning."

"This morning ... you mean, outside, when you fainted? You found out then, when Rory was helping you?"

"Yeah."

Kari gave her a hug. "You're holding it together really well then. I think I would be a crying mess right about now."

Tamara made a sound that was closer to a groan than a laugh. "I'm not a crying mess?" She wiped her hand over her wet cheeks and showed Kari her fingertips.

Kari laughed and brushed Tamara's hair back from her face. "No, I'd say you're handling it beautifully. You're standing here, talking normally, and not in the corner having hysterics."

"It's tempting," Tamara admitted. "To be in the corner having hysterics, I mean. If I thought it would get me anywhere, I might try it."

"Are you going to keep it?"

Tamara pressed her hand against her stomach. "I ... don't know what I'm going to do."

"Of course, you'd want to talk to Alarin first. After all, it's his child, too. I never liked those girls who think that it's only their responsibility, only their bodies."

Tamara scowled. "That's not why I'm not sure," she muttered. "He's not the one who is going to have to go through pregnancy and childbirth. In my opinion, he's got no say in what I choose to do with this child." Though she didn't know whether it was Merran or Alarin who was responsible for her condition, she did know it was her choice to do what she wanted, no matter who contributed the sperm that had resulted in this mess.

"You're going to tell him, though, aren't you?"

Tamara shrugged. "I don't know."

"Tam, you have to. Alarin's a good guy. He'll want to help."

Will he? Especially with the question of paternity? If Merran is the father, will Alarin take responsibility? she wondered. *Will I even want him to?* If the baby was Alarin's, she suspected Kari was right about Alarin's reaction and desires, but she couldn't introduce the question, and she wasn't sure she wanted to. Tamara pressed her lips together. "I don't want to talk about it anymore. Let's go." She turned on her heel and made her way back to where Alarin, Damiar, Rory, and Sharynn waited for them.

What happened? Alarin asked on her intimate level, as she and Kari came back to the table, the strong tone coming through that usually meant he was willing to use his coercive talent if he had to. Tamara privately thought of it as his "bossy" voice. It usually annoyed her, but today, she didn't care. She had more things to worry about than whether or not Alarin was trying to push her around.

Not a good time to discuss it, Tamara sent back. *Not in front of everyone.*

Watching her steadily, he looked like he might give in, but she'd forgotten about the Azellian ability to easily read a full human, and Kari, still in the throes of her own emotional reaction to Tamara's news, was easy for every Azellian at the table to read. Tamara knew she'd made a mistake—she should not have told Kari in public, around the other Azellians—as soon as the expression of shock and disbelief crossed his face.

Rory got to his feet. "Come on, Kari, Damiar, Sharynn. Let's leave them alone." He glanced at them over a shoulder. "She is physically fine," he told Alarin, placing a slight emphasis on the word physical, before he ushered the others out the door.

Alarin was silent for a few minutes after the others left. "Is it true?"

"Rory says it is," she said, feeling cold and miserable. She slumped on the cold plastic of the chair. "He's a Healer, so he probably knows what he's talking about." She knew she sounded sullen, but she didn't try to modulate her tone.

Alarin shifted in his chair. "Is it mine?"

Tamara shrugged noncommittally. "Rory couldn't tell yet."

179

"How far along?"

"Ten weeks."

Alarin was silent as he did some mental calculations. "It might not be, then."

"It might not." She felt frozen, as if the cold from outside had seeped into her whole body. Her lips were numb. "Does it matter?"

Alarin was quiet for a moment. "Does it matter to you?"

"No. Yes. I don't know." At least he wasn't angry, Tamara thought. He had a touchy temper sometimes, but he seemed to be very controlled right now. Of course, her own emotions were in such a mess she wasn't sure she could have heard any of his emotional upheaval if she tried.

"What are you going do?"

"Why does everyone ask me that? I don't know." The first hints of anger made her say the words far more sharply than she intended. Tears would be hard on the heels of anger, so Tamara pushed her chair back. She didn't want to cry in public. "I want to go home."

Alarin got up too, and for the first time, she saw uncertainty in him. "I can take you home, if you want."

She stood there, feeling isolated and alone, and terrified. "I'd like that. Please."

He came around the table. "Can I hold you for a minute?" he asked, his voice especially soft.

Tamara shook her head. "When we get home, please," she said, feeling the tears constrict her throat. "If you touch me right now, I'm going to burst into tears ... or scream. I'm not sure which, and neither is appropriate in public."

He nodded and did no more than support her with his telekinetic abilities as they headed for the car, then home to where Tamara could come unglued in private.

Chapter Six

Late one morning, after he'd escaped into the mountains for some much-needed rest, the ringing of his personal cell phone dragged Merran out of a sound sleep. Rubbing his eyes and trying to chase the cobwebs from his mind, he stumbled out of bed and into the kitchen to grab the phone. Glancing at the blinking numbers on the screen, he frowned. The number was not Ketiana's, unless she was calling from a location he didn't know about.

"Hello?" he answered the phone in English rather than Azellian, just in case the caller was someone other than Ketiana.

"Merran," Alarin said. Merran could hear the strain in his voice over the phone. His friend had not used the video function to call, so Merran couldn't see Alarin's stress, but it was clear enough that something wasn't right, even without visual confirmation.

"What happened?" Merran asked in Azellian, automatically reaching out with his mind across the miles that separated them to brush up against solid shields that only imperfectly covered the churning concern underneath.

"Where are you?" Alarin responded in Azellian, but he ignored the invitation and the touch of Merran's mind. "Ketiana wouldn't say."

"Not far actually. In the mountains. On a much-needed vacation. What's happened?"

Alarin took a deep breath. "I thought you might want to know that Tamara's in the hospital."

"What?" Merran demanded. "When? Where?"

"She's at Denver Mercy," Alarin replied slowly, as if the words were being dragged from him. He kept his shields high and tight, relying instead on spoken words. "They're keeping her in the hospital on enforced bedrest. I ... it wasn't easy for me to decide to call you," he admitted, his tone almost hostile, but Merran could clearly read the fear and worry behind the hostility. Alarin didn't often leak through his well-developed shields, but he was most certainly doing it now.

Merran hesitated for a moment. He knew what he wanted to do, but he also knew that his relationship with Alarin depended on his next actions. "Do you want me to come down?" he asked, carefully putting a relaxed note into his voice that he didn't feel. Tamara was in trouble, but he had to take the time to dance around Alarin's sensibilities. He knew he should be amazed that Alarin had called him at all—and he was—but Merran didn't know quite what to make of it.

"It's up to you," Alarin replied, his tone still faintly hostile. "It doesn't matter to me."

Doesn't it? Merran thought to himself, extremely aware that Alarin was still not accepting the casual mental touch Merran offered. There was more to this invitation, he thought. More to the call than he knew. What could be wrong with Tamara? "Are you going to tell me what happened to Tamara?"

"Come down and visit her yourself," Alarin replied and hung up the phone.

Merran stared at the phone in his hand. There was something not right about the whole thing. On the surface, it appeared that Alarin was extending an olive branch, but the way he ended the conversation—what had happened to Tamara?

Merran raced through the necessary preparations to leave, telling his skiing buddies that a family emergency was sending him home. It wasn't until he sat in the car, speeding home as fast as he dared, that it occurred to him to wonder why, with a new Healer available, Tamara had ended up in the hospital at all. The Healer, a bright young man named Rory Memaxthal, could have healed anything physically wrong with her, although it was possible that an illness had laid her low. Even then, Azellians with access to a Healer rarely had to go to a hospital. Maybe it was psychological? Had she done something to herself? His mind raced through possibilities, matching his breakneck speed down the hill to the downtown area. He chafed at the slower speeds in the metro area, and arrived at Denver Mercy a little under two hours later, much faster than one normally could have gotten off the mountain and across town.

As he exited his car, he noticed that the air was much warmer than in the mountains, with a light smell that promised spring. He normally loved the humid, soft, green scent of spring, something Azelle, with its harsh desert environment lacked, and it curled around him, reminding him to take a deep breath despite the anxiety that rode him. After several deep breaths of the gentle air, he was able to soothe down some of the frantic energy that filled him. He walked into the hospital, the scent of antiseptic stinging his nose, the pain and fear of the patients in the building slamming into his shields and ramping him back up again. The benefit of the breaths he'd taken outside was drowned in the flood of anxiety rising through him as he stalked up to the admitting desk.

"Tamara Carrington's room. Please," he said, adding the last as an afterthought.

"Are you a relative, sir?" the woman asked, glancing up from her computer screen to acknowledge him. "She will not see anyone but those on the accepted list."

That took him by surprise. Such a restriction was something normally reserved for celebrities or people who were being hounded by the press. Was she being hounded by the press? And if so, why? "Merran Corina," he snapped. "Am I on the accepted list?"

Her eyes widened, but otherwise there was no sign of weakening on her part. "Let me check, sir."

Merran stood impatiently as she checked the list of accepted visitors, tapping his fingers on the counter. He didn't bother to modulate the force of his irritation. Most humans couldn't stand up to him in a mood like this, and he didn't use it often, but it sometimes helped to get what he wanted. That she'd resisted him thus far was pretty impressive for a human.

"I'm sorry, sir. May I see your ID?" she asked, her tone firm.

"Am I on the list?"

"Merran Corina is, sir, but I must establish your identity."

"My—" Merran stopped, belatedly remembering the labors he'd taken to shift his appearance, dying his hair blond and letting it grow into an unkempt thatch, along with a dyed blond circle beard that now framed his mouth and chin. He suddenly realized he hadn't bothered to shift it back before he flew down the mountain. "Fine," he said, pulling out and handing to her the license that established his true identity.

She studied the picture, then peered at his face. After a moment, she nodded. "Room 453, Sir." She handed the card back to him.

Merran took the license, shoved it in his pocket, and turned to get on the elevator. After getting off the elevator at the fourth floor, it took him a moment to find the heavily shielded room that was Tamara's. He stopped at the door and hesitated a moment, smoothing down his hair—suddenly feeling unusually nervous. The door was closed and he knocked quietly.

The young man who pulled open the door was not known to him personally, but he recognized the new Healer from his mental array even before he introduced himself. "Merran Corina, I presume," he said, then an expression of amusement crossed his face. "Rory Mennak Memaxthal. Alarin told me he had called you. I didn't expect you to arrive this quickly. What did you do, fly down the mountain?"

Merran stood impatiently in the doorway, ignoring the young Healer's amusement. "Yes, yes. How is she?"

"Fine. This is mostly precautionary."

"What's wrong with her?"

"That's for her to tell you." He stepped back.

"Why all the cloak and dagger? Can't someone tell me what's wrong with her?" Merran demanded, frustrated that no one was answering his questions. Rory shrugged and waved him into the room.

Merran entered, turning the corner to see Tamara sitting up in the hospital bed with tubes running from her arm to a bag that

fed her intravenously. She looked pale but normal, except for …
Merran stared at her, his eyes going wide. It wasn't possible! Tiny
unformed thoughts brushed across his mental screens, seeking,
probing, and trying to learn the boundaries of her mother's life.
He was hardly aware that Rory had stepped out and closed the
door behind him—only that distant part of him that monitored
everything around him registered they were alone. *How is this
possible? Tamara is … pregnant?*

Tamara met his gaze and burst into hysterical giggles that
ended in throat-tearing sobs. Merran's heart, which he thought
he'd managed to heal during his time in the mountains, leaped
into his throat, aching from the stark terror and unfocused anger
that poured through the shielded room. Her normal shields were
in rags, and the force of her projection was enough to rock him
back on his feet. No wonder they had her shielded. He stepped
closer as he put out a hand. Pulling from an old acolyte training
ritual he'd learned during his years at the Temple, he spoke in a
low voice, using an Azellian dialect he was certain she didn't know,
repeating over and over, "Strength comes from the knowing of
ourselves." He murmured the words, as he came close enough to
stroke his hand through her aura. "You are complete and whole.
You are strong enough to do this, my beloved. You are strong and
loved." The word beloved slipped out, and he was suddenly glad
she didn't know the dialect and that no other Azellian was in the
room. It was part of the ritual, but it made him feel distinctly odd
to call her that, given what had passed between them these past
few months. It might be sort of true—she certainly was closer to a
beloved than anyone else, but he didn't need to complicate things
by using a word like that with her.

The spikes of emotion smoothed a little and her sobs subsided to hiccoughs. "Wh-what are you doing?" she asked, staring up at him as her breathing slowed under his ministrations. "What language are you using?" The dialect distracted her, as he intended it should, even as she let his projection soothe her. She was far from calm, but she was coherent at least.

He sat on the chair that had been placed by the head of the hospital bed. "It's a meditation ritual I learned years ago," he replied, letting his hand drift down to rest on hers. "It's not quite as effective as if you did it yourself, but it helps. The language is an old version of Azellian. The Keepers at the Temple use it for benedictions and teaching. No one speaks it anymore. Rather like Latin for humans." He used the touch to calm himself too, to paste a veneer of calm over his own shielding. Inside he felt anything but calm, but he hadn't been ambassador for six years for nothing. He knew very well how to control his own projection without regard for his own true emotions. "It helps make things seem less … overwhelming."

Tamara's hand shook slightly as she pulled it from his to brush a lock of hair out of her face. She sounded oddly calm as she said, "Don't lie to me. I'm an empath myself, and I've spent some time behind your shields. I know you're not nearly as calm as you're acting."

Merran leaned back, pulling his hand away. He shrugged, but didn't entirely dispose of the guru-like calm he'd pasted over his mind. "Will running around the room shrieking like a banshee get me anywhere?"

Tamara choked. "It might make me feel better," she muttered. She eyed him. "You look good. Even sort of relaxed. Although the hair color is a little distracting. Where have you been?"

Merran spread his hands. "In the mountains."

Tamara lifted her eyebrows. "The mountains? We all thought you were offworld. What were you doing in the mountains?"

"Skiing," Merran said, his mind not entirely on the conversation, thinking instead about the impossibility of her condition. "Never mind about me. What ... how ... how did you end up here ... like this ..." he trailed off, unable to finish the sentence.

"I don't know," she snapped, her voice thickening. "I thought Azellian women didn't get pregnant by mistake. I thought that you Azellians had control and didn't get women pregnant by mistake. Because God knows this is a mistake. An awful, terrible mistake." Tears slid down her cheeks. "God, I hate this! I just *hate* it! My emotions are a train wreck. One moment I'm calm, the next I'm sobbing like my heart is breaking." She slammed her palm on the bed beside her. "I just hate this!"

"It's a very natural reaction to a rather severe shock," Merran soothed, not sounding entirely like himself—but then he didn't feel like himself either. Had he ... no, it wasn't possible. It had been ages since he'd had intercourse with Tamara—just about three? four? months ago. How far along was she anyway? Was he the one responsible? Sometimes he got so distracted ... but she knew how to keep from getting pregnant too. Surely she would have taken care of it, even if he'd not done a thorough enough job ...

"Oh really? How do you know what I'm feeling?" Tamara demanded, glaring at him, her nostrils flaring, her eyes snapping blue fire at him through the tears. "How in the hell do you know what I'm going through? It's not exactly your body, is it?"

He twitched at the strength of her reaction. She couldn't have read him through his shields, could she? "I can sense it," he answered, finally, opting for what he thought might be the least irritating.

His effort was wasted. "Oh, and how many pregnant women have you experienced to make you such an expert?" she asked snidely.

Merran took a breath. He wasn't the only man she'd slept with, he reminded himself. Why did he have the impression she thought the baby was his? It could be Alarin's just as easily. "Rory's told you the same thing, hasn't he?" he asked, trying to keep his veneer of calm. It wasn't easy, especially not with her railing at him. It would have been much easier if a tiny part of him hadn't been terrified that she was right, that it was his fault.

"Don't try to distract me. Just answer the damned question."

"Question?"

"Don't play games, Merran. How many women have you gotten pregnant before?" The question was blunt and wasn't exactly what he'd said or thought they were talking about.

Merran choked and coughed. She did think it was his fault. "Uh, none, as you know very well," he said, clearing his throat and sitting up straighter, trying to control the flush that crawled up his cheeks while holding on to his shielding and his temper at the same time.

Tamara made a strangled sound. "I don't know," she replied, barely audible through her tears. "That's the point. What do I know? Nothing. I don't know you. I don't know anything about you, and suddenly I'm carrying your daughter." She threw her arms in the air, almost dislodging the intravenous feed. "This ... this parasite that is making me so sick I can't even eat anything, that is tying me here and will change everything in my life. I'm not ready for this, Merran. Why? Why? I'm not old enough to have a baby!" A sob exploded out of her at the end of her rant, and she buried her head in her hands, hiding her face.

Merran lost control of his flush. He could feel the heat crawl up his cheeks, but managed to control everything else, from his shielding to his temper. Considering the force of the unshielded emotions rocketing around the room, he had to give himself a momentary acknowledgment for holding onto his shields. "Are you telling me you know for sure it's mine?" he asked, trying to sound less panicked than he suddenly felt.

Tamara lowered her hands, taking a deep breath. Her nostrils flared. "Rory tried to guess based on her mental array, but she's not being particularly cooperative," she admitted sullenly, staring at her hands.

Merran braced himself. "Then we don't know for sure?" Relief poured through him at the thought. Tamara made a disgusted sound, and he knew she was picking up more than he meant to show her. "I don't think it's possible that it's mine. Why do you think it's mine?"

Tamara gave him a look. "Why isn't she?" she asked acidly. "Are you trying to deny that we had a sexual relationship? Funny, I seem to remember some very sexual moments between us. As in, it's damned possible she's yours." Sarcasm poured off her in waves.

"Uh, you and I haven't had intercourse in nearly four months," Merran pointed out sharply. "If not more." It had been more. It had to have been. It couldn't have been him.

"Actually it was less than that," Tamara said, clenching her fists on the blanket covering her legs. "Believe me, I counted out days as soon as I found out. It's possible. I'm thirteen weeks along."

Merran took a breath through his nose, losing the battle to stay calm as he fought down the surge of panic by telling himself she was wrong. She had to be. He refused to think about it. "All right, fine. In the end it doesn't matter anyway. You're pregnant and that's that."

"What are you going to do?" Tamara asked, her voice getting thicker, as if tears were building at the back of her throat. He could sense the fear that backed all this anger, and he shared it. What, by the grace of the *aarya,* was he going to do it if was his child? *A daughter? I have a daughter? No.* The words echoed through his mind, shocking him. He didn't question that Tamara knew the sex of the child she carried—any Healer would have told her that immediately. But a worm of doubt that this baby could be his crawled through him.

He stared past her head at the windows. The sun poured in and mocked the momentous change that had just come into his life. His mind raced through the problems, consequences, and possibilities, his ambassador training kicking in to help. "Whatever I have to."

"Which is?" Oddly enough, her voice was neutral. Considering how her emotions had been careening around the room a moment ago, it was almost as odd as if she'd screamed at him. Actually more so. He'd expected the screaming.

"I'll support whatever you decide regarding the baby. You'll have whatever money you need, of course. I'd help you through, no matter what. The embassy has an excellent daycare system. You can finish college at least." His voice didn't sound like his own. *Welcome to Earth, I'm Merran Corina, Azellian ambassador. My daughter is in the daycare unit downstairs.* His hands trembled, and he pressed them together to keep her from seeing it. He couldn't come unglued. Not now.

Tamara's nostrils flared. "Money?" Her voice rose at the end of the word. "Money? You're not going to let it change your life, are you?" She was pretty much screaming at him by the end of the question. "You're not even going to let it dent that so calm exterior of yours!"

"Tamara, be reasonable," he said, trying for calm and not defensiveness. "We don't know for sure if she's mine in the first place and in the second—"

Tamara made a sound, interrupting him. "Oh, so you think she's not yours? I'm thirteen weeks along, Merran. Have you really forgotten that afternoon about three months ago? In your office? Between meetings?"

He scowled, his own emotions in enough turmoil that he couldn't hide them anymore. He got to his feet and paced, raking his hands through his hair. A terrible, horrible feeling that she was right spread through him, and with it came the resentment and anger he could feel so clearly in her. He'd been so distracted that day; the whole thing had hardly counted as being together. If she hadn't taken care of her end, it could very well have been the day that was about to change their lives. Actually it made sense. It was the last time they'd had any intercourse at all. And, no matter how quick it had been, it could very well have led to this.

"Do you remember?" Tamara pressed. "It's even likely," she reminded him, "you weren't with it at all. Remember? You were so involved in that treaty you didn't even say goodbye when I left. Do you remember?"

"Yessss," Merran hissed, his temper igniting. He stopped at the foot of the bed. "I remember." He took a deep breath. She didn't need him yelling at her, as much as he'd like to explode out his own frustrations back at her. It was highly probable that he hadn't made sure she wouldn't get pregnant that day. But she'd taken care of it, hadn't she? She knew how.

"If you want full proof, we can do a paternity test," she pointed out, paradoxically calm. It was as though finally rousing him to the same level of panicked anger and fear she had allowed her to become calm. "The hospital is right here. If you need the proof."

"No!" Merran exclaimed, leaning down to press his hands against the bar at the foot of the bed. "No," he said more calmly, mixed emotions pouring through him. He knew for certain he was not wrong in what he had to do. He could feel her expectations, the pressure of what she wanted him to say, and he braced himself to disappoint her. "Tamara, listen." He took a deep breath. "It doesn't matter in the end. Even if she is mine, even if I am the one who got you … I can't acknowledge her. I can't. You would become the focus of the paparazzi. I don't want my child raised in the public eye, Tamara. I don't want to do that to you either. I can work it so you are supported monetarily. But don't you see that I can't be what you want me to be? I can't be your husband, your lover, and I can't claim her as my daughter. I can't change what I am." He stood up. "I can't be what you want me to be, Tamara," he repeated. She was wide open, and he could clearly read the fear and disappointment in her. "Look, I'm not running away from my responsibilities. I'm trying to think of what's best for you both, no matter if I am her father or not." He took a deep breath and came to the side of the bed, sinking to his knees. "Look," he said again, trying to get through to her, although he could tell she wasn't listening. "If she is mine, and I'm willing to admit it is a possibility, a very strong possibility, I do want to be a part of her life. I just can't be what you want me to be." He reached out a hand to hover above her stomach. The baby's unformed thoughts reached out to him, and he was helpless to them.

Tamara's color heightened as he spoke, and she pulled herself away from him, cupping her hands over her abdomen. "Just get out of here," she said with a coldness in her voice he'd never heard before. "Alarin and I will deal with it. You don't have to do a damned thing. We don't need anything from you." She stared at her hands. "Your precious life doesn't have to be changed at all."

Fear that she might keep him away stirred something within him. "Tamara, don't. I do want to be a part of her life, as much as I can be." He tried to maintain calm.

Tamara lifted her blue eyes to meet his, the expression in them as cold as the glacier he'd hiked in the mountains last summer. "Ha! You aren't willing to give up one portion of your precious life for me. You aren't willing to change for her. So fine. Don't. You don't want to participate, you don't have to. Leave us the fuck alone. We'll do it on our own. I don't need you. We don't need you." Venom poured out with her next words. "It's always on your terms, isn't it, Merran? You want me, but you don't want to commit to me. You get me pregnant and you'll support me monetarily, but you won't acknowledge that you had anything to do with it. Someone else always cleans up your messes, don't they? What would you do if Alarin weren't here?" She made a sound. "Scratch that. I know exactly what you'd do. You'd do the same damned thing. Cut me … cut us out of your life. Well the baby doesn't need you doing that to her. You'll play with her emotions the way you did with mine and walk away like you did to me. She doesn't need that. She'll have a father," Tamara sliced her hand through the air. "Just not the one who biologically produced her."

That angered him. As a matter of fact, he was abruptly so furious he could hardly speak. He got to his feet and leaned over the bed. "I walked away? I walked away? Excuse me, who ended our relationship?" He spat the words at her. She stared at him, eyes wide, huddled against herself as far away as she could get. "Have you forgotten? The last months of our relationship you turned down just about every offer I made to spend time together. I'm surprised you agreed to the one that got you pregnant!" He took a deep breath, fighting to control the urge to throttle her. That would definitely be harmful to the baby, and though right now he didn't like her mother too much, the baby still brought out a protective urge in him he didn't know he had. "Because I care about you and Alarin so much, more than I care about my own happiness, I chose to walk away rather than rip you two up. Now to hear you say I'm running away? That I ran away from you?" He clenched his jaw tightly. "That I play with your emotions with no consideration for them? Who just spent time away trying to put himself back together after our breakup? Who is determined that no matter how selfish and outrageous you are being, that he is going to do everything he can to contribute to his daughter's life, as far as he is able?" His hands trembled and he stood up, pacing away from the side of the bed. "You know what you are?" he demanded, twirling to face her again. "You're nothing but a selfish child, Tamara. Would you prefer I acknowledge her, then take her away from you, to send her to live on Azelle? I can do that, you know. She'd be raised normally, away from the public eye, on Azelle. My sister would be thrilled to raise her niece for me." He made the threat quite deliberately, trying to hurt her the way she'd hurt him.

"That's enough," Alarin's voice cut through the tension between them, forestalling Tamara's response. Merran twitched. He hadn't sensed the young man's approach, much less heard him come in. How long had he been standing there? "Long enough," Alarin said, answering his unspoken question, coming further into the room. "Neither of you mean it, so let's not say anything more damaging until we've all cooled off enough to talk about it rationally." The force of his will gripped both of them, holding them immobile. Merran could feel Tamara fight it, but he let Alarin take control, his surge of temper abruptly draining away, leaving that horrible ache that had driven him to the mountains in the first place. Alarin turned to Merran. "Just go, Mer. We can discuss what our next step is later, after she's had some rest and she and I have had some time to talk about things."

Tamara twitched at that, but Alarin did not release her, making it impossible for her to say anything. Merran pulled his shielding around himself, rebuilding what the force of his anger and hurt had shattered, and gave Alarin a formal, polite bow. "I'll be at my apartment."

Alarin's mind touched his on his private level. *I'll talk her into letting you have some say in all this, Mer,* he said mentally, letting a surge of reassurance in. *She's just frightened and scared of the future.*

You think the baby's mine, too, don't you?

Chances are, Alarin replied. *It's very likely, since I don't remember any times when I was so distracted I forgot to make sure I wouldn't get her pregnant.*

I thought Greg taught her how to take control herself, Merran said, feeling somewhat calmer, but still not happy. It was a comment he had been intending to throw at her, but had never managed to get into the argument. Why was it all his fault? It wasn't really. She had the ability to make sure nothing resulted from their activities together, too.

He did, but it makes her queasy, so she doesn't like to do it, and she got out of the habit with the two of us because she thought we handled it.

Why the hell didn't she tell me that? Merran demanded hotly. *It would have saved us a whole lot of headache.*

I don't know. But she didn't, and she feels guilty. It's some of where her hostility is coming from, I think. She just needs to feel loved and assured that she hasn't screwed up her whole life.

How do you feel about it?

It's Tamara. I want to marry her no matter what happened or whose child she is carrying. I will be the father you can't be, Mer. I've had quite a bit of time to think about this, and I mean it. I'll raise your daughter as though she's mine, combine her with the other children we have, and no one will know the difference. As soon as Tamara's calmer, which may take until after the birth, she'll agree that it's the best thing, Alarin reassured him. There had been hostility a few hours ago from Alarin, but he must have heard more of the conversation than Merran had realized, or found some other reason for his sudden reconciliatory attitude. That anger was gone, and Alarin seemed quite calm about the whole thing—far calmer than he, Merran, was, as a matter of fact.

I'm full-blooded Azellian, Merran reminded Alarin. *We have to register her birth with the Temple, and we can't lie on her Azellian birth records as to who her father is. If she's my child, it will be obvious pretty quickly that she's not a Raderth to any of us who can sense her, including the Keepers at the Temple, who are pretty good at this sort of thing.*

So we lie on the human birth records and not on the Azellian ones. Alawahea, Mer. Merran could clearly feel the warmth in his friend's mind, the strength that he showed only his closest friends. Apparently, there was a silver lining to this—he and Alarin seemed to be on their way to repairing their damaged relationship. Odd that it would take an accidental pregnancy to do it, but Merran would take what he could get. Although right at the moment he was sorely tempted to walk out of Tamara's life for good, he knew he'd regret it in the end, and he appreciated that Alarin was trying to prevent that from happening.

He bowed to them both, still smarting from the words he and Tamara had exchanged. It took him a few minutes to collect himself after he'd closed the door—firmly, although he managed not to slam it—to thicken his screens around his internal turmoil enough that he could face the rest of the world with any kind of equanimity. He avoided Rory, the young Healer who was currently involved with talking to one of the pretty young nurses at the nurse's station, and made his way out of the hospital to his car, trying to process the enormity of the change that had stormed into his life as he drove home.

Tamara languished in the hospital, chafing at her enforced captivity. She felt distinctly sympathetic toward zoo animals, especially since the teaching hospital had three or four groups of students in to discuss her case each day. Unable to keep down anything, the smell of any type of food nauseated her so badly she ended up with the dry heaves. It was just one more intolerable, infuriating part of her situation, and she raged against her body, the baby, her changing future, her gender, and even nature itself. In a tiny part of her mind that was still rational, she knew she was being ridiculous, that her behavior was stupid and counterproductive, but it was how she felt, and she was helpless against the force of her emotions.

She had been in the hospital about a week, and the doctors still had not figured out how to help her keep down food—even Rory was stumped. Since she was about to enter her second trimester, everyone hoped her violent aversion to food would resolve itself.

If she hadn't treated Merran so badly, he might have been able to determine whether there was another reason for her inability to keep anything down, but he hadn't spoken to her in days. Alarin could have, too, but she blocked him as well. As much as she knew she should be trying to help herself, she had to admit that she didn't want to feel better. She just wanted it all to go away. Maybe if she lay there and just gave up, it would.

She was doing just that, staring at the wall with unfocused eyes, when a familiar voice said in English, "Apparently, things have fallen apart in my absence. What has gotten you to the point you are trying to will yourself to death?"

She jerked out of her reverie and turned her head to see Greg standing there with his hands on hips, his aura sending amber glints off his sandy hair. In the months he'd been away, he'd lost weight, although he looked pretty much the same as always otherwise, down to the affectionately irritated expression on his face. Tamara stared at him, a thousand different emotions leaping to her throat and damming up inside her. Then, to her faint horror, she burst into hysterical tears, her vision completely disappearing in the storm of her sobs.

His warm arms enveloped her in a tight hug as he spoke to her softly in Azellian. She didn't process what he said, just let the language flow over her soothingly. As he held her and spoke, her emotions drained away, pouring out and away from her body and his. She shared the memories of the past week with him— even though her short-term memory sucked right now, she remembered enough. Greg listened gravely, without judgment, and shifted the memories away, along with the guilt and self-pity. In their place welled delicious, warm peace. With peace came the awareness that she had been cruel to her unborn baby, to Merran, and to herself. Her sobs subsided, and she lifted teary eyes. "I've been ridiculous," she murmured, hugging Greg tighter, feeling the strength in his stocky body. He shared it with her, as he always did.

"Then it's time to stop it, isn't it?" Greg asked, releasing her as he leaned over and grabbed a tissue from the box beside her bed. With a look of compassion mixed with authority, he handed her the tissue.

"How much do you know?" Tamara sniffed, wiping her eyes and blowing her nose.

Greg shifted to perch himself on the edge of the bed next to her. "You just shared most of it with me."

"I mean about M-Merran's side," she said, wincing as she said his name.

"Very good, you remember that he has a perspective," Greg said gently, reaching over to brush a lock of hair out of her face. It had gotten stuck to her cheek during her crying jag.

"Don't tease me," Tamara frowned at him, but the expression lacked ferocity. She was too relaxed for that.

"Well, I'm glad you're starting to realize this isn't just about you," Greg replied, shifting a little. "Now if we can just get you beyond this little passive self-destructive urge you've got going. Your body is going to feed your baby before it does you, you know. Right now, you're doing yourself more harm than her." He continued without giving her a chance to answer. "As for Merran, he's the one who called me. I know all about his reactions to this."

Tamara took a deep breath as guilt washed over her. "He's the one who got me into this."

"And if you'd taken the precautions I showed you how to do, then you wouldn't be here. There are two sides to this story, my dear. It took both of you to land you where you are."

Tamara choked as another wave of guilt washed through her.

"Anyway, it doesn't matter who contributed to this situation. It's done. And now you get to deal with the consequences. You can give her up for adoption ... there are plenty of Azellian families that will take her. Or you can raise her yourself, considering Alarin's willing to help and so is Merran. He can't help you the way you think you want him to," he said, raising a hand to forestall her protest, "but he can do what he can to help ensure that your life won't be negatively impacted by her arrival. You can still have a life, Tamara. It may not be the one you thought you were going to have, but you can have one ... and one that is quite fulfilling."

As always, Greg's clear-sighted calmness ripped away the emotional roadblocks Tamara had been building in front of herself. Even as she teared up again—Greg seemed quite unmoved by her emotionality—she was grateful for his calm strength. "Not all Healers can do what you do," she sniffed, blowing her nose and struggling to control the new tears. "How can you always tell exactly what's bothering me so immediately?"

Greg smiled at her. "I'm your friend as much as your Healer, Tam," he said, getting off the bed. "I trained you, and I'm a Tenricth. It makes a difference. To say nothing of the fact that Rory is more squeamish than I am about emotional issues. As a Memaxthal, he's not a therapist by preference."

"How did you know that I was talking about Rory?"

Greg grinned. "Because he's the only other Healer that I know who has worked on you." He touched her head, and she could feel him brush his mind across hers. "He did a good job of shielding you from both the baby's pushes and from your own ability to project your emotions on others, though. A very good job. Excellent, in fact, considering he doesn't have your projection ability. And your daughter is going to be one hell of a projector, too, for it to be showing up this early. Hmmm, he's got more talent than I thought," he said almost to himself.

"What do you mean?" Tamara asked. She could feel a slight push against her shielding.

"Your own shields are in tatters," Greg replied, withdrawing his hand and not answering her question. He leaned against the edge of the bed. "That's very normal when your baby first starts to tug at them." He frowned at her. "However, for them to remain in tatters means you have let them stay in tatters. You haven't been doing the exercises I taught you, have you?"

Tamara flushed and looked at the covers. "I've been too upset and sick to do anything."

"No excuse. We talked about this before I left, Tam. You and I have spent considerable hours training you to shield from everyone around you, so you don't get overwhelmed by their emotions and don't overwhelm everyone with yours. Breathing exercises, focusing exercises, meditation. Have you done any of them?"

Tamara's cheeks burned. "I was depressed, too," she said, somewhat sullenly, although she knew Greg was right.

Greg raised an eyebrow.

"Fine. I'll start the focusing exercises right now."

"Good." Greg walked toward the door. "While you do those, I'm going to get you something to eat."

Given her current relationship with food, she felt a vague sense of panic at the thought, but a look from Greg was enough to get her to focus on the repetitive, intense focusing and breathing exercises he'd made her do when he first started to train her after her Awakening.

By the time he came back, she was too focused to feel nausea, and Greg helped her block out its return as she started to eat. The food didn't taste the same, but it wasn't nauseating. Without the nausea, she was hungrier than she expected, but, because it had been a while since she'd eaten solid food, Greg limited her intake. Then he sat on the edge of her bed and forced her to look at him. "Now that you've eaten and things don't seem quite so bleak, we need to talk about Merran."

Tamara flushed again. "I know I was overreacting when I said he couldn't have anything to do with her. I was angry and I wanted to hurt him. He said ... he said he could take her away. He won't do that, will he?"

Greg shook his head. "Of course not. Merran cares about you and this baby. He can't contribute the same way Alarin can, but he can be a part of his daughter's life, if you let him."

Tamara took a deep breath. "We know for sure then?"

Greg shrugged. "Both he and Alarin made a pretty good case for it being his. You corroborated that when you gave me your memories. Alarin, however, is willing to be the overt father, to protect you and the baby from those people who would want to force themselves into her life. She doesn't need to be in the public eye constantly, and as Merran's daughter, she would be, and so would you."

Tamara shivered, wrapping her arms around her stomach protectively. "Nothing can happen to her," she said, surprised by the sudden desire to protect this tiny, helpless being. She could almost sense the baby's half-formed thoughts, the tiny tugs at her that insisted she be loved and protected.

"All children have a certain amount of coercion to them," Greg said, reading her efforts. "The psi goes dormant with birth, reemerging at Awakening. Good thing, otherwise, parents would constantly have to fend off childhood psi demands."

Tamara shivered again. "I can't imagine being a non-psi giving birth to a psi child."

"That is one reason why we Azellian men have to be so careful around humans. When it does happen, it can be very damaging to the relationship between the mother and child. To say nothing of the sanity of the mother. She doesn't understand what is happening and can't get away from it." After a momentary pause, he added, "I'm going to tell the hospital you're ready to be released tomorrow. You seem to have recovered quickly." He poked at her shielding, and she tightened it automatically.

"I'm not ready to go," she replied, suddenly afraid to leave the hospital. There was something so comfortable about being here, about being taken care of.

"You have classes to return to," Greg reminded her. "If you don't want this to impact you negatively, you're going to be too busy to do anything but study for the rest of the school term."

"What about my short-term memory?" she asked, again feeling that irrational panic. What was happening to her? Her body was again being an alien thing, with emotions she didn't understand and urges that didn't make any sense. "It sucks."

"I'll teach you some techniques to fix your studies in your long-term memory."

"Are you back for good, then?"

"You think I'd miss your first child's birth? Like every good Healer, I go where I'm called, and you've been calling me quite loudly."

Tamara felt a mix of guilt and pleasure. "What about Ather?"

"I've done what I can for Ather. The plague is as under control as it will ever be and they don't need me anymore. You do. Now, take it easy, enjoy your last day in the hospital, and we'll get you out of here in the morning."

Tamara lay back, completely aware that Greg knew exactly how she was feeling. Greg wasn't going to let her sink into self-pity or despair, not without brow beating her out of it. That knowledge relaxed her enough that she could let the awareness of her baby spread through her mind. She allowed herself to brush across the tiny, unformed mind and was immediately deluged by the intensity of her need. The baby craved her love and her devotion, and soaked up as much of it as Tamara could give her.

Late that afternoon, as she ate her second meal of the day— quite successfully and without any nausea, although she continued to do her focusing exercises just in case—Greg stuck his head in the room.

Tamara looked up. "Hmmm?" she asked, sipping her cup of juice.

"Visitor for you. You feel up to it?"

Tamara shoved the tray to the side. "Who is it?"

"It's a surprise," he replied, a look of amusement in his eyes as he pulled his head back out.

The door opened wider to reveal Janille, her gray hair pulled back tight against her head, looking as inscrutable and calm as always.

"Janille," Tamara said, sitting up higher in bed and smoothing down the front of her hospital gown. "How did you know I was in the hospital? We've kept it pretty quiet."

Janille walked over to the bed and held out a card. "I know most everything that goes on in the embassy and with those close to it," she replied, without any hint of pride, just a simple statement of truth. "You worked for me. I came to offer congratulations and wishes for you to get well soon." She said the words as a means of explanation. The question was, how much did she know? Most people assumed it was Alarin's—the doctors certainly had, and no one had disabused them of the notion. If the plan that Alarin would claim the baby as his was to work, it had to stay that way.

"Thank you," Tamara replied quietly, taking the card.

Janille offered her a polite bow, turned as though she intended to leave, but then stopped in the middle of the move. She turned back to Tamara. "Forgive my curiosity," she said after a moment's hesitation. "But dare I ask if he is the one who contributed to your condition?" There was the slightest emphasis on the "he."

Tamara flushed and spread her hands. "We can't tell for sure until later, of course," she said, not willing to reveal too much about the truth to anyone who was not in their inner circle. Even Rory didn't know who the true father was. Just that it might not be Alarin. Janille gave her a long, steady look that made Tamara's flush deepen. She kept forgetting that though Janille had never once asked any questions or offered any opinions, she knew quite well that Merran had had a physical relationship with Tamara. There had been some very embarrassing moments, which Janille had helped make less embarrassing by never mentioning or ac-knowledging them. But because of those moments, Janille, more than anyone, knew about the physical side to their relationship. "However," she appended hastily, well aware that Janille would not reveal the information to anyone, and that if anyone deserved to know, it was Merran's long-suffering secretarial assistant, "there is a strong chance."

"Good," Janille said, a faint smile touching the edges of her mouth. "Maybe he'll learn that there are more important things in the world than work. Children always shift your perspective about what's important, and he needs to obsess less about his job. I have three grandchildren in the Denver area, and they keep me sane."

That one statement revealed a couple of things about Janille that Tamara had never realized before—first, that she was quite fond of Merran, and second, that she had children and grandchildren of her own. The older woman—Janille was almost old enough to be Merran's grandmother—had never shown anything but a smooth, professional exterior to anyone at the embassy, and never discussed her personal life. Janille's comment also made Tamara realize that there were more important things in the world than remaining focused on her own self-pity and selfish anger. She felt tears prick at the back of her eyes and fought not to start crying in front of Janille.

The older woman bowed to Tamara and left. With her departure, Tamara let the tears flow down her face unobstructed, cupping her hands over her abdomen. Lost in faraway thoughts, for the first time she began to think about how they could include Merran rather than push him away.

She didn't call him until she got back to the apartment the following morning, having successfully eaten three times the previous day. Once home, it took a few hours to talk herself into contacting Merran before she got up the courage to actually place the call. *What if he refuses to speak to me? What if he is still angry? Could he still want to take the child away?* She worked herself into something of a panic, then firmly told herself to call anyway. It was better than wondering. Anything, even rejection, was better than wondering.

Janille answered the video call on the second ring. "Ambassador Corina's office, Janille speaking. How may I help you?"

"Janille, is Merran available?" Tamara asked, as she looked

at Janille's calm face, trying not to allow her voice to tremble. Admittedly, it wasn't easy.

"Hold a moment, please," Janille said, her tone and expression completely neutral. "I'll see if he has a free moment."

Tamara was on hold for so long she had enough time to think she shouldn't have called, convincing herself that Merran was going to refuse to talk to her. She bit at her nails as she waited. What would she do if he refused to talk to her? What would she do if he were too angry to do anything but hang up on her? What if … so what if? She was giving him what he said he wanted, wasn't she?

His face appeared on the screen, and she jumped. "Corina," he said. Merran sounded short, almost irritated. His face was etched with the lines of exhaustion, deep shadows visible under his eyes. He looked disheveled, with his odd-looking blond hair tousled, a stripe of his normal black showing at the roots, and his tie loosened, as though he'd tugged on it in frustration. Had he slept in that shirt? He'd shaved off the blond goatee, but a proto beard had begun to shade his cheeks and chin in a heavy, dark five o'clock shadow. It would be a beard in a few more days if he left it untended. In short, he looked terrible, and it shocked Tamara.

"Merran? You look exhausted!" she exclaimed, unintentionally blurting out the comment.

"Yeah," he said, sounding almost as tired as he looked. "I haven't been sleeping well for some reason." There was a distinct edge to his voice as he spoke. He rubbed his eyes. "What do you want?" he asked, crossing his arms and frowning into the camera. "I'm in the middle of a meeting."

"Is that why you're in the conference room?" she asked, recognizing the walls behind him. She ignored his edginess, suddenly not sure how to broach the subject with him and trying to work

up to what she wanted to say. She hadn't expected him to be so …
irritable.

"Yes," he replied. "Janille told me it was important. What's
wrong?"

She looked down at her hands. "Um, I'd-uh, I'd like to know
if you'd like … um … if you … I'd like you to come by to meet the
newest member of our family," she stammered, digging through
her rehearsed speeches and discarding all of them.

He stared down at the top of the table, remaining silent and
absolutely still. His expression was indecipherable, his shields
preventing her from reading anything at all. He could have been
thinking about his meeting for all the expression he was showing.
Her heart pounded in her throat. "Oh … does this mean you've
decided to forgive me?" he asked, looking up after a moment.
Though the question was innocuously worded, there was an un-
dercurrent of bitterness to his voice that she'd never heard before.
He sounded sarcastic. His eyes were dark and unreadable.

"Fine," she snapped, her temper igniting. "Don't come. Excuse
me for trying to offer you an apology for my behavior the other
day." His jaw tightened. "Never mind," she said, waving a hand.
"Forget I said that." She took a deep breath. "Look, do you want
to get to know the baby or not? If you do, come over tonight after
work. I'm home."

He took a long, noisy inhale through his nose and let it out
through his mouth. "I'll see if I have time," he said, then added,
almost as an afterthought, "Thank you." He cut the connection abruptly, leaving her shaking. She glared at the phone and
screamed, letting out all the rage that had suddenly built up. He
was being such a jerk! She burst into tears.

"What's the matter?" Alarin asked, coming into the room and

dropping his book bag on the bed. "Who's got you this upset?"

"A-a-asshole," Tamara sobbed, trying to catch her breath. "He-he's such an asshole."

Alarin didn't quite smile. "Merran, I presume, since I think there aren't many others you're quite that angry with?" He sat on the edge of the bed.

Tamara rubbed her eyes fiercely. "I-I-I tried to offer him an olive branch and h-he threw it back in my face," she gasped, trying to calm her hysterics, but not having much luck. "I-I thought you t-told me that he w-wanted to get to know the baby. H-he certainly didn't act it," she managed to get out.

Alarin reached out a hand to soothe her aura. "He does, *akila*. And he'll take your olive branch, you'll see."

"If he's going to act like that, I don't want him to," Tamara said, as her breathing calmed enough under Alarin's ministrations to allow her to speak without stammering. The feeling that she was going to throw up her breakfast faded too, much to her relief.

Alarin shifted in his seat. "Shhh," he said softly, stroking a hand down her aura again. "You don't need to get yourself sick again."

Tamara closed her eyes, then put her head back. "Why is he being such a jerk? I said I was sorry."

"Merran's going through something very similar to you," Alarin said. "He doesn't want to be a father any more than you want to be a mother. But it's done, and now he has to deal with the consequences."

"But he's not dealing with them, Alari, that's the point. We are. You and me. Why is he still acting as though I'm trying to force him into a shotgun marriage?" Tamara demanded, opening her eyes and sitting up.

"A what? A shot … what? What's a shotgun?"

Tamara waved her hand and snorted, choking in half-laughter at the expression on Alarin's face. "In the olden days, fathers would force men to marry their daughters when the men got them pregnant. They sometimes did it at the end of a shotgun, which is a type of weapon."

Alarin raised an eyebrow. "Ah. It makes quite a bit more sense. Colorful terms English has. We do not have that concept, of course. Azelle is quite a bit less complicated about these things. On Azelle, if the mother and father do not want the baby, another family will adopt it without question. Usually relatives of either parent. If a marriage occurs, it is because they want it to occur. Like we are doing." He slipped an arm around her shoulders. "I am so happy you said yes to marrying me, but I want to be sure you understand that when I asked you, it was not because of your pregnancy. We're just moving up the timetable—I wanted to marry you anyway. You know that, right?"

They'd discussed marriage shortly after the revelation of her pregnancy. Tamara was still not sure she was ready for it, but it wasn't for lack of loving Alarin. It was more because she wasn't sure she was ready to be a full-fledged adult. True, the baby took that option away from her anyway—and marriage seemed such a small step compared to caring for an infant and raising a child. "Why are you so much better about this than he is?" she asked, snuggling up under his arm.

"Because I want a family, Tam-*ala*. Merran never thought about having children, never wanted them. He doesn't want a wife, either. He struggled with being accepted growing up, and his childhood was rough, especially because there was no father as he grew up. Have you ever heard him talk about wanting a family?" Alarin asked.

Tamara shook her head.

"Well, trust me. This is not easy for him. He wants to contribute, to know the baby, but it scares him, and makes him question his life," Alarin replied. "Not a comfortable position to be in, when you've dedicated your life to a position like he has."

"Did you see him?" she asked, feeling her temper and defensiveness begin to fade under Alarin's calm.

Alarin nodded. "He's not sleeping at all, I'm told. Spending nights in the office. Ketiana's running interference again. She's about to force him to take more time off."

Tamara took a breath. "I didn't realize," she said softly. "He certainly looked like crap, though."

"Just don't take his moods too seriously. He's going to have them, and he'll get over them. It disturbed him pretty badly to think you weren't going to let him have access to the baby at all."

Tamara flushed. "I'm sorry, all right?"

Alarin waved a hand. "Hey, I'm just explaining Merran's behavior, not judging you. You asked him to come over tonight, didn't you?" he asked, changing the subject.

Tamara nodded.

"He'll be here, then. You'll see. The *aarya* couldn't keep him away. I'll get dinner made. We'll talk him into staying awhile," Alarin said, getting to his feet. He leaned over and kissed her. "He should probably be offered the chance to communicate with her," he commented, looking down at her belly. "If it doesn't bother you too much."

"He'd better not be a jerk, or I'll kick him in the ass."

Alarin grinned at her. "Hey, pregnancy has made you positively aggressive."

"Damn right," she said. Tamara sniffed and Alarin handed her a tissue. "I have to go to the bathroom," she complained. Alarin helped her off the bed—she wasn't yet ungainly enough to need the help, but it was nice to have him there being so supportive. Of course, the thought that she would eventually actually need help to get up was enough to make her grit her teeth in irritation, but she ignored it. She couldn't spend the rest of her pregnancy irritable and angry—as attractive as that sounded, she knew it was nothing more than feeling sorry for herself, and Greg had shaken her out of that. *Mostly*, she thought ruefully. If Merran kept his head, then she'd keep hers, she told herself as she went into the bathroom and closed the door behind her. But if he turned out to be a jerk, then she'd do exactly what she said she would. Kick his ass. Bracing herself for what she feared would be a difficult meeting with the father of her baby, she pulled herself together and went into the kitchen to help Alarin prep for dinner.

Chapter Seven

Merran changed his mind three or four times that afternoon about going over to Tamara's and Alarin's after work. Then changed it again. He had honestly not expected Tamara to call and offer him the opportunity to meet the baby, and he hadn't treated her very well when she did. He felt vaguely guilty about that, but his inner turmoil was too strong for him to worry about it. Alarin might be willing to act as the father, and Merran knew it was necessary, but it didn't change the truth of the matter. He was a father, but how the hell had it happened? He had never wanted children, never wanted to continue the patterns that had produced him. He had not known his father for very long. As much as he loved his niece and sister, he hated the pattern of rejection and approval-seeking that went on between himself and his much older brother. What would Junian say about a half-human brat his non-Council half-brother accidentally sired with a human? He could hear Junian's smug tones now—even despite extensive efforts to let it go, the sting of his brother's continuing rejection of him still had the power to bite. No, Junian would have no time for Merran's offspring either. The fact that Tamara was half-Azellian, and half High Council at that, would be irrelevant to Junian.

He pressed his hands against his temples and stared at the treaty paragraph he'd read five times so far. Why did he care what Junian thought anyway? It was useless to ever ask for Junian's approval, and he knew it, but he still seemed to keep trying. Youngest ambassador ever, countless treaties to his name, fame and fortune—now it all meant nothing in the face of this unborn child who made him feel helpless, terrified, and twelve years old, facing the death of his mother and the uncertainty of life all over again.

The door to his office opened and he looked up. Ketiana came in looking cool and collected.

"You don't need to say it," he said in Azellian. "I can't work like this."

Ketiana looked faintly surprised, but responded matter-of-factly in the same language. "How long do you need?"

Merran sighed. "I don't know. I was actually doing pretty well, feeling up to working again, then this."

Ketiana came to sit in front of the desk. "Do you want to talk about it?"

Merran shrugged. "Not much to talk about." There was actually, but Ketiana wasn't the one to talk to. He'd had a long talk with Greg the night before, when Greg had stopped by to tell him Tamara was getting out of the hospital, then again this morning when Tamara had interrupted.

"It's yours, isn't it?" Ketiana asked bluntly, surprising him.

He blinked at her. "What?"

"Tamara's baby. It's yours."

Merran winced, the words shocking him to the core. They burned to hear them from someone else's mouth. "Why do you say that?" he asked, after a brief interlude of considering and then discarding all kinds of responses to her question.

"Other than the fact that I am a Dorvath and a clairvoyant? There's very little that would knock you on your ass to this extent, except that," Ketiana replied. "You haven't looked in a mirror lately, have you?"

Merran took a deep breath. "I know I look rough ..."

"Rough?" Ketiana asked. "You look like you haven't slept in a week. You also have the look of a man who's just had a board between the eyes. You've been walking around in a daze since you got back from vacation and visited Tamara in the hospital."

All of it was true. When he did sleep, it was to screaming nightmares in which his daughter lived the life he'd had, or in which he relived some of the less pleasant aspects of his own life. He thought he'd left everything behind, but the knowledge that he'd created a new life brought it all roaring back. Nothing helped right now—not meditation, not losing himself in the *aarya*Song, nothing. It had to be experienced, and he was helpless in front of the force of it. He took a deep breath. "Fine," he said. Even though her ability to see consequence probably told her exactly what was happening, ambassadors were trained not to give straight answers. Oblique ones were all right. "I'd appreciate you not mentioning the possibility to anyone. Alarin is claiming the child as his, and they're going to be the official parents. The only ones who will know anything resembling the truth are the Keepers."

"And you, and anyone else who's seen you this past week. You need to get out of the office at least temporarily, Mer, if you truly want to convince people nothing's wrong. Fortunately, we didn't reveal to too many people that you were back, and you've only sporadically been in the office these past few days anyway. You'd better get yourself under control, though, or more people than me are going to figure it out. I'm sure Janille knows, too."

Merran had wondered about that, especially when she'd interrupted his meeting with Greg earlier that day to tell him he had a very important phone call—and didn't tell him who it was. He sighed. "All right, all right," he said, raking a hand through his hair again. "I'll take a few days to recover my equilibrium and get myself back on track. At least I don't have any meetings, since I wasn't officially back." He rubbed his fingers on the desk. "I'm staying in Denver, though," he told her. "I have some … thinking to do that requires me to be here."

"Fine. But we'll have to come up with something for the media or you're going to attract the wrong kind of attention." She studied his black-and-blond striped hair. "You might want to do something about your hair too. It's rather eye catching, and not necessarily in a good way."

"I'll dye it back to my normal color."

"But no matter what color your hair is," Ketiana said carefully, "you're going to attract media attention if you're not careful."

Merran sighed. "I know," he muttered irritably. "Too many damned people know as it is."

"Don't hide it," she suggested, going in a direction with her comment he didn't expect at all.

"What?" Merran demanded, staring at her, certain he hadn't heard right.

"Don't hide your interest. After all, Alarin is your friend, Tamara is … was? … your employee, and they have a new baby coming. We'll do a press release and make it seem boring and mundane. You want to celebrate the birth of your good friend's baby. If you manage to get yourself under control, they'll never know the truth."

Merran was silent for a few moments. "That will bring attention to Tamara."

"A little, yes, but isn't that preferable to the media discovering the truth? You know as well as I do that a little misdirection works better to hide the truth than acting as though you have something to hide. We've manipulated the media enough in the matter of your image that a little leavening in the form of your enjoyment of your friends' joyous news will perhaps help camouflage your true interest in their child."

Merran shuddered. "I still have to think that through before we make an announcement, but I think you may be right. I don't like bringing anyone's attention to Tamara and Alarin at all, but I'll mention the idea to them and see what they say. I'm seeing them tonight," he said decisively, his voice sounding stronger, losing some of the lost despair it had held earlier. He leaned over and made a note on his tablet, then said, "I'm going to take a shower. You don't mind handling the office for a little while longer?"

"Of course not."

Merran walked into the bathroom connected to his office. "Oh," he said, leaning back out of the door. "Remind me to give you a very large bonus this year."

Ketiana grinned. "You bet I will. Now get showered before you stink up the office any worse than you already have."

Merran felt better than he had since he'd found out about the baby and even grinned as he closed the door behind him. The shower and shaving didn't take too long, nor did dressing, although he didn't have much in the office but suits. He was finally able to dig up a pair of slacks and a white tank, over which he slipped a dress shirt. Studying himself critically in the mirror, he frowned. It was slightly more formal than he wanted, but he didn't want to go back to his apartment and dig up more casual attire. It was getting close to dinner, and he wanted to get through this before he got any more nervous than he already was. He hesitated over what scent to apply, then stopped, remembering from somewhere that pregnant women have an enhanced sense of smell. Tamara might not like a scent. Slapping some gel into his hair instead, he tugged it into position. It was short, so all the gel really did was make his hair look wet, but it was too late to do anything else about it. All he was really doing by trying to get "just the right look" was stalling anyway. He opened the bathroom door.

Ketiana was on a video call, speaking in Atheran. She gave him a thumbs up away from the camera, but her expression of polite disinterest didn't change a whit. The person she was talking to would never have noticed her distraction. Merran grinned and bowed, grabbing his coat as he left the office, his face settling into more thoughtful lines. Ketiana had done such a tremendous job of running the embassy while he was gone that he had to think seriously about giving her more responsibility. In the outer office, Janille silently handed him car keys and watched him leave.

He distracted himself with thoughts of what more he could start having Ketiana do, as he walked toward the lot where the embassy kept its spare cars. He hoped a personal car would be camouflage enough, since he never went out in anything other than the limo, and the media had been slow to catch on that he was gone or that he'd returned. It helped that the Nuvo Film Festival was in town and the media had star power galore to follow—not just their colorful ambassador. Of course, news like this—Azelle's playboy ambassador fathers child—would create quite the headlines and would add to the speculation of who slept with whom at the Nuvo Festival. He shuddered again. *The rumors would spread faster than wildfire*, he thought to himself. Whatever they could do to avoid that would be good. He got into the car and started it up.

It occurred to him as he drove over to the school that he'd only rarely been on campus and had never visited Alarin and Tamara before. This was an historic occasion for him, as he normally avoided drawing attention to his friends by visiting them. After he pulled into a parking spot on the street, he pulled down the mirror on the sun visor and frowned at his uncharacteristically blond thatch that had started to show its dark roots, giving him a reverse skunk look. He wondered if there was a hat in the car. Climbing out, and scanning with his psi to make sure no one was observing him, he popped open the trunk and started to laugh. Sitting quite primly in the trunk of the car that Janille had obviously prepped for him, was a black, ten gallon Stetson hat, very much like the thousands of others that Denverites had been favoring since the days when the area was first tamed and settled by the cowboys of the old West. Beside the hat was a beautiful pair of intricately decorated, very *pointy toed* cowboy boots, made out of stiff, dark brown leather. As he picked up one—it was his exact shoe size—a glint of silver caught his eye, and he reached out to touch a thin black string of a bolo tie, complete with a large silver-and-turquoise pendant.

Merran grinned to himself. *Janille. She knows, all right.* And, as was typical of Janille, she gave her tacit aid without his asking or her mentioning a thing. Although a cowboy sauntering up to Alarin and Tamara's room might be a bit odd, it was better than Merran Corina walking up to the apartment—and no one would expect to see Merran Corina dressed up as a cowboy. He pulled the items out of the trunk and got back into the car to tug on the boots, using the open car door to hide what he was doing. He slipped the bolo tie around his neck, adjusting the pendant to a comfortable spot around his neck, and slapped the Stetson on his head, covering up the eye-catching black streak in his still mostly blond hair.

When he finished, he was surprised at how much camouflage the items provided. The boots and tie didn't exactly go with the black pleated dress slacks and the crisp white Oxford button down shirt—jeans and a denim or flannel shirt would have been better—but it worked, and his hair was covered. Once he pulled the heavy, long wool coat over his haphazard ensemble, he certainly didn't look like himself, which pleased him.

All the same, he took care to avoid people. Fortunately, that wasn't too difficult, as everyone seemed to be at dinner. It was quiet, and he ran into no one on his way from the parking lot to the apartment. His scans revealed no one watching him either.

Tamara and Alarin's apartment was the only one heavily shielded; even if he hadn't known where it was, he would have found it easily. The shielding was powerful and expert, and he could taste the flavor of Alarin as he touched the outside of the firm, shining shields with his mind. He walked up the staircase toward the second floor, his boots clicking on the cement as he climbed to the landing. He had to duck around a corner only once as a young woman and man, draped over each other, came up the stairs to the second floor. However, they didn't even notice him, much too lost in the spiraling pleasure they'd begun with each other. Merran had to smile as he slipped into the hall. The apartment they entered was most certainly not shielded, and it seemed like they were not going to make it to the bedroom. He had a moment of half-bitter thoughts about the possible consequences of their actions—not something he'd ever considered since he'd been trained to make sure he didn't impregnate someone—then he firmly blocked them out of his mind and went up to the shielded door and knocked.

Alarin opened the door. A delicious smell spilled out of the apartment as Alarin momentarily stared at him, a look of shock crossing his face before he burst into laughter. "Come in," he said, when he'd caught his breath enough to speak. "Quite a disguise, I must say." He closed the door behind Merran. "Changing jobs?"

"No. Not really."

"I don't know. Looks good on you. Where's the horse, though?"

"The pants and shirt don't exactly go with the boots and hat. Or the long coat." Merran pulled off his coat and hung it on the coat tree.

"Or the muscle shirt under your dress shirt. I don't think I've ever seen you this ... haphazard."

"I had limited choices. And I didn't come up with the idea of a disguise until I got here. I used what I had available."

Alarin laughed. "The embassy keeps cowboys in the trunk, does it?"

Merran flashed a brief smile, respecting Alarin's cheer, but too nervous to share it. "Janille can be creative apparently. It was her idea."

"Well," Alarin said, his eyes dancing with barely suppressed mirth, "you'd better get at least the hat off or you're going to send Tam into cardiac arrest."

Merran snorted and took off the hat, hanging it on the coat tree in the entryway with his coat. "Where is she?"

"Resting. She tires easily still, although it's not quite as bad as it was at the beginning. I've got dinner almost ready. We should be eating in about half an hour. Do you want to go in and say hi?"

Merran's heart leaped. He couldn't quite control the tremor that spilled through his hands. "Uh. Maybe she should wake up first. I don't want to wake her."

"Go in," Alarin said firmly, taking the decision out of his hands. "She's awake, which you would know if you weren't shielding so hard. There's someone who wants to meet you."

Merran remembered the feather touches of the unborn baby's mind against his. At the time he'd had too much to process to let it affect him, and since then, he'd tried to block out all thoughts of having anything to do with the baby. Frankly, after their fight at the hospital, he hadn't expected Tamara to let him have anything to do with the baby at all. But she was, and here he stood, nervous as he hadn't been since his predecessor Saren died and he'd been forced to negotiate a treaty Saren had thought impossible to negotiate, while pretending that Saren was still alive. Actually, he was more nervous at this moment, because back then he'd known he could convince the other side to do as he asked, but right now he still wasn't at all sure he was ready to be even a remote father. He took a deep breath and went to the closed bedroom door, knocking softly.

"Come in," Tamara's voice called from inside the room.

He opened the door, trying to hide the tremors that shook his hands, but knowing that it was almost impossible. Her shields were back to normal, but he didn't relax his own. He didn't want to feel the baby's insistent touch yet. Merran looked at Tamara and was taken aback by the glow of her face—for all her struggle with the idea of being a mother, pregnancy had given her a luminosity that made her beautiful. "Hi," he said, not daring to say more. Emotion was going to make his voice crack, like it hadn't since he was thirteen and his voice changed.

"Hi," Tamara said, looking at him. She said nothing more.

"You look beautiful," he remarked, startling himself. He hadn't meant to tell her that. He hadn't meant to break the silence at all.

She raised her eyebrows. "I don't know if I'd say that. It doesn't show yet, but I feel like I'm starting to puff out." She touched her belly.

"You're beautiful," he said, shaking his head. "You glow."

She flushed, color spreading up her cheeks. "Thank you. Alarin says it too. Maybe I have to start believing him." She gave him an arched look. "Of course, I know he's biased. He has to tell me I'm beautiful … he wants to marry me. What's your excuse?"

Her attempt at humor, at pretending everything was okay, touched him. Instead of laughing, though, he suddenly wanted to cry, and the emotion shocked him. His shields wavered, weakened under the force of his emotions, and he knew he was leaking. He couldn't help it. He loved her. She was the mother of his child, and the *aarya* help him, it changed his view of her. He hadn't expected to feel this way, and he feared it would take him apart.

Tamara slid her legs off the side of the bed. "Merran?"

Locked in a struggle not to show her too much and control the emotions surging through him, he couldn't answer.

Tamara came to his side. "Merran?" She reached out to touch his arm. "Come, sit," she invited.

He let her lead him to sit, too involved in keeping his emotions from overwhelming her through the physical link of her hand on his arm.

There was a moment of silence, then Tamara slid her hand

down his arm to his hand. She picked up his hand and studied it for a moment, tracing her fingers across his palm, up his fingers. His skin tingled, and oddly, the emotional firestorm that still coursed through him calmed, the desire to cry fading so he could control it. Very softly, she placed his hand on her stomach.

As soon as his hand touched Tamara's belly, the baby reacted, surging through his shields with a force he didn't expect an unborn child to have. Her mind twined around his, not thinking, not quite yet, just needing and seeking, accepting and touching. She demanded him to accept her, to love her, and he responded with a ferocity that surprised him. He adored her, he told her without words, and it was true. She was wanted, needed, and perfect in every way.

The baby released him after she'd gotten the assurances she wanted, and Merran came back to himself, surprised to find himself crying. Silent tears slid down his face as he pulled his hand back from Tamara's stomach.

Tamara smiled at him, her own eyes wet. "Demanding, isn't she?"

Merran sniffed and leaned over to pull a tissue out of the box beside the bed. "Takes after her mother," he said, as he wiped his eyes and blew his nose.

"Hey," Tamara protested, but because of the happiness she radiated, her objection lacked heat. "What about her father?"

"Absolutely not," he replied. "Her father is always easygoing and reasonable."

Tamara snorted. "Right, not stubborn at all," she said softly, brushing her fingers against the back of his hand. "Are we all right? Is this going to work?"

Merran leaned over suddenly and kissed her. The kiss was not a passionate one, but he wanted her to know how he felt. He let the gentle brush of his lips against her cheek communicate it to her. "It will work," he said, as he pulled her into a hug, his mind enveloping both her and the baby at once. "I promise you that."

Her arms tightened around his waist, and he stroked a hand down her neck, resting his face against her hair. The feel of her body in his arms was difficult, because, despite his determination to let her go, he vividly remembered making love to her and he still wanted to on some level—but the baby was there in her little demanding way, and she provided the bridge that allowed him to offer her mother support and caring untarnished by his more selfish urges. *Actually, I'm not entirely sure that I could perform with the little imp observing everything—no wonder many Azellian males refuse to sleep with their mates while they're pregnant.* The thought made him smile, and he broke the embrace. Reluctantly, the baby let him go, but only after he'd assured her that he wasn't going to leave them—apparently she'd seen farther into him than he'd let anyone see before, even Tamara. The thought was not a comforting one.

"There now," he said, pulling back and sniffing as Tamara's stomach growled insistently. "All this emotion is making me hungry."

Tamara laughed tearily. "You're not the only one." She sniffed as well. "And I need a tissue."

Merran leaned over to grab two more and handed them to her. "You ready to go out?" he asked after she'd blown her nose.

Tamara nodded and dumped her tissue in the trash. "Yes. Alarin's going to wonder what we've been doing in here."

"He already knows," Merran replied, getting up and helping her to her feet.

"I feel like I was beaten with a padded stick," Tamara muttered.

"You're not the one who just got coerced by a fetus." He shook his head. "She's quite a projector, that little girl."

"Takes after her father." She gave him a sideways glance. "Poor child."

Merran grinned and held up his hands. "Me?" he asked, pressing his hands against his chest and giving her his best innocent look. "You're the stronger projector, my dear." He reached out and pulled open the door.

"Hah. You're stronger than I am."

"You're both damned strong projectors," Alarin said, coming in from the kitchen, his face showing signs that he'd experienced some of what the two of them had gone through in the bedroom. "It's a damned good thing she's going to go latent with birth. She got to you, too, I see," he said to Merran. "She's already decided that we are all going to be part of her life, whether we want to be or not. Dinner's ready."

Alarin was right, Merran thought to himself as he moved toward the table. The baby had made the choice already—that all three of them would be involved in her life. He could no more abandon her now than he could cut off his arm. It was going to be a tricky, careful balancing act, but it was clear that he wouldn't be able to walk away from his daughter. As they sat down at the dinner table, he prepared to broach the subject of how to work this out.

❋ ❋ ❋

Later that night, Tamara tossed restlessly, unable to find a comfortable position. She turned over and dozed, then shifted again.

"What's the matter?" Alarin murmured as she flipped for

what seemed like the hundredth time. He shifted to give her space. "Merran's ideas about how to work this out bothering you?"

"No, I'm actually relieved that he has an idea about how to handle things. I just can't get comfortable. And no, it's not the baby. She's actually sleeping right now, amazingly enough. It's my dad. I'm not looking forward to telling him. I'm almost afraid to talk to him. He's going to be so upset. I mean he didn't want me to get too involved with you and now to find out that you and I are going to not only get married, but we're going to be parents within the next five months …"

Alarin pulled her closer. "*Alawahea*, Tam-*ala*."

Tamara glanced at him dubiously. "Maybe everything will be fine, but that won't help me if he kills me."

"He won't kill you, *akila*. He might be disappointed or worried, but he won't kill you."

Tamara sighed, warming to the affection in Alarin's use of the Azellian word. "Maybe if I finish my degree, he won't be so worried about it. Merran is certainly convinced I have to finish my degree. Enough so that he is setting up an elaborate plan to be able to contribute financially without anyone knowing."

Alarin rolled on his back. "He still loves you."

Tamara coughed in embarrassment. Alarin hadn't been there to feel Merran's conflict, to know that if it hadn't been for the baby, he would be gone from their lives, no matter how he felt or didn't feel about Tamara. She knew it. His feelings—and hers—were too mixed up for them to have remained friends without the child's presence. He might care about her—she thought love was a bit strong a word—but he would have chosen to pull away, if it weren't for the baby who roused such powerful feelings in him. She'd sensed his reaction to the baby, sensed his helplessness toward his own emotions. He was bound, as irrevocably as she was, to this tiny life they'd created, and she suspected guilt and strong feelings for his child were stronger motivators than any tender feelings he held for her, no matter what Alarin thought. "What about your parents?" she asked, changing the subject. The last thing she needed to do was trigger Alarin's insecurities. The time when they'd affected their relationship was not so far in the past that she felt she could ignore them. "They're not going to be too happy either."

"Don't worry about my parents. My father can foretell the future," he said ruefully. "He's probably already known for years that I was going to be the father of a child that isn't entirely mine. He's most certainly known who I would marry and the date of my marriage." He put his arm around her. "He would never say anything either supporting my choices or berating them, though, so we don't need to worry." A faint hint of bitterness threaded through his voice.

"Did he tell you who it was?" She tried to keep her voice soft and calm. Alarin rarely talked about his family. *If he's willing to talk tonight, I'm definitely listening!*

Alarin shook his head. "No, Father doesn't share the visions with anyone. They aren't his to share, he says. So he doesn't. But he always knows. And he always holds himself aloof from all of us. It is one of the ways precogs stay sane. There aren't many who allow the talent expression. When they do allow themselves to see the future, they adjust by withdrawing. I grew up with nurses and caretakers. My mother has always been more interested in her status and her society parties, my father, his visions. There wasn't much left over for children." Alarin's voice had become oddly mechanical, as though he spoke by rote, and Tamara could hear the pain in his voice.

Tamara hugged him, moved by that pain. "What a lonely existence. Lonely and isolated. But you aren't, you know. You have me, you have all the other people in our lives who love you and care about what happens to you."

Alarin turned over to hug her. "The baby's sleeping, eh?" he asked, nuzzling her neck, pressing himself closer to her, then sliding his hand over her stomach and down her side.

Tamara snuggled against him. "Uh-huh."

"Then how about we get a private moment to ourselves?" He kissed her nose.

"If she wakes up in the middle?" Tamara could remember a couple of times when that had happened and the effect it had had on Alarin. She'd never seen a more effective mood killer.

Alarin grinned. "Then she gets a crash course in anatomy and forgets all about it during the trauma of her birth." He slipped his mind through her shields.

Tamara reached up to kiss him, relaxing her shields enough to let him in. "I love you, Alari."

Alarin answered her without words, wrapping his arms around her, both of them losing themselves in the moment and their intimacy. Later, after falling asleep again, Tamara felt the moment of happiness stretching underneath her, and she let it fill her. She didn't have to tell her father yet, but by the time she did, surely she would figure out how to approach it.

❄ ❄ ❄

Tamara woke the following morning to a ringing telephone, which jerked her out of sleep. At least it wasn't on the other side of Alarin this time. "Hello?" she asked sleepily, looking over at the clock.

"Tammy?" her father's voice added to the adrenaline rush. He sounded odd, not quite right.

"Dad?" She sat up in bed. "What's wrong?"

"Can you get in touch with Justern quickly?"

"Justern?" Tamara asked, as Alarin turned over and propped his head up on his arm. "Maybe. I don't know. It depends on what time it is on Azelle. Why?"

"I just got a call from the president. He wants to talk to Justern personally. When he couldn't get a hold of Merran, he contacted me, as Justern's attorney."

"About what?" Tamara asked, turning on the video feed. She wanted to see his reactions, not just listen for them. "Dad, Justern has put … is putting his life back together on Azelle. Why would he want to bring it all up again? Are they still trying to pursue Justern on Azelle to get him to pay up? They found him innocent on Azelle! Or is Joely admitting she was wrong?"

The tiny screen that revealed Peter's face and shoulders didn't clearly show his expression, and her father was too controlled for her to read his emotions. He made a sound. "That would be a miracle from on high. No, I believe Merran has been campaigning for Justern these past few months, working toward getting him pardoned from the highest levels so he does not have to continue to worry about an ongoing effort to collect him from Azelle. And maybe to eventually allow him to come back here."

Tamara, who had talked to Justern religiously each week ever since he'd been exiled back to Azelle, knew that Justern was still struggling with the pain of the accusations that had been brought up against him and the rejection and blow his pride had taken. "You can't get a hold of Merran?"

"No, I can't reach him. He's on a leave of absence," her father said, sounding exasperated. "Or vacation or something. Either way, he's not available. I've tried his cell and the embassy, but nothing."

"All right, all right." She was quite aware of why Merran was unavailable right now. "I'll call Justy. I'll try to contact him now and have him call you."

Peter relaxed slightly. "Thank you, honey. By the way, I'm going to be downtown today for a deposition. I'd love to meet you for lunch at O'Reilly's. It's been a while since I've seen you, and I'd like to have lunch with my daughter. Are you going to be free?"

Tamara tensed. She had no real reason to say no, but she didn't think she was ready for this—yet. She had to consider that even though she wasn't showing, at least not in the form of a protruding belly, it wouldn't be long before she did, so the sooner the better. Alarin touched her arm gently, and she felt his warm presence beyond the phone screen, supportive and buoyant. "What time?" She tried to sound normal and not wary.

"Around noon."

She took a deep breath. "All right. I … uh … have some stuff to talk to you about anyway."

"Like what?" Peter asked, his tone sharpening. Although Tamara had technically inherited her sensitivity to emotions from her Azellian mother, her father didn't lack for a sometimes psychic sense about people. Greg had said her father might be human psi. There were times, like now, when she believed it was possible.

"I'll tell you later, when I see you at O'Reilly's. I have to call Justern now. Bye, Dad," She hastily hung up the phone.

It took her a few moments to get her composure after their conversation. "Shit, shit, shit, shit," she muttered, pressing her hands against her temples.

"It will be all right, you know."

Tamara looked up at him. "Sure. Tell me that after he's throttled me and killed you. How does it feel to die for someone else's sins?"

"He's not going to kill anyone." He levered himself so he could sit up in bed, sliding an arm around her shoulders. "He might want to, but he's too much of a lawyer to give in to those primal urges."

"Thanks. That's a very helpful visualization." She shrugged her shoulders so his arm slid down her back, making sure he heard the sarcasm.

"Oh come now, Tam. You're being theatrical. Remind him that this is his first grandchild. Any anger from him is going to come out of a sense of protection. Tell him we're getting married. He'll get used to the idea."

"He'll disown me." Her pregnancy didn't help with the stability of her emotions.

"I doubt that. He's not an ogre, Tam, no matter what you believe. He might be angry and disappointed at first, maybe, but he'll come around."

Tamara made a sound. "That's if I survive the coming around part."

Alarin grinned. "I'm sure you'll survive. He may not, if the shock is great enough, though."

"Oh great," Tamara replied, responding to Alarin's attempt to lighten her mood. "Just great. I kill my own father. Just what I need. What do I tell the baby when she gets old enough?"

Alarin laughed. "*Alawahea, akila.* It will be fine. Just wait and see."

She leaned over. "What time is it on Azelle?" She looked around him at the clock.

Alarin frowned, doing some quick calculations in his head. "Late," he said. "I'm not sure exactly what time it is, since the time shifts slightly between the two planets, but I'd say it's late night."

"Too late to call Justern?"

"Probably not," Alarin replied. "Justy tends to stay up late, or he did the last time I spent any time with him."

"I'll take a chance. He got a personal phone a month ago, so I won't wake up everyone else in the house." It was also easier to focus on Justy than spend the next few hours worrying about her lunch meeting with her father.

She dialed Justern's phone, using the video option, and tried not to think too much about her meeting with her father. She hadn't told Justern about her surprise pregnancy either, mainly because she hadn't come to terms with it herself until the last few days. Maybe if she tried it out on Justern, she'd figure out how to tell her father.

The phone rang twice, and a woman's face appeared on the screen. "Hello?" she said in accented English. "Tamara?"

"Mellis?" Tamara asked, rather surprised to find the young woman answering the phone. The last time she'd talked to Justern, they'd decided to go their separate ways. "Hi! Long time no talk to. How are you?"

"Fine, fine. Good … really good. Justy and I are catching up." She made a face. "Not that I'm back, really. We're just … scratching an itch." Her English was still very good, even despite her absence from Earth.

Tamara laughed. She hadn't talked to Mellis since the end of last semester when she'd decided to leave Earth with Justern. Tamara had forgotten how very earthy Mellis could be. "Oh, is that what it's called?" she asked, still chuckling. "Very picturesque. Thanks for the image. I'm not interrupting, am I?"

"No, we were pretty much finished," Mellis replied frankly. "Justy's on his way back from the bathroom." She leaned over and spoke off screen. "It's Tamara."

"Tam?" Justern's face appeared in the video screen as he took the phone from Mellis. "Is something wrong?" Like Mellis's English, his English was still quite good, even despite the fact he'd returned to Azelle and was no longer using it as often. His accent was slightly heavier, though, and more musical.

"No, no." Alarin slid out of bed to pad into the bathroom as she spoke, leaving her to talk to her half-brother in private. "Not at all. I thought I'd call and bug my favorite brother. Apparently, I have good timing."

Justern grinned and she could see him relax. He leaned back, resting the phone on the table beside the bed as he stretched his arms above his head. His change in posture revealed that he wore nothing above the waist—and probably nothing below it, but thankfully she couldn't see that. His chest had filled out, revealing less boyish contours and more of the musculature of a man. Tamara often forgot that he was younger than she was and quite a bit younger than Merran and Alarin. "Good or bad, depending on your point of view."

"You guys on again?" Tamara asked, referring to the fact Mellis had answered the phone.

"Nope. Not at all."

"Then what's this? Mellis told me you were scratching an itch."

Justern's grin widened. "We're recharging. For the next stretch of sexlessness."

Tamara snorted. "Which will last, what? A week?"

"If that," Justern answered with another grin. He glanced off screen and waved. "Bye, Mel. See you later, when you get back from Nemorantxl."

She could hear Mellis murmur something in return, then Justern turned back to the phone. Tamara heard a door close in the background. "So what is going on, Tam? You never call me in the middle of the night, and we're not scheduled for another call until next week." His tone went from the lighthearted to serious.

She should have known that Justern would pick up on the fact she was calling for a reason. Even though his family talent might have been to project illusions visually, he was still quite good at picking up unspoken attitudes. "Well, I, uh, have a couple of things to tell you." She looked down at her hands, where they rubbed unconsciously against her belly. She looked up again at the phone resting on the bedside table.

"Good or bad?" Tension crept back into his body. He pulled his arms down and sat up.

"Depends on your point of view. Uh, the first one concerns me. I'm uh … well you're going to be an uncle." She spoke in a rush.

Justern's eyebrows shot up. "You mean you're ..."

"Yeah. I'm going to have a baby," Tamara said, surprised at how hard it was to say the words to someone else. She had the opportunity to see Justern left completely speechless, though, and that was rather amusing.

"Well," he said, after a moment. "That's certainly not what I expected you to say. You don't sound thrilled, though. Are you happy about it?"

"It wasn't the easiest thing I've dealt with. But I've come to terms with it. Alari and I are getting married too. Not precisely because of it, of course, but it's moved our plans up a bit."

"Is it Alarin's?" The question was normal—but blunter than she expected.

"Uh …" Her brain raced. He knew about the tangled relationship between herself, Alarin, and Merran, although she'd told him she'd broken it off with Merran. "Let's just say to the outside world, Alarin has a daughter, no matter her true heritage."

"Whew. How's he taking it? The biological father, I mean. I already know Alarin's probably got it all handled. He's very good at that."

Tamara could feel the flush burn up her cheeks. "About like I am. Uneasily. It's easier because the rest of us are going to be the ones overtly raising her. He gets to pretend nothing's changed." She could hear the lingering bitterness in her voice and consciously added, "Well, actually, it's not so bad as that. He's working on a convoluted plan to be part of this, as much as he can be, while keeping her protected from the paparazzi's interest in him. So she is Alarin's and my daughter, and that's as far as it goes."

"So he's going to be an uncle. Well, that works. He's already been one and knows how to handle it. Wow. Pregnant. I'm gone from Earth for a short time and you turn your life upside down."

"It wasn't on purpose. But it's done and we get to deal with it."

Justern cocked his head. "Not on purpose? How not on purpose? Hasn't Greg shown you how ... "

Heat rushed up her body to settle in her cheeks. "Yes, but I got used to trusting that they would take care of it. There was one time ..." She rubbed her eyes. "Let's just say that we were distracted. Not really paying attention ... and it happened."

Justern blinked. "Ah," was all he said.

"The wedding will be this summer, after the semester's over." She deliberately changed the subject, very uncomfortable with the turn this one had taken. "If you were able to get a full pardon, would you come back for our wedding?"

The color slid from his face. He went very still. "Don't tease me."

"Hasn't Merran told you he's been campaigning for you to be pardoned so that this persecution will end?"

"He told me," Justern replied, his voice remote, "but I thought it was extremely unlikely that it would actually work."

"Well, my dad called me this morning to tell me that the president of the United States wants to talk to you. Why else would he want to talk unless it's to discuss a pardon?"

"So you don't *really* know what he wants, do you?" Justern's eyes stared at her steadily.

"Not for sure, but considering Merran's efforts and the president's desire to speak to you, I thought maybe ... just call my dad anyway and talk to him. He's the one who spoke to the president."

Justern shifted on the bed and took a deep breath, closing his eyes briefly to calm himself down. "All right. I'll call him. As for your first question, if ... and that's a big if ... I get a pardon, yes, definitely, I'll be at your wedding."

"Good. Oh, Justy, I didn't tell my dad about the wedding or the baby yet so don't mention anything, please?"

Justern shook his head. "I won't. Has Alarin told his family yet?" he added abruptly, as though the thought had just occurred to him.

"I don't think so."

"Oh."

"What?"

"Just that it's going to come as something of a shock." A grin tugged on the edges of his mouth. "It's going to turn the Raderths upside down, and that's something I can enjoy, no matter how it comes about."

Tamara shifted on the bed uncomfortably. "Really? Alarin doesn't think it's going to be that big of a deal."

Justern laughed. "Ho, it's going to be a big deal all right. Really big. As in Azelle-shattering. At least that's how they're going to treat it."

"But he said his father already knows!"

"Probably, but he most certainly hasn't told anyone, so the others are going to react rather predictably. They're going to hate it. This is going to be fun."

"Fun? How so?"

"You're on Earth, my sweet sister. You're not going to feel much of it. But here on Azelle ... let's just say that Alarin's news will shock them to their core. They were absolutely insufferable about the whole Carrington-Dorvath-Memaxthal affair, which involved our mother, as you'll recall. Now ... well, they've got what's coming to them. It's better that everyone thinks your baby is his. It makes the whole thing even funnier."

Tamara closed her eyes. "Justy ..."

"Don't worry about it, Tam. I'm just enjoying seeing the Raderths get their comeuppance. Alari is the best of the bunch. Kyla's not too bad, either, but the rest? Well, they've lorded it over the rest of the families for centuries, touting their perfect heritage, untouched by scandal or imperfection. They're perfect and the rest of us are flawed. Seeing one of their own being independent and doing what he wants—I've always admired that about Alarin—and now he's going to continue what he's always done ... shaking up the status quo."

Tamara shook her head. "Just call my dad, will you? Now you've got me worried and I have to catch Alarin before he goes off to class."

"I will. Don't worry too much about it, Tam. It's an Azellian thing. It won't affect you on Earth, and one day it will blow over."

"Like my own history has? I can't get a visa to Azelle to save my life."

"Except your baby's father is full-blooded Azellian, as is your future husband. I might not play politics as well as Merran, but I'm absolutely certain that he's going to get her and, by extension, you a visa now."

"Our mother was full-blooded Azellian and that didn't stop them from sending me and my father away."

"Yes, but Mother didn't have Merran on her side," Justern replied. "Mer's really good at getting what he wants, Tam, and your pregnancy, for all that it frustrates you, will open doors. I suspect you'll have a visa to come to Azelle before the baby's born, with a written invitation from Kendrick Raderth himself."

Tamara stared at him. "No way. You've got to be kidding."

"You wait and see. You'll have a visa by ... well, let's say in the next couple of months. You could always have the wedding here."

Tamara took a deep breath. "We'll see. Merran might actually manage to get me a visa, but there's no way in hell he's going to get one for my father, and I want him to be able to be at my wedding. Besides the wedding, though, if there's a chance you can come and go freely, I'd like my daughter to know her Uncle Justern too."

"I'd forgotten about that part. All right, fine. I'll call your dad right now and not mention anything about weddings, babies, or anything else."

"Thank you." She felt a vast relief. "Bye, Justy."

"Bye, Tam," Justern said and hung up the phone.

Tamara slid off the bed and padded into the kitchen to find that Alarin had left her a note. She hadn't sensed him leave—which put off her confronting him about his family's reaction. Going back into the bedroom, she got herself ready for a luncheon she was not looking forward to, no matter how reassuring Alarin had been.

※ ※ ※

Tamara met her father at O'Reilly's at noon, making sure she got there first and was sitting when he came in, her bulky, loose sweater hanging well over her hips. As he came into the restaurant, joining her at the table and leaning over to kiss her lightly on the cheek, Tamara made sure she shielded the baby as hard as she could as his lips, cold from the outside, brushed her cheek. She remained firmly seated. She wasn't sure about her ability to shield herself from a full body hug. The unborn baby had a mind of her own and a steady determination to bond everyone to her. Although Tamara's father was not psi the way she or the Azellians were psi, Tamara suspected her daughter would capitalize on his sensitivity the moment she had any contact with him, which could prove to be a good thing. However, it wasn't necessarily the way Tamara wanted to tell him about her new status.

"It's good to see you, sweetheart," her father said, settling down across from her. "How have you been?"

"Good," Tamara said. "How's Jill?" she asked, referring to her father's long-time secretary.

"She's doing great. Keeping me organized, as usual," he said, nodding at the waiter. They chatted about his work, little family details, and her classes until the waiter came over to take their order.

She still hadn't figured out how to tell him exactly, but the pressure to disclose recent events in her life was growing as the waiter delivered their sandwiches. "Uh, dad," she said, once the waiter left and a moment of silence fell between them. "I … have some news. You're, uh, you're going to be a grandfather," she blurted. It wasn't the most political way to have dropped the news in his lap, but at least it was finally out.

Peter froze, his fork halfway to his mouth. He set it down and looked straight at her. "Say that again."

Tamara stared at her plate of food. She suddenly wasn't hungry anymore. "I'm … pregnant."

Peter didn't say anything for quite some time, doing nothing but breathing while putting his best lawyer face in place.

Tamara pushed at her salad with her fork. "It was accidental. We … took precautions, but you know there's always a failure rate with every method," she said hastily, trying to cover the increasingly uncomfortable silence between them. "I'm keeping the baby, but I am finishing college. And we're going to get married." *As if that will make it all better … but maybe it will. Yeah, and pigs will fly soon, too.* "Things aren't going to be easy, but I am not going to give up on college."

Peter's eyes gleamed as he looked at her, but from anger or unshed tears Tamara wasn't sure. "Tell me one thing, Tamara. Is it that damned ambassador who is responsible for this?"

Tamara stared at him in shock. How to lie to her father? She hadn't expected him to make that connection; he'd known of her brief relationship with Merran, but she'd also been very careful to tell him it had ended. "Actually," she said, knowing that her father's ability to spot lies was pretty well developed, but also hoping he was emotional enough to miss her stretching of the truth, "it happened after I started seeing Alarin."

Peter made a sound. "I don't know that that's any better. At least Merran has a job. Alarin's a student, honey. How is he going to support you?"

The complex arrangement that Merran was putting into place to support his daughter was going to pay for any expenses associated with the baby and would provide more than enough to support Tamara while she was a student, but Tamara couldn't tell her father that. "Alarin has an internship with an IT company and it's looking very likely that they will hire him on a permanent basis. We are also getting married, so you don't have to worry about family gossip."

"Family gossip is the least of my worries right now," Peter said with a sharp sound that was somewhere between a cough and a sarcastic laugh.

"Dad, please," Tamara whispered, adrenaline rushing through her so strongly she could hardly breathe. "Don't be mad at me."

Peter shook his head. "I'm not angry, Tamara. I'm worried. I know what it's like to have a child you didn't expect. I hate to see you repeat my mistakes." His eyes took on a haunted look.

"I was a mistake?" She felt the sharp jab of pain lance through her.

"No, yes. I don't mean that I didn't and don't love you, Tamara," Peter's eyes focused on her. "It was just hard, honey. Very hard. Particularly before I met Jeanine. I don't want to see you struggle, Tamara. Have you thought about alternatives?"

Tamara took a deep breath. "I have. At length. She's three-quarters Azellian, Dad. Even at fourteen weeks, I can already sense her. I couldn't … I couldn't have an abortion, and I know I can't give her up for adoption. I've made my decision, Dad. I hope you can respect that and give her your love, too."

Peter looked down at his food, and she saw him blink away something that looked suspiciously like tears. "You are so much like your mother," he said finally, staring at his plate. "She had such determination and inner strength." Tamara could hear a note in his voice she'd never heard before. Peter had told Tamara of her history, but she'd never felt emotions like the ones coming from him now. She couldn't always sense her father, but she did in this moment. Chagrin, fear, love, and pride spilled through him. No real anger, although it did flare momentarily, but he understood too much to stay angry at her. "It always amazes me how life comes around full circle." He pulled himself back together and the sense of his emotions faded. He stared at the table.

Tamara let the silence extend for a while, then, wanting to change the subject, she asked, "Did Justy call you? I talked to him this morning. He said he'd call you right away."

"Yes, I talked to him." Peter shook himself and came back to the present. He took a deep breath. "You mentioned a wedding. Am I allowed to have a say?"

Tamara lifted her head and stared at him. "Of course. We'd love your input."

"Then I want you and Alarin to come down to the house this weekend. We have a wedding to plan and a family to figure out how to manage." He sighed and rubbed his cheek. "I'm going to get a lecture about how I allowed my daughter to be corrupted by those damned Azellians."

Tamara coughed, trying to suppress the laugh that threatened to erupt. "Grandmother's going to be quite unsurprised, I suspect. She already thinks I'm evil incarnate. Do we have to tell her?"

Peter rolled his eyes. "Eventually, yes. But we'll wait to tell her until we can't hide it anymore." He paused, then added dryly, "Maybe by then she'll be too senile to care."

Tamara giggled. "Dad! I'm shocked! Okay … not really. How is she doing?"

Peter shrugged. "Not as well as we could hope, but that's not an unmixed blessing." He paused and then continued. "You're turning two families on their ears, you know. Your grandmother isn't the only one who is going to have trouble with it. The Raderths are going to have collective apoplexy over this as well. I'm not as unaware of Azellian politics as they might think. Alarin is the prodigal son, the heir of the senior branch of the family. They're not going to take the news well, that he's marrying a human, especially Peter Carrington's daughter."

"Everyone keeps saying that," Tamara said. "What does that mean, anyway? What is this big deal? Why are the Raderths going to be so upset? Why does it matter what happened between you and my mother? I know the family story, and the results, but not the reasons."

"You know how Azelle is set up politically? By clan?"

Tamara nodded. "Yes, and that there are eight families who are on the Council."

Peter nodded. "Yes, the Raderths have been the foremost family of Azellian politics for a very long time. The head of the Raderth family, who is Alarin's grandfather Kendrick, is very opinionated. He was instrumental in making sure that Jasmian and I were separated."

"He was? Why?"

"Because I was human, and he couldn't stand to see a human disrupt a politically motivated marriage between Jasmian's family and Kendrick's wife's family. I got in the way, and he made damned sure I was taken out of the picture. The Raderths will do anything to get what they want, Tamara. If they can block you coming to Azelle and marrying their prodigal son, they will."

Tamara groaned. "Just what we need. Do you think they will succeed?"

"It depends on how willing Alarin is to go against his family. I've had a few conversations with him since he started dating you, and he seems very different from the Raderths I experienced more than twenty years ago. Still, it's extremely difficult to reject all your upbringing and follow your own way. There aren't many people who could do it."

"Alarin says his father probably already saw this marriage for us and knows."

Peter frowned thoughtfully. "Hmmm. I'd forgotten about Galadrian."

"Can he really see the future?"

Peter shrugged. "They say he can, but he doesn't get involved if he can help it. He certainly didn't prevent them from kicking you and me off the planet twenty years ago. Although ..." he trailed off and poked at his salad.

"Although what, Dad?"

"Galadrian said something to me once, before I left Azelle with you." Peter frowned, putting his fork down. "He said, 'Take very good care of your girls, Peter. They will change the course of a galaxy.' It stuck in my head all these years. I had no idea what he meant at the time. I still don't—although I did have two daughters, so maybe it does mean something, but I can't tell you what." He focused on her as a shiver rippled up Tamara's spine. "Galadrian is quite ... different from the other Raderths in that family. He's not like any other being I've ever met anywhere. When he looks through you with those eyes of his ..." Peter shuddered. "He's about the only one on Azelle who could prevent the Raderths from trying to interfere in your relationship with Alarin." He picked up his fork again. "But God knows if he will."

"Should I not go to Azelle? Do you think it will be dangerous for me? Alarin said we will have to, to register the baby with the Temple."

Peter's eyebrows went up. "I'd forgotten about that. Yes, he's probably right. All Azellian babies are required to be recognized by the Temple and the *aarya* who live there. Jasmian and I registered you just before you were born, too. I'm not sure how you're going to get a visa, though. Kendrick will block it with everything he has."

"Justy thinks Merran's going to play the political angles and get a visa out of it."

Peter looked thoughtful. "Merran's talented enough. He might just do it." He took a breath and extended his fingers to touch the back of her hand. "I'm so sorry my youthful carelessness put you in this position, honey."

Tamara looked at him and turned her fingers to squeeze his. "It's not your fault, Dad, and don't you dare take responsibility for it. You aren't responsible for the years of prejudice or Kendrick Raderth's behavior, nor are you responsible for my or Alarin's choices. I just want you to be a part of your grandchild's life."

Peter took a shaky breath. "Well, I wasn't quite ready to be a grandfather yet," he winced as he said the words, "but I will be."

Tamara smiled, and they finished out a lunch that ended much more pleasantly than it had begun. She went home after that feeling much better about everything—her future, her pregnancy, and the impending changes in her current life. There was so much to look forward to, and she found herself thinking about it positively for the first time since she'd discovered her pregnancy. Her father had taken it well, and it gave her the courage to face the other people, like the Raderths and her own grandmother, who might not.

Chapter Eight

"So the media got a whiff of the fact that I was in the mountains skiing and are blowing it way out of proportion." Merran frowned at the computer Ketiana laid in front of him. "Is that all?" He leaned back in the heavy leather office chair that he'd reclaimed following his and Tamara's reconciliation a few days earlier. He still didn't know what he was going to do in the long-term about working his life to include a daughter, as unacknowledged as she might be, but that was a problem for a later time.

Ketiana motioned with her hand and the page on the tablet changed. "You've assigned Jamie to go to Dorbin, and he's going next week," she said. "Ambassador Ki'i and he came up with an agreement, and he's going to see if he can manage not to kill those psi-sensitive Dorbin plants, to the point the Dorbin are willing to release them to us. I have no idea how you managed to get the Dorbin to agree to that, Mer, but it's impressive. Even if I'm not sure why we need those plants so badly."

Merran made a sound between a chuckle and a sigh. "Those plants have some very powerful properties that help in healing. The Healer enclave on Azelle is truly drooling to get their hands on them."

"But there's an Azellian ambassador to Dorbin, isn't there? An Azellian assigned to Dorbin?"

Merran shook his head. "No, there isn't. Corporeal beings don't do well on Dorbin. Jamie is a former Keeper who used to spend large amounts of time with the *aarya*. Non-corporeal races don't have the same perspective as those of us with a physical body, Kate, and sometimes that can be really unpleasant for those of us with a physical body. Jamie's training with the *aarya* will help him bridge that gap."

"We're lucky we have Jamie and that you have a good relationship with the Dorbin ambassador, then."

Merran's success at getting the plants had come from his willingness to play host to the Dorbin, and he suspected Jamian was going to be required to do many things that a normal *umanaarya* would find distasteful, but he didn't tell Ketiana that part. "We are." The intercom interrupted him, and he leaned over to acknowledge it. "Yes, Janille?"

"Justern Memaxthal on line two," Janille said, her voice only slightly altered by the electronic media that filtered it. "Did you want me to take a message?"

"No, I'll take the call. Tell him I'll be with him in a moment."

Ketiana got to her feet. "I'll go back to my office. Let me know if you need anything else." She left the office as Merran answered the phone.

"Corina," he said briskly, clicking on his computer and revealing his friend's face. "Hey Justy. I haven't talked to you in a while. How have you been?"

"Fine. Better than what's been happening to you, apparently. Congratulations, or would sympathy be better?"

"Congrat—" Merran halted mid-word. He controlled his flush firmly and took a deep breath. "Congratulations for what?" He knew he sounded stiff, but he didn't try to mitigate his tone.

Justern cocked his head. "When I talked to Tam last night, she told me that things have shifted course rather dramatically for her and that she and Alarin are getting married."

Merran made sure he had on his best ambassadorial face. "Yes, I knew that. What does that have to do with me?"

Justern gave him a look. "Maybe because she told me there was a reason she and Alari are getting married so soon."

"What did she tell you?" Merran asked coolly, feeling suddenly irritated at Tamara. Hadn't they worked this out? How were they supposed to say the child was Alarin's if she told everyone the opposite?

"She didn't tell me anything at all, but I pretty much figured it out myself." Justern corrected the impression immediately. He paused, then frowned. "I'm not stupid or blind, Mer, and I knew more about your little complications than you thought I did. She and I talk frequently." He sounded almost belligerent as he continued, a misplaced effort to be a protective brother. "How could you get so careless? She doesn't need that complication in her life."

Merran's eyebrows shot up. He put his hands up. "I got care—wait a minute, Justy. I'm going to pretend you didn't say that." He took a deep breath to control the automatic defensive reaction. "Mainly because I know you didn't mean it, and because people who live in glass houses need to watch the stone throwing." He made sure he enunciated his words, crushing his desire to lash back at Justern. Of all the people on Earth and Azelle, Justern shouldn't be the one complaining about carelessness. "I assume your motivations for berating me about carelessness are because you want to make sure I'm taking care of my responsibilities. Well, you can be sure I am. Now that we have that settled, why else are you calling?"

Some of the belligerence faded, and Justern managed to look sheepish. "I'm sorry, Mer. I just …"

"Got all brotherly on me," Merran finished for him. He softened his tone a little. "It's fine, done, over with. Did you need something else?"

Justern took a deep breath. "I talked to Peter Carrington."

Merran waited, letting Justern take his time.

"The president wants to talk to me personally."

"Did Peter tell you what the president wants?" Merran asked, keeping his voice level and neutral. He knew President Jerry Foster well enough to expect that the president wasn't going to make it easy on either Merran or Justern, and he wished that he'd taken the time to research what was going on before he'd taken Justern's call.

Justern nodded. "If I'm willing to offer a public apology for the carelessness," he swallowed hard, and Merran suddenly understood the comment moments earlier, "that ended me up where I ended up, he will offer me a full pardon that will put a stop to years of endless appeals processes and the constant pressures to pay up."

Merran blinked. What was Jerry thinking? The whole thing had been a major embarrassment to a government administration that had agreed to allow alien exchange students. Why would he want Justern to go so public regarding his behavior? Merran was suddenly wary about what the president was going to ask for in exchange from Azelle. "He wants you to apologize?"

"And he wants me to apologize to that *shiia* Joely—" the words stuck in his throat and he had to stop to clear it. "Peter says it's to end this nonsense for good. As badly as I want to come back for Tamara and Alarin's wedding, I don't know if I can apologize, Mer. I didn't do anything wrong except be at the wrong place at the wrong time. But at the same time, I'm going to be an uncle. I don't want to be forbidden from visiting my niece just because I'm being stubborn. Who knows when the Council will unbend enough to let Tamara come here?"

"Let me contact the president before you agree to anything. I need to find out what's going through his head before I recommend that you do anything. It may not be necessary for you to talk to the president at all."

"Thank you. Peter didn't really recommend anything one way or another. He said I should contact you directly."

"And I will take care of it. Right now." Merran jotted a note on the computer pad in front of him. "I'll call you back later."

"Until later then."

The intercom beeped immediately afterwards, before Merran could dial out. "Idara Tenricth here to see you," Janille announced, her voice absolutely neutral as always. "Shall I send her in or schedule an appointment for her later?"

Merran twitched. *Idara? Why is she here?* "Send her in, Janille." *Might as well get it over with.*

The door opened and Idara walked in. Merran blinked. She looked somehow different from the Idara he remembered on Azelle. She was still tall, elegant, and stylish, her clothes and hair perfect, but she lacked the arrogant confidence she'd had on Azelle. As a matter of fact, she seemed almost shy. "Hi, Merran," she said in Azellian, looking down at the floor and glancing up from under her eyelashes. "Thank you for agreeing to see me. I ... didn't expect you would be willing to, after ..." She trailed off, thinning her shields politely, waiting quietly for him to take her invitation.

Merran got to his feet, reaching out to touch her mind lightly with his. She was well shielded, her personal thoughts behind a thick screen, with only carefully controlled surface thoughts available. "It's good to see you, Idara. Come in, sit. How's the semester going?" he asked, as he walked over to the deep brown leather couch and sat down. He could have put the desk between them, but despite her sometimes annoying habits, she was one of Merran's misfits, and a friend by extension whom he'd known for years. During their several conversations last semester, when she'd contacted him because Alarin wouldn't communicate with her, she'd shown him she had changed, that Alarin's departure had brought a few things home to her. Apparently, her stay on Earth—something Merran had never thought he'd see in his lifetime—was changing her even more.

Idara drew a thin screen over her public thoughts, too, thin enough for him to read the truth in her mind, but not so thin that he was bombarded by unpleasant emotions. She sat on the matching armchair across from the couch, her restless fingers the only things that betrayed her nervousness. Her surface mental state reflected nothing but polite calm, not a peep leaking through heavy inner shields, not even to one with Merran's sensitivity. "Good, really good. I'm learning so much. They do things so differently here." She gave him a rueful little smile.

He rested his arm across the back of the couch, setting his left ankle on his right knee. "What have you noticed?" There was definitely something different about her—what was it? She was a blank wall, unreadable, but there was something that wasn't typical. He normally didn't project at fellow Azellians, but he let some of his goodwill toward her leak, relaxing his shields just slightly, silently encouraging her to do the same.

She smiled at him, and some of her defensive tenseness relaxed. "Although they don't have our abilities, I've been amazed at the depth of knowledge these people have. I can't believe how much there is to learn from them."

"So you've been spending some time with humans?" he asked, enjoying what he heard in her voice.

"Oh yes. Part of that is because I've had to. The five of us who came weren't friends, and I find ..." She shrugged, lifting her hands up. "All Francyne seems to do is worry about things like how she is High Council and Malinna is not, so how could she be doing better than Francyne is, or how is it that she's more popular than Francyne is ... " She didn't quite flush, but Merran caught the whiff of embarrassment off her anyway. "I mean, here it just seems so meaningless, those family politics we think are so important. They just seem so ... arbitrary..." She stumbled over her meaning and trailed off at the end.

Merran rescued her. His own non-High Council, *urro-ken* mother's legacy was one of the reasons he liked living on Earth, away from the Azellian obsession with family names and bloodlines. "It is arbitrary. I'm glad you think so, too. What about the other Azellians?"

Her smile this time wasn't entirely genuine. Her eyes didn't reflect it at all. "Rory's nice, but he's a Healer, and that means even with Greg back, he's spending all his time at the hospitals. Now that Greg's back, I'm going to spend what time I can with him, of course, as much as he has to spare, but he's a Healer too. Damiar's got a new relationship, which means he's got his hands full, and Sharynn, well, she and I have spent some time together, but we just have such different tastes," Idara said, rubbing at the grain on the chair, making a soft swishing sound. "I miss our group. It's so awkward between Alarin and me. He was so angry about me coming here. I even tried to be really nice to Tamara when I first met her, and he just got so upset. I didn't mean to offend her or him, but he took it the wrong way, so I I just figured it would be better to ignore him and leave them alone."

That showed a level of maturity Merran did not expect Idara to have. "Probably a good idea. He's got quite a bit on his mind." Ruthlessly, he suppressed his own momentary guilt about his role in just why Alarin had a lot on his mind. Idara did not need to pick up on that little complication between the three of them.

"That leaves you," Idara said, glancing down at her fingers again, twisting them in her lap. "I ... I was hoping y-you might have some time to spend with me. I mean, I know you're busy," she added hastily as he stared at her in shock. "Maybe too busy, but once in a while maybe could we go out or something? Do something just for fun?"

She was afraid he'd say no, that he'd push her away. Merran could taste her fear and the loneliness that leaked from the edges of her shields. It struck an answering chord in him, a chime of consonance that had never been there between them, that frankly, he'd never in a thousand years expected would be. Idara was beautiful, yes, but she had never attracted him and never found him attractive. What had changed? She sat in the depths of the armchair in his office, looking so lost, and so extremely vulnerable. They had known each other for just about twenty years, and he'd never in that entire time considered that he would ever be in the position where Idara asked him out on a date, even a friends-type date. It had always been Mellis with whom he'd shared a bed off and on, never Idara. But Idara had been as much a part of his life as Mellis, if in a totally different way, and he couldn't callously turn her away. He vacillated, and in the end the silence went on too long.

Idara flushed. "I'm sorry," she said, getting to her feet and almost stumbling over her own legs as she went for the door. "I have no right to ask you … I'm … I'm really sorry. I'll leave you alone."

"Ida, wait," Merran said, sensing that if he turned her away now, it would damage something permanently between them, and he couldn't do that. Maybe it was his own weakness for the past he'd tried so hard to fight off, but he couldn't just slam the door in her face. He reached out and held the door shut with his mind. "Wait." He came around the couch. She faced the door, refusing to turn around, staring at the door handle as he came up behind her. "You just took me by surprise, that's all. I am really busy, but I can make time for friends, if you're flexible."

She turned to place her back against the door but kept her eyes downcast. She was nearly as tall as he was, he noticed with that part of his mind that never stopped monitoring his surroundings. When they had been younger, in Merran's misfits, Idara had always been Alarin's girlfriend. She'd been part of the group, but by extension. He'd never been physically close to her, like this. Right now, she stood so close their auras almost brushed. "Friends?" she asked faintly and lifted her dark eyes to his.

Merran went breathless for a moment, the consonance between them humming so strongly he could almost feel her against him. One step, one tiny step and he'd be able to brush his aura against hers—how long had it been since he'd slept with an Azellian woman other than the human-raised Tamara? A very long time. Years maybe. There weren't many Azellians on Earth who weren't embassy workers, and despite his aberration with Tamara, he didn't sleep with his employees. He didn't sleep with friends who remembered things about him he'd rather forget, either, he told himself sternly, firmly thickening his shields. Especially not when he'd just broken up with a woman because he didn't have time to spend with her—and when he had a secret daughter on the way. "Of course," he said briskly, stepping back and quite deliberately breaking the tension between them. "We've known each other for twenty years, Ida. There are things we'd both rather forget about our histories, so let's make an agreement. We'll let the past go, all right?"

Idara smiled. "Deal. You didn't answer my question," she reminded him, not quite flirtatiously.

"Which one?" Merran asked warily, pulling on years of training to maintain a neutral posture.

"What do you do for fun? If you don't tell me, I'll just have to come up with something on my own."

"Fine. I ski," he said curtly, already beginning to regret his somewhat impulsive decision to accept her offer.

"Hmmm, sounds promising. I haven't been skiing up north in the mountains around Nemorantxl in years, but I used to love it as a kid. Before my family decided it wasn't appropriate for me. I'm sure it won't take me long to get it back. How about this? We go up to the mountains and go skiing. Could you get away this weekend?"

Despite his misgivings, it sounded tempting. Maybe it was his recent sojourn with the skiers in the Rocky Mountains, maybe it was his own desire for company, but he shrugged and capitulated. "I've got some time free next Monday, if you don't have too many classes. I'll set it up and call you to confirm."

Idara's smile spread across her face and she looked delighted. "That works great. Mondays are pretty light for me; I only have an evening class that I could skip if we don't get back in time. I'm so glad," she said as she opened the door. "I'll talk to you later then."

Her mind brushed his as she left. *I know you're probably doing this because you feel sorry for me, but I do appreciate it,* she murmured in his mind. *I promise we'll have lots of fun. Even though you've known of me for twenty years, Mer, I think we haven't really known each other at all. I'm looking forward to getting to know who you really are.*

He acknowledged what she said and watched her leave, not sure if he'd done the right thing or not. Turning back to his desk, he tried not to think about Idara. Fortunately, his afternoon was such that he didn't have much trouble with that. After a long, agonizing conversation with the president, in which he discovered exactly what he wanted as a return favor for Justern, Merran didn't have much time to worry. The president's proposed deal would require some heavy arguments with not only the Council, but the Healer Conclave, too, since the president wanted more Healers on Earth.

That afternoon, Janille also fielded no less than fifteen requests for interviews—the media had most certainly discovered that he was back at work full-time. He hardly had a moment to think about anything at all, much less his impulsive date.

✳ ✳ ✳

Later that night, across town, Tamara leaned over to answer the phone ringing on the coffee table—or tried to. Although she still wasn't showing, she didn't like to bend over. "Could you get that?" she asked Alarin, stopping mid-motion as she made a grimacing face.

Alarin grinned at her, leaning over easily to grab the buzzing phone and handed it to her. He muted the television.

"Hello?" she asked, swiping the phone to accept the call, facing the camera.

"Tam?" It was Kari. "Are you watching *Celebrity Reviews Tonight*?"

Tamara shook her head. "No, we were watching a movie," she replied, settling back against Alarin as she spoke. He rested his arm over the back of the couch. "Why?"

"Turn on Channel 8. They're talking about Merran Corina. Call me after."

Alarin flipped the station, unmuting the sound as Tamara hung up the phone.

"Next on *Celebrity Reviews Tonight,* a segment about Merran Corina, that elusive bachelor. *Celebrity Reviews Tonight* recently discovered that he has just returned from a very hush-hush, private trip to the mountains of Colorado, posing as an unknown skier, not in the celebrity town of Aspen, where he usually spends his time skiing, but in another, much less known resort in the Rocky Mountains. Was he there for a secret tryst? Does he have a secret lover? Or was there another reason for the normally high-profile ambassador to hide himself away? Our reporter on-the-spot, Kaylee Carpenter, was able to catch up with one young man who spent time with the ambassador." The screen flashed to a tanned, very fit young blond man, a pair of skis slung over a shoulder and a knit cap on his head, anchored by his ski goggles. He stood near a very pretty reporter wearing the Hollywood version of ski chic, including a puffy pink down coat that set off beautifully her dusky skin and dark hair.

"Yeah, he skied with us quite a bit. Hated to come off the mountain, actually. First one on, last one off. Great skier. He liked the black diamond runs the best. Anything that tested his physical abilities. You mean, he's actually that alien ambassador from Azelle? I didn't think Azellians had that kind of stamina." The young man shook his head. "Man, you think you know someone. He said his name was Michel Caron and he was from Nova Scotia."

"Besides testing the limits of physical endurance, did he spend time with anyone in particular? A woman maybe?"

The young man frowned and shook his head. "Not that I know. He spent most of his time on the slopes. He certainly got quite a bit of attention from everyone because he was a great skiier, but he was kind of a loner, you know what I mean?"

The show switched back to the hostess. "Know what you mean? No, we really don't. A loner? That doesn't sound like our very popular media star." A series of old stories and pictures linking Merran to this starlet and that actress flashed across the screen. "But his unprecedented escape to the mountains does give rise to the question as to just what Merran Corina *was* doing in the mountains under the assumed name of Michel Caron and what might have driven him up there. Today, exclusive to *Celebrity Reviews Tonight*, we have a woman who claims to know the ambassador's secret heart. Janice Cooper is a woman who professes to have been the ambassador's confidante some years back. She will share with us what she knows about the ambassador." The hostess smiled her empty, bright white smile at the camera, then the program flashed to a dowdy older woman with long dark hair parted exactly down the middle.

Tamara looked at Alarin. "Janice Cooper? Who the hell is she to Merran?"

Alarin made a sound. "Probably no one important."

The phone buzzed again and Tamara jumped. "Hello?" she asked, turning on the camera feed.

"I have some good news for you," the subject of the television show said into the phone. He looked mostly relaxed, sitting behind his desk at home with his feet up on the desk, wearing a t-shirt Tamara knew as his favorite and a pair of boxer shorts barely visible above the line of the desk.

"Speak of the devil," Tamara commented dryly to Alarin.

"So, Mer, who is it?" Alarin asked, leaning into the camera range. "Mellis?"

"What?" Merran made a tent of his fingers. "Who is what? What are you talking about?"

"*Celebrity Reviews Tonight* has a whole segment dedicated to you and your escape to the mountains. They think you had a secret lover or were hiding out there for some other reason." Alarin grinned into the phone.

Merran said something in Azellian, which made Alarin grin wider.

"Hey, no fair speaking a dialect I don't know." Tamara shoved at Alarin.

"And you don't want to know besides." He pulled her close. "It wasn't very nice."

Merran made an inelegant sound with his lips. "Don't they have anything better to talk about?"

"Nope." Tamara gave him a cheerful smile. "The Nuvo Festival is done, celebrities are laying low, so the hype is all about you and your love life."

Merran rolled his eyes. "Human media. It's so ridiculous sometimes."

"Do you know someone named Janice Cooper?"

"Who?"

"Janice Cooper. Turn on Channel 8. She's telling the hostess that you and she were lovers at one point and you told her that you were coming off a very intense long-term relationship." Tamara studied the television. "You slept with her?"

Merran was silent as he flipped the station to match theirs. "Holy shit," he swore succinctly in English, then added something in that Azellian dialect Tamara didn't know.

Alarin laughed. "Apparently you did?"

Merran didn't quite flush, but he did run his hands through his hair in his typical nervous gesture. "I was … really young. Of course, I wasn't an ambassador then. I'd just arrived from Azelle and loved the high I could get from humans. I was not particular about whom I got that high from, either." He listened to the broadcast for a moment. "By the *aarya*, I did not have that level of relationship with her." He said something in Azellian, then added, "I spent one night with her and then moved on to the next one. She's making most of that up."

"Fame brushes by her and she wants a piece of it." Tamara slid down on the couch a little. "You are the closest she will ever come to her fifteen minutes of it."

Merran snorted and ran a hand through his hair again. "They are trying to dig up as much as they can about my love life again. I've heard enough," he muttered and turned off the television on his end. "They are being ridiculous, and the more left unsaid about this, the better I will be. Acknowledging any of this will give it importance it should not have." He sounded almost robotic as he spoke, and Tamara knew he was upset, although, as usual, he showed very little outwardly.

Tamara shifted to alleviate pressure on her body. She took pity on him and changed the subject. "What's your good news?"

Merran took a deep breath and visibly composed himself. "I called to tell you I managed to get you and the baby a visa to Azelle."

"You what? How did you manage that?" Alarin demanded, leaning over so he could see the phone too. "Who did you tell them was the father of the baby?"

Merran shrugged. "I didn't tell the Council anything, just re-submitted the visa request Tamara put through before."

Alarin frowned. "Then how did she get the visa? You had to have done something. What did you do?"

Merran twisted his neck as though he were trying to relieve pressure. "I registered her pregnancy with the Keepers at the Temple," he finally admitted. "There wasn't much the Council could say to reject her visa when the Keepers stepped in. They need both our signatures on the registry, and the Keepers are going to want to communicate with both Tamara and the baby."

Alarin shook his head. "How long do we have?"

"We'll have to wait for the winter storms to end. Then we have to get her there and back before she enters her third trimester. It really isn't good to take an expectant mother into space during the last trimester. It can trigger a premature birth."

For the first time in a while, Tamara saw tension creep back into Alarin, that same tension he'd had while struggling with having to share her with Merran. She put her hand on Alarin's arm. "We can go after the semester's over, right after finals, before we get to the third trimester. I have a feeling we're going to need Alarin there. We have to keep up the appearances, after all, and it would look strange to have me and you go without Alarin. It will give him the opportunity to tell his family about me too."

Alarin twitched. A strange expression crossed his face.

"What?"

"He hasn't told them yet," Merran guessed. "You should probably do that before we arrive, you know. It's going to create political waves at the very least and an uproar at the worst, Alari."

Alarin's nostrils flared, but he said nothing.

"Justy and my dad also think it will be a big deal, even though you don't think so, Alari," Tamara said, alarm spreading through her at Merran's confirmation that Alarin's news would be a problem. The baby was still too small for her to feel anything but the tiniest of flutters, but she responded to her mother's alarm anyway. The oddest mixture of panic and soothing warmth spread through Tamara. Tamara stared down at her stomach, more than a little spooked by the baby's efforts. Having her own emotions out of control was bad enough, but having another's spill through her was positively disturbing.

Alarin burst out laughing and the tension shattered.

Merran raised an eyebrow. "What's she doing?" he asked, guessing that it was the baby that changed things. "Tamara's got the weirdest expression on her face."

"Trying to control her world already. She's going to be a feisty little thing," Alarin replied, as he put his hand over Tamara's stomach and helped soothe the baby's ruffled feathers.

Tamara lifted her head after a moment. "She's trying to calm me down. We got sidetracked. Is this going to be a problem, Alari? You told me your father already knows."

"His father most emphatically hasn't told anyone," Merran replied for Alarin, who was still communing with the baby. "It's his mother, his grandfather Kendrick, and the rest of the Raderth clan who will have the problem with it."

"They'll be fine with it," Alarin said firmly, lifting his hand and leaning back against the couch again. "They have to be, because it's what's happening. If they don't like it, they can join the cavers."

Merran made a face. "I'd rather you didn't use that particular epithet, thank you very much."

"Sorry. The point, however, is the same. There is nothing that my mother and grandfather can do to stop me from marrying Tamara," Alarin said firmly.

"Even if Galadrian doesn't support you?"

"Even if." Alarin hugged Tamara against his shoulder. "I don't care what my family thinks, we're going to get married and raise this baby together."

Tamara rested a hand on her stomach, feeling it grumble under her hands. "You and I are going to talk about this more later, Alarin, but for now, I have a visa, and we'll go to Azelle as soon as we can. So, are we meeting you for dinner, Merran? We're hungry, this baby and me."

Merran nodded. "Yes. Absolutely."

"Then we'll meet you at your place in an hour." They said goodbye, and she hung up the phone. When she stood up, Alarin hugged her, letting her wrap her mind around his. She rested her head on his chest, as he pressed his lips into her hair. She relaxed into his embrace, and they stood like that for a few moments before the ringing phone pulled them apart. Alarin reached for it this time.

"It's Kari," he said, handing it to her.

Tamara pulled herself together enough to talk to her friend about meaningless stuff, including the earlier celebrity gossip show. Having a child was already changing her, she thought, after the conversation was over. She didn't care as much about things that were truly irrelevant, and sometimes Kari seemed to care too much about them. She had plenty to deal with juggling the loves of her life in the face of the new reality they were all going to be sharing than to worry about Merran's reputation with the media.

Chapter Nine

Between his impulsive date and the child that tried to ensnare him in her emotional life, Merran found himself feeling overwhelmed. What had possessed him to agree to a ski date with Idara? Besides their history, most of which involved Idara steadfastly ignoring him, she was Alarin's ex. That was bound to create more tensions, not less, between him and Alarin.

Although he'd changed his mind several times about going up to the mountains with her, when Idara met him at the embassy Monday morning to head out, he was relatively composed. He walked into the lobby area of the embassy before dawn and found Idara sitting on a bench in the corner of the lobby, decently shielded and calm. She wore a fashionable green ski suit, a pair of skis propped against the bench next to her. Her dark hair tumbled over one shoulder as she read something on her phone. She looked as well put together and stunning as she always did, and with his new awareness of her still lingering, it bothered him. His breath caught a little in his throat, aware as he hadn't been until recently of the potentials between them. *She is just a friend. Just a friend*, he told himself. The potentials were that and nothing more. Idara was Idara, after all, and he'd never been sexually interested in her. He wasn't going to start now.

Idara wasn't obviously scanning around herself, but she must have been, because she looked up and saw him approaching. Her face split into a wide, welcoming smile. "Hi," she said in Azellian. She caught his glance over at the skis propped against the bench. "My friend Jenna suggested I get a pair of skis down here because it's cheaper and easier," she said as greeting and explanation.

"She's right." He gave her the proper bow and greeted her, despite his misgivings, with a polite touch to her mind. "You ready?"

"Absolutely!" She returned the greeting as he picked up her skis, noticing that he wasn't carrying anything else. "You already packed the car?"

Merran shrugged as they walked toward the door. "Yes, just wanted to get a jump on it. We've got a long drive ahead." He slung her skis over a shoulder and made sure he didn't slam into anything on his way out the door.

"Definitely prepared." Idara smiled at him as she walked beside him.

"Always."

"No spontaneity?" Idara asked curiously as they reached the car and Merran slid the skis into the compartment built for that purpose. "That doesn't match the Merran of the past."

Merran didn't answer until they sat in the car and he started it up, heading for the one mountain town with the security for him to ski as himself—Aspen. "I'm surprised you knew that much about me." He glanced over at her as he pulled out of the back parking lot of the embassy and merged onto the surface streets to make the three-and-a-half-hour drive up to Aspen.

Idara laughed impishly. "I might have been distant, but that doesn't mean I didn't hear Mellis and Charina talk sometimes."

Merran raised an eyebrow. "Charina?"

"Why not Charina? As your niece, she was in the perfect position to know her uncle quite well. There may have been certain … types of spontaneous behavior you indulged in that she didn't get to witness, but there were most certainly others. Remember the time you and Alarin dared each other to a breath-holding contest?"

Merran coughed and rubbed his cheek. "It would have worked better if we hadn't tried it underwater."

"Or the time you built a rocket and tried to set it off? Let's see, we nearly blew up the cave we were in. I remember running as fast as I could to get out of there. I was almost forbidden to have anything to do with you after that. If it hadn't been for my mother's concern that I stay on the Raderths' good side …" She stopped abruptly and continued hastily, "Anyway, I was nearly grounded. My childhood was peppered with scoldings I got because of something you did. Of course, that was in between your other pursuits." Idara gave him a sly look out of the corner of her eye.

Merran didn't flush, but he most emphatically didn't look at her either. After leaving the Temple the first time, before coming back as an acolyte, he'd welcomed his adolescence with a vengeance, using his looks and charisma to get him quite a few willing partners, especially after he'd figured out how to act and speak in order to hide his *urro-ken* heritage. It was that spontaneity and interest in the opposite sex that had gotten him the reputation he still had here on Earth. It was an undeserved reputation now, and most certainly had been for the past year, even before Tamara had come into his life. Mostly.

"Mellis stopped being able to talk to Charina quite so much once the two of you started having sex. Chari cut her off when she got too graphic, so Mel and I used to talk quite a bit. What she liked the most about you was your spontaneity. You didn't care where or who or why. It was something I envied, actually. Alarin was never that ... free. Ever."

Merran lifted a hand. "Whoa, whoa, whoa. We don't need to go down that road right now." As true as it might have been, he wasn't going to discuss it with Idara. "I didn't realize you and Mellis had that close a relationship."

Idara shrugged. "It was one of those things that I didn't really advertise. Mother wouldn't have approved." She looked sheepish. "Mennak is High Council, but not quite high enough for her."

"How did your mother take to you coming to Earth?" he asked, hoping to shift her off his sex life and onto other subjects.

"Greg had already pushed all those buttons with her, so it was relatively easy. She thought I was chasing Alarin, so she didn't say much." Idara looked down at her hands. "Of course she doesn't know my true reasons for coming to Earth. *Everyone* thought it was because I was chasing Alarin. I wasn't, and I'm not." She twisted her hands in her lap and was silent for a moment, then said in a voice that had an unusual hint of shyness, "I used to go over to Mel's and watch Earth television shows, especially the ones about modeling and fashion. The Emmys, the Grammys, the Golden Globes, the Oscars, reality shows about the fashion industry, anything I could find ... I would really like to become a model. I've been researching it. It's not the easiest industry to get into, but I love clothes and fashion, and the chance to see myself on billboards and advertisements appeals to me too. I can see my-self doing that. The idea of mating an influential man on Azelle just doesn't have the appeal to me it once did. Since I've been here on Earth, I've gotten a taste these past few months of something totally different. Something I can do, myself, without someone to hide behind."

"So in setting her daughter free, your mother loses her alto-gether. I can't say I disapprove. High Council families' tendency to push their daughters and sons into subservient positions for gen-erations has never been to my taste. One of the reasons I pushed for the exchange program."

Idara widened her eyes at him. "I used to be jealous about your family. That your family didn't do what mine did around arranging marriages. I mean, you weren't forced into a relation-ship you didn't want. The Corina elect their leaders from within the family, not hand them down from oldest son to oldest son, so they don't care who marries who. Didn't your sister take the fam-ily leadership from your older brother?"

"She did," Merran agreed, then smoothly shifted the subject away from his older brother. Junian was not a topic he was going to discuss with Idara, newly converted to a more liberal attitude or not. "You are certainly beautiful enough to be a model. I might be able to get you some connections into the modeling industry. There are friends of friends who might be able to set you up. If we run into them in Aspen, I'll be sure to introduce you."

"You'd do that? Thank you! You really think I'm beautiful?"

Merran raised an eyebrow and glanced at her. "Insecurity? You?"

Idara flushed slightly. "Well, things have been different here on Earth. I haven't had any of the guys I know even approach me since I got here." She stared at her hands. "Alarin's so in love with Tamara, I don't think he even sees other women anymore. And you, well, you're different too. Not so interested in sex." She glanced up at him. "Or not in sex for its own sake. Who changed you?"

Merran choked again and gripped the steering wheel. Idara seemed to insist on bringing the conversation back to where he didn't want it to go. What was she doing? They were just friends. No sexual interest at all. Why did she care how he felt about sex anyway? "What do you mean?"

"I know you better than you think. You're ... softer. Less hard edges than you used to have when you were just out to claw your way up in the world. And I know that you didn't change until recently. So who was it?" Merran opened his mouth to protest, vehemently, but Idara interrupted, waving a hand. "You know what? It doesn't matter. I don't really have a right to know, and it's not that important to me." She glanced at him. "No, what I would like, if it's possible, is for you to teach me."

"Teach you what?" He could barely keep up with her mercurial subject shifts.

Idara leaned a little toward him, smiling up at him. "If I'm going to be a model, I need to learn a little more about other men than just Alarin. If you'll help teach me, I can use some of your ... glamour."

Merran blinked at her. "You want me to teach you how to be seductive?" He couldn't believe his ears.

"Something like that. I already understand fashion. Now I just need to understand how you manage to walk into a room and make all the women and half the men fall in love with you."

Merran shifted in his seat as he dodged through the traffic of other skiers heading up to the mountains. "For one thing, you exaggerate my powers. For another, just how am I supposed to teach you how to be seductive?"

"Have sex with me. I'll take what I need from your mind."

Merran stared at her for a moment, then returned his attention to the road. "Excuse me?"

Idara giggled. "Oh, come on, Merran. You have been away from Azelle way too long if an honest proposal throws you this far off balance."

"It's not the proposal. It's who it's from."

Idara shrugged and looked somewhat embarrassed. "Why?"

"I didn't think I'd ever see the day that Idara Tenricth asked me to have sex with her," Merran replied, still a bit dumbfounded. They'd played with the edges of possibility for the first time only recently, but he most emphatically didn't expect her to request an assignation this boldly, this fast. "To teach you how to be … sexy. I still can't quite wrap my mind around it. Is this the Idara who told me once, when she even deigned to talk to me, that she didn't understand how other women could fall for me over and over? There was never any sexual interest between us, Ida. Where is this proposal coming from and why me?"

"Are you interested?" she challenged, crossing her arms and lifting her chin. "Forget our past. Forget what I've said to you before. You're different, I'm different. We're different. I'm making the offer now. Are you interested?"

Merran shook his head. "I can't just forget our past, even if we both have changed." He rubbed his jaw.

"If we didn't have a past, would you be interested?"

Merran shifted in his seat uncomfortably. "Maybe. Maybe not. Oh hell, Ida, I've changed too. I'm not into having sex with a woman just because I can anymore. I have too many other ... responsibilities."

It was Idara's turn to stare at him open-mouthed. "The *aarya* damn me to the caves. You have changed. What about your reputation?"

Merran sighed. "As you can see, it's no longer deserved or even wanted. But I don't have much choice. I don't fight it because it keeps them from looking too hard at my life ... and there are definitely some parts of my life where I'd rather they not look. Misdirection, I believe they call it." He met her gaze steadily. "Your turn. Why me?"

Idara shrugged. "Because you won't laugh at me, or make fun of me. Because you're not interested in relationships, and you won't keep me from doing what I want to do when I want to do it. Because I trust you."

Merran managed to hide his shock, but it took some effort. "You trust me?" He kept his voice as neutral as possible.

Idara gave him a swift glance. "Of course. You never once threw in my face that I treated you terribly for so many years when I called you regularly to talk about Alarin and my relation-ship. You, as a matter of fact, started encouraging me right from the beginning to get my own career rather than try to ride on the coattails of Alarin's. You are, as much as you try to hide it, one of the most considerate, compassionate people I know. I think you would give your shirt off your back to help someone else if they asked. And I know that if we have sex, it will go as far as I want it to go and no further. You're safe."

Merran stared at her for a moment, then turned back to the road. "Damn, Ida."

She smiled and uncrossed her arms. "You asked."

"Yeah, but …" Merran trailed off, lifting his head and taking a deep breath. Silence fell between them for the rest of the trip up the mountain.

He didn't speak again until they pulled into Aspen and he headed for one of the more distant parking lots. "Are you ready?" he asked, looking off at the distance, deciding it was time to get moving and face the media crowd he could see gathered at the edge of the parking lot.

"Ready for what?"

"For the circus that's my life. You want to know what it takes to be a model? Well, come with me and I'll show you." He looked over at her. "It's lots of image. Don't be too surprised at anything I do or say. I haven't decided on whether or not I'm taking your whole offer, all right? I'll tell you outright when I do. Until then, it's all part of the game. No matter what I do."

A smile spread across her face. "You offering to teach me?"

"About certain things, yes," Merran replied, opening his car door. "As for the others, I haven't decided."

Idara rubbed her hands together. "That works for me," she said as he got out of the car and went to the back to pull out the skis. She opened her door and got out, slamming the car door shut as she looked pointedly at the four skis he held in place with his mind as much as muscle. "Showing off?"

Merran glanced over at her and smiled. "It's all about image. Brace yourself," he added, as they walked toward a crowd of people at the edge of the parking lot. *Keep your mind open. The crowd will tell you how to play it if you listen carefully enough.*

Idara acknowledged his mental comment, and he could sense her open up a little to pick up the thoughts of the reporters coming at them.

Merran stepped out of the yellow tape that blocked the parking lot from the more public areas of the ski resort. The nice thing about Aspen was the strict rules about where reporters were allowed to be versus where they weren't. Cameras flashed in his face as he and Idara stepped onto the public walkway and a big burly bodyguard-type appeared out of nowhere behind them. Aspen catered to the rich and famous by offering them guards as part of the package to go up there. It cost an arm and a leg, but it worked, and Merran sometimes preferred the relative anonymity of the guards they provided to bringing one from the embassy. Today, because he was with Idara and didn't want the whole embassy to start buzzing with rumors, he'd chosen to leave the embassy guards behind, although he hadn't expected this level of media to be up here. It looked like some major news channels were even here—so much for not spreading rumors.

"Ambassador," a dozen voices called, trying to catch his attention, each yelling a question they begged to be answered. "Ambassador, is this your new girlfriend? Ambassador, do you come skiing often? Ambassador, are you going to attend the wedding of your Azellian friend? Ambassador, is this your secret lover? Ambassador, did you have an affair with a college student and get her pregnant?"

Merran couldn't hide the shock that reverberated through him, and though he knew it would be better to let the questions go rather than stop and answer any of them at all, he halted so abruptly the bodyguard nearly ran into him. "Where did you hear that one, Alicia?" he asked, pinpointing the source of that last question. It was a jet-set-following reporter he knew fairly well, who had interviewed him more than once. He'd slept with her, too, more than once, although she'd gotten involved with her current husband and been the one to dump Merran (on Merran's active encouragement, actually, although she didn't know that).

Alicia met his eyes boldly. Smiling warmly, she sidled up to him, a petite woman with a much larger personality than her figure implied. "Oh, you know rumors. They spread so easily and can be so misleading. I thought I'd go to the source and ask directly."

Merran offered her a little bow. Her cameraman followed not far behind, the other reporters perking up intently to hear his answer. "Then you also know that there aren't many truths buried in rumors."

"Oh, there usually are," Alicia replied, the triumph in her voice obvious. "With a little digging, there are usually some truths to be found in all rumors."

Merran also knew her well enough to realize that she already knew most of what she wanted to ask. Trouble was, which part? If he confirmed the affair part, the other part would end up being considered true too. He knew better than this, and if he didn't handle it just right, he was going to blow everything he, Alarin, and Tamara were trying to do for the baby.

Idara stepped forward and slid her arm around Merran's waist. "Well," she said, adding a sultry lilt to her voice that Merran had never heard before, "the college student part is true, but I'm most certainly not pregnant, am I, Mer?" she asked in accented English, looking up at him with an adoration she'd never shown him before. Hell, she'd never shown Alarin that kind of look, either, at least not that Merran had ever witnessed. He wasn't entirely sure it was feigned, but she'd also just rescued him from the trap he'd walked right into, so he played along.

He lifted a hand to brush her long hair out of her face, imagining it was Tamara standing there, keeping that part of his mind well shielded from Idara. He'd never have been this open with his emotions with his real lover, but Idara—well, she wanted to play the game, so he might as well let her play it. He lowered his head and kissed her, putting quite a bit of mock passion into it. Idara responded enthusiastically. "No, sweetheart, you're not," he replied, pulling out of the kiss and lifting his head as the flashbulbs went off. "Unless you forgot to tell me?"

Idara laughed—and it even sounded genuine. She was a much better actress than he'd ever believed possible. "I always share the important stuff, you know that, love. I think that would be *very important.*"

From the shock on Alicia's face, they carried it off. "Who are you?" she demanded.

"Idara Tenricth," Idara said politely, offering her a little bow, disengaging enough from Merran to make it pretty. "Pleased to meet you."

"Where did you come from?" Alicia wasn't particularly polite about the question.

Merran cleared his throat and interrupted before Idara got too carried away. "Now, now, Alicia, play nice. Idara is an old friend from Azelle. She's been on Earth for a short time, studying at the university."

"And she's your lover?"

Merran looked over at Idara. She was too tall to fit underneath his arm, but she did help him present a strong front. "Would you say that you're my lover, dearest?"

Idara pouted, a cute little expression that looked odd on her elegant face, but she did make it look believable. He'd seen that expression before—she had used it on Alarin as often as she could when trying to manipulate him. "I hope so, love. Because I came all the way here for you."

Alicia was still highly suspicious, but her shock was making it easy for him to read her. She had heard a rumor all right, a rumor not from the embassy, but from campus. He chased down the rumor in her head, rummaging around in there very carefully, while she was still trying to figure out what to say. Much to his surprise, he knew the originator of the rumor—a young woman who'd approached him more than once for a job, offering to sleep with him to get it. He'd turned her down at least three times last semester during the embassy gatherings for the exchange students. Apparently, after the *Celebrity Reviews Tonight* airing, Kellie Darren had slyly implied that she was both pregnant and his lover. As badly as he'd have liked to have a few words with Kellie Darren about spreading rumors, it was better to let it go. The truth in it hit too close to home. Besides, now the media had something else to chew on, with Idara offering an alternate explanation he could now happily "prove" correct.

"And there you have it," he said, pulling Idara in tightly against him and kissing her again, very aware of the cameras pointed at them recording every moment. "Now if you'll excuse us, we have a date with some powder."

Snow had started falling softly again as they made their way to the slopes, celebrities of all types passing them, many stopping to say hi to Merran and quite a few others offering admiring comments to Idara. They played up the lovers part thoroughly enough that after dinner, during which Idara managed to charm the socks off three or four potential agents and photographers, they retreated to a single bedroom. Merran hadn't been intending to stay the night, but given that Idara had two interviews in the early afternoon the following day, he couldn't exactly run off and leave her behind, not if he was truly a lover trying to help her get her career off the ground.

As soon as the door closed behind them, though, Merran collapsed onto the stiff armchair the suite provided. Looking over at the couch that seemed a lot more comfortable, he announced, "I'll order a set of extra sheets and take the couch." He rested his head back and closed his eyes briefly.

"That will give the game away," she reminded him, stripping off the top three layers of clothes as she sank into the couch wearing little more than a camisole and a thong. He'd seen her in less on Azelle, but the sight of her sprawled on the couch in her underwear bothered him more than if she had stripped everything. "We can both sleep on the bed."

Merran gave her a disgruntled look. She grinned and spread her hands, blinking at him innocently. "What? I thought you said there was no sexual interest between us, and that bed is huge."

"I didn't know you were quite that good an actress. You played it wonderfully today. Why did you end up rescuing me?"

"Think about it. It could be useful to have someone who is willing to play as a smokescreen."

Merran frowned at her. "Smokescreen?"

"I'll play your lover, redirect the media, build my career, and get some of your publicity and glamour to rub off on me. So to speak." She gave him another heated look he didn't know she had in her.

Merran sat up. "How far is this ... smokescreen to spread?"

"As far as you like. You already know I'm willing," Idara said, sprawling a little more indolently on the couch and spreading her legs wide.

Merran got to his feet and, turning his back on her, paced to the window. He stared out at the dark slopes lit only by the lights that lined the lifts. "I thought you wanted to be taught how to seduce someone. Seems to me you know quite enough already."

"I haven't had the experience I need." He sensed her come up behind him. She didn't quite touch him, but stood close enough that their auras brushed. He could, far too vividly, imagine her naked, and he felt his body react. Maybe it was the pretending they'd done, but he was suddenly interested. Very interested, no matter what he'd told her earlier in the car. "You can give me that experience." Her fingers trailed through his aura as she brushed the thick sweater on his back.

Merran flipped the shutters closed and turned to face her. He lifted his hands to grab her wrists and push her back. The movement jiggled her body, and he realized she wasn't wearing a bra. Trying to control his reaction, he had to close his eyes briefly. No matter what his head said, his body was certainly willing enough. He was suddenly glad his shielding was as solid as it was and his sweater hung long on him, since his jeans were abruptly *very* tight. Why had he never noticed how attractive Idara Tenricth actually was? She was almost as tall as he was, athletic, and surprisingly buxom for an Azellian woman. Tamara and her generous curves had changed his taste in women, he realized as he acknowledged that he wanted to run his fingers over the silk of Idara's camisole and cup her breasts in his hands. "Ida," he said, feeling and sounding strangled, "this is not a good idea. Alarin and I are on touchy enough ground as it is. I don't know what he'd do if he knew …"

Idara laughed a light little tinkling sound. "We just played it up for the world, Merran. He already knows, believe me. How is this going to make things worse?"

Merran took a deep breath in and back out through his nose. He glared at her. "This way, I can tell him honestly that nothing happened, that we played it up for the cameras."

Idara pulled the camisole off in one smooth gesture. Merran closed his eyes again, suppressing a groan. "Why does it matter what Alarin thinks?" she asked, stepping up against him, rubbing herself against his sweater. She lifted his sweater and pressed her warm hand against his stomach, tugging gently on the hair that dusted his mid-section. "He will probably be thrilled to know that I've really moved on." Holding up his sweater, she lowered her mouth to nip lightly at his skin.

Merran shuddered at the touch of her lips against his abdomen. She glanced up at him, an expression on her face he'd never seen before, not even earlier that day. His empathic talent told him she wanted him, almost as badly as he wanted her, but it was the hint of mischief, of passion, that caught him. She kept her eyes locked with his, even as she carefully undid his jeans and shoved them and his underwear down off his hips. He closed his eyes and she moved down, teasing him, his body tightening pleasurably as she continued to actively arouse him.

He gave in, leaning down and pulling Idara up to kiss her ferociously, drawing her tightly against him, his mind shoving past her light shields to slide into that area of the brain that controls sexual desire. Idara made a sound at the back of her throat as he stimulated that area, sliding her hands to scratch across his bare skin. An involuntary groan crawled up his abdomen and into his throat. It had been a long time for him, and his body ached almost unbearably. He didn't count his impetuous one-night-stand when possessed by the Dorbin, and neither did his body.

He let Idara up for air only long enough to strip off his clothes. She watched him, her dark eyes wide in arousal. He could feel her as she watched him undress, her eyes dilated in desire. She reached out to brush her fingers across his erection, and it responded, sensations skittering through his body and up his spine as she slipped her mind around his, sliding into a link without much effort. He used the access she allowed him to trigger a cascading series of orgasms, using his empathic channeling talent to rebound the sensations of her own climax back at her until she collapsed to the ground, pulling him down with her.

He landed on top of her. If he hadn't been quite so sexually frustrated himself, he might have managed to avoid intercourse, but as intense as his participation in Tamara and Alarin's sexual encounters had been, he missed the sensation of being inside a woman, and the afternoon Tamara had conceived—months ago—had been the last time he'd allowed himself to fully participate in a sexual encounter. Idara was warm and welcoming, her body and mind wide open. He took her invitation and let himself sink into her body, starting up a hard and fast rhythm he hadn't let himself experience in a long time—certainly not with the very inexperienced Tamara. Idara matched him, meeting his rhythm with her own stimulation, using her psi to increase his arousal. He had only enough awareness outside of the spiraling pleasure to make sure his lower level shields were firmly in place—he could not have Idara wander his mind without barrier—then he let the pleasure spill up his entire body. When he came, it was explosive, as if he would scatter to the four winds.

Too relaxed to move once it was over, Idara stared up at him and smiled, a slow, sultry expression. "Damn. How did you do that?" She stretched, her body moving against his in a sensual dance that made him shiver. "That felt … amazing. I've never had anyone play inside my shields like that. Is it a Corina thing?" She shivered voluptuously and eyed him. "How long has it been since you've had decent sex anyway? You were … quite wound up."

Merran rolled off of her and sat up, pulling his knees close. "Little tricks you pick up along the way." He got to his feet and padded into the bedroom, slipping on one of the complimentary robes and bringing another one out for her.

Smiling, Idara took the robe he held out to her. She sat up and slipped it over her bare shoulders, her dark hair spilling over the white terrycloth fabric. "Those are some tricks." She climbed to her feet with his help, not bothering to tie the robe closed. "I told you I needed more experience. I didn't realize until just now how much more experience."

Merran didn't respond, walking on bare feet to the chair and dropping into it. His robe gapped, but he ignored it as he sank into the chair and crossed his arms over his chest.

"So tell me one thing. Two things actually. Do you want my help in misdirecting the media or not? And is that trick you did, playing inside my shields, a Corina thing, or can anyone do it?"

"No. It's available to any of us. You just have to know where to look to set it off. The only thing I can do differently as a Corina is project your own excitement back at you." Which he had done quite effectively. It had worked amazingly well, since surprisingly enough, Idara was quite passionate and very responsive. He wouldn't have expected that of her. As long as he'd known her, she'd been rather remote and somewhat cold—he'd never gotten the impression that she and Alarin were particularly passionate as a couple. Before their connection had stopped, he'd ridden enough of Tamara's lovemaking sessions with Alarin to know that lack of passion certainly wasn't Alarin's fault. After tonight, he realized it wasn't Idara's either. Even though there was nothing more than gentle caring between Idara and Merran, Idara was quite an enthusiastic and generous lover. "As for your other question, we can have a public relationship, but I do not want intimacy. I am not after a true lover."

Idara smiled. "Of course not. Neither am I, for that matter." She stretched her arms high above her head. Merran met her eyes steadily, not letting his gaze wander lower. "I'll drag the cover sheet out here and give you the comforter. I'll make do with the other sheet and the blanket." She disappeared into the bedroom area and came back moments later with the sheet and comforter.

"That works," Merran said, getting to his feet to spread the sheet on the couch. It wasn't going to be a comfortable night, but it beat sleeping with Idara. Surging through her shields and into her body the way he had disturbed him. It made him remember the parts of his relationship with Tamara he missed, sometimes keenly, and he didn't want anyone else getting as close as she had. "Goodnight," he called as she disappeared into the bedroom again.

"Goodnight," she replied, and he heard the bed squeak as she climbed into it. He sighed and tried to go to sleep himself. Sleep was long in coming, but he finally dropped off.

Merran jerked awake two hours later, his mind fully alert. What had woken him? He listened with his ears and heard nothing but silence. Casting out with his mind, he brushed across Idara's sleeping form, acknowledging her shields, which flared slightly at his touch, then moved on wider, deeper, higher, and lower, still searching.

He found something, the faintest whisper of awareness, deep in his soul, too fragile and faint to access without some effort. He sat up on the couch, arranging himself into a meditative posture and breathed himself into loosening the ties that shackled his awareness, plunging deep into the river of his consciousness, into that area from which all being sprang.

Warmth spilled through his body, spreading out from his lower abdomen to his toes, up through his chest and out his head, pouring from his arms and fingers, sending a delicious tingle through every part of him and stirring long stagnant energies. With an almost audible snap, he slipped past a sense of self, past a sense of having a physical body, into the soothing rush of being that washed him away, cleansed his stresses, and dumped him, energized and energetic, back into his own body. With the edge of his hearing, in the deepest reaches of the ether, the *aarya*Song gathered, swelling forward, and he could almost feel the anticipation of release, of spring, that was Azelle's Festival.

He jerked out of his meditation so fast it made him dizzy. "Shit," he swore succinctly. "Damn it, damn it, damn it! Ida!" he called, jumping off the couch. "Ida, get up!" He strode into the bedroom. "Ida, come on, wake up." Idara lay sprawled on her stomach, diagonal across the bed, the blanket wrapped around her waist and her long dark hair spread across her bare shoulders like a cloak. Merran felt himself react and sternly pushed the feelings away. Now was not the time. He couldn't afford to lose himself in Festival fervor. Not yet. They had to get back to the embassy.

"What's wrong?" Idara mumbled, lifting her head and blinking at the brightness of the light pouring in from behind him. "What happened?" She turned and sat up, paying no attention to her nudity.

"Festival. It's coming. The *aarya* are building the Song."

Idara stared at him. "They told us we would hear it on Earth, but I didn't believe them. We can really hear it that clearly?"

"As though we are on Azelle. Come on. Get up. We've got to race it back to the embassy. Even if I speed, it's going to take us most of the time we have left to get there."

"How do you know it's happening?"

Merran lowered his shields and let her read the call he'd just begun to sense.

Idara's eyes widened. She threw her long legs over the edge of the bed and stood up, reaching for her clothes. "They told us in orientation that humans don't know about it. How have we managed to keep it from them?"

"By making sure none of us are caught outside the embassy. They know we gather in the embassy once or twice a year. Azelle's year is shorter than Earth's, so it's usually more than once a year. But they don't know why we gather. If I'd known it was going to be tonight, I would not have taken us this far away from Denver." Merran turned on his heel and walked into the other room as his cell phone began to ring urgently, the tones of emergency shrilling through the room and interrupting him. "There it is." He picked up the phone. "How long do we have?"

Ketiana's voice was far more alert than he expected. "The Council just told me the *aarya* are giving us four hours to gather before they release the Song. I was on call tonight. How far away are you?"

"At this time of night? Three and a half hours, maybe less, if I speed. We're up and getting ourselves ready. We'll be there, Katie. Have you sent warning to the others in Denver?"

"They're starting to gather already. Actually, we had a few show up at the door half an hour ago. The guards let them in. It's cold here tonight, Mer. We're going to have to open up all the rooms to fit everyone."

"Do what you need to. We'll be there shortly. See you soon."

Understanding the urgency, Idara gathered her things

together quickly as Merran ran through the online checkout process, then followed Merran out of the hotel. They said little as he raced back to Denver as fast as he could without endangering anyone on the way. There wasn't much to say, except hope they made it back in time.

They did make it back, with only a few minutes to spare. Merran could already feel the *aarya*Song swelling and getting louder in his head as he pulled the car into the parking lot at the embassy. He was hyper aware of Idara sitting in the car next to him, the warmth of her body and the play of her aura next to his.

"Cutting it close," the guard on duty said as they got out of the car. "I'll close and lock the gates behind you, Ambassador."

"Thanks, Jerren," Merran said. "Are we the last two, then?"

Jerren nodded. "Yes."

"Then lock it down and get yourself back inside, too, before the *aarya*Song gets any louder than it already is," Merran said, noticing that the guard's eyes had gone distant, just as the swell of the beautiful, compelling Song tugged at him, too. A wash of energy spilled through Merran, starting up a familiar tingle in his groin and spreading through the entirety of his body, triggering each of his chakras as it went. He pulled himself out of the alluring melody, making sure the guard followed him as he ushered Idara into the building.

The door had hardly slammed behind them before Merran was reaching for Idara. Pulling her into his arms, Festival fervor swept over him, the pulsing melody making every cell in his body vibrate in tune with its sensual beat. Idara responded and kissed Merran, pulling him into an intimate embrace that caused him to shudder against her. As the spiraling ecstasy claimed him, he surrendered memory and awareness to the pulsating, flowing river that linked him to all living beings on Azelle.

Tamara woke hours later, disoriented and confused. A warm arm draped itself over her stomach, just under her breasts; a hard body pressed up against her back. Thick carpeting cushioned her backside, soft enough to be bearable, but scratchy enough that she wasn't totally comfortable. From the amount of skin contact, even with her eyes closed, she could tell she was naked, without any blankets covering her body. Because she didn't sleep naked very often and preferred big loose nightshirts, especially since being pregnant, her current state of undress set off alarms in her head, and her eyes popped open. Alarin lay beside her, sprawled out on his back, looking totally relaxed and completely naked too. Tension crept into her as her brain struggled to process the input it was receiving. If Alarin was lying in front of her, who was draped around her back? She shifted again and tried to see behind her. As she moved, she realized that maybe it hadn't been the best idea. The person who slept against her back stirred and pulled away as she moved her head, revealing that she, Alarin, and the unknown person behind her weren't the only three in the room. She recognized Rory and Damiar, and at least two more men and about four other women in the room, none of whom were any more dressed than she was. At least she recognized the outer portion of Merran's office where Janille usually worked. She scrambled to sit up, panic overcoming any thoughts of staying quiet.

"Shhh, it's all right," someone whispered in her ear, and she recognized Merran's voice. He slipped his arms around her, holding her still but not quite enwrapping her in a hug. It helped relax her, knowing that the man she'd woken up next to wasn't a stranger. Despite the fact they'd had their moments and were no longer officially lovers, Merran was still a friend. "Let's go into my office," he breathed into her ear. "I have clothes there."

Tamara got up carefully and stepped her way around the many still-comatose people, trying to fill in the oddly blank space in her memories as she went. She could conjure nothing but confused images—rather like her memories of Awakening, although there were no traces of pain. Instead of any recollections of discomfort, there was only the swelling, soaring Song, which soothed her even as she remembered it. She followed Merran into the office.

He closed the door quietly behind them and disappeared into the bathroom off his office area, coming out moments later with a dress shirt for her and wearing nothing but a pair of pants himself. His chest looked very much the way she remembered it—muscular and covered in a light dusting of dark hair. That hair had always felt silky against her chest and body, and she'd loved touching it, feeling the difference in texture between soft, warm skin over hard muscle and rough, silky hair. A vivid sensual memory abruptly spilled over her, a recollection of his body slipping against hers, of his warmth enclosing her, then the Song returned and washed away the memory.

"Where are my clothes?" she asked, blushing and looking away as he handed her the shirt. She slipped it on and buttoned up the front of it, careful to not look at him directly.

Merran shrugged. "Scattered." He went over to the couch and threw himself on it, resting his head against the back. Her eyes drifted to him, but she managed not to focus on his bare chest this time. "It usually takes a week or so after Festival to get all the clothes sorted out … if we manage to do it at all. Most of us show up wearing nothing but a trench coat. It adds an odd mystique but prevents too many clothes from getting lost."

"So that was Festival? Last night? The song in my head? The

fact I don't remember a damned thing? That's what everyone has been talking to me about for months? The grand, mysterious Festival that none of you would tell me the specifics about?"

Merran nodded. "Yes. Festival. The *aarya* call it *Kyarinal*, which means all that is possible becomes possible." he said, sounding like he was suddenly quoting Greg. "Throughout the night of Festival, everything is possible, and we explore the possibilities without any judgment or restriction. Most of us don't remember. Which sometimes is better." There was an edge to his voice that made her suddenly wonder what he remembered.

"Did we … uh … do anything?" she asked, looking down at herself and flushing.

Merran shrugged again and lifted his head, but it was his turn not to meet her eyes. "Maybe. Probably. I don't remember." Again that edge. What was he thinking? He was so shielded it was almost like he wasn't there.

"How many people did I … were there? Did I do it with everyone in the room? With everyone?" Tamara asked, feeling more than a little scandalized. The flush in her cheeks deepened.

Merran's dark eyes met hers. She could feel him, even through the thick shields between them. Reassurance spilled from him, reassurance mixed with a peculiar gentleness. "Don't worry about it, Tam. *Alawahea.* Just enjoy having shared the *aarya*Song and let it go. No one's going to remember anything about what happened, and it's not like any of us are going to pass judgment about it. We all go a little wild during Festival. It's part of what it's about."

"*Alawahea,* right." She hesitated. "But I woke up in your arms. Not Alarin's."

Merran lowered his gaze to the floor. "Yeah. I know."

"Is that normal?"

"It is when I'm the father of the child you're carrying," he answered. He gave her a faint smile. "Nothing's changed in any other way."

"What do women normally do after Festival to keep from getting pregnant?" She relaxed slightly. He was right. Nothing else had changed. Waking up in his arms was just a pleasant trip down memory lane. He was still who he was and she was still who she was—and she was still marrying Alarin in the summer. She could let it go.

"They have a couple of days after Festival to take care of things if they don't want to get pregnant," Merran replied, sounding distracted. "And if they do, well, Festival babies are treated differently from most children on Azelle. As you know, formal adoption doesn't normally exist on Azelle, since the extended family almost always takes a child in. Festival babies are the exception, because the father is unknown. They can be adopted by any family looking for a child, no matter who the father is." He looked away momentarily and then continued. "I can sense Alarin's waking up," he told her. "Go ahead out and I'll stay in here and start the cleanup process." He got to his bare feet and padded to his desk.

She obeyed him, even though she wasn't ready to face the roomful of naked people again. She paused at the door. "Merran."

"Hmmm?" he asked, looking up.

"Thank you for the shirt."

"You're welcome." A wealth of unspoken words stretched between them. Despite what she'd said to him about not remembering, she did have a flash of something, of the very familiar sensation of sliding into Merran's mind, sharing with him as though they'd never broken up. It was as hazy as a dream, but this morning there was a thread she could almost see, a thread that ran through her, the baby, and into him. Opening the door, she slipped out and closed it quietly behind her.

This time the sight of eight, no nine, other people—of which she only recognized three or four—hardly startled her, although she hastily turned her eyes away. They still slept in abandoned poses, totally relaxed and completely naked. Even as she made her way over to Alarin, stepping over sleeping bodies, she managed to ignore them.

Alarin stirred and moved as she sat next to him in a cross-legged pose. He opened his green eyes and looked up at her. "Morning," he murmured, stretching and sitting up. His mind wrapped sensuously around hers and she welcomed him, letting him in completely. His presence didn't precisely chase away the lingering touch of Merran's, but she had another flash of memory. She and Merran might have shared something during Festival night, but so had she and Alarin. She embraced the memory— this time she did have a stronger memory of Alarin's body against hers—and allowed the disturbing sensations from Merran to slip away. "Merran's?" he asked, reaching out and tugging on the shirt hem.

Tamara nodded. "Yes. I woke up early and was a little … disturbed. He's in the office."

Alarin glanced at the people sleeping on the floor. "Let's see if he's got something for me." He got up gracefully, slipping past the people who were beginning to stir on the floor.

Tamara followed him back into Merran's office. Merran was standing and leaning over his desk, this time with a half-buttoned shirt added to his attire. He looked over as they entered. "Morning," he said to Alarin. "Late morning anyway."

"What time is it?"

"Eleven." He glanced at Alarin, who dropped lithely onto the couch. "Did you want some clothes?"

"If you've got some. You two are dressed, so I'd like to be."

"The weather is not terribly conducive to wearing nothing anyway," Merran said, getting to his feet and heading for the bathroom again. "It's too damned cold, even though we turned up the heat as high as we could last night." He reappeared with a shirt and pants for Alarin and tossed them to the young man. "I hate winter Festivals."

"It wasn't bad for my first Festival on Earth. I don't miss the sand in my various body parts like we experience at home, but I do miss the sensation of being outside. Does Festival happen outside, ever?" Alarin asked as he slipped into the clothes. They didn't quite fit right, but they did cover the important parts.

"Sometimes, but with Denver's cooler evening temperatures, even in the summer, we usually end up inside. It's a little chilly to sleep naked in sixty-degree temperatures."

Alarin looked down at the floor. "I noticed when we got here last night that the floors were covered. You lay down carpets for everyone?"

"Would you want to sleep on marble and wood? One of the reasons we asked the Council to give us some warning, so we could prep the embassy."

Alarin studied him. "You were up in the mountains yesterday, weren't you?"

Merran didn't answer. Tamara came to sit on the couch by Alarin, ready to interfere should the redhead's temper get the better of him. She hadn't reacted quite the same to the news that the playboy ambassador had new eye candy on his arm, but Alarin had been rather upset—probably because it was Idara, *his* ex-girlfriend.

"We saw the newscast," Alarin's voice had a hint of anger in it.

Merran shrugged. "We played it up. It prevented the media from sniffing out Tamara."

"With Ida?"

Merran paused as he appraised Alarin. Tamara relaxed slightly. It was hard to be tense when one was so utterly relaxed—whatever had happened last night, it felt absolutely wonderful. The world felt fresh and clean and newly scrubbed. It seemed like Merran, at least, shared her feelings in that regard, because he didn't react to Alarin's irritation at all. "What's bothering you? That I was with Ida or that Ida was with me?" he asked matter-of-factly.

"I don't know," Alarin said flatly.

"Either way, Ida is using me as much as I'm using her. We both know it," Merran said unemotionally. "She wants to be a model. She thinks I can help her do that."

"Can you?" It was impossible to tell exactly what Alarin was feeling from his voice, but he *seemed* physically as relaxed as she and Merran were.

"Sure." Merran leaned back. "Last evening, she made all kinds of contacts. I run in the circles she needs to be in, and I can open doors that she can't open herself. Already, I have to reschedule two interviews this morning with modeling agencies that were supposed to take place today up in Aspen," he continued thoughtfully.

"It doesn't matter, Alari," Tamara interjected, placing her hand on his arm. "Neither of them concerns us, right?"

Alarin shook his head. "I just can't believe you and Idara ..." He trailed off and shrugged. "Whatever. All right, fine, it's your life, do what you want to do. Just remember that Ida tends to fall for people she can't have. She's very good at lying to herself."

Merran spread his hands. "If you've got a better idea, I'm

open to suggestions for how to prevent the media from finding out about Tamara. Ida and I can always have a huge breakup on the newscasts."

Alarin sighed. "I don't have any better suggestions." He shook his head. "I don't have any worse ones, either. I just hope you know what you're doing."

Merran snorted. "Well, I wouldn't go that far. But I'm trying." He got to his feet. "If you'll excuse me, I need to start the process of getting the embassy put back together." He offered them both a short bow and left the room. As he left, a certain tension spilled out with him. *We might have come a long way since the ending of our three-way relationship, but we still have quite a distance to go,* Tamara thought to herself.

She curled up next to Alarin, resting her head against his shoulder. "What now?"

"We go home as soon as we feel fully awake, then get showered and move on with our day," Alarin replied, slipping an arm around her. He rested his head against hers.

"Did Merran seem strange to you?" Tamara asked, after they'd cuddled for a few minutes, lightly linked.

"We are all a little odd the morning after a Festival," Alarin replied, sounding sleepy. "It has something to do with the energies the *aarya*Song releases in us. Hmmm," he said, pulling her closer. "I wouldn't give this up for all the power or fame in the world."

Alarin finally stirred after what felt like the entire day had passed, but was probably not more than an hour later. "We should give Merran his office back," he murmured as he nuzzled her neck. "I think he's managed to get most of the others awake and out."

Tamara shifted her legs into a more comfortable position and got up stiffly. "I'd like my clothes back," she said wistfully, adjusting the long shirt so it didn't ride up quite so high.

"Let's go find them," Alarin suggested, getting up and holding out a hand. "I don't know where we wandered last night, but it couldn't have been too far." Hand in hand, they went in search of their clothes.

They finally found most of Tamara's attire in one of the conference rooms downstairs, although she had no recollection of having been in there the previous night. Tamara got dressed as Alarin watched the door. She was still missing a few important pieces of her outfit, including her underwear, but at least she'd managed to get herself completely covered. Merran either avoided them or was too busy to talk to them again, because she didn't see him except from a distance during her hunt for her shoes. Had they shared their bodies during Festival? That thought was not one she pursued for long, though, because down that path lay far more disturbing memories—like how many people had been in the room when she'd woken up and the uneasy idea that she might have slept with more than just Merran and Alarin. By the time they left the embassy, she decided to let it go. It wouldn't lead anywhere for any of them. *Far better to let sleeping Azellians lie,* she thought to herself as she followed Alarin out of the embassy and back to their normal life.

Chapter Ten

Merran performed his duties mechanically, cleaning up after Festival without much enthusiasm, his mind still on the Festival he'd told Tamara he didn't remember. It was true, for the most part. He didn't remember most of it clearly—no one ever did, not if they'd truly given themselves up to the Song. He did remember melding with Tamara, however, the excuse of Festival allowing him to indulge the desires that had tormented him since they'd broken up. He did love her, and the brutal honesty of Festival, during which one's deepest desires are brought to the forefront and allowed expression, had ripped the pretense away. He didn't remember if there had been a physical release or not—it was almost irrelevant anyway—but there had most certainly been a mental communion, the likes of which he'd never felt before. Their daughter provided the bridge across which he'd poured himself into her. It had been very different from the connection they'd established at her Awakening, but not necessarily any less intense.

The added dimension of a child of his body—there was no longer any doubt in his mind that the baby was his—had heightened the strength of the connection to a point he wasn't sure he could walk away from if he wanted to. How much of it did Tamara remember? He didn't know and didn't want to ask, but there was something in her behavior toward him that told him she knew their connection had changed.

"Merran?" a voice interrupted his thoughts. "Are you all right?"

Merran jerked back into himself, taking note of Greg, who stood directly in front of him. "Hey, Greg," he said, trying to recall the past few moments. He'd been so far away he probably wouldn't have noticed if a marching band had stepped in his path.

"You're a thousand light years away," Greg commented, echoing his thoughts. "What's got you so distracted this afternoon?"

Merran glanced around to see his assistants and embassy employees helping to roll up carpets and clean up what was left from the Festival frenzy they'd experienced last night. "Not here. Let's go up to my office."

Greg followed him upstairs. "You were with Ida last night, weren't you?"

A vivid memory of Idara up against a wall, enthusiastically encouraging him, washed through him and he winced. "You saw that?"

"It was early enough in the evening that I think quite a few people saw that. Not that most people will remember it."

"I'm surprised you did. We cut it close enough that if it had been any later, Ida and I would have been caught outside in the cold. Literally."

"I fought it a bit. I was worried that you guys wouldn't make it. I'm surprised that you remember, though."

Merran shrugged as he opened the door to his office. "I always remember more about Festival than most people."

"I'd have expected, considering your training with the *aarya* and being an acolyte, that you would have less control, not more." Greg followed him into the office.

"I didn't say I had too much control, I just have good recall. Too good sometimes. I remember far too much of what happens during Festival. Enough so that it's a curse sometimes." Merran grabbed two waters from the fridge in his office, offering one to Greg.

The Healer took the water and twisted off the cap. "Have you seen Alari yet?"

"Yes. He was upset at my show with Ida yesterday." Merran sat down, sagging back into the chair. "Despite what you saw last night, Ida and I are not lovers," he said to Greg, pushing away the thought that technically they had been. "In case, as her brother, you were worried about it. She wants to be a model, and I am helping her get there. In exchange, she's helping me misdirect the media."

"I know. She told me about it this morning after we woke. It's not a bad idea, actually. It'll help keep them focused away from Tamara and the baby. But if you don't think you're lovers in the purely physical sense of the word, you're deluding yourself. Yes, last night was Festival, so it doesn't count, but she told me you had sex with her earlier in the evening, before Festival started."

Merran shrugged, unwilling to talk about Idara and particularly not with her brother, even if Greg had never been protective of his sister. Whether their relationship in private would go anywhere beyond that night and Festival, he did not want to dwell upon it.

"Just so you know, she now has this idea that you're some type of love guru. She was full of questions about you this morning and whether I knew you could do some of the things you did. I've never seen her so ... giggly."

Merran coughed. "I ... uh ... used what I had at hand."

"If I hadn't known you practically from Awakening, I would have thought you learned all those esoteric sex techniques rumors say the Temple teaches," Greg teased. He winked at Merran. "Pity you're so emphatically into women."

Merran glared at Greg. "Enough already. Don't you start."

Greg leaned back against the couch and eyed Merran clinically. "You know, for someone who claims he's not that interested in lovers and sex, you certainly attract them."

"Yeah, well, I don't mean to." It was hard not to let the exasperation show, so he didn't bother to hide it.

"Don't worry about Alarin." Greg shifted so his head rested on the couch as he put his hands on his stomach. "He'll get over the shock of seeing Ida with someone else. He'll probably even be happy it's you, because it will mean to him that you're not playing for Tamara anymore."

Merran winced and didn't try to hide it. Not from Greg.

"Did something happen between you and Tamara last night?" He sat up and peered at Merran intently.

"Yes. It's the reason I was so distracted downstairs," he admitted. "Read," he invited Greg, lowering his shields. "Tell me we didn't reignite the bond that we forged during her Awakening. Please."

He could feel the Healer shift into professional mode and slip into his mind. Greg was somber when he slipped back out again, all traces of his earlier humor gone, his expression thoughtful.

"What is it?"

"There's most definitely a connection there. It's not the same one, though. Tamara's a part of it, but it's not directly through her. You don't need to worry about that pesky little side effect of sharing each other's orgasms."

Merran relaxed abruptly. "Thank the *aarya*," he murmured.

"However, you now have something far worse to deal with."

Merran's eyes widened. "What?" he demanded.

Greg hesitated and Merran braced himself for something earth-shattering, then noticed the faintest of grins feathering the edge of Greg's mouth. "Infants." The grin exploded into reality. "Toddlers. Teenagers. The joys of parenthood, in some approximation." He gave Merran an arch look. "Oh, how the mighty have fallen. Imagine. Merran Corina as papa."

Merran glowered, but he was too relieved to be truly upset. He hadn't realized how much the bond between him, Tamara, and Alarin had bothered him. His sexual encounters with Idara last night had reminded him how much he enjoyed sex on his own and how much he didn't need to be sharing someone else's sex life. "I melded with Tamara during Festival," he said, ignoring Greg's teasing beyond favoring him with a frown. "I remember that very clearly, even if the rest of it is muddy. How did I manage to not re-trigger that damned bond with her?"

Greg shook his head. "Near as I can tell, the baby took the brunt of it. You used her as a bridge to Tamara, and she's inherited your family's channeling talent from you. It didn't hurt her and kept you and Tamara from reactivating the bond."

Merran let out a breath he didn't even realize he'd been holding. "Is every Festival going to be like that?"

Greg raised an eyebrow. "Like what?"

"So ... I don't know. Driven by my subconscious. I didn't mean to meld with Tamara. I didn't mean to be anywhere near her," Merran replied, hearing the note of forlorn misery in his voice and not mitigating it. "I had her and Alarin stay in my shielded office, partially to shield her from the worst of it, partially to keep myself away from her. It didn't seem to make any difference. We ended up in each other's arms anyway."

"I assume that's a rhetorical question. You know as well as I do what Festival's all about ... release of the blocks we place on our energies. As long as you fight yourself, and hide from your feelings, Festival will bring it to the forefront, and you will do things you don't consciously intend to do."

"What am I supposed to do? Chase Alarin off? Quit my life, my job? Drag her off into the sunset? Throw ourselves on the mercy of the universe?"

"That question is for you to answer. Festival just brings up everything. It's up to us to navigate how to release the blocks and free the stagnant energies."

Merran sighed. "Tamara loves Alarin more than me anyway."

"She trusts Alarin more than she trusts you," Greg corrected, his voice neutral. "However, just because you love her doesn't mean you have to marry her and raise your daughter with her. You're right, she does love Alarin and he loves her. But you can't deny yourself the ability to show you care too. However you choose to do that, you have to express your feelings for her to yourself and accept them within yourself, or you will find yourself out of control during Festival and doing things you'd rather not. Tamara's pregnant right now, but what about the next time? Do you want a Festival sibling for the baby? You know how these things go, and you two have already gotten pregnant once without meaning to."

Merran choked and closed his eyes. "No. No more kids. Not for me. I don't want to spend the next ten years hiding from Festival, but I'll do it if I have to." He opened his eyes and stared at Greg challengingly. "Anything other than what happened last night."

Greg studied him. "Why are you fighting so hard against admitting that you love her? Why can you not just enjoy it? Let it flow freely and Festival won't be a problem."

Merran eyed Greg. "Enjoy what? The fact that I'm supposedly in love with a woman I won't allow myself to have? Enjoy the fact that if I do something to have said woman, I know I'll screw it up and we'll end up hurting each other? To say nothing of the fact that I'd destroy my friendship with someone I've known since we were kids daring each other to reach for the stars?" He let some of his emotional rawness show, the reverberations still echoing through him from his intense melding with Tamara during Festival. "If it weren't for this baby, I wouldn't be dragging us through this hell in the first place. But now we're stuck and I'm supposed to enjoy it?"

Greg was momentarily silent. "You're not fighting your feelings for her because of Alarin; you're fighting because you see love as a weakness, as something to be avoided. You don't need to be consumed by her to love her, Mer. And you don't have to lose yourself in her in order to show her that you love her. At least admit to yourself that you love her and you won't have to act it out during Festival."

Merran waved a hand but didn't answer. He had enough awareness to know Greg was right, but he didn't want to talk about it any further. Greg sensed it and got to his feet. "I'm off, then, to let you get to work. Call me if you want to talk."

Merran nodded. "You know I will." He got to his feet and made his way to his desk. "See you tomorrow." Greg waved and left. Merran looked down at the stacks of paper on his desk. There was nothing better than work to distract him from things he'd rather not deal with, so he let himself get sucked into the tasks waiting for his attention rather than think any further about Festival and his feelings for Tamara.

✹ ✹ ✹

Tamara flatly refused to continue to probe her memories of what had happened during Festival, and life settled more or less into a calm routine of classes and finals, as her baby grew and she and Alarin planned their wedding and the trip to Azelle. Two months after Festival, just after Tamara finished up with her last final, Alarin stuck his head around the door into the bedroom. "Almost ready to go?"

Tamara stared at the suitcase on the bed. "Why are we doing this?" The stress of finals had passed, and while she was glad to be done with school for another school year, she was not that excited about facing the tensions she feared waited for them on Azelle.

"Do you not want to go to Azelle?"

Tamara sighed. "I want to go. I know that now is going to be the easiest it's ever going to be, because we will have a child to take care of shortly, which is going to change our lives forever. And I won't be able to go if I get too much more pregnant. I mean, *when* I get too much more pregnant, although how anyone can be more pregnant—"

Alarin interrupted her with a kiss on the mouth. It wasn't so much passionate as gentle, and it cut off her flood of words. "We're going to Azelle because it *is* the best time to go. Finals are over,

Merran is scheduled to go back anyway, you and I are both done with school for the year, and you are not too pregnant to take the trip. So we're going. And Justern will be meeting us at the port."

Tamara smiled a little at the thought of her half-brother. After so long, it would be good to get to see him again in person. They'd developed a strong relationship these past months, talking on the phone regularly, but it wasn't the same.

"We also have to see what arrangements can be made for people to come to the wedding," Alarin continued cheerfully. Tamara glanced at him warily. They'd set the date for the end of July, although she'd be just about ready to explode by then.

"Have you told your family yet?"

Alarin shrugged. "Not in so many words." His expression hardened. "It will be fine, Tam. It's not like there's much they can do about it. I'm an adult and can make my own decisions."

Tamara quenched the quiver of misgiving. *It will be all right. It will.* She took a deep breath as Alarin grabbed both suitcases and they headed down to where the nondescript embassy sedan waited to take them to the airport. Tamara would have used a taxi service or even the bus, but Merran had arranged it, and she didn't argue.

The short hop from the airport to the interstellar ship in orbit around the planet was uncomfortable enough, turbulent and rough until they left the atmosphere behind, but the trip on the starship through the wormhole to Azelle was even more unpleasant than she'd expected. Five days in cramped quarters was overwhelming. Although the ship had plenty of space to wander, gyms and swimming pools to exercise and play in, movie theaters to distract, and one of the most amazing libraries she'd ever seen, two people in one tiny cabin and shower was way too much.

The baby set up a vociferous racket, broadcasting her discomfort loudly enough that it took Merran, Alarin, and herself to shield the fetus. When they finally arrived, Tamara was relieved to get off the ship and into the shuttle that would take them from the space vehicle to the surface of the planet.

The shuttle touched down on the surface of the planet with a bump, jerking Tamara in her seat as the pilot put on the brakes, making her grab for Alarin's hand. He squeezed it reassuringly as the shuttle slowed and rolled its way across a bumpy surface toward a set of low buildings Tamara could just see out of the tiny portholes that served as windows on the shuttle.

The flight attendant came on, welcoming them to Azelle in both English and Azellian, then they waited again as the big doors were opened and the stairs lowered to the surface. Tamara got to her feet, the anticipation of stepping onto a new planet for the first time in her life making butterflies flutter in her stomach. As she stepped onto the stairway that led downstairs—no jetways for Azelle, apparently—heading down toward the ground, she took a deep breath, feeling the hot, dry air sear her nostrils as she gripped the metal railing. The oxygen level on Azelle was slightly higher than Earth's levels, the gravity a bit lower, so a peculiar sense of euphoria and lightness filled her as she nearly bounded down the stairs. The ship had adjusted its gravity and oxygen content gradually to help acclimatize the passengers, so it wasn't as much of a shock as it might have been otherwise. Thankfully, one positive result was that she felt much less ungainly in pregnancy than she had on Earth. As she stepped onto the packed red sand of the desert, though, all thoughts of heat and weightlessness disappeared. A throbbing vibration pulsed through her legs, a warmth that spread through her entire body and spilled out her fingertips. She shuddered and rubbed her fingers together. "What is that?" she murmured to herself, not expecting Alarin or Merran to hear her.

Merran glanced at her, his eyes distant. "The heartbeat of the planet. You can hear it?"

Alarin seemed to notice nothing different, or if he did, it wasn't affecting him the way it was affecting Merran and her. He was talking animatedly with someone behind them from the shuttle. No one else seemed to be as affected as they were.

"It's incredible," she whispered. She had to force herself to walk through an odd sensation that wasn't quite dizziness. It might have been the lower gravity or her pregnancy affecting her sense of balance. "Can Alarin hear it?"

Merran shrugged. "Probably, but it usually only knocks us empaths for a loop. Other psi sensitives are not quite as affected. If you think it's strong for us, it knocks some Healers off their feet, sometimes quite literally."

Tamara pressed her fingers against her forehead. "Wow," was all she could say.

He touched warm fingers to the back of her hand. His hand was hot, almost feverish, a sensation that she'd never felt from him before. The throb eased back a little, and she caught the faint sounds of the *aarya*Song that had taken her during Festival. She had another very sensual flash of memory, of those hot fingers sliding across her thigh and guiding another, equally hot part of his body into her. For a moment, it was as though she were there again, his body in hers, pulsing to the beat of the Song, the beat that echoed the throb against her feet right now. It made all the energy in her body wake up, abruptly and suddenly, and she felt her body react to the memory far more intensely than was appropriate for the moment. She jerked away from his hand, feeling her face flame.

Merran did not look at her, but she knew he'd picked up on something—her memory or the flash of emotion that had come with it. He didn't show any response to it, but she sensed that underneath the shields he maintained at all times, he felt it. From the connection that suddenly pulsed between them, she wondered if he shared the memory or just her reaction to it.

Quite deliberately, she turned to Alarin. As though to remind her that Merran was not the only man in her life, she was rewarded with another sensual memory, of Alarin's mouth and hands on her body, his tongue burning across her sensitized skin. She hastily shut down any further memories. God knew she did not want to remember anything more. She was done remembering what Festival had brought out in her, although to be honest, both memories might not have even been related to Festival. She'd most certainly been both Alarin's and Merran's lover and felt their bodies in hers more than once.

They moved with the two hundred or so passengers from the shuttle, into the one long low building that looked more like a growth from the ground itself than a building. If it weren't for the Song that teased the edge of her hearing, the warmth that pulsed up through her body, the awareness that she felt so alive and alert that her skin might crawl right off her bones, it would have seemed an ugly, uninteresting planet. However, to psi, Azelle was alive in a way Earth was not. She could hear the mental buzzing that meant other psi lived here, a faint whisper on levels she'd never heard on Earth. The animals spoke on that level, a chatter not unlike the birds on Earth during the spring and summer, although these animal sounds were not audible with her ears. The living beings on the planet welcomed her, inviting her to visit with them, to learn from them, and she found herself listening.

The interior of the building was cool, much more comfortable than outside. Signs and people standing quietly separated her from Merran and Alarin, guiding her toward another part of the building that processed humans instead of returning Azellians. From there, she went through a customs process, not unlike what she would experience on Earth, but the Song whispering in her ear and tugging at her awareness made her feel disassociated, as if none of what she was experiencing was quite real.

As she came out of the baggage claim area, rolling her suitcase behind her, Justern threw himself at her, pulling her into a warm, full-body hug and jerking her out of that absorption with the planet. "The *aarya* save me, I couldn't believe it when Merran called to tell me he'd managed to get you a visa," he said, emotion making his accent stronger than normal. "It's so good to see you, sis!"

Tamara returned the hug. "They didn't have much choice," she said as a grin spread across her face. "The baby is three-quarters Azellian and very definitely psi," she added, disengaging and resting her hand on her belly. "She needs to be registered with the Keepers, apparently."

"And the *aarya* are going to want to know her," Merran interjected, as he came up behind them. "Hey, Justy."

Justern gave Merran a hug, too, greeting him warmly. Alarin joined them, and for the first time, Tamara got to see the old bonds of friendship between the three of them. They started chattering in Azellian, speaking an odd mixture of the school Azellian she'd learned and a dialect she'd never heard before—probably slang. She could only pick up half the conversation, which seemed to revolve around old friendships. A portion of it was mental, too, and not meant for her to hear, until Alarin turned away from the group and slid his arm around Tamara in the familiar way he'd started doing since her pregnancy.

"Come on, let's get settled. Your sister Alerra and her husband Kennan agreed to take us in?" he asked Merran. "All three of us?"

"Yes," Merran replied, a careful tone to his voice. "It's easier than opening up my house for a few days, and will undoubtedly be more comfortable since I don't have much in the way of furniture. That is assuming you're allowed to join us."

An expression flashed across Alarin's face. His arm tensed around her shoulders. "There's no question of that. I told you, I don't care what my family says about my relationship. I'm staying with Tamara."

"Let me take Tam to Alerra's to settle in," Merran said, his tone absolutely neutral. "If you stop by to visit your family now, alone, you'll prevent a whole host of problems later."

Alarin didn't want to go. Tamara knew and could feel it in the tightness of his grip around her shoulders. She slipped a tendril through his shields to curl around his mind. Merran was right, she read in his mind, although Alarin didn't want it to be true. She sent him a strong reassurance, and he relaxed slightly. "I won't be able to get away from them quickly."

"Tamara and I need to go over to the Temple as soon as she has freshened up, or we're not going to get to do it at all," Merran replied, his tone sounding even more neutral, if that were possible, than it had been a moment before. A flash of jealousy flittered across Alarin's face. "I've got to head back at the end of the week and I've got meetings for the next five days solid. Today is going to be the only time we have to do this. You'll have Tamara to yourself after we finish up at the Temple."

Alarin nodded. "Fine. I'll see you tonight," he said to Tamara, leaning in to kiss her. Tamara watched him leave, suddenly feeling uncomfortable.

"How badly is his family going to react?" she asked Justern.

"Depends on how Galadrian chooses to act," Merran answered her instead, as they watched Alarin stride away. "If he steps in and says something, none of them will do anything. If he doesn't ..."

Justern took her suitcase from her, pushing in the handle and letting it float along the floor just behind them as they walked into the tunnels that led to the main cave. "If he doesn't, then Alarin has some choices to make. I wouldn't worry too much about how it's going to go, Tam. Alari went to Earth against their wishes. He's not going to let a little thing like family preferences stop him from marrying you."

"Well, thanks," Tamara said dryly.

Merran glanced over at her. "*Alawahea*, Tamara," he said softly.

"Yeah, right," she said, not quite believing it.

"You live on Earth, Tam. You won't even notice." Justern's effort to calm her worked better than Merran's did, and Tamara was able to relax enough to pay attention to their surroundings.

As the tunnel opened out, Tamara stopped and stared. Dappled sunlight, filtered by the high, arching crystal ceiling overhead, filled the interior of the cavern with light. Spread out in front of her was an enormous open area, covered by a soft moss-like substance that cushioned the hard stone. The sounds of life were muted by the huge soaring expanse above them, so large that it absorbed rather than reflected sound. Although it was a city underground, the city felt *alive*. It *was* a city, complete with a centralized, marketplace bazaar and people walking everywhere. The metropolis was filled with sunlight, pulsating as if it were breathing. It was breathtaking and beautiful—a city of light.

Merran's sister's house was not far away from the entrance to the tunnel. Up a short flight of stairs, into a cave set in the wall of the enormous cavern, Alerra and Kennan's joyous welcome helped soothe Tamara's nerves. Merran's niece, Charina, a sweet girl around Tamara's age, traded jokes and friendly insults with Justern, treating him like a sibling. Merran joked with them, too, treating Charina very much like a younger sister, but Tamara could see that he was playing a role, in the same way he always did on Earth. Underneath that role, he was not at all lighthearted.

Merran let Tamara take time to get a drink, change her clothes, and wash her face, then he urged her out of the house and down the steps, toward the big bazaar. On the other side of the busy marketplace, a huge stone building stretched up to the ceiling, its angled side revealing a pyramid shape. It disappeared into the ceiling and stopped, the top part of the pyramid truncated.

"Is that the Temple?" she asked him, motioning with her head, trying not to look like a gawking tourist, but knowing she'd failed.

"Yes."

"Where does it go?"

"It continues above the surface," Merran said, sounding distracted.

"Merran?" she asked, wanting to take his hand for comfort, but not entirely daring to. This was his planet, his hometown, and he was known here. Would he want to advertise their former relationship? She didn't know and it made her wary.

"Yes?"

"What's going to happen?"

"When?"

"At the Temple. When we go in." He hadn't talked to her about it, and she hadn't thought about asking Alarin in the midst of the uncomfortable space ride through the wormhole between Azelle and Earth.

"What do you mean, 'What will happen?' We'll go in, talk to the Keepers, and register the baby with them."

"Even though she's not born yet? And I don't have a name for her?"

"Yes," he said. "She will be Azellian, so she needs to know the touch of the *aarya*, just like all of us who are born Azellian." He glanced over at her as they made their way through the fair, weaving in and out of people, past stalls set up with crafts and food. It looked like an ordinary Earth market, which surprised her. Except for the robes, the cave, and the alien language, it could have been a farmer's market in Denver. "We may end up in a dream state. Don't be surprised at anything you see or hear. It may look or feel like a dream, or it may look or feel very real. The *aarya* are certainly real, but they communicate with us the way we are the most comfortable, so you may or may not realize you're speaking with one. It's not unlike Festival in that you will be faced with your own subconscious. You may or may not remember what happens."

He was nervous. She could hear it in his voice. That, more than anything, made her nervous, too. Merran? Absolutely calm, unflappable Merran was nervous?

"Is it dangerous?" she asked.

He looked at her more closely as they came to a beautiful, calm garden that soothed her nerves. "Dangerous? No. But you can't be anything but utterly honest at the Temple," he said. "And sometimes that's more frightening than anything else."

On that note, the doors silently swung open. Tamara gasped. Warm, humid air and dappled sunlight spilled out of the interior of the pyramid, filtered by one of the thickest forests she'd ever seen. Was this underground? Energy—life—spilled out from the open door, welcoming them to come in, inviting them to step into the interior of this odd place.

Tamara stepped across the threshold and felt the most indescribably wonderful sense of peace spill over her. The ache that followed the release of tension, tension she didn't even know she was holding, was almost orgasmic, and it made her eyes fill with tears. Those tears spilled over to slip silently down her cheeks. Something about the peace in here, the feeling of release, dissolved her shields, but she didn't feel at all threatened. In this state of calm, shielding didn't matter, because nothing could hurt her. There was no need for hiding, no need for protection in this place. She turned to Merran.

He had an odd look on his face, almost panicked, as if he would hyperventilate. His shields, unlike hers, were not gone, but they looked tattered. His aura pulsed fitfully, throwing off amber darts of light against the foliage beside him.

"Welcome home," a voice said, but it wasn't a physical voice. It echoed in Tamara's head, yet didn't sound like mental speech either. It spoke not in Azellian or English, but in a form of communication that was at once all languages and none. "Why do you fight?"

Tamara stared. Walking toward them was an ordinary human being. At least it looked like a human being. But to her psi, the aura that surrounded this being was intense, far brighter than anyone she'd ever seen before, and the shape of the mind was most emphatically not human. Nor were the gentle, flowing thoughts anything human. A distant sense of wonder pricked at her. It took her a moment to realize the being was completely naked. There was no room in this beautiful place to wonder about that, and she found herself noting it and moving on.

Merran choked. Tamara glanced over to see him stop and shudder violently. "I can't lose my shielding."

The shining being came up to him. The woman's head was taller than his, which made the being far larger than she had first appeared in the midst of the forest. She lifted a hand gently, tenderly, and placed it on Merran's cheek, stroking his skin lightly. There was silence, and Merran collapsed, sobbing. Tamara's heart wrenched at the sounds coming from him, but she didn't dare move.

The being turned to her. "Welcome to Azelle, *umanaarya* daughter. Welcome to your unborn, as well. Come," she continued, apparently ignoring Merran. "We will take you to others of your kind. You will join us."

"What about him?" she asked, motioning to Merran.

"He will join us when he is ready for the joining," the being said cryptically. "Come."

She followed the woman, uncertain, but also feeling calm and safe. Nothing harmful could happen here—she could feel that. The being led her through the thick trees to a spot near a rushing river. It thundered through the space, spilling out of a hole in the distant wall to her left, going who knows where. Tamara thought it would be the most magnificent waterfall if the wall opened into a cliff face.

"It does and is," a voice said softly, in English, surprisingly enough. Tamara looked up to see a different woman come toward her. She was dressed in formal Azellian robes, her hands tucked into her sleeves. A turban was wrapped around her head, and her olive skin was tanned dark, darker than most of the other

Azellians she'd ever seen—maybe it was just the contrast between the woman's bronze skin and the pale color of her robe. The robe shimmered in the muted light. "The underground river feeds and supports the oasis and all the animals that live on the surface. It feeds and supports those of us who shelter underground." She smiled. "I am known as Darra. I am a Keeper, one of those who hold the histories and speak for the *aarya*. Come, join us for refreshments."

Tamara made her way to a group of people sitting in a semicircle around a table. There were no chairs, just thick cushions on the floor.

"Where's Merran?" Tamara asked, looking around, jerking herself out of her thoughts, as the feeling of worry nudged at her, even despite the soothing aura in this room.

"Merran will join us when he is ready," Darra replied quietly. "Please, sit."

"What's wrong with him? Is he all right?"

Darra shook her head. "He is fine. As for what is wrong, if anything, you may ask that of him when he joins us. It is for him to decide if he wishes to share."

The answer wasn't really an answer, but it did tell her what she needed to know, and she decided to accept it and let her concern go. She moved to an empty spot by the table and picked up a piece of fruit with her fingers. No one said anything as she ate, and Tamara found herself slipping into a meditative state quite unlike any she'd ever known. She closed her eyes.

The *aarya* greeted them at the door to the Temple, something the *aarya* very rarely did. To Merran's acolyte vision, the *aarya* was

little more than a shimmer in the edge of his vision. "Welcome home," the voice said, warmth coiling in his stomach and spreading through his limbs. Merran shored up his shields, knowing even as he did, that the effort was wasted. It was possible to maintain shields in the Temple, but not in the presence of the *aarya*, which was probably why one had greeted them at the door—to prevent him from hiding himself. "Why do you fight, acolyte?"

"I can't lose my shielding," he said, his voice a croak. *Not in front of Tamara.*

The *aarya* coalesced into a body, taking on the shape of a woman. She came closer to Merran, reaching out to brush odd-feeling fingers across his cheek. *Be at peace, child,* she said to his mind only. *She will remember nothing of this. Let go of your pain, let the healing flow through you. Surrender yourself and you will be set free.*

The words caused a cascade of reaction in Merran, and all the pain he'd suppressed during these past several months, all the pain of his childhood, the isolation and fear, the child he'd created with a woman he loved, all of it came boiling up, and he fell to his knees weeping. He abandoned himself to it, sobbing all the pain, the fear and anger roaring out of him in a flood of sounds.

The *aarya* sat on the ground beside him as the storm subsided and Merran was left gasping and panting. It—she, this one had chosen to appear to him as a she, although the *aarya* had no fixed gender—sat beside him, saying nothing.

"I have a child," he said, his voice hoarse. "I love her. Already. She's not even born yet and I love her so much it scares me." He looked down at his hands. "I don't know ..." he said softly. "How ... how will I show her? How do I show her mother that I love her? You teach that love expresses itself organically and genuinely when we love ourselves. How do I love myself enough to cover everything that's happened?"

The *aarya* said nothing, sitting quietly by him.

"I spent a large chunk of *Kyarinal* in her mother's arms," he said, after a few moments. "We are now bound by the child we have brought into being. I want to be able to show her that I love her. I want to show her mother that I love her too, but I don't want to lose my friendship with our friend. How can all of this be?" He felt incoherent, but somehow he knew that he was asking for something and the message had been received.

The *aarya* looked at him through large, luminous eyes that weren't any more real than the body it projected. Despite that, Merran could sense the force of the being behind those eyes. He could feel a sense of vast immensity, of awareness so far beyond his that it was utterly incomprehensible to a large portion of his thinking mind. He took a deep breath, letting it out slowly.

As he breathed, the *aarya* spoke, its—her—voice vibrating along his skin and deep into his bones. "You have asked. Are you willing to receive what you have asked for?"

"Yes. I am ready." He closed his eyes.

When he opened them, he was in a small room, lying prone on a cot. Tamara, looking much the same as she had when he'd first met her, no longer pregnant, hovered in the doorway of the room. Here, in this room that was only in his mind, she was naked. He sat up, feeling his body stir at the sight of her. "Hi," he said to her.

"Hi," she replied shyly.

Merran got to his feet. "Come in," he said softly, reaching out to her. She hesitated, but took his hands and stepped over the threshold into the room. As she entered the room, he tugged on her gently, pulling her into his arms. She came to him easily, effortlessly. As she fit into his embrace, her warm body against his, her head against his bare chest, he could feel all the sensations from Festival come rushing back, and he abruptly knew what he needed to do. "I love you, Tamara," he said to her as he hugged her against him, here in this place that was not real. "I love you and our daughter. I love you both so much I can't even begin to express how much." As he said the words, he felt a rush of energy pulse through his body. Abruptly, the image in his arms shifted and changed and became himself as an aggressive, wild child on the streets of the outer caves, the space the *urro-ken* called Azorunt: the place abandoned by beauty. Except it wasn't abandoned by beauty, at least not entirely. There were the *urro*, and the *urro-ken*, and there he was, luminous and beautiful. The little boy, his hair tousled and eyes wary, wriggled free and stared up at him.

"Why did you abandon me?" the boy asked. "I needed you and you left me. I was alone. Without anyone to love me and accept me for who I really am."

"I'm sorry," Merran said softly to his younger self. He'd never questioned that his mother loved him, but yet somehow, in this space, it wasn't his mother's love that was missing. It was his acceptance of himself, of the child he had been, represented by this wary little boy. "I'm so sorry. I'm here now."

The boy stared up at him silently, without words, measuring the truth in what he said. "Will you do it again?"

Merran shook his head. "I love you," he whispered. "I love you."

The boy shifted and became a young, dark-haired girl who bore his eyes and Tamara's smile. "Daddy," she said, and Merran gasped. "It's me, Rashella. Don't you know me?"

"Rashella," he whispered, extending his hands. "Hello, my beautiful, beautiful baby girl."

She stepped into his arms and said, "Daddy, I love you. I forgive you. Will you love me?"

Merran crushed her against his chest, holding her tightly against him as he stroked a hand through her hair. "I love you, my sweet girl. Never doubt that. I love you beyond space and time and into infinity."

Rashella flickered and became the little boy again. "I love you. I forgive you. Will you love me?"

"I love you," Merran told his younger self. "More than you'll ever know."

The image of both his daughter and his younger self dissolved and Merran found himself facing the *aarya* again, the same one who had greeted him. "You are welcome, child of the *umanaarya*. Welcome home."

With tears in his eyes, Merran came back to his body and found himself sitting at a table. A Keeper, wearing robes and a turban, was seated beside him. "Welcome," she said, echoing the greeting the *aarya* had used. "You were told the name of your child, then?"

Merran nodded. "She told me she is to be known as Rashella."

"Rashella Carrington Corina. It is a beautiful name. Her mother joins us soon. Please, take some refreshment."

Merran reached out for a piece of fruit, the taste of it exploding across his taste buds in an eruption of ecstasy. He smiled and nibbled on the fruit, willing himself to wait patiently for as long as he had to. Peace filled his heart and he smiled, feeling love bubble up through his entire body.

✳ ✳ ✳

Tamara opened her eyes to see a small room. Merran lay on a small cot in the corner. He sat up as she hovered in the entryway. "Hi," he said to her in English, his voice soft and uncertain, a tone she'd never heard from him before. He smiled shyly.

"Hi," she replied, his shyness triggering her own. She glanced down at her hands, realizing she wasn't wearing any clothing—and she wasn't pregnant. "Wh-?"

Merran got to his feet. He wore nothing either, and his aura shone around him steadily, a powerful glow that was almost a cloak in and of itself. "Come in," he said softly as he reached out to her. She took his warm hands and stepped over the threshold into the room.

He released her as she entered the room. "Where are we and why am I suddenly not pregnant?" she asked, the words filled with alarm, yet her energy remained quite calm.

"You are not physically present," he replied, turning from her to walk over to the cot. "I'm not either."

"Then what's happening?"

Merran took a deep breath and turned to her. "I have to talk to you. Come, sit." He patted the bed beside him.

"What?" she asked, joining him on the cot. "What's happening, Merran?"

He took a deep breath and looked down at his hands. "Quite a bit has gone between us."

"Uh, you can say that again."

"You asked me a question before." His voice had taken that uncertain tone again.

"When?"

"When I ... when we officially ended it. You asked me if I ever was in love with you." He looked down at his hands.

Tamara put her hand out to touch his arm. "You told me that I was the one who made you come closest to regretting your life. I don't need to know anything more, Merran. It's enough."

He opened his arms to embrace her. Tamara looked at him directly. Here, in this place, she couldn't lie to him. He'd hurt her, and it loomed here, a visible thing between them, an angry energy. "I don't trust you," she said, pain evident in her voice. "You hurt me."

He looked at her steadily, his physical form dissolving abruptly. She found herself staring at herself, as if she were looking into a mirror. She jerked back. "What ... what's happening?"

"It is not your lover you do not trust, it is yourself," a voice said, and she turned her head to see the woman who had greeted them earlier. "He has played a role for you, allowing you to see that which you have hidden from yourself. In this place, you have the freedom to acknowledge that and to truly see yourself. Will you acknowledge what you have not been willing to see?"

"I don't trust you. You hurt me." The words echoed through the air, and she felt a sort of desperation. She shook her head. "No," she whispered. "No. Please. No."

The woman inclined her head. "As you wish. Remember only that which you are willing to accept."

Tamara woke with a start, the baby kicking her in the ribs, a fluttery sensation that hurt. She gasped and looked up. Darra sat cross-legged at the edge of the table. On the other side, Merran knelt, his eyes downcast. He was open, and there was a calm to him Tamara had not seen or felt in a long time—not since she'd first met him, before her Awakening. He leaned over a piece of paper and signed it, then slid the paper across the table to Tamara.

She looked down. It was a perfectly ordinary birth certificate, although it was a little more intricate than the human ones she'd seen. The line with the baby's name was blank. Underneath it, under the father's name it read, Merran Liporinn Corina, son of Jarid Memaxthal Corina and Pelera Liporinn, born in Azorantxl, at half past six in the morning, on day 125 of Arrival Year 1163. The second line asked for her information. Tamara picked up the pen and signed her name. She filled out her father's full name and her mother's, then stopped. "I don't know where I was born," she said, remembering the false birth certificate on Earth.

Darra extended a hand and showed her a birth certificate, except this one had her name under "baby's name." Tamara Dorvath Carrington, it read, daughter of Jasmian Mennak Dorvath and Peter Robert Carrington. She ignored the grandparental information and studied the signature of the woman she'd never met. Jasmian's handwriting was beautiful and flowing, and Tamara continued to stare at it. She'd been born in Uzorantxl, at 10:00 in the morning on day 45 of Arrival Year 1175. She finally filled in the rest of her information on the birth certificate and sat back.

"What is her name?" Darra asked, breaking the silence.

Tamara looked surprised. "We haven't come up with one," she said, glancing at Merran.

Merran shifted on his cushion. "Have you asked her yet?"

"Asked her?" Tamara frowned at Merran.

"She knows who she is," Darra replied for him. "It is customary that the mother meditate and ask the unborn her name. The father," she glanced at Merran, "may and usually does participate in the cases when the father is known. His participation helps the unborn know that she will be honored when she arrives."

Merran shifted again on his cushion. "This father is going to be unknown to his daughter until later."

Darra gave him a steady look. "Then why have you touched her?"

Merran glanced at Tamara. "Because I don't want to be completely out of the picture, just not the father she knows. Alarin Raderth will be that."

Darra fell silent, then continued with a short nod, "Alarin Raderth will perform the overt function of father, then," she said, spreading her hands. "She will return to Azelle when she is ready to be trained and Awakened. She will be raised Raderth, not Corina, and she will be known as Raderth until she chooses to know her true name." She lowered her hands and looked at Tamara steadily. "You will contact us when you know her name?"

Tamara nodded, not sure what she was being asked to do, but not willing to question it either. She looked back at the signature line of the woman she'd never met and found herself wondering if her mother had asked her name before she was born.

Darra's voice pulled her back to the present. "You have bound yourself to Azelle, daughter of Earth, and it has welcomed you. So will your daughter be when she reaches the necessary age. Take what you will of this visit back with you." She gave Tamara a long, steady look. It confused her, but again, she didn't feel the urge to question. "You may return to seek those who are lost to you," she said after a moment. "When you are ready. Now go and return with the name of your unborn."

Merran got to his feet and helped Tamara to hers. He bowed to the Keeper and Tamara did likewise.

The feeling of peace and calm lingered for a little longer after they'd left the strange cavern that was the Temple. It remained with her, in fact, most of the evening and into the night, even as she lay in Alarin's arms, helping to mitigate the nagging feeling that there was something she might have explored, if she'd been more willing to open to the guidance the *aarya* had shown her. As she lay restlessly on the bed, staring up at the ceiling, wondering what she had missed, a strange feeling crept through her, an odd knowing that whispered that she'd get another chance. Comforted, she fell asleep.

She drifted into the strangest dream, a dream about a dark-haired, beautiful young woman who looked like a female version of Merran. She woke with a name on her lips. "Rashella," she said, sitting up.

Alarin groaned. "Tam?" he asked, blinking at her sleepily. "What's going on?"

"Rashella. Her name is Rashella. I just dreamed about my baby as a young woman, and she told me her name is Rashella."

Alarin shifted and rested his hand on her abdomen. He was silent as he listened. "You're right." He slipped his hand around the swell of her stomach. "We'll tell the Keepers in the morning."

She settled back, cuddling up against him. Tamara felt wide awake for some reason, so she twisted. Alarin didn't seem sleepy either. "Alarin?"

"Hmmm?" he murmured, his hand stroking lightly over her belly.

"What time is it?" she asked, looking around the room for a clock. Charina had given up her room for the two of them, she and Merran sharing the floor in the living room. Nothing in the room resembled a clock.

"Early." He slid his fingers over her hipbones and down her leg. He moved against her, and she felt him press against her lower back. "Dawn or a little before."

"How do you know?" She tried to ignore the pressure of his erection against her lower back.

"If you listen, the animals will tell you." His hand wandered down her stomach.

Her breath caught as his fingers slid between her legs. She put her hand on his forearm. "Alarin," she gasped.

"Everyone's asleep," he murmured into her hair. "Even Rashella." He rubbed himself against her, leaning over to kiss her neck. Tamara shivered and made a sound low in her throat. It had been awhile since they'd been able to do anything—Rashella's level of alertness was too much for Alarin most of the time, and the little rascal had taken to sleeping when Alarin wasn't there, waking up almost immediately when he returned, her hungry little mind seeking constantly. She may have caught a nap or two when they both slept, but her restlessness lately had been such that Tamara wondered if she slept at all anymore. Tamara felt distinctly odd about doing anything in this house full of psi users, but if she said no now, they weren't likely to get another chance—that is, if Rashella even let them have this opportunity.

She did, remaining asleep as Alarin teased her mother, aggressively arousing Tamara, sliding into her mind so fiercely he nearly sent her over the edge without his body's additional stimulation. She managed not to cry out, holding her breath as his fingers, body, and mind drove her to explosive release, feeling his body shudder as he pulsed inside her, groaning softly as he found his own release. He pulled her close, wrapping his arms around her as their breath slowly came back to normal.

"God. It's been like forever," she whispered.

She could feel his chuckle as he hugged her tighter. "It will get worse the closer to her birth we get, then you'll need to heal and we'll both be too damned tired to do anything until she hits her teen years."

Tamara shifted and turned to look at him. "You're kidding, right?"

She could see him in the faint light from the window and from the soft light of his aura. He grinned and tucked a strand of hair behind her ear. He kissed her. "Of course."

She stared down at herself and sighed. "By then, I'll be so fat you'll be glad to find it somewhere else."

He hushed her with a kiss. "You are pregnant, love, not fat. And it truly doesn't matter to me what you look like."

Tamara gave him a look. "You've got to be kidding."

He leaned over and kissed her stomach. "Nope. Not at all. You're stuck with me, you realize."

"Oh, I don't know how I'll survive," Tamara replied, snuggling closer. "How did your meeting with your family go, by the way?"

He cuddled her close. "I don't think my mother will be attending the wedding," he said softly, and she could feel the echo of pain in him. "But surprisingly, Father was openly supportive. We won't have any trouble with my family. Father pretty much said our wedding was necessary and ended all the arguments. Mother wasn't happy, but she doesn't interfere when it comes to Father's foresight." Alarin sighed and tucked her closer, hugging her against his body. "He wants to attend the wedding. Are you okay with that?"

She twisted her head to look up at him. "Of course," she said. "I hope he does."

"My sister may come as well."

Tamara smiled. "She's welcome too. Will I get to meet her? Them?"

Alarin kissed the side of her neck. "Kyla's up north working the hot springs this week, so probably not. Mother, you don't want to meet, and that means you will not meet Father either. Their relationship is a little … odd. He backed me, and privately prevented Mother and Grandfather from interfering, but he won't do anything here in Azorantxl to overtly show that he disagrees with Mother. Since he is going to come to the wedding, you'll meet him then. While we're here, Justy and I can show you all the sites where we used to hang out and tell you lots of stories about the old days. Then we'll go home knowing that we have Father's blessing."

She could feel his relief at having his father's blessing—it had been more important to him than he'd let show—and though she didn't fully understand the dynamic between his mother and father, she accepted that it was there and fell asleep cuddled up against Alarin, wrapped in his warmth and ready to enjoy what he could share with her.

Chapter Eleven

A little more than two months after the trip to Azelle, Merran sat at the oceanside listening to the soft slap of waves on the beach. The peace he'd discovered at the Temple during his and Tamara's visit to register their daughter's conception and to introduce Rashella to the *aarya* had lingered, bringing the most profound sense of well-being Merran had ever known. It had carried him through the tricky coordination of the wedding between Alarin and Tamara, now only twenty-four hours away, and was enabling him to relax before the whirlwind began.

"Can I join you?" a voice asked, and Merran looked up to see Idara walking across the warm sand toward him, emerging from a hut. She wore a see-through cover-up over a sleek white bathing suit, her long hair flowing loose over her shoulders and back.

Merran nodded and moved over on the towel he'd spread out. Idara settled herself down on the towel, pulling her knees up against her chest. "This is the most beautiful place I have ever experienced," she said, as she looked out at the waves. "Where did you find it?"

"The embassy does quite a bit of business with the people who own this island," he said, looking out at the ocean surf. "Many of our staff use the island as a vacation getaway, since it's a privately owned island and the tourism is not nearly as crazy as Hawaii next door."

"If Azelle had any locations like this …" Idara trailed off.

"It would be a different planet," Merran replied, smiling a little. He stretched his legs out in front of him and looked over at her. "Sleep well last night?"

"Of course, especially after our nightcap." She looked over at him, a touch of concern apparent in her dark eyes. "You sure that Alari and Tamara will be all right with you inviting me?"

"Yes, I got clearance from both of them. I wasn't sure you'd be able to get the time off, though."

Idara smiled and tossed her head. "There's a photo shoot in Hawaii the day after tomorrow. It wasn't as difficult as I feared it might be to get a few days away to spend with friends." She gave him a flirtatious look from under her lashes. "And to enjoy a night or two of pleasure, as well, of course."

Merran shifted. Over the past several months, his relationship with Idara had settled into something eminently pleasurable for both of them. Their interactions had become mutually satisfying sexual encounters punctuated by occasional phone chats about nothing in particular. Idara provided him with the perfect smoke-screen, playing up the girlfriend when necessary, staying out of his life when he didn't want it. "You got the photo shoot? With *Expanded Vision*? Congratulations."

Idara's smile was brilliant. "Thanks to you and the contacts you've brought me. One of these days, I'll be able to see myself on the cover of a big fashion magazine."

"I don't doubt it for a minute." They both heard the sound of a plane approaching, the low *putt-putt* of the prop engine loud above them, beginning the process of bringing people in from where they'd laid over after their journey from Azelle—first to the spaceport in Denver, then to Hawaii, and finally to this tiny island that was the venue for the wedding. "That's my cue," he said, getting to his feet. "The Azellian contingent arrives today, and I get to welcome them all and make sure they're settled into their accommodations appropriately for their status."

"I'll see you later tonight, then?"

Merran reached out and gave her a gentle kiss, pulling her in briefly against his body. "Yes," he said, letting his hands run lightly over her curves, then he released her. "Until tonight." He watched as Idara made her way down the beach, already looking like the supermodel she almost was. He turned and, smiling to himself, strode down toward the small airport, which was hardly more than a landing strip on the north side of the island.

As he walked, he mused over the changes these past few months. His trip to the Temple had brought him many things, peace being only one of them. His total acceptance of himself, as symbolized by his ability to embrace his inner child during the Temple vision, had dissolved the uncomfortable pressure of Tamara's need for him to be someone he was not, and their relationship had settled into something pleasant and caring, untinged by any lingering sexual desires. He loved Tamara, as he loved their unborn daughter, but the love was very different from anything he'd ever felt for anyone before. It was easy, effortless, and untinged by possession, greed, or any of the usual components he'd always associated with romantic love. *Greg is right,* he thought to himself. *I love her. I love her, but I also know we would never make a good couple, so I can let her go freely, without reservation. How wonderful that feels. Will I ever find someone who will be my mate?* he considered briefly, his feet pressing into the spongy grass as he walked. After his experience at the Temple, his resistance to the idea had dissolved. *It would be nice to find someone I care about in the way Alarin and Tamara care about each other, but I really am okay if I never do.*

Ketiana joined him as he came toward the single building that served as a welcome hut. "Ready for the hordes to descend?" she asked, pulling him out of his thoughts. "I think we have more dignitaries coming to this wedding than we do ordinary people."

Merran smiled. "Yes, we do have a few Council members, including Galadrian. A few Healers, including Alarin's sister Kyla. A former Keeper. Speaking of our former Keeper, has Jamie made it back from Dorbin yet?"

Ketiana nodded at the landing strip. "He even brings with him a wedding gift from the Dorbin to you—some of those plants the Healers want."

"A wedding gift? For me? I'm not getting married. And Alarin and Tamara hardly need psi-active plants that can help Healers."

Ketiana grinned at him. "All right fine, it's not a wedding gift. But yes, Jamie is here with those plants you want. How are you taking it, by the way?"

"Taking what? Alarin and Tamara's wedding? I'm happy for them, of course."

"No lingering regrets?"

Merran shook his head. "None. I'm truly happy for them and pleased with my role in their life."

"You sound very ... balanced."

"I spent a little time at the Temple when I went back to Azelle. The effect lingers."

Ketiana smiled. "It shows. I'm glad to see you've found your footing again. It's good to have you back, Ambassador."

"It's good to be back." Merran smiled at her warmly. "Let's go greet the arriving *hordes* and get this dignitary-studded wedding moving forward."

❋ ❋ ❋

The morning of the wedding dawned beautiful and warm, accompanied by the tropical breezes of the ocean island that were always pleasant. Tamara woke to the smell of sand and fish—part of the unique smell of the ocean. It had made her rather nauseous at first, but she'd gotten used to it. Alarin had chosen to sleep elsewhere the previous night, as a nod to the traditional Earth manner of bride and groom being apart the night before their wedding. Tamara herself had argued, considering her extremely pregnant state, but he'd gotten it into his head that it was honoring her father and family to do so. Reluctantly, she'd finally given in.

Somehow, Merran had managed to get all one hundred and fifty wedding guests to the island—Tamara didn't want to think about the expense it had cost Merran to ferry that many people to a tiny island off the coast of Hawaii. Several extra huts had been thrown up to house the influx of people, and most of the guests were cheerful enough about their accommodations. She maneuvered herself out of bed, lumbering over to the bathroom and pulling a large muumuu over her head. She didn't bother with underwear—it was too warm. Getting dressed had become quite a challenge these days with little Rashella growing so large Tamara seriously wondered how far her body could stretch before the skin split and the baby popped out. Except for the fact it sounded painful she would have welcomed something like that. Rashella had gotten so restless lately that some of the baby's vigorous kicking woke Alarin, too, even as they bruised internal organs and her mother's ribs. Tamara was anxious for the baby to be born and the physical discomfort of the pregnancy to end.

As she made her way out of the hut and down toward the beach, Tamara rested her hand on her belly, feeling little Rashella shift inside. The sound of the ocean soothed her, reminding her of the peace in the Temple of Azelle, and she walked slowly through the soft, moist sand. Everyone had arrived yesterday, creating considerable chaos, but today it was quiet, with people still sleeping off the pre-wedding party of the night before.

"Beautiful morning," a voice said from her left as she walked past a large stand of palm trees. She glanced over to see an older man, who looked strikingly like Alarin, get to his feet. He spoke in English, his accent heavy but understandable.

"Lord," she said, trying to bow over her stomach and failing. She'd met Alarin's father briefly for the first time yesterday and had nearly pitched into his arms when she lost her balance on the uneven roadway. She hadn't had a chance to spend any time with him alone in the press of friends and family, but had found him incredibly intimidating in even those few moments. Now, dressed in a light Azellian robe, his hair mussed by the ocean breeze as he lounged on the beach, he was certainly more relaxed, but she wasn't entirely sure he was any less intimidating.

"Galadrian," he said, coming closer and bracing her with his telekinesis as she wobbled. "You are soon to join our family. We cannot have you call me Lord as though you were some supplicant."

Tamara tried not to feel too breathless, but with the baby crowding her lungs, stomach, and everything else, it was nearly impossible. She had no intention of calling Alarin's father anything, much less Galadrian, which sounded far too familiar. "Alarin and I are both so glad you could make it."

Galadrian offered her a deep bow. "I would not have missed my son's wedding."

"And his mother?" she asked, not sure she wanted to know, but knowing she needed to ask.

Galadrian smiled, and the expression bore a depth of something Alarin's lacked. *He has seen pain*, Tamara thought suddenly, her empathy sparking even though she could not read his mind at all. Seen it, experienced it, and then moved beyond it to … *what is on the other side of pain*? Tamara blinked, confused. Where had that thought come from? She pushed the confusion away and focused on what her soon-to-be father-in-law was saying. "Melyssa chose not to come. My daughter, Kyla, however, did." His nostrils flared. "Despite appearances, you are welcome in our family, Tamara."

Tamara shivered. The Raderths had not been nice to her on the trip back to Azelle, but they had done nothing overtly hostile; they had simply ignored her. Fortunately, Merran's sister's family had more than made up for the Raderth refusal to show any hospitality, welcoming her with joy. "Thank you."

Galadrian gave her a look that made her think he could see right through her, and Tamara suppressed another shiver. The man had green eyes, not unlike his son's, but she couldn't meet his steady gaze. He looked down at her stomach, freeing her from his unnerving regard. "May I?" he asked, and she knew what he was asking to do.

She nodded, shifting so he could have better access. He rested his hand lightly against her stomach. She could feel the communion between them, Rashella growing still under his touch. Galadrian's hand was warm against her extended belly, and Tamara felt tension wash from her. He was no Healer, but his touch was not far from it. After a moment, Galadrian lifted his head and stared into the distance.

"She will be strong," he said in a soft sing-song voice. "And in that strength find her weakness. In her weakness, she will learn of her power." Tamara trembled under his fingers. A slight smile spread across his face and he looked at her. "You will have a beautiful daughter, *akila*. And she will be welcomed into the Raderth Clan as long as she wishes to claim it."

Tamara twitched a little. They hadn't told Alarin's family the true parentage of Rashella, but Galadrian obviously knew.

He lifted his hand and gave her a surprisingly formal bow. "Felicitations on your upcoming marriage and welcome into the Raderth Clan. I believe there is someone who would like to speak to you."

Standing at the edge of the palm trees was a familiar figure. Merran slid down the steep slope towards her as Galadrian stepped away, disappearing around the edge of the huts. "Hi," he said, looking tired as he came to a stop a few feet from her. "How are you feeling this morning?"

"Unnerved," Tamara replied, staring after Alarin's father. "Why does he make me feel like I'll come unglued in his presence? Like all the little parts of me might just go spinning off into the void?"

Merran laughed. "That's Galadrian," he replied, the edge of amusement lighting up his face and animating it. "It's an offshoot of seeing more than most other people do about possible futures, along with the *aarya* training he underwent so that he could survive the onset of his talent. I think he enjoys his effect on people and cultivates it."

Tamara shook her head. "He can see the future and he married Alarin's mother anyway?"

Merran's grin widened. "Well, there's no accounting for attraction. How is little Rusha this morning?"

Tamara pressed her palm against her stomach, feeling a sharp little elbow or heel press back. "I'm more than ready for her to be born. Greg, who knows the exact day she was conceived, told me it will be another three weeks at best, if she's not to be premature. Maybe even six, if she goes full term." She made a face.

Merran noticed her gesture and smiled. "She's getting restless, Alarin tells me."

Tamara nodded. "She's kicked the crap out of all my internal organs. I don't think the little imp sleeps at all anymore, and she's constantly tugging at my psi. She's as curious as a cat and about as persistent."

"Who else does that sound like?"

Tamara laughed. "Not me, that's for sure. She must have gotten that from you."

Merran smiled, but the expression was a bit distracted. "You ready for today?" he asked, changing the subject and looking up at the deep blue of the early morning sky.

Tamara sighed. "It's not what I would have expected or thought I even wanted, but yes, I'm ready. And except for being a bit stressed by all this, and more than ready to give birth, I'm happy."

"Things are turning out for the best, aren't they?"

"Yes, they seem to be turning out pretty well." She hesitated. "Tell me one thing, though. You didn't pay for that charter plane yourself, did you?"

Merran's soft smile turned into a wide grin. "Why?"

"Because it's not fair. I mean, you've already started up that trust fund for Rashella and me. You don't have to foot the lion's share of the bill for our wedding too. You already had to get this island set up for guests at the last minute, and I know I've been difficult ..."

He shook his head, holding up a hand to forestall her. "Don't worry about it, Tam. It's not necessary for you to help. The Council picked up the tab, considering we do have no less than three Council members attending this wedding, several Healers, an ex-Keeper, and more than a few politically important members of the embassy, including myself. I asked the Council for the funds and they gave it to us, although I would suspect Galadrian had something to do with the ease of the donation."

Tamara sagged in relief. "Thank God," she murmured. "I didn't think, well ... usually it's customary that my father or I should be responsible to pay for wedding-related expenses. I honestly didn't know how we'd manage it, but I also didn't want you to take on that burden."

Merran reached out to brush a lock of hair from her face, his fingertips lingering on her cheek. "I would have talked them into it anyway, especially as it is much easier to secure an island like this than it would have been some building in Denver."

The feel of his hand against her cheek made her breath catch in her throat. Tamara closed her eyes and tilted her head briefly into his touch. "I'm ... really sorry things got so complicated, Merran."

"Nothing to feel sorry about, *akila*." His warm arms pulled her into an embrace, and in response, Tamara wrapped her arms around him as well, feeling his solid warmth. Although the hug wasn't as tight as normal—her belly was far too big for her to get any good bodily contact with anyone—she could feel Rashella move restlessly and kick. Tamara's eyes flew open and she frowned. Merran looked down at her. As he released her, a grin appeared on his lips and a laugh in his eyes. "Doesn't like people hugging her mother, apparently."

Tamara pressed her hand against her abdomen, soothing her daughter. "You should see how she gets when Alarin tries to hold me. I'm not sure she's going to have the patience to wait to be born. This baby is ready to face the world and take it by storm."

"Take it by storm she most certainly will," he said softly. He added something in Azellian, something she only caught the tail end of. "... *may the aarya protect and guide you and our daughter, Tamara. Felicitations on your mating and may your life be blessed with every joy.*" He leaned over and brushed a very light kiss against her mouth, then turned and disappeared over a hill.

Tamara stared after his departing figure for a few moments, touching her fingers against her mouth briefly. Something had changed in Merran during their trip to Azelle. He'd found peace, and it was obvious. And though sometimes she still wondered if she was doing the right thing, marrying Alarin and raising Merran's daughter with him, there were other times, like now, when she could feel some of that peace and know it would all be well. For the first time, she could feel some of what Greg, Alarin, and Merran were talking about when they spoke of *alawahea. It is as it is,* she thought, feeling the relaxation spill through her. *And it is perfect.*

Movement caught her eye, and Tamara turned to see someone

else loping toward her, the lean young man looking even more mature than the last time she'd seen him on Azelle, having filled out more and starting to come into the promise of his rakish, handsome good looks. He promptly blew the image of dignity that the suit he wore lent to his image by leaping over a bush and throwing his arms around Tamara. He kissed her exuberantly and enthusiastically, lifting her, baby belly and all, and whirling her in a circle. "You got a visa," Tamara said breathlessly, as soon as he'd released her. "You made it!"

"I told you I would," her brother said, gripping her shoulders tightly. "Considering half the Council is here for your wedding, it wasn't all that hard. You'd think you were marrying some fancy diplomat instead of Alarin Raderth."

"You got the pardon, then?"

"I did. And I didn't even have to apologize."

"How did you manage that?"

Justern shrugged lightly. "I have no idea, but Merran twisted some arms and sprinkled some magic and here I am." He let his hands slide down her arms to rest lightly on her stomach. "And how is my little niece this morning? Good morning, Rashella." Rashella, with her usual ferocious demand, linked firmly with her uncle, refusing to release him until he broke free, his gray-blue eyes suspiciously moist. "Damn, she's strong."

Tamara grinned. "She does have two empaths for parents."

"And a determination to make everyone who meets her fall in love with her." Justern brushed a hand across his eyes. "She's going to break hearts one day. As well as other things."

"Good to know you haven't changed any," Tamara said, punching him lightly on the arm.

"Do you know any reason why I should?" Justern asked,

slipping his arm around her shoulders and hugging her.

Tamara leaned into his strength, grateful for the support. "Not at all. Just glad to see you in such good spirits."

"It's a wedding. Of my big sister. Why wouldn't I be happy? Even if you are marrying Alarin Raderth."

"Would you prefer it was Merran?"

"Even if it were Merran, I would be saying the same thing. There just isn't anyone who is good enough for my sister." Justern hugged her shoulders again and released her. "Of course, that cake looks suspiciously good, so I suppose I'll have to celebrate with the rest of you."

Tamara laughed. "It's so good to have you here, Justy. It's the perfect wedding gift."

Justern gave her a lopsided grin. "That's good, because it's about all I got you."

Tamara kissed him on the cheek, feeling the scratch of his newly shaven face. "It's perfect."

Another voice interrupted them. "Tam? Tam, what are you doing out here? We have to get you dressed! The ceremony is in two hours!" Her sister, Andreya, sounding very much like their mother, Jeanine, came flying across the sand. She came to a halt in front of Tamara and Justern, hesitating. "Ah, hello," she said, frowning at Justern. "Justern. I … didn't realize … you were … here."

Justern bowed elaborately. "Nice to see you again, Andreya. I just got here, so I want to catch up with Greg, Alarin, and Merran before the ceremony starts. I just had to say hi to my favorite sister first. See you later, Tam." He gave Tamara a final kiss on the cheek, bowed again to Andreya, dropped a kiss on her hand, and then left, disappearing around the corner of the huts.

Tamara watched the blush crawl across Andreya's face. "Justern? Seriously?"

"What?" Andreya asked defensively.

"I know that look." Tamara turned her sister around. "The last thing you need to do is get involved with my brother."

"He's really hot, so sue me," Andreya said.

Tamara shook her head. "Not my brother, Andreya. Leave him alone. The last thing he needs to do is get kicked off the planet again. Besides, Dad would kill you," she warned. "After tearing my brother apart into little pieces. You're not legal, Drey."

"Oh please," Andreya retorted. "Dad isn't going to notice anything today except you."

Tamara shook her head. "Yes, well, he's my brother, Drey, and you're my younger sister. Isn't that a little too weird?"

"He's only nineteen, right, and not related to me, is he?"

"Well, no, but you're only sixteen. Way too young for him, Drey. And it's still weird."

Andreya laughed. "He's only three years older than I am, Tam. I have friends who have done a *lot more* than flirt. You're just trying to distract yourself from your nerves by focusing on me. Stop worrying about me. We have to get you dressed, and Kari's waiting up at the hut to help, so why are we still standing here talking?"

Tamara trotted across the sand beside Andreya, toward the hut to get ready for her wedding. Andreya and Kari helped fit her into her dress, which had a high waist that didn't precisely hide her stomach, but didn't emphasize it either. Kari smiled, the shine of tears in her eyes as Tamara stood in front of the long mirror. "You're so beautiful, Tam," she said, and gave her friend a hug. "Glowing and radiant. I'm so jealous."

Tamara smiled back at Kari. "Don't be. You've got Damiar."

"I know," Kari replied, dashing away tears carefully so as not to mess up her makeup. "But everything will be different, now that you have a husband and a baby." She kissed Tamara on the cheek. "Well, enough about how things will change. You've got a wedding to get to, so I'm going to take my place," she told Andreya. "See you out there in a few minutes."

Andreya gave the dress a final tug as Kari left the room. "There. As perfect as I can make it."

Tamara turned to her sister. "I wish Mom could be here to see this," she said softly.

Andreya cocked her head and smiled, her expression sad. "Me too. I like to think she is looking down on us and wishing us well. Wherever she is now." She straightened her own dress and cleared her throat. "Everyone is waiting for us," she announced, "so let's get you over to Dad and get this party started."

Tamara followed her sister out to where her father waited, looking very distinguished in his tux. "You look beautiful, honey," Peter said as she came up to him. He kissed her cheek lightly. "Alarin's a lucky young man."

"Thanks, Dad," Tamara said. "Are you really okay with me marrying him?"

"I'm happy to see you so happy," Peter said gently, as she placed her arm through his, holding the bouquet of flowers in front of her. "I am so proud of you, sweetheart. Your mother— both of them—would be so proud of you, too."

Tamara blinked away tears and turned with her father. Walking slowly down the aisle to where Alarin stood waiting for her, looking extremely handsome in his tuxedo, she felt the look of love exuding from his eyes. Beside him stood Merran and Greg, each one of them wearing tuxes and identical smiles of joy. The urge to cry vanished, and a soft smile appeared on her face, remaining there throughout the day. Nothing, not even the sight of Andreya's flirting with her half-brother, or the awareness that he might just repeat old patterns, could wipe it away. Her own private triangle had been laid to rest, and for this day at least, she knew everything was perfect in her world. What had Merran called it? *Kyarinal*: All that was possible had indeed become possible.

Acknowledgments

Every author lives in a complicated web of relationships that contribute to the creation of a story, but there are some very special people I'd like to acknowledge as having contributed intimately to *Triangle*. First, my editor. All authors are very grateful to their editors (or should be!), but I have a very special thanks to extend to Donna Mazzitelli. Without you, Donna, this book would be very, very different—especially as the editing process turned into a total rewriting project. You deserve awards for your editorial skill and kudos for the editorial magic you weave. I am honored to be a part of your cast of authors!

I'd also like to thank my family and friends. Your words of encouragement and excitement about the first book and your desire for more helped encourage me to persist, even despite the sometimes frustrating moments when I faced the certain knowledge that this story had to be rewritten. Persistence is the mark of any successful author, sometimes in the face of intense self-criticism and doubt about whether one's story will work out. It has—and the very special people who support and care about me are a very large part of this outcome.

A very special thanks goes out to my endlessly supportive and patient husband, Troy. It's not easy to live with someone whose head is in the clouds most of the time, and yet you remain as excited about all of this as I am and let me ramble on and on about some new plot twist or backstory that has come up.

Most of all, thank you, blessed, wonderful readers, for sharing the world I am building and the very real people who live in it. Thank you for reading and falling in love with these characters who continue to show me more dimensions of who they are. I hope you enjoy the continuing adventures of Tamara, Merran, Alarin, and the entire crew!

About the Author

Sara L. Daigle has been creating stories since she first forayed into the world of writing at the age of eight. As an avid reader, growing up in a small town without much access to a library, and before the birth of the Internet, Sara devoured her mother's extensive stack of science fiction and romance novels to keep her literary thirst quenched. Soon afterwards, she began writing her own stories and entertaining her friends by composing plays for them to act out.

A passionate interest in astronomy, anthropology, and linguistics, coupled with this early background in science fiction and romance, led Sara to merge the two fields and create a series of interlinked stories built around a fictional planet's culture and its interaction with ours. Her first book, *Alawahea: Book One of the Azellian Affairs*, has won numerous awards, bringing to life her message of tolerance and the journey to acceptance and self-love.

Sara currently lives in Denver, Colorado, with her husband and three very loving and energetic dogs.

Let's Stay Connected

TO STAY CONNECTED, please be sure to find me online by visiting my website at www.SaraLDaigle.com. You can also contact me at Sara@SaraLDaigle.com. I would love to hear from you!

And one last favor …

If you have enjoyed *Triangle*, please be sure to visit my Amazon book page and leave a review.

Thank you!

ALSO BY SARA L. DAIGLE

Tamara Carrington always felt different. One event in high school left her wondering if maybe she really was a freak, although she'd managed to leave that experience in the past—buried deep within her psyche. With the arrival of exchange students from the planet of Azelle to her college, Tamara's long-buried memories threaten to erupt. As Tamara's emotions build and her friendship with the Azellians grows, so does the knowledge of secrets within her own family.

With the deterioration of her mother's health, Tamara doesn't know where to turn for answers or solace. What has her family been hiding? Why does she feel inexplicably drawn to the Azellians? What will happen if she unleashes her long-suppressed passion? Will she survive or even recognize herself afterwards? Wanting answers, yet being afraid of what she might find, Tamara wonders if it would be better to remain asleep.

About the Press

Merry Dissonance Press is a book producer/indie publisher of works of transformation, inspiration, exploration, and illumination. MDP takes a holistic approach to bringing books into the world that make a little noise and create dissonance within the whole in order that ALL can be resolved to produce beautiful harmonies.

Merry Dissonance Press works with its authors every step of the way to craft the finest books and help promote them. Dedicated to publishing award-winning books, we strive to support talented writers and assist them to discover, claim, and refine their own distinct voice. **Merry Dissonance Press** is the place where collaboration and facilitation of our shared human experiences join together to make a difference in our world.

For more information, visit MerryDissonancePress.com.